PRAISE FOR THE WORKS OF DEREK GUNN AND

THE ESTUARY

"Gunn weaves a terrific tale."

—Apex Science Fiction and Horror Digest

"[Gunn's] books are not comforting paranormal romances; they are violent and visceral supernatural thrillers."

—International Thriller Writers

"The action comes thick and fast, with only a few pages to punctuate the fights, and battle scenes are where Gunn excels."

—Whispers of Wickedness

"Mr. Gunn has written a action packed, blood soaked thriller that will keep you hooked until the last page. I am shocked by how much I enjoyed this story… I cant wait to see what he gives us next."

—Horror World

"Gunn keeps the action moving and provides unexpected developments that keep the reader turning the pages."

—Monster Librarian

"Keeps the reader turning the pages."

—Horror-Web

DEREK GUNN
THE ESTUARY

Permuted Press
The formula has been changed...
Shifted... Altered... *Twisted.*
www.permutedpress.com

To Mary and Mick—See what happens when we come to stay for the weekend.

A PERMUTED PRESS book
published by arrangement with the authors

ISBN-13: 978-1-934861-24-0
ISBN-10: 1-934861-24-3

Cover art: Johann Bodin
Interior by Ryan C. Thomas

10 9 8 7 6 5 4 3 2 1

Prologue

March 1944

The sea roiled with barely tempered agitation as if the surface was fighting hard to hold back the chaos beneath. Intermittently the turbulence would break through and the waves would dash thunderously against the desolate, ragged rocks that lined the harbour.

The sky was covered with clouds that seemed to boil in sympathy with the restless sea and reflected its distress almost as accurately as it did its slate grey tone. As if to complete the vista of desolation a fine mist of rain fell from the sky like steam in a small room and drenched the figures that stood motionless along the pier.

A cold, biting wind pulled at the men's long black coats like invisible hands playing with the immobile figures, exposing darker uniforms beneath. Hans Gruber sighed as he looked along the line of guards. *What the hell are the SS doing here?* The day had begun strangely with the visit of Oberbefehlshaber der Kriegsmarine Grossadmiral Dönitz himself. It was well known that the war was going badly, they had already lost Africa and the Allies were already surging through Italy, but the presence here of the head of the German Navy was unsettling to say the least.

Gruber had seen for himself that the Allies' shipping in the Channel had markedly increased and the previously feared and dominant German Wolf Packs were becoming less and less effective as the Allies continued to patrol with their seemingly illimitable number of Destroyers. The two-fronted war was grinding the once proud and powerful German nation to its knees and the Russian front had turned into a meat grinder, taking Germany's youth and devouring whole battalions, spitting back only the wounded and haunted.

The appearance of Dönitz had been surprising enough but Gruber had been shocked to see the black uniformed SS arrive shortly afterwards. They had taken over with their usual arrogance, storming in and clicking their fingers, ordering food and coffee like royalty at a hotel. Gruber had stood to intercept their commander but Dönitz himself had put a gentle hand on his shoulder and shook his head.

The SS commander had sneered at him and had proceeded to order Gruber's men to take up positions back along the road while he sent his own men along the dock with no word of explanation. *Just who were they guarding?* Gruber wondered as he watched the men lined along the pier. They looked like statues in the night despite the biting cold. Even his own men, well used to the sea and the variances of weather it was capable of throwing at them, were huddled in shelter from the cold in the few barracks that lay dotted along the entrance to the compound.

When the commander had settled himself and only the three of them remained in the room Dönitz finally stood and approached the large table in the centre of the room and began the briefing. His usual erect, confident bearing that Gruber had seen at many briefings throughout his years in the Navy had changed dramatically. Now he wore an uncharacteristic, almost haunted, frown and his shoulders were slightly hunched. It seemed to Gruber that the damage being done to the Kriegsmarine was in some way reflected in the Admiral himself like some parody of Dorian Grey.

Dönitz was well known for his abhorrence for Hitler's pet killers and had advanced within the Kriegsmarine despite this due to his natural leadership and the results he had achieved throughout the war. His success had made him many enemies, especially as his continued success had made him untouchable. Now, however, as Dönitz's effectiveness was waning Himmler had obviously convinced Hitler to force the Admiral to allow more active involvement by the *Schutzstaffel*.

"How long do we wait?" Gruber asked as he turned from the small window.

"As long as it takes," Dönitz's spat and then his face softened and he nodded an apology. *It must be serious,* Gruber thought, *the Admiral is not one for apologies.*

Gruber snapped his head towards the window again as he heard a deep rumble. At first he thought it was aircraft coming across the sea to spill their carpet of death over a country already dying from within. There was no shelter in the harbour and no underground facilities, any such protection would be noticed by the enemy and would only invite their attention. The rumble grew until the table in the room began to vibrate and then Gruber jumped as a half-empty bottle of wine fell to the ground and shattered.

Not aircraft, he realised suddenly as he saw tiny pinpricks of light far out across the water. Their transport was nearly here. The trucks in the forecourt suddenly coughed into life and their hooded headlights splashed an eerie, sickly-yellow glow over the docks as they trundled down the narrow incline towards the pier. Gruber shivered and wondered idly why everything associated with the SS had such connotations.

What had started as a small regiment of bodyguards had grown to the most feared force in the world. Rumours of large scale murder, ritual and dark forces were rife in the conventional Army and Navy but no-one questioned the authority of the SS. No-one dared.

"Come," the SS commander snapped and disappeared out into the rain. Gruber looked over at Dönitz and thought for a moment that the man shivered before grabbing his hat and coat and following the SS officer. Gruber's heart was hammering in his chest. Their mission was vital to the Reich's survival but, as he walked out into the rain with his superiors he wondered if a nation ruled by such fear was for the best after all.

The trucks came to a halt and their engines died. For a moment everything seemed to stop. Silence descended over them like a blanket except for the howl of the wind which, in this desolate place, was so common Gruber no longer noticed it. He studied the sleek black bodies of the trucks before him. The engines ticked quietly as they cooled and rain hissed as it touched the heated bonnets and sent spits of steam in the air like angry hell-hounds fresh from a demented chase. Then the moment was gone and the doors opened and more black-clad soldiers spilled from the vehicles.

Gruber began to move forward but Dönitz again placed his hand gently on his shoulder. "Leave them to their dark business, Captain," his voice was low but carried the authority that Gruber was used to. "You will play your part soon enough."

The soldiers moved to the back of the trucks and pulled aside the covers. The material seemed to crack as the soldiers struggled against the wind and it took a number of them at each truck to tame the rampant fabric. From his position just behind the first vehicle Gruber could only see a deeper darkness inside the first truck and he felt a shiver run down his spine, he couldn't shake the impression that he was looking into a gaping maw.

The first of the soldiers appeared from inside the truck and handed a small canister to one of the men below. Each of the guards around them remained stone-faced as the trucks were unloaded but, as the man with the canister turned, Gruber was shocked to see the terror in his face. The man quickly disappeared down towards the pier and was quickly followed by another and so on until a stream of men stretched down to the end of the pier. Somehow a number of small, sleek submarines had materialised at the pier without him noticing and already their hatches were being opened.

Suddenly there was a loud thump and one of the canisters fell to the ground. Gruber snapped his head towards the sound and saw the man that had dropped the canister turn and try to run. He was restrained by guards and there was a brief scuffle and shouted curses until the man finally collapsed as he was struck by a rifle. Gruber felt a cold hand creep up his chest and squeeze his heart as he saw even the stone-faced guards look at the canister with terror.

For a full minute nobody moved but each pair of eyes were riveted on the small metal container as it lay on the ground. Gruber looked questioningly at Dönitz but the man remained impassive. Finally an officer, resplendent in his leather coat, recovered his own wavering composure and shouted at the men. For a second it seemed that the men debated with themselves whether they were more fearful of the officer or the canister but, finally, a man moved towards the container, lifted it and headed down to the pier.

The SS officer approached them a short time later and saluted sharply. His face was young but a hardness in his eyes made him appear far older. He smiled as he clicked his heels and the silver DeathsHead insignia on his cap flashed in the dark. "Admiral," Gruber had never heard Dönitz's title used with such irreverence before and he was so shocked that he missed much of what was said, "…. so we now hand over the mission to your people. Herr Himmler would have preferred our own, of course, but we have no-one skilled in the operation of these," he paused as he smiled again, "toys."

The insult was calculated and delivered with perfect timing. Gruber felt himself moving forward even before the Admiral could stop him but the guards on either side of him were quicker and restrained him before he could lash out. "Control your men, Admiral," the officer taunted and then turned sharply and signalled for his men to leave.

Within minutes the trucks roared to life and began their laborious climb back up the cliff face. Gruber turned to Dönitz but the Admiral cut him off. "Captain, your cargo has been loaded. It's time for you to gather your men."

Gruber felt as if the Admiral had slapped him. Dönitz was well known for his rapport with his men, Gruber himself had been commended by him many times and felt that they had an understanding, a mutual respect for each other's abilities. He had never known the Admiral to act like he had today.

Whatever this mission was it was obviously being done without the approval of the man in front of him. There was a new wind of change tearing through Germany, corrupting everything it touched. Gruber sighed as he turned to collect his men. The submarines bobbed at the moorings in the small harbour below but there was something different about them. Gruber paused as he studied the small craft.

He had commanded these two-man submarines for two years now and knew them intimately. He had always looked on his command with pride but something had changed tonight. The squat shapes in the water no longer looked sleek. Their dark hulls, which usually gleamed in the darkness, now seemed to merge with the shadows around them. He groped for the correct word to describe the lines of vessels in front of him but it wouldn't come. Finally he turned towards the barracks. They had work to do.

Malignant! He thought and felt a shiver run through him as the word popped into his head. *God help us,* he thought, *what are we about to do?*

Day 1

Chapter 1

Wednesday 11.00 AM — 11.30 AM

John Pender looked at the page and sighed. It was blank. The stark whiteness of the sheet seemed to mock him, daring him to try to write on it. He had already attempted to fill similar pages many times this morning but each effort had resulted in another crumpled sheet being tossed into the wastebasket nearby; actually most of the balls of paper lay on the ground around the basket, but that wasn't the point.

God! This was more difficult that he had expected. Using his old typewriter wasn't helping but the battery of his laptop had died last night and the electricity was still off after yesterday's storm. The heat in the small loft room was stifling and the fan on his desk lay as immobile as the mid-morning air.

Pender stood up and crossed to the window, opening the main side panel wide. There was no breeze off the estuary at all, just the stink of old seaweed and stale air heavy with salt. He looked out over the bare sand and sighed. The view was very different to what he remembered from his youth.

The estuary had always been full of water, the sheltered, natural harbour full of boats bobbing gently in the blue water of the Atlantic Ocean. Children, himself and his sister among them, had jumped from the old pier and swam out to the furthest buoy, the first there got to ring the bell and be King for the day. He smiled at the memory and sighed as he looked out at the dry, barren waste in front of him.

The construction of a new marina and shopping centre in the town itself had necessitated the placement of a dam at the mouth of the estuary so work could progress more quickly. It had been scheduled to take three months and was already overdue by a month and still there was no sign of it being completed.

The unseasonable heat of the last week or so had dried out the normally soaked estuary bed. He had lost many a pair of boots in the hungry, sodden sand on his many explorations once the tide had gone out; once he had nearly lost more than his boots when his feet had stuck fast up to his knees and he had to be rescued by a line of men working in a chain lest they too got stuck.

The estuary stretched for over a mile in width from where he stood to where the seaside town of Whiteshead lay on the other side but in all his years trying to explore the great expanse he had never succeeded in getting more than a hundred yards out before he had to return or risk the wrath of his mother for losing another pair of boots.

Now, though, the estuary bed was hard, the sand baked by the merciless sun, and children, his own three included, now ran on ground far further than he had ever dreamed of going. He could see them now in the distance playing rounders with kids from the neighbouring houses. They had fitted right in since they had moved here two weeks ago; nobody seemed to be suffering any withdrawal symptoms from moving out of the city.

He had been born here in Whiteshead and had always wanted to return. His wife, Julie, was a city girl but had fallen in love with the house on the estuary on one of their weekend breaks last year. He had spent the last ten years writing for numerous newspapers, rising to the respected position of deputy editor late last year and his job was flexible enough to allow him to work from home, with only the occasional trip back to Dublin to attend meetings.

The deciding factor had been a letter from a publishing house informing him that they would like to print one of his short stories and were interested in looking at any other work he might have, especially in novel length.

This had been a major boost. Julie and he had always dreamed of living by the sea; they could visualise the sun gleaming, the water lapping gently against the shore and he would be writing in the loft looking out over spectacular views. Unfortunately the water didn't lap anymore, the sun baked rather than gleamed, there was no electricity and the only things he had managed to write so far were either in the bin or lying on the ground beside it.

He pushed himself away from the window. This novel writing was more difficult than he had thought. Oh he had plenty of ideas swirling around his head but structuring them was a big problem. He had wanted to write since his school days but work and a lack of facilities both for learning the craft and publishing anything he might actually write had led him to put his writing aside as he concentrated on his journalism. He had enjoyed his years as a junior reporter, even the shitty stories as he travelled the country for local fairs, new store or hotel openings and canvassing local opinions to a new bypass of some town or other.

He had worked hard and it had only been with the encouragement from Julie that he had picked up his pen to write fiction at all. The first story had come easily enough but he still felt a little reluctant to send it off, somehow the story was much more personal than anything he had written for the paper. Julie had ignored this reluctance and had sent a copy of the story to every publisher she could find; and one of them bit.

He sighed. He really was getting nowhere this morning so he decided he'd go for a walk over the estuary, maybe the solitude would help.

"Finished the masterpiece already?" he heard Julie call from the kitchen where she sat with a steaming cup of tea and the paper laid open in front of her.

He looked over sheepishly. "I just can't get the first few paragraphs right," he shrugged. "Maybe a walk will help."

"Give us a kiss then," she smiled and grabbed his bum as he bent down to kiss her.

"I could stay, the kids are out . . . "

"Go!" she said with mock sternness. "You'll get a reward when you finish the first chapter."

Pender smiled, "What'll I get if I do two chapters together?" he asked with a lascivious grin.

"Probably sore fingers from all the typing," she replied and went back to reading.

Pender grinned as he left the house. Fifteen years of marriage, three children and she still got him as excited as she had when they'd first met. Julie Pender, or Connolly as she had been then, had been staying over in the same hotel in Westport when he had been reporting on a local summer fair in his early days. She had been there with one of the sponsors of the event, organising the PR and customer hospitality.

They had hit it off immediately when Pender had tried to gate-crash the party. It was, he told her, the duty of every junior reporter to check out, sample and return with all details on every party to the more senior reporters so they could decide which party they would bless with their presence for the night. The existence of free drink and food were the main criteria, although a good helping of attractive females was a definite plus. Pender had reported back to his seniors that Julie's party had none of the required elements and that had left him free to talk to her all night.

They had married two years later, once he had gotten a proper desk job in a reputable paper and life had been great since then. Pender crossed over the road, jumped over the small wall and landed on the hard sand, dust rose weakly in the still air and settled back down quickly, as if exhausted from the effort. The sun was already burning his shoulders through the light material of his T-shirt and his jeans stuck to him. He briefly considered going back to the house to change into shorts but he decided against it and set off over the sand.

There was a little breeze out in the middle of the estuary and he lifted his face and enjoyed the cool air washing over him. In the distance, about four hundred yards away he could see Grainne Uaile's castle. It wasn't really a castle, more of a keep really, and may not have had anything to do with the famous Irish pirate either but Pender and his friends had always fantasised that the keep held her long lost treasure and maybe even her body.

Pender and his friends had tried many times to walk out to the keep but the sand always stopped them. When they were old enough they had tried to take a boat out to investigate but official markers warning of sharp rocks surrounded the structure like solitary guards. The one time they had ignored the signs had seen their boat ripped apart against jagged rocks and they had had to be rescued yet again. They also had to pay for the damage to the boat which had been a fortune at the time.

Pender smiled as he saw the rocks surrounding the keep in the distance, their serrated teeth still reaching high into the air, no less sharp today than they had been all those years ago. The very fact that they could see it but every attempt to get to it had failed had created the legend around what was in there.

One day they had been studying history in school. They were covering the period where most of Ireland had come under English rule but pockets of resistance still held out on the West Coast. The 1570s were a black time but the legend of Grainne Uaile, or Grace O'Malley as some texts referred to her, caught the imagination of the whole class. The Keep became her castle and secret resting place of her still-missing treasure and corpse.

The Keep lay in the centre of the estuary, sheltered from the open sea but occupying a commanding position against any ships that sought to sail into the sheltered inlet. From the distance the stone structure looked small but Pender knew well enough that the sheer size of the estuary had a strange effect on the Keep and tended to dwarf the tower and surrounding battlements when, in fact, the structure was actually quite large.

He stood and looked out at the structure. If the sand was as dry out there as it was here he might actually be able to finally walk to the Keep. He felt his heart begin to thump as he considered the distance. It was still early and . . . With a surge of excitement he had not felt since he was a child he made up him mind and strode purposely out over sand that, quite possibly, had never before been walked upon by another soul, and headed for the distant Keep.

He was so excited about seeing the Keep after all these years that he nearly missed the cry for help. It was only when he turned to check on the children one last time before he was too far away that he saw one of the children jumping up and down. He frowned, the rest of the small group were all gathered in one point and one of the group, it could be anyone at this distance, stood away from them and began waving their hands when he stopped and turned. He couldn't hear at that distance but it was obvious that something was up.

He turned briefly for one last look at the distant structure. Yet another attempt to scale its battlements had been defeated by cruel fate.

"One day," he vowed. "One day soon I'll get to you." Then he turned and hurried over towards the group of children.

Chapter 2

He was out of breath when he finally got close enough to the small group to see that it was his eldest daughter, Emma, who had been waving her arms. She waited until he was quite close before she ran out towards him as if she were reluctant to allow too great a distance to grow between her and the other children. She was the responsible one and automatically took on the role of protector when they were on their own.

"What's up?" Pender wheezed as she drew level.

"Dad, Craig's torn his ankle, I don't know if it's broken or not but it's bleeding badly and . . ."

"It's alright, love," Pender assured her. She had spoken in one long stream, not taking any time for breath or punctuation and it took him a second to fit all the words into their correct order. "Let's go and see."

They hurried over to the children and Pender noted the worried faces of the other kids in the group. Craig was still rolling in the sand shrieking, his hands still wrapped tightly around his injured foot. The blood had already covered his hands and was steadily dripping onto the sand where the parched surface seemed to suck greedily at it.

"Okay, Champ," Pender kneeled down and began to sooth his son. "Let's have a look." He tried to ease his son's hands away so he could get a good look at the wound. He needed to see if the cut was bad but he didn't want to scare the boy anymore than he already was.

"What happened?" he asked more as a way to distract the boy than any real need to know.

"You should'a seen it, Dad. Craig was running faster than Flash to get to base when Peter threw the ball like Hawkeye and he swerved and then tumbled like . . . " Pender looked up at his youngest son. His face was scrunched up in concentration as he tried hard to think of a Marvel character that tumbled really well.

"Hey, slow down there, Jack, or you'll twist your tongue like the 'Tongue Twister'."

"He's not a real character."

"Is too, you'll find him in 'Avengers 291,'" Pender countered and then quickly returned to Craig's ankle while his youngest pondered this new information. He'd be for it when Jack proved that no such character existed, and prove it he would, but for now there was a lull that allowed him to check out the injury.

Craig had stopped shrieking at that stage and Pender lifted his leg and studied the ankle. There was a deep cut along the side of the foot and blood oozed from it steadily. He hoped that the tendons had not been cut but he'd have to get to a hospital to check that. With the electricity down in the area that meant a drive into Waterford. First, though, he needed to stop the bleeding.

He grabbed the end of his shirt and ripped the bottom all the way around. He soothed Craig as he wrapped the material tightly around the foot and grunted as he saw that the shirt quickly soaked up the blood but seemed to reduce the flow. It would have to do for now.

"Dad," Emma called to him from just beyond the group of children. He looked up but the children had formed a canopy as they peered over him like trees shadowing a country road and he had to stand up before he could see her.

"I'll be back in a minute," he assured Craig, who nodded bravely and then made his way over to his daughter. "Whatcha got?" He couldn't really afford to waste time but it might be important to know what had caused the injury.

"This is what he tripped over." Emma removed a lump of seaweed from around a curious looking black lump.

Pender looked down and saw the protuberance jutting from the sand. He leaned down and ran his hand over the smooth material.

"It's metal," he said more to himself than to anyone in particular and examined it more closely. There was about a foot of metal poking up through the sand. It had been completely smooth at one stage but now a jagged tear ran along one edge where it had crashed against something. He knocked hard on the surface with his knuckles and stifled a curse as he rubbed his hand to ease the pain.

"Bugger's not hollow whatever it is," he grimaced. "It could be anything but whatever it is it's big and man-made. But that's a mystery for another day," he got to his feet and went back to Craig.

"Looks like you discovered something pal. We'll have to come back with some shovels when you're feeling better. Okay?" He leaned down and scooped the boy into his arms and the boy nodded. "Grab hold of my neck and I'll lift you up."

Craig wrapped his hand around his father and Pender lifted him, grunting with the effort. *Bloody Hell,* he thought, *there was a time I could*

16

lift him easily. He turned and looked towards their house. The heat haze rising from the road shimmered and gave the impression that the house was much further than it actually was; at least he hoped that was all it was. He set off like the pied piper with the group of around twelve children running around him, their boundless energy already making him feel exhausted.

He reached the house drenched in sweat only to find his car gone from the driveway. He laid Craig on the step and plucked his mobile phone from his back pocket and punched in Julie's number. The phone began to ring as he paced impatiently up and down outside the house. As he approached the front room he became aware of a distant ringing inside the house. The sound echoed the ringing in his phone and when he pushed the cancel button the ringing inside the house also stopped. He snapped the phone closed in a rush of anger; Julie had always had a problem with the concept of why they were actually called *mobile* phones and constantly left hers behind.

There was no telling when she'd be back. He stormed next door but their car was missing as well, as was the next house along. He turned to the group of children still following him.

"Any of your parents at home today?" he asked hopefully but the sea of blank faces that greeted him gave him the answer he dreaded. *Oh well,* he thought, *looks like it's time to try that prick Johnson.*

Chapter 3

The bar was filled with smoke. On the ceiling two large wooden-bladed fans swirled valiantly in circles as they tried to dissipate the smoke but their efforts only succeeded in moving the pall around. The room was packed with people and the smell of drink and stale sweat hit Johnson as soon as he walked through the door.

There were small lights dotted around the room, inset into the many alcoves, but their feeble light could really only be described as a dull glow. Johnson felt the hairs on the back of his neck rise and he looked around guardedly; his intuition had been just about the only reliable thing in his life for the last six years since he had joined the Her Majesty's Service. With the exception of Kate of course.

He had learned long ago to trust that intuition but he hadn't seen Kate in six months and his rising excitement smothered the small voice in his head that tried to tell him this was a bad idea. The music boomed from speakers that hung from the ceiling every few feet and he could feel the throb and pulse of the beat run through him as he made his way down the packed stairs.

He looked out over the sea of bodies, trying to catch a glimpse of her but the light was too bad and sweeping searchlights gyrated dementedly and slowed his ability to get used to the darkness. He really shouldn't be here, breaking cover to meet your fiancée was a big breach of protocol but Kate had sent a coded message to him that she needed to see him so he had come running; it was handy when your fiancée was also your handler. Nobody knew, of course. They had been well trained in how to keep secrets and avoid surveillance, even from their own bosses.

It had started innocently enough; she had been assigned to him after his previous contact had been run over in an apparent accident. They had hit it off immediately and both of them could tell that there was an instant attraction. In their business they handled a lot of pressure and as a result they tended to party hard when the opportunity arose.

What started out as just sex, a way to find release from the pressure of the job, had somehow grown into something much stronger. Johnson knew that they couldn't keep their relationship a secret for long and worse than that was the fact that his mind kept wandering when they were apart, a dangerous activity when you were undercover. His current assignment was due to finish in about six months, sooner if they moved the weapons before then, and he had already decided to resign at that stage.

His knowledge of German had been an asset when he had first joined British Intelligence but lately it had become a millstone around his neck as more and more terrorist activity was being discovered there. Germany was in the grip of a failing economy. Despite a growing unemployment problem they still had a large financial commitment to support new entrants to the European Union and this waste of funds as some saw it left many disgruntled. This dissatisfaction offered a fertile breeding ground for terrorist and anti-European groups.

Johnson's heart skipped a beat and then began to pound in his chest as he caught a glimpse of her at a booth in the corner. She had cut her hair he noted as he pushed his way through the crowd reciting 'excuse me' like a mantra as he pushed through the throng of people.

He reached the table, feeling like he had just swum the channel, but her yelp of delight as she looked up and threw her arms around his neck made the fatigue melt away. He pulled her close, feeling her small body press against him. He pushed her back slightly to get a good look at her when he heard a scream behind him.

He snapped his head around, dropping into a crouch automatically, and scanned the room carefully. The screaming grew in volume as more people joined in and he paled when he saw four men wearing motorcycle helmets and brandishing shotguns push their way through the crowd. The men advanced easily as people threw themselves out of their way, heedless of where they landed.

Johnson reached down to his ankle and unsnapped the small Smith and Wesson SW99 from its holster. At only seven inches in length it was perfect for concealment but still packed a hell of an impact. He motioned for Kate to blend into the crowd on her right and he began to creep in the opposite direction.

Just his luck to be caught up in a robbery, if 'control' found out he had been meeting Kate outside of normal operations they would both be in for it. The men spread out, mingling through the crowd as if looking for someone. They had made no demands since they had come in, which was unusual, but Johnson kept his weapon hidden as he looked for an opening.

There was a shriek of pain as one of the men grabbed a woman and threw her by the hair onto the now empty dance floor. Johnson's heart stopped as he saw that that it was Kate that lay sprawled on the ground and he fought against his urge to rush forward and open fire.

"Ah, there you are," the lead man spoke as he approached Kate. His voice was badly muffled by the helmet but his accent was unmistakable—German. "Now, perhaps you can tell me where he is." The man reached down and lifted Kate's chin to face him with the barrel of the shotgun.

She looked up at him but remained silent. *She has guts,* Johnson thought proudly despite the danger of the situation. They had obviously been rumbled, one of them had been followed but it was not yet clear if they knew who she was meeting. Johnson was in the process of moving into a better position when the man faced the crowd.

"Come on out, Regan. We know you're here and it would be a shame to blow this pretty lady's head off now wouldn't it?"

Shit! That meant that they had somehow broken his cover. Johnson made his decision quickly. He couldn't let anything happen to her. He put the gun in his pants pocket and pushed out through the crowd with his hands in the air. Maybe there was still a way out, but not until Kate was safe.

"There you are, my boy," the man turned to face him. The man's helmet covered his face entirely, the deep red resembling blood as it reflected the dull lighting, but Johnson knew exactly who stood before him.

He was about to reply with some macho comment when the man turned back towards Kate and pulled the trigger. The pellets shredded her flesh at such close range and rammed her ruined face back against the floor with a crack that almost rivalled the initial blast.

Johnson stood still in shock. There had been no warning, no bravado, no threat and it took his senses a few seconds even to realise what had happened. The scream began deep in the pit of his stomach and built to such power that when it reached its peak he was no longer thinking rationally. He bellowed his rage and his loss in one wild howl and then . . . woke.

Wednesday 12.15PM – 12.45PM

David Johnson sat bolt upright in the bed and felt his heart hammering in his chest. The covers were sodden and twisted around his body like ivy coiled around a tree trunk. The image of Kate's shredded face still lingered in his memory as he extracted himself from the covers and stumbled to the toilet.

He'd been having the same damn dream for a year now, ever since it had happened but mostly after a night of heavy drinking. Last night, like too many others, had descended into a drunken haze. He stood over the toilet as he relieved himself but gripped the wall beside him to give him balance against the swirling in his head. He crossed to the sink and splashed water on his face, the cold water hit him like a slap.

He was still fuzzy when he returned to the bedroom and it was a while before he heard the banging on his door.

Pender hammered on the door again. He knew Johnson was in, Johnson was always in. He never went out, his shopping was delivered, his milk was delivered and even the laundry came and collected his clothes and delivered them back the next day.

Pender felt his anger grow; it was more worry for his son in fairness but his inability to be able to help him found an easy release as he slapped his hand hard against the door.

David Johnson lived right next door to them and his car was plainly visible in the driveway. Why he had a car at all, let alone a brand new 7 series BMW, when he never went out was beyond Pender. However, the gleaming vehicle offered him his best chance to get Craig to the hospital so Johnson would either open the door or he would break it down, either one worked for Pender.

Johnson was a mean-mannered git, at least that was how he had seemed in their one meeting on the day they had moved in. Pender had seen him working in his garden from his bedroom window when they were unpacking and had gone out immediately to greet him. To say his reception was cold was an understatement. Johnson had actually blanched when Pender had suddenly appeared over the fence.

Johnson had immediately dropped to the ground and had thrown the spade he had been using straight at Pender, narrowly missing him. He had apologised once he had recovered, explaining that Pender had given him a fright, but had then returned to his work, making it obvious that further conversation was not welcome. Since then Pender had seen him a few times but neither man was disposed towards conversation so they had left it at that, until today.

"Johnson," he shouted again, "open the damn door, this is an emergency."

He continued to hammer the door until, finally, he saw movement through the frosted glass. He stopped banging and waited impatiently while he heard a number of bolts being released and the door opened.

Johnson looked terrible. His face was ashen and gaunt, no - haunted was closer to the mark Pender judged. The smell of stale cigarettes and alcohol oozed from the house and Pender was tempted to put a handkerchief to his nose but thought that might be too much as he was the one looking for help.

"What the hell do you want?" Johnson growled as he shied away from the bright light that filled the porch.

"It's my son," Pender tried to remain calm, "he's had an accident and my wife is out. I need to get him to the hospital. Can you help?"

"Not my problem," Johnson answered and made to close the door.

Pender lost it. He stepped into the hall and pushed Johnson back against the hall wall. He was well used to barging into places he wasn't wanted from his early days as a reporter. "Listen, I really am sorry about this," he continued in a reasonable voice but his tone left no room for argument. "I asked for your help and you are going to give it one way or the other. My son is bleeding and I can't stop it. I need a first aid kit and then I would really appreciate the use of your car; you are welcome to come along, in fact that would be preferable as I need someone to look after the other children while he's being examined. I wouldn't ask normally but, as I said, it is an emergency."

Johnson looked at him for nearly a full minute; his eyes flickered over to the boy sitting in the porch with his foot in his hands and then to the group of kids that crowded as close as they dared to see what would happen next.

"Okay," he said at last, "bring him in and I'll get dressed. There's a first aid kit under the kitchen sink."

Pender didn't even have time to mumble a thank you before Johnson had disappeared. He lifted Craig up, motioned Emma and Jack inside and closed the door on the other children to a chorus of disappointed moans.

He found the first aid kit and lifted it onto the counter. That was the first thing he would buy when they got back from Waterford, they just hadn't thought of getting one before. The kit was well stocked, very well stocked in fact. There were phials of liquid with names that he couldn't pronounce, a number of hypodermic needles and even one bottle with 'Morphine' stencilled on the side.

Pender didn't know much about medicine but one thing he did know was that morphine was a controlled substance and you couldn't just go into a chemist and pick up such a large bottle. That would keep he decided as he grabbed a roll of bandages and turned to Craig.

He had sat the boy on the kitchen counter and placed his foot in the sink. Gently he removed his sodden shirt remnant and splashed water on the cut. Craig jumped but otherwise stayed silent. He was very pale and lethargic and Pender was worried that he hadn't been able to stop the blood. The stream of water cleared the sand and blood away easily and he got his first good look at the injury.

The flesh was torn cleanly and stretched about three inches along the side of his foot. It was impossible to be sure how deep it was but it was still bleeding. He began to dry the cut and then apply the bandage but Craig's exclamations of pain had him starting over each time he tried.

"Here let me do that," Johnson suddenly appeared beside him, took the bandage and began to wrap it tightly around Craig's foot, ignoring the cries of the child. "It's harder when it's one of your own but it won't stop the bleeding if it's loose," Johnson remarked as he continued to ignore the whimpers of the boy and ensured the bandage was tight.

"Thanks," Pender replied somewhat sheepishly. "Listen," he began, "about earlier I . . ."

"Don't sweat it; I'd have done the same. Anyway, it's about time I rejoined the human race and now is as good a time as any."

Pender looked at him quizzically.

"Long story," Johnson replied with a grin. He still looked pale but there was something about him that hadn't been there before. "Right," he said scooping some keys from a perch over by the door and turned to the others. "What are you waiting for? I thought you wanted to go to the hospital."

Chapter 4

The road around the estuary was about two and a half miles long. It was beautifully scenic, passing as it did along the water's edge and shrouded by majestic oak and cedar trees on the other side. Unfortunately it was also one of the most dangerous stretches of road in Ireland.

There was just enough room for one car and a bicycle to pass each other. Sharp, blind corners appeared without warning every hundred yards or so and potholes conspired with loose gravel to force the unwary driver off the road. Luckily, Johnson was neither unwary nor a bad driver. He guided the powerful BMW with confidence through the many corners and soon reached the main road where he proceeded to increase his speed well past the normal limit.

"If the Police stop us they'll probably give us an escort to the hospital," he said as he noted Pender's surreptitious glance at the speedometer. The Waterford road was notorious for speed traps and the threat of penalty points had finally caused most motorists to slow down.

"Listen," Pender began awkwardly, "I really appreciate this. I am sorry . . ."

"I told you, it's fine. I needed something to slap me out of the rut I've been in anyway. At least this is in a good cause."

"Want to talk about it?" Pender offered

"Not just yet. I've taken enough steps for one day."

They lapsed into silence and Pender busied himself with checking on Craig and reassuring the other two. He dialled home just in case Julie had returned but the phone rang until the automatic message came on. He decided against leaving a message as he knew that no matter how he phrased it Julie would leap into her car and rush to the hospital. One accident was more than enough for one day.

They arrived about twenty minutes later and Pender jumped out with Craig and left Emma and Jack with Johnson as he went to park the car. He rushed through to the A&E section and purposely fished the blood-sodden shirt from the bag he had brought with him and laid it over the plaster. The nurse took one look at the dripping appendage and ushered him into a cubicle and disappeared as she went to look for a doctor.

Twenty minutes later he was thrown out of the cubicle by a stern faced nurse as a doctor started to stitch the wound closed. He found Johnson easily enough; he just followed the high pitched giggles outside and found the three of them throwing pennies against the wall.

He hadn't realised how tall Johnson was before now but as he approached him he realised that he was a good two inches taller than he was himself, putting him at close to six foot.

"How is he?" Johnson asked before the other two got the chance, although Jack used the distraction to whip the three pennies into his pocket.

"He's fine," Pender sighed, "it's deep but a few stitches and a bit of rest and he'll be fine."

"Good," Johnson nodded and seemed genuinely pleased. "Emma tells me you're a famous author."

"Not quite," Pender smiled, "but maybe some day."

"Is Craig's leg going to fall off?" Jack piped up as he pulled at Pender's ragged shirt.

"No, son, he's going to be fine."

"Emma said it was going to fall off."

"Did not," she retorted and then the two of them resorted to arguing in words of as few syllables as possible.

Johnson grinned at the two of them. "They're great kids."

"Thanks," Pender replied not too sure if he was being sarcastic or not. He smiled when he saw that his companion had been serious. "Thanks a lot."

He finally got through to Julie on their way back and was just in time to stop her running out the door. One of the neighbours" kids had gotten to her first and from his graphic description Craig's leg was all but hanging off. He finally managed to assure her that all was well and that they'd see her soon.

The drive back was much less hectic than the previous mad dash and Pender found himself relaxing with Johnson and revising his earlier, hasty impression of the man. He had jet black hair, thinning at the sides and a little on top but his height kept that from all but a close scrutiny. He had a roman nose that, while prominent, fitted his rugged features well and didn't appear over large. He had piercing blue eyes that sparkled now as they played 'car colours' with the kids.

Each contestant picked a colour of car and received a point for each one they passed of their chosen colour. Of course, turning off the road into a laneway to avoid certain colours was strictly against the rules but Johnson kept pleading that he had simply taken a wrong turn. By the time they pulled off the main road the mood in the car was relaxed, even Craig had perked up and joined in the fun.

The sun was on its downward slide as they pulled into Johnson's driveway and shadows were already lengthening. Far out in the estuary a large group of people gathered around the area where Craig had had his accident and Pender jumped from the car and crossed the road to see what was going on.

"Can you see anything?" Johnson came up beside him.

"No, it's too far." Johnson shrugged and returned to the car in time to see Julie hop over the small wall separating the two houses and run to the car to check on Craig.

"Need any help?" Johnson asked as they approached the car.

"No, I can take it from here. Listen, I really appreciate what you did today."

"Don't mention it," Johnson held up his hand to forestall any further thanks. "I really enjoyed it, despite the seriousness of the situation. It's been a while since I've had that much excitement."

"Stick with us and I can promise you plenty, Mr. . . . "

"It's Dave."

"John." Pender replied and shot out his hand and clasped the other man's hand.

"Listen, if you're not doing anything later maybe you'd like to come for dinner. I'm lighting the barbeque."

Johnson looked hard at Pender for some time as if his mind was running through every conceivable outcome and then he simply smiled and nodded.

"I'd love to."

"Great, come around anytime after 7."

"I can't wait."

Pender turned and put his arm around his wife. "Julie, meet Dave Johnson, he's coming for dinner tonight."

Once they had settled Craig on the couch, reading with a can of Coke and some crisps close to hand, Pender wandered into the kitchen and hugged his wife.

"What happened?" she asked. "All I got was a garbled message that his leg was pumping blood."

"I tried to call you but you left your mobile behind," he said with a mock stern look.

"I know, I know. Just tell me what happened," she punched him lightly in the shoulder.

Pender sighed. "They were playing rounders out on the estuary and he tripped over something and tore his foot. The doctor said there'd be no permanent damage and he should be fine in a week or two. He gave me some tablets but only if the pain gets really bad. A couple of spoons of Calpol should do the job."

"What did he trip over?"

"I'm not sure. I had a quick look but whatever it was it is well buried." He slapped his hand to the side of his head. "That reminds me. There was a crowd over that way when we came back from the hospital. Word sure spreads quickly down here."

"So, we finally met our neighbour."

"Yea, I'd have been lost without him. I feel bad that I threatened him now."

"You didn't," Julie gasped.

"Yep. First I nearly battered his door down and then I barged my way in and threatened I'd steal his car if he didn't help."

"Oh my God. How could you just …"

"Listen, Craig's leg was pumping blood. You and all the neighbours were out. I panicked, okay? Anyway, it's sorted. I'll cook him dinner and give him a few beers, it'll be fine. He's a really nice guy actually. That reminds me, we have to get a first aid kit."

Julie nodded and then suddenly lifted her head. "Where are Emma and Jack?" She asked realising she had not heard any bickering in quite a while.

"I don't know, they could be in the garden."

"Take a look will you?" she asked as she headed for the stairs. "I'll check upstairs."

They met back in the kitchen in a few seconds.

"They're probably out in the estuary along with half the neighbourhood." Pender said and crossed to the door. "I'll go get them."

"I don't want them anywhere near that estuary until they find out if it's safe. There's been enough excitement for one day."

Wednesday 6.00PM – 7.00PM

Pender strode out towards the group congregated in the estuary. As he drew nearer he could see that there was a ring of people comprising mostly of women and some men, who were still in suits; obviously curiosity had gotten the best of them as they had come home from work. Children ran around and through this outer ring. In total he could see around twenty people.

As he drew level he saw that the formation was more a horse-shoe shape than a ring with a gap left open at the far side. He frowned as he saw sand flying through the air at regular intervals but it wasn't until he was a lot closer that he saw that there were people inside a trench that surrounded the shape that had injured Craig earlier.

The men had been busy and had already dug down about ten feet all the way around the growing shape. The trench ran about thirty feet in length and eight in diameter. He nodded to a few of the neighbours as he came abreast and watched the men as they sent showers of sand towards the space left by the crowd. The children ran through the growing mound in daredevil runs as they tried to avoid the flying sand and screamed in delight when one of their number got hit.

There were five men digging and already they had revealed quite a large black shape. He could see now that it was obviously a ship of come sort.

"So this is what Craig found then," Pender said as he nodded to the people he knew. He was a little peeved that his son's discovery had been hijacked and wanted them to know that it was a Pender who had found it originally, the fact that he had literally fallen over it did not change the fact that he had discovered it.

"Looks like a U-Boat to me."

Pender snapped his head to the left and looked at Peter Williams as if he were mad. Williams was in his late seventies but was fit as a fiddle and nodded to Pender as the man turned towards him. He still ran the local supermarket, although he spent most of his time sailing on his boat if the truth were known.

"It's a bit small for a U Boat isn't it?" Pender tried to keep the incredulity out of his voice but the hurt expression on the man's face testified that he hadn't tried hard enough.

"Midget sub," he said gruffly. "Germans caused bloody havoc with the little buggers from '44 right to the end. It could be a Seal or a Salamander by the looks of it. My buddy got sunk by one at Dunkirk in '45 and we chased the bastard for days but never got him."

Pender nodded. "Sorry, I thought you were joking. What's it doing here?"

"Who knows," Williams scratched his head. "Most of these were sunk by bad weather rather than allied guns. They weren't very heavy you see. Maybe he was blown off course."

The two men lapsed into silence as they watched the other men work. The craft was upside down and all they could see was the metal hull of the shape stretching the entire length of the trench. The metal had been a dull black at some stage but rust had spread along most of its length, although the metal itself was still sealed. In fact the only damage seemed to be the protective casing that held the propeller. It was now a jagged mess and the propeller itself had been ripped off. It had been this jagged metal that had torn Craig's foot.

Pender was so engrossed in the craft that he jumped when Jack grabbed his leg and gave him a hug.

"Dad, we found treasure," he shrilled happily and pointed at the vessel.

"Looks like you did at that," Pender agreed and rubbed the boy's blonde hair where upon a cascade of sand immediately flew in every direction.

"Come on," he grinned, "let's get you home. Emma," he shouted when he spied his daughter heading for another pass at the sand mound.

"Oh, Dad, can't we just stay for a while longer?" Jack pleaded.

"No." he insisted as he motioned for Emma to head home.

"But . . ."

"We're having a barbeque,"

"Alright," Jack shrugged and promptly forgot his disappointment as he raced his sister back to the house.

Pender took one more look at the slowly forming shape. A sudden cool breeze whipped in from the sea and he shivered. The kids were about twenty feet ahead of him and he judged that that should be enough of a head start. He took off after them screaming a horror-house evil laugh and grinned at the shrieks that rose ahead of him.

Behind him the digging continued.

Chapter 5

The sun had finally dipped below the horizon and plunged the estuary into darkness. A half moon peaked intermittently from behind small clouds that seemed to tease the dry earth with their promise of rain before moving further inland.

"It's too bloody dark," John Maguire shouted from the far side of the metal shape. As if in agreement there was a loud clang and a muffled curse and the others sniggered at Maguire's misfortune.

"I'm starving," moaned Tom Wilson.

"You're always fucking hungry," snapped Peter Geraghty, "can't you forget about your bleedin' stomach for more than a minute?"

Aidan Perkins laid down his shovel with a snort of disgust and pulled himself up over the lip of the trench. "All right lads," he could sense the growing atmosphere as fatigue set in, the copious amount of whiskey that had been consumed didn't help either, of course. "I think we'll have to call it a night, we'll get back to it in the morning."

There was nobody else around. Their audience had soon grown weary of the slow progress as the air grew colder. *Fuck 'em* Perkins thought. They'd not get a share of any salvage due. That old codger Williams had been right. As they had revealed more of the shape it became obvious that it was, in fact, a small submarine.

Must be worth something to somebody. He took another gulp from a bottle of Jameson Whiskey and swayed slightly as the sudden movement of his head and the copious amounts of alcohol they had consumed over the day made him dizzy.

"Hold on a second," Frank O'Neill called from the centre. "It's starting to wobble; we must be close to the bottom. If we push from this side we might be able to push it over."

Just then the moon cleared the latest cloud cover and its silvery light splashed over the men and the dark shape before them. While there was ample light to see what they were doing now the shape itself seemed to defy the light and wrap the shadows around it.

"Okay lads, a few more minutes," Perkins relented, "let's try and push this bugger over and see what we've got."

The men set to work. They had heard of the strange object in the sand from Maguire's youngest son who had run home and gushed out the news of sunken treasure. Perkins and his cronies had been playing cards; they played cards every day, ever since the footwear factory had closed down six months ago.

There wasn't much industry in the area and those that were here weren't hiring and Perkins and his crew were happy enough to laze around and draw benefit rather than go to the trouble of looking for work in another town.

The prospect of buried treasure would not only be financially rewarding but would give them something to do. They had arrived around one o'clock with four bottles of whisky and five shovels and had worked hard all day as the prospect of salvage fees grew with each spade of sand. They hadn't eaten all day but the whisky had taken their minds off their hunger until now.

The submarine leaned far over and then Maguire slipped and the whole vessel fell back towards them and threatened to bury them underneath. The other men braced themselves against the trench wall until Maguire got back to his feet and then they pushed hard to get the momentum back to the other side.

The submarine seemed to hang immobile for an age and then, finally, it fell away from them with a creak of metal and a wet popping sound as the moist sand below finally gave up its prize after sixty years.

The men fell over on top of the vessel as it crashed onto its side and they whooped and hollered as they scooped the remaining sand from the revealed hatch.

"Are they still out there?" Johnson asked as he lifted the beer to his mouth and took a long drink.

"Yea, crazy bastards. It's too dark to be messing about with a lump of metal that size."

"They must have found something," Johnson smiled as he heard the whoop of raised voices in the distance.

"Either that or they've drunk too much of the whiskey I saw beside the trench."

The two men returned to the patio and smiled at Julie who looked up from her game of chess with Emma. Craig had gone off to bed early and Jack had been sent up at nine, he had of course appeared back down three times so far with yet another toy he just had to show to Dave but he seemed to have settled now.

"So, Dave," Julie began as she moved her rook to take her daughter's castle. "Anyone special in your life?"

Johnson paused, causing Julie to look up from her game.

"There was once," he began. "She died."

"Oh, I am sorry," Julie flushed as she saw the pain on Johnson's face. "That was unfair of me . . . "

"It's alright," Johnson interrupted, "it's just that I'm not used to talking about it."

"We're good listeners if you want to start," she said and turned from the game giving him her full attention.

"Maybe another time," Johnson agreed and took another gulp from his bottle.

"How about your profession, is that too personal?"

"You'll have to excuse my wife but she has a very active curiosity."

"That's okay, I'm sure there must be all kinds of weird stories about me."

Julie nodded. "Yes there are; inherited wealth, big score on the stock market and Lotto winner are just the nice ones."

"Don't forget 'mad murderer in hiding'," Emma piped up and then saw her father's sharp look and went back to rearranging the chess pieces behind her mother's back.

"I can imagine," laughed Johnson. "Nothing so dramatic I'm afraid to say. After my fiancée died last year I needed some time to get away from it all. The house is rented and the car was the down payment on our house. Sorry to disappoint you."

"Anyway," Pender broke the awkward silence by producing another three beers. "You, young lady can go to bed while your parents get our resident mad murderer well and truly drunk."

The hatch was set in the middle of the submarine. It jutted out about six feet from the body of the vessel and spanned just wide enough for a man to slide through. The hatch was rusted shut and the antenna that used to adorn its back lay bent and broken in the wet sand below.

Perkins slid down under the hatch cursing as the damp sand quickly soaked his clothes.

"This better be bloody worth it," he mumbled to no-one in particular but ensured it was loud enough so the others could hear him. He gripped the circular handle on the top of the hatch and pulled it anticlockwise.

"Bugger's stuck," he grunted. "O'Neill, get down here and help me."

"But it's all wet," O'Neill whined.

"Get your arse down here ya wimp or so help me I'll come back up there and ram your head through the bulkhead and forget all about the goddamn hatch."

"Alright, alright, keep your hair on," O'Neill stumbled towards the edge and then sniggered as it suddenly struck him that Perkins was bald. He was still laughing when he slipped and fell into the trench.

"Watch it you stupid fuck," Perkins admonished him. "Here grab hold and turn when I do."

O'Neill stifled another fit of giggling when the moon came out again and reflected off Perkins's gleaming pate and grabbed the lock and put all his strength into it.

"It's moving," Perkins's face was red with exertion. "Keep going."

There was a clang deep inside the vessel and the wheel suddenly spun easily and both men scraped their knuckles against the outer guard and let loose a stream of obscenities.

"What happened?" Maguire dropped down beside the men and bent towards them but the angle was too sharp for him to see without lying in the wet sand. "We heard a noise, are you alright? Is it open?"

"Yea, it's fuckin' open," Perkins shouted as he stuck his grazed knuckles into his mouth. "Maybe you'd like to come down here and go in first now all the work's done."

"Well, if you want …"

"Get real, Maguire. No-one gets inside this baby before me. I need a light, anyone got a lighter?"

Maguire fished in his jeans for his lighter and pulled out a pack of Marlboros. He flipped the lid and pulled a Zippo out, then grabbed one of the cigarettes and lit it before passing the lighter through to Perkins.

"Jesus, take your time why don't you?" Perkins snapped the lighter from him, flicked the top and thumbed the wheel. The sudden light was blinding in the compact area around the hatch and Perkins blinked furiously until he could see properly. A heavy scent of paraffin assailed his nose as he brought the lighter closer to the wheel.

There was a clasp just below the wheel that was loose enough to draw down now that the wheel had released it and he reached over to pull it down. There was a hollow clunk and the hatch groaned and then slid open.

A pungent odour of rotten flesh and stale air made him gag and he felt bile rise in his throat and threaten to empty his stomach, it was probably the lack of food that saved him from puking up all over himself.

There wasn't much room to move but he used his legs to slide himself along the ground. He pushed his hand through into the darkness, illuminating his way with the lighter. He couldn't see anything at first and had to force himself to stop thinking of the small black hole as a gaping, ravenous mouth.

Slowly he began to make out dials and tubes. Just above him the flickering light revealed the top of a small ladder and he grabbed it with his free hand and pulled himself into the hole.

There was even less room inside than he had thought, although he was trying to crawl down the ladder when the submarine was on its side. He reached the bottom and swung the light slowly from side to side as he tried to get his bearings. His feet were standing on a piece of equipment with numerous dials and two screens and he tried his best to move without causing any damage, he didn't want to go to all this trouble and find out later that he had stood on the only thing of real value on the whole vessel.

"Did you find anything?" O'Neill's head popped in through the open hatch and Perkins nearly dropped the lighter in fright.

"Jesus, ya nearly scared the shit out of me. Get down here and help me out. Tell the others to stay where they are, there isn't room to piss down here."

"Sure smells like someone did a lot more than that."

"Just get down here and mind where you put those clumsy feet of yours."

Pender gripped the banister as his head swam. *Too many beers,* he thought as he steadied himself and then continued into the boys' room. Craig was already fast asleep, spread-eagled in his normal bizarre position (Pender couldn't see how he could possibly wake up refreshed each morning and not crippled with sore and strained muscles). He had had a busy day; Pender smiled at the boy as he pulled the covers back over him and did his best to straighten out his tangled limbs.

God, he sighed heavily as he thought of the blood pumping from

Craig's foot. *If it had been just a bit deeper...* He forced the thought aside and kissed his cheek. *He's fine and that's what matters.*

He rose and crossed to Jack's bed and stood looking down at his angelic face.

"Alright you, I know you're awake."

Jack opened one eye and grinned up at his father. "How did you know?"

"That's my secret. Now what has you awake, it's late?"

"I had a bad dream."

"Monsters again?" Pender sat on the side of the bed.

"Uh huh,"

"I told you not to look at 'The Mummy',"

"But I like it. Except for the scary parts. What if a Mummy comes for me?"

"I'm here," Pender answered as he squeezed his hand, "I'd never let anything hurt you."

"No matter what happens?" he asked in a small voice.

"No matter what happens," Pender agreed and smiled.

"Promise?"

"Promise," Pender insisted and stood up.

"Okay then," Jack rolled over and pulled the covers up to his chin, his fear already forgotten.

Pender wiped a small tear away from his eye as he stared at the boys.

Way too much beer, he thought and then went back downstairs.

Perkins found the captain strapped to what looked like the command chair. He was badly decomposed; the scattered remnants of yellowed skin were stretched tightly over stained bones. Shadows danced over the emaciated flesh in the flickering light from the flame giving an eerie facsimile of movement. The interior of the submarine was cramped at the best of times but in its current position Perkins was forced to brush past the corpse with his cheek a mere inch from the putrid flesh and he closed his eyes as he moved on.

He had fifteen feet to travel before he reached the end of the vessel but it took him a good ten minutes and all he found for his trouble was a second decomposed body and a pile of yellowed papers that looked official but were written in some foreign language. Aidan

Perkins wasn't stupid by any means but he wasn't well educated and any language that wasn't plain English was grouped under 'Foreign' as far as he was concerned.

"Look at this," O'Neill exclaimed from the front of the vessel. Perkins snapped his head towards the weak glow of Maguire's lighter.

"What is it?" he said as he began to move back past the rotting corpse as fast as he could.

"I don't rightly know," O'Neill was holding something in his hands but it wasn't bright enough to see properly.

"Well don't go dropping it, you hear?" Perkins cursed his luck that the only thing that they had found so far was in O'Neill's hands, bloody fool couldn't even hold his pecker steady long enough to hit the toilet bowl. Hopefully if he could just . . .

"Shit!" O'Neill cursed just as a ring of metal hitting metal reverberated around the small confines of the submarine.

"What the fuck have ..."

"It's okay, it's okay I caught it before it hit the ground. It only knocked off the wall a little bit, it's fine."

Perkins was just about the shout some more abuse at him but he was nearly there and he didn't want to give O'Neill another excuse to drop whatever it was he held.

"Oh, that wasn't loose before," O'Neill said and then threw the thing away from him as it began to hiss loudly.

"What have you done now?" Perkins finally reached O'Neill and belted him over the head with the flat of his hand.

"It started to hiss, Aidan. I panicked and ..."

Perkins began to bend down to the still hissing object when suddenly a thick green smoke started to belch from one end.

"Oh fuck," he began and then started to cough as the smoke rapidly filled the interior.

"Quick, get out," he turned and tripped over O'Neill who was already half way up the ladder. He paused as a coughing fit racked his body. His eyes began to stream with tears as the toxic smoke billowed around him and rose towards the hatch, oozing out over the opening like the thick fog he had seen in a Dracula movie.

"Give us a fuckin' hand," he shouted in between bouts of coughing. He felt a hand grab his collar and pull him towards the hatch. He looked up and saw John Maguire's face through the haze and tried to pull himself along.

Maguire pulled him out and then the others helped lift them both back up over the trench and onto the sand. Perkins lay on the sand wheezing but already his coughing had subsided and soon he was able to sit up and look around.

The air had grown very cold while they had been in the submarine and his light shirt was no protection against the biting chill.

"O'Neill," he whispered breathlessly, "one of these days I am going to cut those bleedin' hands of yours off and stick 'em straight up your arse. What was that thing that you dropped?"

"I don't know, Aidan, honestly. It wasn't my fault." He pleaded and looked at the others for support but they were well used to O'Neill and his clumsiness, mostly it was funny but this time he could have cost them money and that was unforgivable."

"Help me up, I'm freezin' me butt off here," Perkins shot out his hand and the others rushed to comply. "We'll head home. We can return in the morning when that stuff is gone and see if there's anymore. O'Neill, you can stay outside next time."

The men stumbled across the desolate estuary towards the roadway, the combination of fatigue, drunkenness and coughing making them unsteady. Behind them the green smoke boiled out over the hatch and quickly dissipated into the chilled air.

Day 2
Chapter 6

John Pender sat in the loft and stared at the blank page again. The day had begun early for him as he had woken with a sore head and had gone downstairs to take a Panadol. Once up he decided that he'd try and get some work done after losing the whole day yesterday.

He sipped at a cup of strong coffee and looked out over the estuary as he tried to arrange his thoughts. It was only six in the morning but, already, the faint glow of the rising sun peeped over the horizon. Dark pools of shadows clung valiantly to rocks and debris on the bed of the estuary until the wall of advancing light banished them into oblivion. A thin layer of early dew left glistening droplets everywhere that shone in spectacular colours before the heat of the rising sun savagely vaporised them.

Far out in the estuary the submarine lay motionless like a dead whale.

The night had gone well, too well if the throbbing in his head was anything to go by, and they had gone to bed around one in the morning. He had noted dull pinpricks of light out by the submarine as they had finished and Dave and himself had agreed to take a walk out and see what was going on later in the morning. Pender looked at his watch, he couldn't really call on Dave until at least nine o'clock so, with a deep sigh, he laid aside the coffee and began to type.

After a while the words began to flow.

He didn't hear the noises as the children tumbled from their beds and pounded downstairs for their breakfast. He barely even noticed as Julie came up with a refill, although he did stop briefly as she traced her nails on his bare back and made a grab for her that she deftly dodged.

"Nearly finished the first chapter," he warned and winked at her and she raised her eyebrows and gave him a wiggle as she went back downstairs.

It was ten o'clock before he finished. His back and fingers ached but he felt wonderful as he looked at the lower left hand side of his computer and saw how much he had written. He stretched, picked up his mug and made his way down to the kitchen singing Rod Stewart's 'Tonight's the Night'.

Dave was already sitting in his kitchen tucking into a big plate of sausages and bacon and he nodded briefly before shovelling another forkful into his mouth.

"We decided not to disturb you," Julie smiled and crossed to the oven and produced another plate full of steaming food. Pender hadn't realised how hungry he was until the smell hit him and his stomach growled loudly as he sat down.

"Sleep well?" he managed between bites and Johnson nodded as he cleaned his own plate with a scrap of bread and popped it into his mouth.

"Great," he beamed. "I slept like a log for the first time in months."

"You two be careful out at that wreck," Julie warned and then scooped up the car keys and called the children. "We're off to the tennis club so we'll see you in a few hours." She crossed to Pender and kissed him on the cheek, nodded at Johnson and headed out.

"Thanks for breakfast," Dave called after her and she waved in response.

"Doctor, thank you so much for coming so quickly, I didn't know what else to do." Miriam Perkins was fifty five, slightly overweight around her waist and face but a handsome woman nonetheless. This morning, however, she looked ghastly. Her face was pale, her hair awry and the bags under her eyes testified to a hard night.

"That's alright, Miriam. I'm here now," Theresa Winfield soothed the woman, taking her arm and leading her into the kitchen. Winfield was relatively new to the area but she had taken over from her uncle after he retired and had inherited his patient list. She wasn't yet considered a local by any means, that would take at least three generations in this part of the country, but she had been well received regardless, especially by the men. She wasn't in the class of a supermodel by any means, her slightly short frame accentuated her somewhat sturdy build but her beaming smile and distinctive auburn hair had already assured her of plenty of attention.

"He came home late last night, out drinking with his cronies again," she spat this last part with a look that told of long suffering. "He was coughing badly when he came in and he fell into bed. I was so annoyed with him, as he had left the front room in such a mess, that I ignored him initially."

"His breathing was ragged but I'm used to him wheezing and spluttering like an old tracor. He just won't give up those cigarettes no matter how many . . . "

Theresa gently laid her hand on Mrs. Pender's arm, interrupting her tirade as she took a handkerchief from her pocket and handed it to her.

"Sorry. Anyway, this wasn't a wheeze it was much worse. It was like he was trying to breathe through a pipe but someone had blocked the other end. I got him some Vic and put nearly half a bottle on him but it didn't help. His face was so pale that I stayed up and just held his hand until I felt I could call you. I tried to keep him drinking water but he can't seem to swallow."

"Okay, Miriam." Theresa stood up, "I'll have a look at him." Mrs. Perkins stood up but she put a hand on her shoulder,

"You stay here and rest, I know the way."

Doctor Winfield blanched as she entered the bedroom. The smell was appalling, reeking of decay and the pungent, heavy stink of menthol. Perkins lay on the bed, grey and still like a corpse; in fact she had seen a few corpses looking a lot better. His skin was almost translucent and clung to the bones of his face like dry leather. He didn't acknowledge the doctor as she crossed to the bed.

She felt for a pulse and found a weak, irregular flutter after several attempts. Theresa frowned; she had never seen symptoms that had such drastic effects in such a short time. She laid her hand against the man's forehead; it was cold to the touch. She brought her stethoscope up to her ears and placed it on Perkin's chest; his lungs wheezed with a loud gurgling, as if someone had placed his lungs underwater and they had somehow learned to draw breath. She turned, opened her medical bag and took out a hypodermic needle.

"I'm just going to take a blood sample," she said in as cool a voice as she could manage but Perkins continued to ignore her. She was surprised to see her hand shake slightly as she searched for a vein; it was eerie the way the man just stared ahead, if it wasn't for the faint pulse and the gurgling in his chest she would have sworn that the man was already dead.

It wasn't hard to find the vein; the flesh had sunk in on itself so badly that the veins stood out like grotesque ridges. The needle pierced the skin but Perkins didn't react at all. A crazy voice in her head whispered, *don't worry it's just a little prick with a needle* and she nearly giggled as she whispered the joke her uncle had told her many years ago, "I know that but what are you going to do with it."

She placed a thermometer under Perkins's arm and held it there after two failed attempts to get him to hold it in his mouth. *Far too low,* she thought as she read the dial. She would have to courier the blood sample up to Cork Regional Hospital immediately with the electricity still off in the local clinic. She would ring Professor Matthews and discuss the case with him, see if she was missing something. It certainly wasn't any virus she had ever seen, and it wasn't pneumonia, which had been her initial thought when she had received the phone call.

She replaced her instruments and headed back to the kitchen where a cup of tea waited for her, a chocolate biscuit lying in the saucer beside it. Mrs. Perkins looked up as she appeared and her eyes pleaded silently.

She pulled a bottle of cough mixture from her bag. "Give him two spoonfuls three times a day," she said handing over the medicine. It wouldn't do a damn bit of good but it would make Miriam feel that she was helping. Her uncle had always said that where there was a family involved you always had to consider more than just the patient. She picked up her tea and felt a pang of guilt as the woman took the bottle and held it as if it was a magical cure.

"I'll send a blood sample off and . . . excuse me," she broke off as her phone beeped. "Hello, Doctor Winfield," she answered, smiling reassuringly at Mrs. Perkins. Her smile froze and she put the cup of tea down suddenly, causing a loud clatter.

"I'll be right there," she clicked off her phone and stood up. "I have to go; I'll ring later when I have the results. Don't worry," she touched her arm, "we'll soon get him back to normal."

She rushed to her car and threw her bag on the passenger seat. The call had been from her secretary who had received calls from the wives or girlfriends of three of the other men that hung around with Perkins. They were all complaining of wheezing and racking coughs.

What the hell is going on? she thought as she started her car.

Miriam Perkins prepared a cup of tea and placed it on a small tray along with a spoon and the bottle of medicine that the doctor had given her. *She's such a nice girl,* she thought. Most city folk wouldn't have come so quickly or so early in the morning.

She stifled a yawn, she really would have to get some sleep later or she'd be like a bag of cats for the day. Aidan Perkins had become an infuriating man, opinionated, rude and downright mean but he loved her and had given her a good life, at least until he had lost his job.

She loved him without question, but she did miss the way he used to be. They never did have children, it wasn't from lack of trying she recalled with a blush, but God had seen fit not to bless them and she was certain that he must have his reasons. The closure of the factory had been the turning point, no she corrected herself, it was the months of searching for a job in the time after that had changed him, made him bitter.

She wiped at a tear in the corner of her eye as she reached the bedroom, took a deep breath and opened the door. Aidan lay as before with his eyes closed, his grey pallor made worse by the brightness of the white sheets.

"Now, love," she forced a smile. "The doctor's given me some medicine and I've made you a nice cup of tea. I don't want no arguments now," she continued as she poured the pink, viscous liquid out onto the spoon.

She leaned forward and Aidan opened his eyes, looked at her and lifted his head forwards. She smiled as he opened his mouth and then screamed at his teeth down bit down hard on her fingers. She screamed, more in shock than in pain initially and she ripped her hand back away from her husband. She was about to shout at him, give him a piece of her mind after her looking after him all night and all, when a sharp pain in her hand made her stop in mid breath and bring her hand up in front of her. Something was wrong she thought but her mind was slow to grasp what had just happened. The pain in her hand suddenly intensified and she suddenly felt light-headed. She looked dully at her torn hand as she wondered why two of her fingers were missing. Suddenly she began to scream hysterically and she scrambled from the bed as she saw her husband loom before her, two of her fingers dangling from his mouth.

Her head swam as she tried to run towards the door and she stumbled. The tray in her lap fell and caught between her legs, tripping her and sending her head first against the side of the open door. Her vision blurred and her head ached but the pain kept her focused just enough to allow her to scramble against the wall. She tried to rise to her feet but her head was so dizzy.

There was a thump behind her as her husband fell out of the bed. He lay there for a second as if his limbs wouldn't respond and then slowly he began to pull himself towards her.

"What are you doing?" Her mind couldn't process what was happening. Distantly she was aware that she should get up and run, but she just couldn't. She couldn't accept that Aidan would hurt her. It was the illness, that's what it was. He'd be okay if she could just get him back to bed and take the medicine.

She was still thinking that when he pulled himself level and ripped out her throat.

Thursday 10.30 AM – 11.30 AM

They set off after breakfast and settled easily into a comfortable conversation on the way. Johnson chatted easily and smiled more on their short trip than Pender suspected he had smiled in the previous twelve months.

There was nobody at the submarine and he wondered if Perkins and his cronies had already looted it or if it had gotten too dark for them by the time they dug it free.

"Looks like they got it open anyway," Johnson remarked as they drew level and looked down at the open hatch.

"I hope they haven"t damaged anything. I'm sure the museum would be interested in our little find."

"They might at that," Johnson agreed and pulled a rucksack from his back and fished out two powerful torches, two pairs of gloves and paper masks that fitted over the nose and mouth.

"Regular boy scout aren't you?" Pender noted as he saw items.

"Never hurts to be careful, you never know what's in there after all this time. Shall we?"

"That's what we came out for," Pender replied and took one of the torches and put on the mask and gloves, feeling rather stupid that he had come out in just a T-shirt and jeans.

"I don't suppose we can haul it right side up; it would make it easier to move around."

"If this is the best the 'Fantastic Five' could manage, drunk and all as they were, I doubt we'll be able to do much better. We'll have a quick look and if there's anything of note we'll go and get help and straighten her then. What do you think?"

"Fair enough." The men dropped to their knees and crawled through the hatch into the darkness.

Theresa Winfield made a quick stop at her surgery and asked Georgina to send the sample urgently to Professor Matthews in Cork Hospital, scribbling a note to go with it with her mobile telephone number. The office felt strange in the gloom and Georgina looked bored without her computer.

"If it's still off by eleven, go on home," she told her as she left and noted that the girl brightened up considerably.

The interior of the submarine was tiny. The air stank, even through the light filter in the mask, and walking on the walls was definitely something Johnson decided was best left to Spider-Man. He pushed past the corpse strapped to the command chair and wondered briefly how someone could live in something so small for long periods of time. He imagined being on your own deep beneath the ocean with the enemy hunting you, dropping depth charges systematically as they searched for you. He shivered as a feeling of claustrophobia gripped him.

"You okay?"

The question snapped him out of his reverie and he nodded.

"Just trying to imagine what he would have gone through."

"They." Pender added absently.

"What?"

"According to Williams these were two-man subs."

"Two men lived in this?" he swept his hand around and cursed when he knocked it against the bulkhead.

"Yep, but I'm sure they were close."

"Hey, look. Williams was right," he pressed himself tight against the wall and allowed Pender to lean into the small room at the back. Pender nodded at the corpse and then reached out for the pile of paper beside the bed.

"They're in bloody German," he said in disgust as he put them back.

"You were expecting Chinese maybe," Johnson grinned as he picked up the pile.

"No, of course not. I just meant that I can't read them."

"But I can," Johnson smiled and folded the papers and put them into his rucksack.

"Cool," Pender nodded impressed and then turned and began to make his way forward.

Johnson liked Pender. He could have killed him yesterday morning when he had barged in but it had been just what he had needed. It was well past time he got himself straight. Kate was gone. He would never forget her, and he never should, but she would whup his ass if she knew how he had been living.

Pender's family was so full of vitality that it had reminded him that life could be good as well as bad. They seemed happy to involve him in their life and their easy manner was just what he needed to ease himself back into a routine that wasn't destructive.

"Hey, I've found something," Pender knelt down to lift something from the ground. "It looks like a canister of some sort."

Chapter 7

Julie Pender watched the children run onto the tennis courts and settled herself on a wooden seat to watch them. Even Craig hobbled happily behind them and stood in one place as he hit the ball back across the net. The sun bathed her in heat and she lifted her head to its glare and luxuriated in its warmth. *God, it's gorgeous here,* she thought and sighed as she realised how close she had been to throwing this kind of happiness away.

She hadn't intentionally, or even consciously, set out to be unfaithful but the long periods of being alone while John was away had left her empty and desperate for adult company. Initially, John had been away as a foreign correspondent, and later when he had become deputy editor there had always been a deadline to meet or a story that just had to be checked before they went to print.

Weekends blurred into week days, and soon the only difference between them was the fact that that the children were home more. She had given up her job years ago to look after the children, not that she regretted that for an instant, but they needed her less and less now as they became more independent with every passing year and she had begun to feel less appreciated. *No that wasn't exactly right,* she mused, *useful, yes that was more accurate,* she decided.

It wasn't so much that she and John and had grown apart but other things just sort of got in the way and they had both let themselves fall into the trap of taking each other for granted. John certainly just assumed that his clothes would be cleaned and ironed and meals ready on the rare occasions that he did actually make it home. She too was just as guilty, performing these tasks like a mute servant and allowing her own needs to get pushed aside without so much as a whimper.

It was the lack of attention that had bothered her most. The romance of bringing home flowers or coming home and whisking her off for a surprise lunch had just seemed to stop, although she wasn't entirely sure when. It wasn't that he loved her any less, she was certain of that, just that life had got in the way. He just wasn't there to comment on an outfit, a new hairstyle or grab her when the kids weren't looking and give her a big hug. She missed that most of all.

She realised now as she sat in the sun that she had never stopped loving him, even when she had allowed herself to be put in a situation where she was open to temptation. *Jesus,* she thought, *how corny can you get?* It was just like one of those damn 'bodice ripper' cheap novels she had always refused to read, no matter how bored she got. New swimming instructor, lonely woman left on her own by a negligent husband . . . No, that was unfair, she reprimanded herself, John hadn't been negligent, just absent.

The thrill of someone noticing her and paying compliments when she had made an effort made her feel alive. She grimaced as she remembered putting on her makeup and doing her hair, despite the fact that it would all be ruined in the water anyway, just so he could see her. Barry Collins, the name did nothing for her now as she sat and watched the children play.

It had come to a head, as of course it had to. It had finally come to a point where she could no longer fool herself that she was merely flattered. *What exactly was the point where a dalliance became an actual affair?* She had known that she had to make a decision and that decision had the potential to ruin more lives that she had any right to risk. When she had actually faced that choice she was surprised at how easily she had been able to come to a decision. *The right choice,* she smiled as she looked over at the children.

They had never actually gotten physical; she was more grateful for that than anything else in her entire life (she would never have been able to hide it from John if she had.) The chance of buying the house and moving here had come at just the right time, although she hoped that she would have said no when, if, she corrected herself, anything had been about to happen.

Leaving her friends and brother behind had been hard at first, although it wasn't as if she was a million miles away—she could always travel back up to Dublin anytime she wanted—but the rewards had easily outweighed the sacrifices. Even the small-town 'click' hadn't gotten her down as she ignored the people that required you to be a particular 'set' and concentrated on those that accepted you for who you were, there weren't many but it was quality that mattered with friends not quantity.

John had obviously been more aware of their growing apart than she had given him credit for and he had jumped at the chance to work from home more. Since they had moved here he hadn't got much writing done but they had been like a married couple again. *Newly weds,* she thought as a thrill flowed through her as she planned out his reward for later.

She stretched out her long, shapely legs. *Not too bad for late thirties,* she thought as she looked down their bronzed length. It was amazing how fragile happiness was, how easy it was to lose but, conversely, how easy it was to regain if you had something strong to build on.

She looked out and smiled as Jack went to hit the ball, missed and swung around in a full circle. *This is perfect. Life just couldn't be better,* she thought, She'd been given the chance for a new beginning, a chance to have things even better than they had been and nothing, she vowed with grim determination, was ever going to get in the way again.

"Theresa, why the hell are you wasting our time sending us samples of dead people?" The gruff tone of Professor William Matthews blared into Theresa Winfield's ear.

"What are you talking about?" she snapped back more harshly than she had intended, and way more severely than was warranted when talking to a man of Matthew's standing and calibre. The day had begun badly with the early call to Miriam Perkins and had quickly deteriorated from there with four more emergency calls, all with the same symptoms.

"The sample I sent you was from a live patient," she added with a more conciliatory tone.

"Impossible! The PH level was below 7.2."

"But his heart was still beating."

"Are you certain," Matthews asked in his familiar 'now you and I both know that you are wrong and that I am, as usual, right' tone. "I've lost count of the amount of doctors who have mistaken a pulse for their own throbbing fingers."

"I'm not an amateur," Winfield complained petulantly. "You should know; I trained under you for God's sake."

"Okay, but you know as well as I do that those readings are impossible," Matthews relented with a grudging acceptance. "You really should have sent the sample much earlier when the patient first showed these extraordinary signs."

"What do you mean?" She snapped defensively, "Perkins only got sick in the early hours of this morning. According to his wife he was fit as a fiddle yesterday."

"That's just not possible," Matthews insisted but his customary assurance was beginning to waver. "Not even Ebola works that quickly."

"I know. That's why I sent you the sample immediately."

"How's the patient now?"

"I haven"t had time to check yet . . . "

"Christ, girl. What have you been doing that's more import . . . "

"I've got four more cases with the same symptoms," Winfield interrupted with a hard edge to her voice. Matthews may be her Professor but how dare he question her priorities. There was silence on the other end of the phone and Winfield used the opportunity to transfer the phone to her other ear, bloody mobile phones always left her ears burning with sustained use.

"Epidemic?" Matthews whispered, his tone was heavy with fear.

"I don't think so, it's been five hours since I saw Perkins and I feel fine; exhausted yes, but no ill effects. That would put me within the time frame that he got sick originally so I don't think it's airborne. None of the wives or girlfriends were sick either and they should definitely be showing signs by now. It's more like something they came into contact with."

"Strange," Matthews mused. "I'll send the sample to Dublin, I don't think they'll find anything different but they do have better equipment and you never know. Check on the first patient and keep me informed. Theresa," the softening of his tone was abrupt and all the more poignant as it was so contradictory to the personality of the man on the other end of the phone.

"You do realise that I'll have to inform the Department don't you? It's way out of my league, let alone yours."

"Do what you have to, Will. I'll keep you updated of any changes."

"Be careful, Theresa. Take every precaution you can, good doctors don't grow on trees you know."

"I will," Winfield broke the connection and sat in the car for a few minutes.

Jesus! The conversation with Matthews had brought home to her the severity of the situation. Up till now she had been too busy to think of the implications but now that she had had time to consider the situation she felt an icy touch of fear grip her.

The chemistry within the body functions in an alkaline environment and the blood must maintain a pH of 7.35. If it drops below that to 7.2 or lower, quite simply—we die. At that level the oxygen cannot be transported throughout the body. It was quite impossible for Mr.

Perkins to have a pH that low and still be breathing.

She lifted her records file from the back seat and punched in the Perkins' number. Her fear grew with every unanswered ring.

"Hold on a second," Johnson warned and Pender stopped in mid-crouch and looked back at him with a puzzled expression.

"What's up?" he heard Pender ask as he straightened, the words echoed hollowly in the confined space.

"Let's see if it has any markings on it before we go lifting anything," Johnson replied as he shone his torch on the object. "It might be dangerous." The thin beam from Johnson's torch sliced through the darkness and created a narrow tunnel of light that splashed over the object, illuminating a grey bullet-like canister.

The object was about a foot long and some six inches in diameter and it lay lodged between two dials, held precariously in place by a loop of thick cord. Johnson bent under the object and looked at it from below

"It looks like it has been dropped," he grunted noticing the large indentation on the side and then he straightened up and moved backwards, crushing Pender's toe in his haste.

"Hey, watch it," Pender complained as he stumbled back, avoiding further injury.

"Sorry, but there's a nasty looking warning on the side. I can't read it all at this angle but I did see the words 'Das Giftas' and that means it's toxic."

"Is it open?"

"I can't tell but I don't plan on shaking it to see. I think it's time to let someone who knows what they're doing take over."

"Fair enough, we can call from the house. "Who exactly do you call for this kind of thing anyway?"

"Haven't a clue," Johnson replied as he pulled himself out into the fresh air. "God," he drew in a huge breath and let it out slowly, "what kind of men could stay in one of those things for weeks and not go mad?"

"I certainly couldn't do it," Pender admitted and helped Johnson to his feet. "Come on let's see if those documents can tell us anything."

The creature that had been Aidan Perkins stumbled out of his house and into the street. Behind him he left the torn remains of his wife of twenty two years. Emptiness gripped him. It had relented somewhat when he had bitten the woman but once the blood had stopped flowing his insatiable gnawing hunger returned.

His limited thought processes sent him out in search of more food and the hunger drove him on despite the stiffness of his body.

Dan O'Sullivan took the corner a little too sharply eliciting a grunt of annoyance from his colleague as he spilled tobacco over his lap.

"Jesus, Dan, watch where you're going. This stuff is expensive you know," Frank Humphries complained as he picked small clumps of tobacco from his lap and sprinkled them back into the cigarette paper.

"Those things will kill you, you know."

"Not before you do if you keep driving like a maniac."

"Yeah, yeah," O'Sullivan teased as he brought the ambulance to a stop. "What have we got?"

Humphries licked the length of the paper and rolled the cigarette before popping it in his mouth. He reached back for a clipboard and ran his finger down the length.

"Perkins," he mumbled as he lit the cigarette and blew smoke out the window. "We're meant to bring him to Cork Regional. There's a note that he might need a respirator."

"What's wrong with him?"

"Doesn't say."

"Okay, let's go get him. And put that thing out, you'll get us both fired."

O'Sullivan walked up to the door and knocked while Humphries finished his cigarette and opened the ambulance doors. He leaned in and pulled down the ramp, securing it in place and then reached in, unlocked the legs on the stretcher and pulled it out onto the road. O'Sullivan was still knocking on the door when he came up behind him.

"No answer?" he asked as he sat on the stretcher.

"No," O'Sullivan replied as he tried to see through the frosted glass in the front door.

"Try the window; see if you can see any movement."

Humphries nodded and lifted his leg over the fence enclosing a small grassed area. He shielded his eyes and looked through the window. "I can't see anything, they've got net curtains."

"Try the back," O'Sullivan called as he used the flat of his hand to bang hard on the door.

"There's no way around," Humphries called as he returned to the front door. "Want to break it down?"

"Oh yea, and get done for criminal damage. That's a great idea."

"Just a suggestion," Humphries said and laid his hands out flat. "We gonna leave then?"

"I suppose, why don't you call it in on the radio first."

Humphries shrugged and headed back to the ambulance.

Alan Peters was unlucky. He wasn't quite sure if the fact that he knew that he was and accepted it was a good thing or not but the knowledge didn't change his luck either way so he didn't spend a lot of time thinking about it. Some people won raffles or lotteries; they arrived just before the train left or found parking just beside where they wanted to be. He didn't.

That wasn't to say that his life was unsuccessful or depressing, merely that he didn't receive that extra little push that launched others ahead of the pack. He had accepted this long ago and had set himself a path early on that ensured that he would get to where he wanted to go without outside help. His humble beginnings certainly hadn't done him any favours, but there were millions like him and millions more even worse off. He had never considered this a matter of luck merely of circumstance. What made Alan Peters different from those other millions was the fact that he did not wait around for some imagined higher power to take an interest in him.

`From an early age others could see a single mindedness in him that left him excluded. It wasn't that he disliked people; it was more the fact that they merely didn't fit into his calculations. There were times, of course, when he actively sought out those that might be of use to him, but not many; you could only go to others so many times before they began to come to you, and he didn't want that.

He had made his own destiny and that could not be considered luck, merely a matter of cause and effect. Luck had nothing to do with his success; he had planned out his life, had calculated his decisions and had carved out an empire that included property, land and industry that spread over the entire country, and beyond as fledgling states joined a Europe desperate for investment. His drive for immortality was all-consuming, his empire and so his name, would live on for years after he was dead and gone.

He stormed from his car, still angry with the news that had brought him here this morning. The new centre wasn't going well. The recent elections had upset the balance of power within the local council and councillors who had supported him before, their loyalty bought and paid for long ago, had been replaced in an unexpected country-wide backlash against the current government.

The new councillors wanted a full review and had questioned why work had been allowed to start, indeed it was almost finished at this stage, when final approval had yet to be signed off. What had been a mere formality last week now threatened a multi-million Euro investment deal. What made things worse was the fact that the new councillors were not from the usual party system, which would have merely required another pay-off. These were from a growing 'Green' element that had concerns about the environmental impact of the proposed structure.

Bloody do-gooders he fumed as he strode towards the council offices with his staff struggling to keep up behind him. He didn't see the figure that tottered towards him until they actually collided and he fell heavily to the ground as his momentum worked against him.

His staff immediately flocked around him but he pushed them away with a snarl that was more feral than coherent. "Stupid, blind motherfucker," he muttered as he pulled himself to his feet and approached the figure that had collided with him.

"What the hell do . . . " he shouted as he grabbed the man's lapel. *He's wearing fucking pyjamas,* he thought incredulously and then the smell hit him and he recoiled from the figure. He stank of stale sweat and something else that he couldn't quite place, something sweet but cloying. Bile rose in Peters' throat and he released the man in disgust. *It's not worth it,* he thought, *especially so close to the council chambers.*

Suddenly he felt a violent tug on his sleeve and the material of his light summer jacket ripped. He looked back in shock as he saw the man standing before him with the torn sleeve in his hand. He was so stunned that he merely stood there with his mouth open, the cool breeze softly caressing his bare arm and bringing goosebumps to the surface.

His brain seemed to click back into gear and he raised his arm to the man in front of him, reaching again for the lapel. The man's face had remained curiously impassive throughout the entire incident and Peters felt an intense anger grip him. He balled his hand around the man's lapel, squeezing hard and pulled the man towards him, screaming incoherently at him.

His chief aide immediately stepped between the two men, gently but firmly pushing his employer away from the other man. He was dimly aware that his aide was talking to him but the words were meaningless. His tone, however, steady and calm, slowly filtered into his brain and he began to regain control.

It was then that the man leaned in towards his aide and tore the flesh from his cheek.

Julie stood at the jeep's door as the children settled themselves. She checked their seatbelts before she slid into her own seat and carefully pulled out into the afternoon traffic, not that the few cars on Main Street could really be considered traffic.

The sun shone mercilessly and Julie leaned forward to turn the air-conditioning up to high as her blouse grafted itself to her back. The boys began to whisper in the back, a sure sign that something was up, and Julie glanced briefly in the mirror to check on them.

She saw the man tumble onto the other side of the road a split second before the truck hit him. The man seemed to be propelled backwards at some speed and she could almost hear the crunch as the heavy goods vehicle hit him squarely before the driver reacted and swerved.

The driver of the truck responded far too late and too severely. The truck struck the man and then he disappeared beneath the front tyre just before the vehicle swerved and came across the road towards Julie.

She only had a split second before impact but managed to shout a warning and turn the front of the jeep away from the advancing truck. The truck screeched, or was it the same screech from before—she wasn't quite sure? The front edge of the heavy vehicle caught the back of the jeep and swung the car around before finally coming to a halt.

Nobody seemed to move for a few seconds, time seemed to stand still in a surreal dream-like way, and then suddenly the boys were shouting excitedly. She turned in her seat, Emma held her arm quietly but her eyes brimmed with tears of shock and pain and outside the first of the screams began.

Julie snapped open her seatbelt, tearing at the belt when it got tangled. She threw open the door and almost collided with the truck that was buried into the back end of her car. The back door was ruined and the way was blocked so she ran around the other side and wrenched open the other door to check on her daughter.

"Are you okay?" her voice was over loud but she barely noticed as the blood pounded in her ears.

"I'm fine," Emma said between sniffles. "I hit it against the door."

"More like it hit you," Julie noted as she nodded at the metal bulging inwards from the accident. "You two okay?" she looked at the boys who were half-way between awe that they had been in an accident and shock that they could have been hurt. They nodded mutely.

Julie examined them briefly anyway, running a hand over arms and legs, braced for a cry of pain that never came. Satisfied, she withdrew from the car.

"Stay there while I see what's happening."

Alan Peters stared at his aide and cringed. Somewhere a dim voice whispered, *that could have been you, you know. Lucky, lucky you.* His aide, Matthew O"Rourke hopped from one foot to the other as he gripped his ruined face. Bright red blood poured from between his fingers and a litany of curses poured from his mouth.

It had happened so fast. One minute he had been about to hit the man in pyjamas and the next O"Rourke had stepped in and the bastard had bitten him, torn half his face off to be more accurate. What happened next was still fresh in mind. His memory replayed the event in slow motion for him as he stood looking at the scene but not seeing it.

O'Rourke had screamed bloody murder and had lashed out at his attacker. With a strength borne of shock and pain he caught his attacker square in the chest and sent him reeling backwards out onto the road.

The man hadn't uttered a word, or even a grunt, throughout the entire exchange. He hadn't even screamed when the truck had hit him and he had disappeared under its wheels.

He looked down now at the road and saw two motionless legs sticking out from under the now stationary truck. He motioned for his other two companions to take care of O'Rourke as he pushed past his injured aide.

Constable Denis O'Malley had missed the accident. He shouldn't have missed it, as his beat would have brought him right opposite the scene, but the advertising hoarding extolling the cool refreshing flavour of a new ice cream had been too much for him. He had been in the process of tearing open the packaging when he heard the screech and then the scream.

His Sergeant would kill him if he ever found out and he dropped the ice cream, as if it announced his guilt and ran out of the shop. He pushed his way through the crowd that inevitably formed around accidents and tried to assess the situation.

There was a truck in the middle of the road, pulled sideways with its front fender buried in the back end of a light blue Jeep. People were screaming on the footpath. For God's sake, he thought *it's only a bloody accident*. He had only been in the force a short time himself but already he had seen far too many accidents.

It wasn't until he moved towards the footpath that he saw the body.

Chapter 8

Dan O'Sullivan banged again on the door and looked back towards the ambulance. The hospital had given them a second address when they had called in but there didn't seem to be anyone here either.

He was about to return to the vehicle when he heard a scraping at the front of the house. He paused and then returned to the door and pressed his ear against it. *There,* he thought as he heard another scrape. Suddenly there was a click and the door opened an inch or so and then stopped.

"Hello," he called as he tried to see in through the crack. "I'm from the hospital." There was no reply. "We're here for a Mr. O'Neill." There was a scraping at the door and it started to close.

Maybe they can't open the door, what if unlocking it was all they could manage and they now lay in the hall waiting for help?

O'Sullivan shot his hand out, stopping the door from closing and then pushed gently. It swung easily so he pushed further to reveal a narrow, heavily-shadowed hall. A man tottered backwards to avoid the door and O'Sullivan sighed in relief.

"Hi, I'm Dan O . . . "

The man grabbed him as soon as the door swung open and pulled him forward. The action was so surprising that O'Sullivan lost his balance and sprawled into the hall where he fell heavily against the bottom of the stairs. He looked up and saw a man in bright blue pyjamas. There were dark patches staining his front but the poor light in the hall clouded the details. O'Sullivan tried to rise but the man loomed forward and gripped him around the throat.

The hands were freezing, their touch seemed to suck the very warmth from his body and O'Sullivan felt fear for the first time. He had been attacked many times in his career; patients that were too scared or too ignorant to let themselves be helped, relations that turned on you in their grief or rage, even jealous lovers who had found him in their homes and assumed the worst. But this was different.

The man leaned in towards him and O'Sullivan retched with the sudden rank smell. He tried to scream for help but the hands around his throat were like vice grips. He tried to push the man away but the angle he was in gave him nothing to brace himself against and his hands groped ineffectively at the man.

The entire attack had happened in an eerie silence, broken only by the scuffling noises as O'Sullivan tried vainly to pull himself out from the stairs. Even the man's tight grip on O'Sullivan's throat, though, couldn't prevent the scream of agony that ripped from his throat as his attacker bent lower and tore the flesh from his face.

Frank Humphries replaced the radio and took a final drag on his cigarette. The administrator had told them to stay where they were until they could clarify the situation. Two homes with no answer was beyond co-incidance. He would wait until they contacted the local doctor. He stood up, stamped on the cigarette butt and headed back to O'Sullivan. He had almost reached the garden gate when he heard the scream. Humphries wasn't a coward by any means but the scream made him pause. There was something terrifying about it that ... he didn't have time to finish his thought. He looked up the garden path and saw that the door was open.

Suddenly a figure flew backwards out the door and sprawled on the path in front of him. Humphries looked down at the man at his feet and blanched. The man was grey, his face completely devoid of any colour, except for a deep red stain that ran from his mouth and continued down the entire front of his pyjamas.

Humphries automatically leaned towards the man to help him up and felt his hand gripped tightly. He stumbled as the man pulled him closer and then a searing pain shot through his arm as the man bit into the soft flesh on the inside of his arm.

The pain was beyond anything he had ever felt and consciousness began to slip away from him. He tried to pull his arm back but the other man held him tightly and bit again into his arm. This time the pain was too much and his eyes fluttered upwards and he fell forward.

Dan O'Sullivan lay panting in the gloom, sucking great breaths into his starved lungs. The pain of the bite had lent him a strength that he didn't know he had. He lay on the floor and the pain in his face throbbed terribly. He brought his hand up and it came away wet.

What the fuck is that guy on?

Slowly, he pulled himself to his feet. A racking cough gripped him suddenly and he braced himself against the stairs as his body recovered. He tried to call for help but his tortured throat was raw and he could only manage a hoarse cry. He moved towards the door, holding his hand over his eyes as the sunlight threatened to blind him. He got to the door just in time to see the man in pyjamas tear Frank Humphries' throat out.

"I've put a call into the Department of Marine but I don't think the guy I talked to was qualified to do anything. He said he'd pass the information on though," Pender grabbed a coke from the fridge as he put the phone down and went into the sitting room to join Johnson. "Any luck?"

Johnson sat on the sofa with the documents laid out before him on a small coffee table.

"There are about twelve sheets in total," he said as he straightened up from the table. "Some," he continued and lifted a few sheets, "are copies of inventory orders, weather forecasts for the time, fuel orders and maps."

"No orders relating to what they were doing?"

"No, and that's certainly not normal," Johnson lifted a can of coke from the table and sat back in his chair. "The German's were successful in the early part of the war due, among other things, to their efficiency. You couldn't move ten feet without papers, orders and permission from a litany of people. It took the allies quite some time to get a handle on the level of documentation needed to successfully infiltrate occupied territory. They just didn't operate without orders."

"Sounds like you know a bit about it."

"Not really, I had a case a few years ago that dated back to the war so I had to get some background."

"A case?" Pender leaned forward, "You never did say what it was that you did."

"Not now, John," he said softly, "I'm sorry but I'm just not ready yet. I know it's a leap of faith and I will tell you, but give me a few more days." The two men looked at each other and Pender pursed his lips and nodded.

"Fair enough. So what are they?" Pender asked as he indicated the pages on the table.

"Ah, these," Johnson said brandishing the pages, "are our saving grace. These are a few pages from the diary of one Hans Gruber, Captain of the *Seehund*, that's 'seal' for those who don't speak German, in the proud service of *Unterseebootwaffe*, that's the German Submarine Service to you."

"A diary," Pender sat up, "that's great. What does it say?"

"Let me see," Johnson ordered the papers and began to read out load.

March 1st 1944

We left today in the rain and the mist. Spring is always so bleak here on this barren rock, but at least the long winter is finally over. God, how I hate the perpetual darkness and biting cold that are the norm during December and January.

Our mission is disturbing but imperative if we are to disrupt the allies' planned invasion. We had a visit from Grossadmiral Dönitz himself today, a singular and distinctive honour but also one that underpins the gravity and importance of our mission. We knew that an officer of merit would be coming to inspect us but none of us expected the Oberbefehlshaber der Kriegsmarine himself. It was just as well we were well turned out and that our small navy gleamed.

"Hold on a minute," Pender brought his hand to his chin and stroked it unconsciously. "You said, 'small navy', is that the correct translation? Does that mean there is more than one of them out there?"

"I don't know, Johnson replied, "but that's the literal translation."

"Fair enough, we'll come back to it," Pender sat back in the sofa and Johnson continued.

The sea was angry today as we left harbour, the waves rolled incessantly as the wind pitched us to and fro. We had to dive while still in the harbour to avoid being ripped to shreds on the rocks protecting the harbour mouth. Once below the surface we made good time but our signals reported wild weather for the rest of the day.

March 3rd 1944

This is the second day underwater. These vessels were never meant for extended dives and the air is thick with the smell of sweat and diesel but we dare not surface. My calculations put us another four days away from our destination, I long to look up at a clear sky again and feel the wind on my face.

I have plotted a course that avoids the main shipping lanes and, hopefully, the allies' Northern Patrol, although their sonar is superior to ours so I am not sure if we can slip past undetected. We have been ordered to land on the West Coast of

England but with their head quarters being in Liverpool this will be difficult. Hopefully the other teams will have an easier time of it.

Our mission is critical to the invasion as the entire Russian Front is supported by the Allies out of the port of Liverpool. The merchants carry guns and supplies to the Russians in a seemingly endless steam and are protected by the battleships and destroyers operating out of Liverpool. We must find a way.

March 4th 1944

As we draw nearer to our goal Ernst and I grow more nervous. It is not just the worry from the constant patrols that pass overhead, although that is more than enough. We have had to travel the last two days so close to the coast that every crag and rock could rip through our shell and commit us both to a watery grave at any moment.

However, it is our cargo that worries us most. We were not told much about the canisters that take up so much of our living space but the scientists were adamant that we release their contents into the water supply as close as possible to major towns.

They gave us injections, of course, but I fear that these were more for effect than any preventative measure. A chemical deadly enough to warrant this effort so close to the Allies' expected invasion must be powerful indeed.

How the war has changed! Our once mighty German Army held to a standstill on the Eastern Front by mere peasants, defeated in Africa and Italy and now we resort to poisoning our enemies instead of meeting them honourably. I would have no part of it but for the relentless bombings on our civilians that the Allies are engaged in. Still, my heart is heavy and my soul, I fear, damned.

March 5th 1944

We are terribly off course. The sudden storm has carried us far from our destination and our small craft is not powerful enough to fight its pull. We must bide our time and wait out the weather, I hope it does not get worse. These Seals were really not designed for such long journeys. I dreamed again last night of the sky and the rain, oh to see even the barren wastes of our port again.

"That's it," Johnson dropped the last page on the pile and looked at Pender.

"Jesus! If that storm hadn't blown up we could all be speaking German now."

"Quite possibly, we'll have to inform the police. Those canisters obviously contain a poison of some sort."

Pender nodded and reached for the phone.

Constable Denis O'Malley pressed the button on his radio and announced his number; his voice was barely recognisable with the shock of the sight before him. The body lay at a grotesque angle. The front wheels of the truck had rolled directly over half the victim's body, crushing the left leg, chest and head. From one angle the victim merely looked asleep but from the other side his face had been shredded and pulped by the heavy tyres.

"347, go ahead," the radio crackled as the despatch answered him.

"Control, there's been an accident on Main Street, one fatality. Please send an ambulance and backup."

"On the way, Denis," he barely recognised the voice of his colleague through the static.

He let the radio fall back to the shoulder clip on his uniform and crossed to the driver of the truck who stood white-faced on the path looking at the body beneath his truck. He pulled out his notebook and flipped it open.

"Right, sir, can you tell me what happened?" he tried to keep his voice even and controlled but the image of the victim kept swirling in his mind.

The man turned towards him but merely stared at him, reciting the same words 'he just ran out in front of me, there was nothing I could do' over and over like a mantra.

"Constable," O'Malley whirled towards the voice and saw an attractive woman standing before him. The woman wore white shorts and a blouse that flattered her tanned skin. Her shoulder length brown hair framed an oval face and clear blue eyes looked quizzically at him. He realised with a start that he was staring.

"Sorry," he apologised and blushed, "what can I do for you, Miss?"

"I'm Julie Pender," she said and pointed at the Jeep, "I own the Jeep."

"Ah," he said understanding, "are you alright?"

"I'm fine but my daughter was hurt ..."

"Constable," another woman approached him with a bag in her hand. He recognised her immediately.

"Doctor Winfield, just in time. I've called for an ambulance but now that you're here this woman . . . "

"Hi, Julie," she interrupted and nodded.

"Theresa," Julie nodded and smiled.

"Oh, you know each other—good."

"You don't raise three children, Constable, without making it your business to introduce yourself to your local doctor," Julie smiled despite the situation.

"Quite so," O'Malley agreed, "you were saying your daughter was . . ."

"Is Emma okay?" Theresa asked quickly.

"Just a knock, I think. But if you could spare the time?"

Theresa Winfield looked at the constable and he nodded. "The victim is dead so you might as well."

She nodded and headed over to the Jeep.

Constable O'Malley turned and approached a group of people on the path. One of them was sitting on the ground rocking forward and backward with his hands held tightly to his cheek. As he pushed his way through the crowd he noticed the blood.

"Officer," he turned as a tall, black haired man approached him. "My colleague was attacked by that man," he said pointing towards the truck. "Have you called for an ambulance?"

"One is already on its way, Mister . . .?" he let the word trail off in a question.

"Peters, Alan Peters," he replied. "This is Matthew O'Rourke."

O'Malley wrote the names into his notebook. "Now, sir. Doctor Winfield is also here so we'll get her to look at Mr. O'Rourke as soon as she's finished. You say he was attacked. Can you give me the details?"

Theresa Winfield examined Emma's arm carefully, taking particular care around the bluish bruise that had already appeared.

"She was lucky," she said as she nodded at the ruined metal, "a little higher and it would have hit the bone. As it is, it's just a bruise. It'll go in a few days, give her Nurofen if it hurts too much and make sure she rests it."

"Thanks, Theresa." Julie sighed, relieved.

"No problem. How are you two?" she looked over at the boys who sat quietly in their seats. They looked at her and mumbled a reply.

"I think they're a little shocked," Julie said and winked at them.

"Don't underestimate shock; the best place for them is home right now."

"You're probably right. I'll just clear it with the police officer and then take them home."

Theresa nodded and the two women walked over to the path.

Theresa waved goodbye to Julie Pender and allowed herself to be directed to a man sitting against a shop window with a blood soaked handkerchief to his cheek. She knelt down beside him and gently lowered his hands so she could see the wound.

"Now," she said, "what have we here?" Her eyes bulged in shock as she saw the damage to the skin. She was aware of someone beside her reciting a story of what had happened but she was only distantly aware of it. She forced her eyes away from the wound and busied herself looking in her bag for a few items as she allowed herself a couple of seconds to recover from the shock.

The skin, and indeed a large chunk of flesh, from the man's right cheek had been torn away. There were jagged edges around the wound and in the centre there was a small hole through which she could see the man's teeth. *It's gone right through* she thought as she stared at the wound.

"What?" she began and had to cough to clear her throat. "What did you say caused this?"

"That bastard bit him," the man behind her stated. "He came from nowhere and attacked me and then poor Matthew got in the way and he bit him."

She dabbed at the blood around the wound, thankfully the bleeding had just about stopped. She heard a siren in the distance and looked at the man again. "The ambulance is here. I'm just going to get them and they'll take you to the hospital."

The injured man nodded but his eyes just stared ahead. *Shock* she thought, *Can't say I blame him, I'd be screaming my head off.*

The paramedics arrived with a wheelchair. Theresa filled one of them in on what she knew while the other man lifted the patient into the chair.

Theresa caught Constable O'Malley's eye and she crossed over to him.

"What a day," she sighed. "You let Julie go then."

"Yes, I can get her statement later, better to get the children home."

"Do we have an ID on the victim?" she asked.

"Not yet, would you mind taking a look? I didn't want to disturb you before but . . . "

"Certainly, lead the way."

"It's not pretty I'm afraid," O'Malley added as he led her to the truck, "but it would certainly speed things up if you recognised him. I'm afraid I haven't quite got round to all 15,000 inhabitants yet."

Theresa leaned in under the truck and looked in at the body.

"Jesus," she muttered as she saw the damage to the man's head. Half the skull had been crushed almost flat by the truck's wheels but the left side was still relatively undamaged. She studied that side and suddenly went pale.

Oh my God!

"It is gruesome isn't it?" O'Malley said as he saw her reaction.

"It's not that," she replied as she came out from under the truck. "That's Aidan Perkins but . . . "

"Perkins . . . " O'Malley wrote the name in his notebook and then looked at Theresa quizzically.

"It's just that I treated this man earlier this morning."

"It's no good beating yourself up, I'm sure you couldn't have ..."

"No," she interrupted, "you don't understand. When I visited him this morning he was at death's door. He was so bad that I put in a call for an ambulance to collect him along with four other patients who had similar symptoms. He certainly wasn't well enough to walk let alone attack someone."

"How are the other patients?"

"I don't know. I was on my way to Cork hospital when I got stuck in this traffic jam."

Chapter 9

John Pender heard the keys rattle in the door and rose from the couch to greet his family.

"Hi there ..." he began

"Dad," Jack burst into the hall, "there was a big truck and it squashed a man and then ran straight in to us and ..."

"What happened?" he asked as Julie walked in behind them.

"There was an accident in town ..."

"God, are you alright?"

"We're fine, but the car took a beating."

"Told you," Jack nodded as his mother confirmed his news.

"What happened?" Johnson asked as he joined them, having heard the brief conversation.

"A man stepped into the road and a truck swerved and ploughed into side of the car. Emma got a bit of a knock but the doctor said she was okay."

"You've already been to the doctor?" Pender asked concerned.

"No, she was at the scene so she had a look there and then."

"And the man?" Johnson asked as he poured hot water from a saucepan on the gas stove into a mug and added a teabag.

"Dead, I'm afraid."

"Oh my God, did the kids see it happen?"

"No, but they're pretty shaken up," Julie gratefully accepted a steaming mug of tea and sat down at the counter.

"You guys okay?" Pender asked the children and they all nodded. "Jesus, that's two accidents in two days. We'd better be careful; they say they come in threes."

"That's a cheery thought," Julie replied. "How did the big adventure go with you two?"

They filled her in and Johnson gave a brief overview of the diary's contents. "You hear that guys," she shouted into the living room, "that wreck out in the estuary is off limits okay? It's dangerous."

"Did you call anybody?"

"Yes, we informed the police and the Department of the Marine, but there's been no response yet."

"Electricity still gone?" she asked and nodded at the saucepan.

"Yea, just as well we have a gas cooker."

Julie lapsed into silence and sipped at her tea. "Are we safe here?" she asked suddenly and Pender frowned.

"What do you mean?"

"That wreck," she nodded her head towards the estuary. "That gas. It couldn't affect us from here if it got out could it?"

"I doubt it, but to be honest I don't know. What are you thinking?"

"I'm probably being ridiculous but with so many accidents ..." she let her words trail off as she looked at her husband.

"Do you want to move into town for the night?

"No," she said and after a second's thought nodded emphatically. "The kids have gone through enough excitement for one day. I'm probably over-reacting. We'll leave it until the morning and see how things are then."

"Are you sure?"

"Yea, I'm sure we'll be fine."

The phone was answered just as Theresa Winfield was about to break the connection.

"Hello," the voice at the other end sounded distracted.

"This is Doctor Winfield from Whiteshead, I'm ringing to check up on some of my patients. They would have been sent by ambulance this morning."

"Doctor Winfield," the voice repeated the name in a low tone a number of times as if the nurse was looking down a list. "I don't see anything here, doctor."

Theresa Winfield gripped the phone tightly as her fears grew. She had called for the ambulances earlier that morning once she had seen how bad each of the men were. Perkins had been bad enough but when she had seen the other men with similar, and in O'Neill's case even worse, symptoms she knew she had to get them to hospital. She had rung Cork Regional Hospital and put in a priority call for all five patients to be collected immediately. She had been on her way to the hospital when the accident had happened and finding Aidan Perkins on Main Street was the last thing she had expected.

"Are you sure?" she persisted. "The request was referenced to Doctor Matthews; maybe they are listed under his name."

The nurse mumbled the name as she checked through the list

again.

"I'm afraid not, doctor. We haven't had many ambulance cases today at all in fact."

"There must be some mistake," Theresa insisted as her mind tried to make sense out of what was happening. "Can you transfer me to despatch please?"

"Of course, doctor, hold please."

There were a number of clicks on the line and Theresa waited impatiently as she tapped her fingers on the steering wheel of her car. She had already tried the number of each of her patients and the phone had rung out in each case. *There must be a mistake,* she told herself, *patients don't just disappear.*

"Despatch," a bored voice announced suddenly and she jumped.

"Oh, hello. This is Doctor Winfield in Whiteshead. I called ..."

"Winfield. Yep, we logged a call from you at ten fifteen for the collection of five patients from Whiteshead."

"Thank God, yes," she sighed in relief, "I'm trying to check on my patients and Administration doesn't seem to have any record of them. Can you confirm what time they reached the hospital please?"

"Let me see," the voice at the other end replied and there was a pause. She could here a number of tapping sounds as the clerk typed the information into a computer.

"Umm, that's strange," the voice announced and then a flurry of tapping noises filled the line. Theresa felt her heart thump faster in her chest.

"Is something wrong?" her voice was nearly drowned out by the furious tapping noises.

"I'm not sure," the voice replied, "I remember the call. I had just come on shift and I despatched two ambulances because there were five bodies—sorry patients—involved. They left at ten forty but I can't see a delivery time. In fact," there was another flurry of tapping, "we got a call from 149 at eleven thirty saying that there was no answer at the first address and that they were going to continue on to the second and try again on the return journey. And after that there's nothing. There's a listing for another ambulance call an hour and a half ago."

"Yes, that was for a road accident. It's a separate incident," Theresa offered.

"Yea, we sent another car and they called in thirty minutes ago. They're on route and should be here soon. Hold on and I'll call the other two on the radio."

Theresa's mind raced furiously. Cork city was an hour away and it was now after three in the afternoon. They should have arrived ages ago. The seconds ticked by and she could hear the clerk talking in the background. It seemed an age before she heard the phone rattle as he picked it back up.

"Doctor, I can't seem to contact them at the moment, it might be a radio fault. Can I take your number and I'll call you back if I have any updates?"

Theresa gave the man her number. She didn't even hear his last words as she lowered her phone and started the engine. She'd have to check on her patients on her own.

Thursday 3.30PM – 5.00PM

John Maguire's house was closest. He lived on the edge of town on Marlborough Street, aptly named for a man who always had a cigarette stuck in his mouth. It still took her over twenty minutes to get there with the traffic still backed up after the accident on Main Street.

John Maguire lived with his two sons and together they ran one of the town's two petrol stations. He had been third on her call sheet earlier this morning and he had been the reason she had called the ambulances. His breathing had been way too laboured, it didn't help that he insisted on smoking despite his difficulty. His two sons were the image of him, right down to the cigarettes in their mouths and she had had to warn them to keep their father's room free of smoke, no matter what he threatened them with.

Maguire had been conscious when she arrived but had quickly lapsed into the trance-like state she had seen from both Perkins and O'Neill. His face seemed to turn grey as she watched and the racking cough he had had when she arrived seemed to ease as his breathing grew shallower.

The boys had been able to tell her that O'Neill and Perkins had entered a miniature submarine they had found out in the bay. They hadn't got any more information from him as his coughing had been constant and he had been violently sick ever since. They did know, however, that the other three, their father included, didn't actually go into the vessel. Maguire had, however, pulled Perkins out when some gas had been released.

This information was crucial and Theresa had rushed out to check on the final two men, calling the ambulances as she went. She had hoped that the other two men would be less affected if they had not been too close to the craft. She needed information from them so she could get a team to check the wreck. If they could get a sample of the gas then they would be better able to understand how it was affecting her patients.

Unfortunately, both men had been in the same late stages of the illness by the time she had got to them. Whatever this gas was it was certainly powerful if it could work that quickly and spread through the air.

She had put in a call to Matthews but had gotten his voice mail. She left a message for him outlining what she had found and asked him to call her. So far he hadn't returned her call and she had then been involved in the accident after that.

The day was disappearing rapidly.

The garage appeared in front of her as she came around the corner and she indicated and pulled off the road. The Maguires lived in a small house right beside the garage and she parked in the forecourt and got out.

A big Mercedes sat at the pumps and the owner was knocking on the office door with his credit card in his hand. Theresa crossed to the house and knocked on the door. There was no answer. She knocked again and turned when the Mercedes driver began pounding on the office door and calling for attention. He looked over at her and they both shrugged and returned to their knocking.

Theresa took out her phone and dialled the Maguire's number. She could hear the ringing through the door and snapped off the phone in frustration as it rang out. The Mercedes driver had moved off to the side of the garage and headed around the back, calling as he went. His original shout had now become an angry curse.

Theresa tried Doctor Matthews number again as she leaned against her car. She shivered as the sun slid behind some clouds. She looked up and frowned as she saw the cloud cover quickly spread across the sky like oil through water. A cool breeze came in off the sea and she opened her car to get her jacket.

She knocked again at the door. She heard a noise from over at the office, there was a heavy thump followed by a crash and she returned to her car to get a better view. The forecourt was still deserted; there was no sign of the Mercedes man.

She was about to give up and try the Perkins house when she saw the Mercedes man stumble around the corner clutching his throat. There was a dark patch staining his shirt and Theresa paled when she realised that it was blood. Her mind screamed at her to turn and run but she remained rooted to the spot. Indecision warred within her. One half of her argued that she must try to help while the other insisted that she run.

The man fell to one knee and raised a hand towards her. That was enough; her training took over and she reached into her car for her bag and ran to him. The blood spurted from his neck; whatever had cut him had ripped the artery. There was no way he would survive such a wound with what she had with her. The man tried to scream but only a choked gurgling came out. He flailed madly as Theresa tried to get a good look at the wound. She pulled one hand away but the man was beyond reason. He lashed out and his hand caught her just below her chin.

Her head swam as her teeth knocked together with the force of the blow. She was sent sprawling to the ground and knocked over her medical bag. The man tried to stand but the loss of blood was already sapping his strength. Theresa tried again to calm him and used her weight to force the man to lie down. He tried to resist but she was prepared this time.

She eased the man's hands away from the wound and pressed a cotton bandage against the wound. *Oh My God,* she thought. She had only gotten a quick look but the wound was ragged around the edges.

What the hell is going on? She had seen this type of wound earlier today. The man had been bitten.

She didn't hear the movement behind her until it was too late. She felt a hand grab her hair and pull her violently upwards. She screamed as she felt her hair torn from her scalp. She felt a second hand grab her arm. The grip wasn't tight but the pain in her head was more than enough for her to scramble to her feet.

She turned towards her attacker, bringing her knee upwards as she turned. She had a fleeting glimpse of a grey face and then her knee connected with the man and sent him sprawling backwards. He lost his grip on her hair but Theresa was overbalanced and she stumbled and fell forward towards her attacker.

She landed on his chest, hands outstretched, and immediately rolled to the side, narrowly avoiding his groping hands. She scrambled to her feet and fell again as the man swiped at her legs and brought her down on her knees. She cried out as she landed heavily. The pain was intense as she tried to rise and she stumbled when her legs wouldn't support her. She rolled over a number of times away from the man and lay panting as she looked back to see where he was.

The man's back was towards her as he rose unsteadily to his feet. She looked over briefly at the Mercedes man but he had stopped moving, the pool of blood around him already beginning to congeal. Her attacker turned towards her and she gasped as she saw the face of John Maguire. He looked worse than he had before; his face was so sunken that the dark ridges of veins protruded like cords of rope but his eyes still had the same glazed look.

He turned towards her and she tried to get to her feet again but her knees collapsed again. She cried out but there was no-one around. She pulled herself towards her car, oblivious to the pain in her legs as she dragged her bleeding knees over the tarmac.

Maguire moved slowly towards her but his stiff shambling was still faster then her crawl and he reached her just as she grabbed the open car door. Her hand locked around the handle and she went to pull herself up when he grabbed her jacket. She heard the material rip but he kept his grip and pulled her towards him.

Theresa gripped the handle harder and screamed as her arm was wrenched. She felt her grip loosen as her hands sweated and then she was falling back as the handle slipped from her grasp.

The back of her head struck the ground hard and she lay stunned as her vision filled with stars. A dark haze threatened to cloud her vision completely and she shook her head violently, ignoring the nausea. Maguire stepped in front of her and she brought her two feet up to her chin. Maguire leaned in towards her and she shot out her legs, catching him in the chest and sending him flying backwards.

The exertions caused her head to swim dangerously but she forced herself to breathe deeply and the nausea receded. She looked over and saw Maguire fall to the ground. She crawled back to the car door and grabbed the handle. Her vision clouded again, some remote part of her brain calmly informed her she was probably concussed but she ignored it. She pulled herself into the car, grabbing the steering wheel to pull herself further in.

She lay panting on the front seat and screamed as she felt a hand grab at her ankle. She turned awkwardly in the seat and lashed out again at Maguire, only this time it wasn't Maguire. It was his son, Peter. The same glazed eyes looked in at her, the same grey face, its muscles limp and sagging looming in her fading vision.

What the fuck is going on? She screamed in pain and anger as she kicked at him. She felt elation as she saw the man fall back out of the car but the pain from her knees shot through her like a wave. She fell forward and felt the darkness close in. She lashed her hand against the steering wheel, howling with the pain but using it to hold onto consciousness for a little longer.

She reached out a trembling hand and gripped the door handle and pulled with her last remaining strength. The door closed with a heavy thump and she raised her hand to snap the lock. It was too far. She raised herself up and reached again. Her head swam and darkness loomed. She reached out but her hand fell an inch short.

She collapsed to the floor and hit the metal pedals. The last sound she heard was the dull thump of fists against glass, as the sound followed her down into unconsciousness.

Evening

That night the weather broke. Thick black clouds rolled silently in from the sea, their mass heavily pregnant with moisture. Darkness came early with the sun's fading light being extinguished prematurely by the impenetrable cover. The lack of electricity allowed the darkness free reign as it draped over the town like a heavy blanket. Here and there a few pinpricks of candle light were all that kept the ebony shroud at bay.

The clouds sat bloated over the small town, seemingly impervious to any further force from the rising wind that had brought them here. They seemed to sit motionless in the air for some time as if waiting for something. Then, as if following a previously prepared plan, the rain began to fall. It fell lightly at first, as if reluctant to waste the water on such a small town, and then the force increased dramatically as the rain began to thunder on roofs and dance on roads and paths.

Out in the bay the waves gathered their momentum, pulling the tides back relentlessly until finally releasing their ferocious power against the harbour wall. Spray shot high into the air and the thunder of their violence was like artillery shells exploding. The wind swept down and carried the spray far into the town, hurling swaths of sea water against buildings and cars.

Alarms roared into life as the wind buffeted windows and vehicles with impunity. Dogs and cats sheltered as best they could, those not lucky enough to have found somewhere safe were swept up by the wind and flung savagely against walls. Pubs closed early and shutters were raised.

People made their way home or to their cars bent forward against the driving rain. Umbrellas tore or were whipped violently from their owners' hands, disappearing up into the blackness above. Here and there election posters, still on lamp posts after last week's election, flew past, some striking the unwary and eliciting more than a few curses from their electorate.

There were, however, a few figures that tramped through the weather, oblivious to the elements. They did not feel the biting wind or the torrential rain. Sometimes they would be knocked down with the force of the storm but they merely picked themselves up and continued on in search of something to tame the wild hunger that filled them with a singular purpose. The screams that followed their passing were snapped up by the wind and swept away, lost in the violence of the storm.

Day 3
Chapter 10

Friday 5.30AM – 6.20AM

The incessant buzzing reminded her of bees. She saw herself in a field, the sky was a perfect blue and a gentle breeze played with the daisies and buttercups, swaying their flowers to a beat only they could hear. The long grass tickled her bare legs and to her left she could see her father, busily gathering honey from the hives. A flood of pleasure surged through her, feelings of love and contentment enveloping her like the warm breeze.

In the distance she could hear the drone of lawn mowers and the heady scent of cut grass was almost intoxicating. Every detail was clear. She could hear the tiny bees, their individual wings beating furiously, the noise growing louder and louder, the pleasant background murmuring growing in strength until it blocked out everything.

Pain replaced pleasure as the breeze became a wind and the sky darkened with swarms of insects. Dark shapes appeared in shadows and fear replaced contentment. Her whole body ached, throbbing to the beat of the droning bees; the pain so intense, growing as the bees drew nearer, filling every pore. Growing and growing and …

She woke.

The pain remained but the images were already fading rapidly. She clung to the images of her childhood and tried to close her eyes, to recapture their warmth but the buzzing persisted.

She opened her eyes, her left eye stared at a metal pedal while her right eye remained dark. She raised her hand and pain surged through her body, bringing a wave of nausea with it. The buzzing continued and she touched her eye, her fingers groping gently as she felt a mostly-dry substance caked over the right side of her face.

Blood she realised and with the revelation the memories flooded back. The attack, the Mercedes man . . . *Oh God, the doors.*

She forced herself to move, ignoring the dizziness that threatened to pull her back into darkness. She gripped the steering wheel above her and pulled herself up. Her body ached from too many cuts and bruises but she gritted her teeth and forced the pain to one side. Survival was paramount.

Slowly she pulled her head level with the top of the steering wheel. Sunlight blinded her, the light burning like lasers after the gloom of the floor. Her left eye filled with water and she nearly lost her grip on the wheel. She sent a silent prayer of thanks that she had not yet opened her right eye or the pain would surely have made her lose it.

She levered her arm through the steering wheel and angled her bottom up onto the passenger seat. She lay there for a second, breathing heavily. Finally she wiped her eye and groped at the door lock, snapping it to the locked position with a dull clunk.

She had now idea how long she had been in the car but it had been getting dark when she had fallen unconscious. Had she really gone through the night on the floor? What the hell had happened to Maguire and his son to make them attack her? The car had been unlocked and yet they hadn't attacked her. Why? The questions swam in her head as her numbed mind tried to make sense of the last few hours.

She forced the caked eyelids of her right eye open and blinked repeatedly as her vision clouded with tears. She looked around, keeping her head low so as not to attract attention. The garage forecourt was empty. Mercedes man was gone, the ground was still stained red where he had fallen, despite the rain, but the body was gone. If someone removed the body then why didn't they see her? Where was Maguire?

The buzzing began again - had it ever actually stopped? She jumped at the sudden intrusion? It took her a few more seconds to realise that it was her phone. Someone was calling her. Her thoughts were still confused as the pounding in her head competed with the concussion. She had begun to wonder if she was totally alone or even if she was still dreaming. She fumbled for the instrument as a drowning man reaches for a lifeline.

"Hello," she almost shouted as she finally found the phone and jabbed blindly at the buttons in her haste to make contact with someone—anyone.

"Theresa," the man at the other end of the line sounded relieved. "Thank God. Where the hell have you been? I've been calling all night."

"William?" her speech sounded alien to her and came out slurred. "What time is it?"

"My God, woman you can't have been asleep all this time. I've been trying to contact you since yesterday evening."

"What?" The realisation slowly started to filter through the haze in her mind. "I was attacked, … hit my head …"

"Jesus," Professor Matthews whispered. "Listen, you've got to get your head together. There isn't much time. Things have spiralled out of control while you've been out."

"What are you talking about?" her voice was high pitched, close to panic.

"Your message about the submarine and the gas," Matthews prompted, his own voice strained with excitement. "The bite victim you sent from the accident," he explained, "he arrived yesterday evening and quickly exhibited the symptoms you described. We quarantined him but he attacked the nursing staff last night. He became completely rabid, uncontrollable. The Department are all over it. I've had military people questioning me all night."

"What happened to the patient?"

"Dead, they had to kill him," Matthews sighed. "I've never seen such relentless ferocity."

"Did he hurt anyone else?"

"Just scratches, thank God. We have everybody he came in contact with isolated, including me," he spat the last comment with an anger she had never heard from here before.

"What about my other patients?" she interrupted as the thought of the missing patients suddenly popped into her head.

"That's what I'm calling about?" Matthews snapped, concern in his voice. "We need to know what this gas has done to them. Did it affect them the same way? Where are they now?"

"I don't know," she replied as she looked out over the deserted forecourt. "I called for ambulances yesterday but none of them were collected. I went round to John Maguire's house, he was one of the one's that remained outside the sub, and he attacked me. I've been out since them."

"Shit!" Matthews cursed. "Look, the army are going to quarantine the town . . ."

"They're what?" Theresa exploded and winced as her response set off a fresh wave of pain.

"Theresa, these people are dangerous," Matthews tried to control his voice. "I shouldn't be telling you this but you just might make it out if you go now."

"Are they contagious?"

"We don't know, we're doing an autopsy but the findings are

strange."

"What do you mean strange?" There was a beeping in her ear but she ignored it.

"We're still doing tests but …"

The line went dead. Theresa snapped the phone away from her ear and looked at it, checking the signal. The battery tab blinked once and then the LCD screen went blank.

Shit. She sat numbed in the car. Nothing moved. *Where is everybody?* She looked at the sun and noted its low position. *It's still early,* she thought and relaxed a little. *Nobody's up yet that's all.* She considered what Matthews had told her. *Should she run, or wait for the army? Was it already too late?*

Too many questions swirled in her head and she felt as if she would explode. She had to at least try to help her friends and patients, but how? She thought hard and then snorted as the answer finally came to her, it was so obvious. She leaned forward, turned the keys in the ignition and headed back into town.

The phone rang, its annoying high-pitched tone bleated persistently in her ear. Julie Pender rolled over and buried her head in the pillow but the irritating tone continued, demanding attention. The phone used to be on John's side but he kept unplugging it, arguing that whoever it was could always call back. She had been quite vocal that someone had to be responsible in the family and had made quite a show of repositioning it on her side. She made a mental note to herself to apologise to him as she reached for the receiver.

"What?" she snapped at the phone as she looked blearily at the clock beside her bed.

"Julie, this is Doctor Winfield."

"Theresa," Julie snapped instantly awake noting that Theresa had used her formal title despite her tiredness. "Is something wrong?"

"Actually, yes," there was a brief pause. "I don't know quite how to say this but … Do you trust me?"

The question puzzled her but her answer was immediate. "Of course."

"Good," she sighed with relief, "gather up your family, right now. Put them in the car and drive to Waterford immediately. Call anyone else you know in town on your way but leave right now."

"Theresa, what's going on?"

"I really can't explain, Julie, but you need to go now. I'll explain later."

"Alright," Julie agreed already shaking her husband. "Listen, take care of yourself and thanks." She looked at the clock's digital display, 6:10. *What the hell was going on?* She mumbled a quick explanation to John but her tone conveyed more than the words. Then she was up and already running to the children's room as John was pulling himself from the bed.

Joshua Hackett rose earlier than usual. Yesterday's storm had forced him to close early and he was determined to make up for lost time. Operating the town's second supermarket was tough enough against that bastard Williams, whose family had been here for generations. Loyalty was important in this town and many of the older and established families wouldn't consider shopping anywhere else, no matter how much lower his own prices were.

Hackett had arrived over twelve years ago but would always be seen as a 'blow in'. Despite the town's growth and desperate need for another general store many people still considered him a thief, stealing business away from a local man.

Both supermarkets were very profitable, although he had to open from early till late while Williams only opened when it suited him. Yesterday's storm had forced him to close three hours early, his staff had flatly refused to work later with no electricity and with the storm growing so violent. He had tried to continue on his own but had finally given up when no-one had come to the shop at all in a time when he was usually very busy.

This morning, however, was a different case entirely. The sun shone, weakly at the moment but it was only six fifteen, and the air smelt fresh and invigorating. Good weather, especially after a bad storm, always pulled the customers in and he rubbed his hands in anticipation of the crowds that would flock to his store this morning. Williams wouldn't open until after ten so he had the whole town to himself until then and he planned on milking the most he could out of it, at least until the new chain supermarket arrived.

The new shopping centre was a major worry for him. A major supermarket chain was taking a huge area in the centre and already he could hear people growing excited with the prospect of lower prices and more brand choice. Williams would be alright, of course, but his own trade was mostly from the newer, and in most cases more affluent, inhabitants. A new competitor, especially one with big marketing drives and shiny new shelves, would hurt his trade badly, especially his profit margins.

He normally opened at eight o'clock but this morning he arrived at the store at six twenty. He almost bounded from his car and unlocked the shutters in one fluid movement. He cursed when he noted that the electricity was still off but he consoled himself with the fact that people had to buy more fresh food than usual as milk and other fresh produce spoilt more quickly without fridges. He could put up with working in a gloomy shop if it meant people spent more money.

His usual routine in the morning included taking in the milk, papers and bread deliveries that were left in front of the shop. These deliveries normally arrived around six thirty while he was still in bed and were always stacked neatly by the side wall when he arrived. This morning, however, he was too early so he pottered around the darkened shop realigning magazines, straightening shelves and restacking the myriad collections of chocolate and sweets that dominated the cash-point area.

He took his jacket off, the shop was quite stuffy without air-conditioning and the heat was already becoming uncomfortable. He heard a noise and turned to see a figure stumble into the shop. Hackett noted that the man walked stiffly but it was early yet and he could be on his way home after a night of drinking.

"I am so sorry," he began with an oily slickness perfected over many years of dealing with the public, "the electricity is still off and we're all floundering a little. Is there something I can get for you?"

The figure remained silent but recovered his footing and continued into the shop. Hackett shrugged, if the man wanted to keep his own council then that was fine—just as long as he spent money.

A truck screeched to a halt outside and a man jumped out and shouted a greeting into the shop. Hackett brightened as the Milk delivery man opened the back of his truck and started unloading.

This is wonderful, he thought as he headed towards the door, *maybe I should open up at this time every morning.* He moved to brush past his customer with a mumbled apology when the man suddenly grabbed him by the arm. *How rude,* he thought briefly as he turned, fixing a smile on his face as he turned to the customer.

"Can I . . . " his question was cut short as the man raised his other arm towards his face. Hackett felt the cold flesh an instant before the man's nails raked downward. Blood burst from three deep scratches on his cheek as the man's nails cut deeply into him.

Hackett was too surprised to scream. He merely stood looking at the figure as he brought his own hand to his cheek. It came away damp with blood and Hackett looked at it in confusion as the figure grabbed his arm and bent his face towards it.

Hackett finally reacted. He wrenched his arm back and was surprised as his action broke the man's grip so easily. His arm sprang back and he hit himself in the face which sent him stumbling back a few steps. The other man followed after him but tripped over Hackett's legs and both of them fell heavily to the ground.

Hackett landed hard and the breath flew from his lungs as the other man landed on top of him. He lay still, gasping for breath as he tried to make sense of what was happening. *Why would the man att...* his thought was interrupted by the most incredible pain in his arm. He looked down to see what could possibly cause such pain when a second searing pain struck him.

His head grew dizzy as the pain flooded his senses. Darkness threatened to take him but he struggled against it. He was dimly aware of shouting in the background but he ignored it as he looked down at his arm. It was covered in blood and a numbness started to spread through him as his body compensated for the pain by pumping adrenaline through his system.

He blinked in confusion as he saw the man tear another chunk of flesh from his ravaged arm. His mind rejected what it saw; the concept was just too far outside his experience. He tried to rise but he just didn't have the strength. The man's weight was too much and his position on top of him meant that he couldn't take a breath. Stars sparkled in his vision and his eyesight grew dim as the darkness enveloped him.

Chapter 11

Damn cheapskate, Hillary Talbot cursed as she exited Whyte's Hotel. She had stayed the whole night with her client and he had still only paid her for the original hour. It may have been her decision to stay because the bloody weather was so bad but he hadn't complained and she had given him more than enough reasons during the night for a sizeable bonus.

"Bastard," she spat. The sun was only just rising and its feeble light did nothing to keep the early morning breeze away. She shivered in her tight skirt and halter top as she made her way around the harbour. There were leaves everywhere, small branches lay strewn on the road and many more bobbed gently in the water, the lethargic swell of the waves in total contrast to the violence of yesterday.

She lived about four miles out of town and there was no way she would make it in the boots she was wearing. They looked great sure enough, hugging her legs and thighs in dull, crushed leather, but the high heels were totally impractical for long walks. She had wanted to call a taxi but her client wanted her out before the hotel staff began to clean the corridors and she couldn't very well ask at reception.

There wasn't a car in sight—that was unusual enough—but she couldn't see a soul on Main Street either. She was well used to leaving her clients early in the morning and knew the town's early routines well. She knew which shops would be open, the delivery vans were well used to her; most of them would even stop and give her a lift after they had dropped off their orders.

But this morning the town was deserted.

She tied her hair back to stop it falling in her eyes and wrapped her arms around herself in an effort to keep out the cold. She stumbled as her heel slipped on a soaked branch and she cursed again. She cursed her father, who had started abusing her at twelve and had forced her to run away at fifteen, she cursed her mother for ignoring the signs and pretending that everything was alright and she cursed the men who used her and cast her aside.

Prostitution was never something she had actually considered but giving favours to a leach of a landlord to allow her to stay one more month when she didn't have the rent was only the start. It wasn't such a long leap to offer her body for money on a regular basis and once you started it was ever so hard to give up.

You still needed to eat and every day brought more demands for money. Depression and self-loathing had led her to take drugs at first and then she couldn't stop. She had fooled herself initially that she would only do it until she got a good job but that argument grew weaker as each month went by. She was now twenty one and already her looks were beginning to fade. Her face was strained and lined and her eyes reflected the pain of a lifetime.

Despite the hard knocks life had dealt her she had a fire in her spirit that was hard to extinguish. She had begun to wean herself off the drugs in the last few months, they only made her feel sick and took too much of her hard earned cash anyway. It hadn't been easy but it did mean that she could afford to reduce the number of clients she had to entertain and that left her more time to try and get her life in order. She had recently begun to attend evening classes in typing and office management and hoped to qualify in a few months.

She saw the milk delivery truck parked outside the supermarket and she quickened her step. *Martin will give me a lift.* She liked Martin Taylor. He was twenty four and not bad looking. His hair was too long and his nose a little too big, but he was always nice and could make her laugh on even her worst days. He had even slipped her a few quid when she had had a bad night. She had offered to make it worth his while but he had never accepted, which was a pity because he was actually the first guy she had wanted to have sex with for an awful long time.

Her heels clicked loudly in the street, their sound seeming to rebound in judgement on her. The shop was open and that was strange, Hackett never opened until eight, but she shrugged, the only thing that mattered was that Martin was here and she wouldn't have to walk. She could hear the engine idling as she approached and then she heard a scream and saw Martin race from the shop and scramble to the van.

She started to run and called out to him. She didn't know what had caused the scream but she didn't want to be anywhere near whatever had caused it. Martin snapped his head towards her as he heard the shout but his glazed look showed no recognition. His eyes shone with fear and then suddenly he seemed to blink.

"Hillary," he shouted as he wrenched the door of the van open, "get in quick, before he comes out."

She ran towards the van. She wondered briefly if he had just robbed Hackett. If she got into the car she would be implicated and she already had enough hassle with the police. Martin jumped into the van and looked at her as he gunned the engine; there was real fear in his face.

"Hurry!" he screamed at her. Hillary made a quick decision and ran around to the other side. As she reached the door a man stumbled out of the shop, startling her. She grabbed at the door handle but her attention was drawn to the figure, there was something not quite right about him. She looked more carefully as he came into the sunlight and she grabbed blindly at the handle.

The man was covered in blood, his clothes were soaked with it, but what held her in thrall was the sight of his face. The man's mouth was covered in blood and his grey tongue licked greedily at the stains around his mouth. He noticed Hillary and changed his direction. He didn't show any emotion, just a glassy-eyed stare that held her rigidly in place.

"Hillary, move it," she heard Martin shouting at her but she just couldn't tear her eyes from the approaching figure. The horn blew and she jumped. The shock wrenched her eyes from the figure and suddenly she realised the danger she was in. She turned and grabbed the door, flinging it open and diving into the seat as Martin gunned the engine and sped away.

She looked back at the figure, expecting to see anger and frustration at her narrow escape but the figure merely changed direction again and continued on in its shambling gait.

"What did she say exactly?" John asked as they sat in the car and started the engine.

"She just asked me to trust her but that we should get out of town immediately."

"Did that mean us or everybody? Should we tell Dave?"

"I don't know, there really wasn't time," Julie replied, the last words carried a harder tone than she intended and she reached her hand forward to John's and squeezed gently.

"I'm going to tell him," John opened the door and ran across to Johnson's house and began to bang on the door. Julie looked at her watch nervously and looked in the back of the car and smiled at the children who sat tired and bewildered in their seats.

The seconds ticked away, their passing seemed to match each loud thump on Dave Johnson's door. Suddenly it stopped and she looked up.

"This is becoming a habit," Johnson yawned as he regarded his obviously harried neighbour.

"Dave, I can't explain now but I think you should get dressed immediately and come with us."

"Are you serious?" The question was out before he realised it. He glanced past his neighbour and noted the full car in the driveway; of course the man was serious. "Sorry," he apologised before John could reply. He was tempted to question further but he could see that Pender was highly agitated. His neighbour hadn't struck him as a man who panicked easily so he nodded and decided to accept the situation at face value. "I'll get dressed and follow you in my car." Pender nodded and ran back to his family.

What the hell is going on? Johnson thought as he rushed back to his bedroom and grabbed his jeans and a T-shirt. John didn't strike him as the paranoid type so something must be up, something big if he had his family in the car and ready to go at six twenty in the morning.

It must have something to do with the submarine, he concluded but worried at why there was such urgency. Had he heard something back from the Police? Johnson passed a window as he grabbed his jacket and quickly looked out over the estuary; there was no activity there so it was unlikely that the authorities had called him.

Questions swam through his head and he considered each one while he got dressed. He was well trained in reacting at a moment's notice and although he was deep in thought he swept through the room, gathering up everything he needed quickly and efficiently.

It only took him four and a half minutes. He paused briefly at the door and then rushed into the kitchen and jumped up on the counter. He punched through the tile above his head and grabbed the package secreted in the alcove. He gripped one end of the oiled rag and caught the Beretta M9 as it tumbled from its protective covering.

It never hurts to be prepared, he thought and raced to the door.

"**What** the hell was that?" Hillary looked over at Martin. His face was deathly pale, completely bloodless and his eyes darted between her and the road.

"I don't know but he attacked Mr. Hackett," his voice was high pitched and close to panic. "He fucking tore his arm to pieces and ate it."

"What?" Hillary snapped. "Are you sure?"

"I'm telling you, I saw the fucker rip Hackett's arm apart with his teeth and eat the flesh."

Hillary remembered the blood on the man's face but her mind still rejected that someone would actually eat raw flesh. Her look betrayed her thoughts.

"I know what you're thinking but I saw it," Martin insisted stubbornly.

"What are you going to do?" she asked quietly not wanting to upset him. She wondered briefly if she had done the right thing getting into the van after all.

"We'll head to the Police Station."

"I can't go to the Police dressed like this," Hillary snapped back at him.

"They'll have much more to worry about than what you've been up to," he relaxed a bit now that they were away from the shop. He smiled reassuringly. "Don't worry; you won't even have to get out of the van."

"Alright then," she agreed slowly and went back to looking out the window. She still hadn't seen another soul.

The Police Station was back the way she had just come. It was housed in a small converted house just off Main Street and catered for four officers and a Sergeant. Martin jammed on the breaks and leapt from the van, leaving the engine running and the vehicle parked at an angle with its rear blocking the street.

His purposely tried to keep his mind focused on getting to the police. He dared not let himself think about what he had seen. His skin still crawled with the images that he couldn't suppress but he refused to even consider what they might mean. He ran around the van and up to the entrance, slamming the door open with such force that the glass wobbled dangerously.

"Hello. Anybody here," he shouted as he reached the small counter. The room behind the counter was separated by a partition with frosted glass at either side of a small wooden hatch. He banged on the glass and pounded the small bell on the counter.

"Hello, there's been an attack at the supermarket, is . . . " He stopped for a second as he saw movement behind the glass. The dark shape was distorted through the glass but there was definitely someone there. He waited impatiently, hopping from one foot to the other. The figure seemed to approach the glass but the hatch didn't open.

"Hello," he knocked on the glass again. "This is an emergency. You're going to need to call an ambulance." The figure moved again and he heard a chair scrape across the floor.

He looked around the small reception area and cursed under his breath. *What the hell were they up to?* He saw a door to his right and crossed to it. He snatched at the handle and almost fell through as the door opened easily inwards. A small corridor greeted him and, at the end, he could see where it opened out into a larger room.

"Hello," he called again as he moved slowly down the corridor. His mind began to imagine all kinds of things as he progressed slowly towards the open room. A thought struck him. It must be Sergeant Donnelly on duty he sighed as he thought of the old Garda. It was well known in the town that he was past retirement age but Dublin didn't have enough senior offices to go around and they couldn't run a station without a Sergeant so they had asked him to continue for a while longer.

Everyone loved Donnelly, most of the town had received a clip across the ear from him in their youth when they had committed minor offences and everyone had a lot of respect for the big man, but he was more than a little deaf. Martin moved with a bit more confidence as he solved the mystery and he smiled as he reached the end of the corridor and entered the office itself.

Hillary sat in the van and worried. She looked at her watch and for a minute she thought that it was broken. The hands showed 6:30. *Surely it's later than that?* She looked around but the only windows in the van were the windscreen and front windows and her field of vision was very limited.

Martin had parked the van at an angle to the Police Station with the back of the truck towards the Main Street. The street they were on was a short cul-de-sac and all she could see were a few dark houses. The whole town could be coming up behind her and she wouldn't see them until they were on top of her.

What the hell is going on? There was definitely something wrong. Whiteshead may be a small town but by six thirty half the town is normally up and about. She should be seeing the early commuters on their way to Cork and Waterford by now. The early shift for the local pharmaceutical plants start at seven but there still wasn't any movement in the town—it was like a bank holiday.

And then there was that man at the supermarket. Now that she had time to think about it she wasn't entirely sure that she believed Martin. Sure he probably saw something but, actually eating someone was just too far fetched. Wasn't it? The image of the man sprang into her mind. The blood on his clothes and dripping down his chin made her doubt her own ruminations. *Could it be true?* She wondered and shivered.

She kept looking over at the Station door, hoping to see Martin emerge with a smile of relief on his face but the doorway remained empty and the area beyond remained gloomy without the aid of electrical lighting. She kept glancing in the rear view mirror but the angle of the van only afforded her a small view of what lay behind.

She didn't like being here, especially being so exposed. She noticed that the lock was still open on the doors and reached over to the driver's door and pressed the button down before doing the same to her own. She looked over at the station door again but there was still no sign of Martin. What was taking him so long? Surely the Police would at least want to investigate?

She considered briefly going in after him but quickly discounted that, she had spent enough time in the station against her will since her arrival in this town and she was damned if she would voluntarily go in. The engine continued to turn over, the diesel engine spluttering loudly in the quiet street. Should she turn the engine off? Would the noise attract more people like that man at the supermarket? Were there any more like him and what exactly were they? The questions flooded through her mind and indecision and fear paralysed her just as effectively as the man at the supermarket had done earlier.

If she turned off the engine it might not start again, the spluttering sounded rough enough as it was. She looked again in the mirror but she couldn't see anything. Her heart thumped in her chest as she warred with herself.

What if Martin didn't come back? The thought hit her like a blow; she couldn't just sit here like a prat. She had to do something. She took one more look at the Station door and then slid over into the driving seat. She should turn the van around to allow them to leave quickly if they needed to; it would also give her a view of the Main Street, just in case. At the very least it gave her something to do.

Alan Peters woke in a foul mood. The meeting with the local council had been cancelled because of the accident and was scheduled for later this afternoon instead. He hadn't slept well as the bed in the Hotel was uncomfortable. He had no toothbrush and his mouth felt like he had licked the carpet—although this had more to do with the amount he had to drink the previous evening than anything else. His head hurt and he had only brought one set of clothes as he had planned to drive back to Dublin after the meeting yesterday.

He washed as best he could and sniffed his shirt dubiously. It would have to do until he got to a shop and bought a new one. He had called reception already but had received no answer so he would have to go down himself. He looked out over the Harbour and saw the chaos that the storm had wrought. He was vaguely aware that there had been a storm but they had started drinking pretty early yesterday and hadn't finished till late.

He briefly considered phoning his secretary and getting her to get him a change of clothes but, in a rare moment of compassion, he decided to let her sleep. He let the door close behind him and made his way down the stairs.

Chapter 12

The smile on Martin's face froze. He had been right on one point; the Garda on duty was indeed Sergeant Donnelly, he recognised the man's massive frame immediately, but everything was far from alright.

The Police Sergeant looked very like the man from the supermarket. He had the same grey, sunken flesh and his uniform was torn along his arm and the material was heavily stained with blood. As he looked, Martin could see that the Sergeant's arm was as torn as his shirt. Flesh hung in ragged tatters from the appendage and blood covered it in clotted lumps.

He backed away and stumbled over a chair, nearly falling but somehow managing to keep his footing. The big Sergeant was already facing him but was trapped behind a small chicken-wire area that surrounded the public counter area. The small enclosure was to further protect the main office in case anyone tried to enter the office via the hatch. The Sergeant had obviously approached the public counter when Martin had first come in but the door had clicked closed behind him, effectively locking him in the small cage.

The Sergeant stood against the wired partition and swung his hands methodically against the wire, oblivious to the wounds he inflicted on his fingers and hands. Martin noted that the cuts forming on the Sergeant's hands did not bleed. The partition wouldn't last long. It was only the fact that the man was hitting the wire at random and not in the same place that had kept it intact so far. It would hold for now.

Martin looked around. The initial shock was fading and his mind began to think rather than just react. If there were two of these things then it was safe to assume that there could be more of them. Martin lived about four miles out of town and he collected his deliveries from the Co-Op each morning about ten miles away before returning and delivering to all the shops. Everyone in town had been alright yesterday so whatever had happened was only recent.

Hillary wasn't affected so it probably hadn't happened to everyone. However, so far he had only seen three people and two of them were affected so the odds weren't great. The fact that the town was so deserted hadn't escaped him either.

He kept an eye on the Sergeant and searched through the station for anything he could use. Police in Ireland aren't armed so there were no weapons but he did pick up two expandable batons that he found in two utility belts hanging along the wall.

Martin smiled as he gripped the small foamed vinyl grip. The baton was only five inches in length as he held it but shot out to a length of twenty one inches when he flicked his wrist. The silver gleam of the baton and the reassuring weight gave him confidence and he held the baton tilted against his shoulder as he approached a door at the far end of the office.

There was nothing else worthwhile that he could see in the room but he wanted to make sure there was nothing else of any value else-where. He opened the door and walked through to a larger room that had been converted into a small jail. There were four small cells with metal bars running from the floor to the ceiling. The first one was occupied but the others lay open.

The first cell held another figure like the others with grey skin and blood smeared over its mouth. The man reacted as soon as the door opened and crashed against the bars, his hands grasping at the air towards him.

The officers had obviously locked him up before he had changed completely but he must have bitten Donnelly in the struggle. Martin turned away from the figure. He still found it eerie that these things, whatever they were, were so quiet. There were no grunts or noises of pain or hunger from them at all, not even the sound of breathing.

Martin had seen enough horror movies to give him an idea of what might be happening but his rationality insisted there must be another answer. He heard the van's engine rise in volume and he rushed back out through the office. He had forgotten about Hillary. *How long have I been in here?* he wondered as he rushed out. Behind him he heard the crash of the chicken-wire finally giving way.

Hillary shoved the van in gear and pulled hard on the hand-break to release the lock. She hadn't driven a van before but she was well used to cars and had even driven a tractor once. The happy memory was fleeting. Her childhood had ended once she entered puberty and her father had come visiting in the night.

She slammed her foot on the accelerator, suppressing the memory savagly, and the van leapt forward in a series of jerks that threatened to stall the engine at any second. She levered her foot further against the accelerator, giving it more fuel but losing control of the steering wheel as the van shot forward and hit the wall opposite.

Her chest slammed against the steering wheel knocking the air from her and the engine rattled, coughed and then died. The silence seemed to fall over her like a blanket. There was a sudden bang on the driver's door and she screamed. She looked out the window and almost cried with relief as she saw Martin bang on the door and point at the lock. She looked at him, confused. He seemed to be mouthing words but she couldn't hear anything.

Then, suddenly, she could hear again and Martin's shouts and his banging on the door were so loud that she cringed. She reached over to the lock and flipped the button up and immediately snatched her hand away as the door flew open as she slid back across the seat.

"What the hell are you doing?" Martin shouted as he jumped into the van. "There are more of those damn things and one of them is right behind me."

"S . . . Sorry," Hillary managed as her senses began to recover after the accident. "You were so long. I thought I'd turn the van in case we needed to get away quickly."

Martin reached down and turned the key. The engine coughed and he pumped his foot on the accelerator, feeding it more petrol and pleading with it to catch. The engine spluttered and then died.

"Shit!" he cursed and looked in the mirror. He could see Sergeant Donnelly stumble from the station. He tried the key again but the engine was flooded. He could smell the diesel in the air and forced himself to wait. Hillary looked over at him and apologised again, then her eyes widened as she saw Donnelly cross the road towards them.

"Try it again," she shouted and slapped her hand on the dash-board.

"I can't, it's flooded," he tried to remain calm but his heart was pounding. He purposely didn't look at Donnelly, that would only make him turn the key too quickly but Hillary's screams were warning enough.

He couldn't help himself, he looked. Donnelly was right next to him and Martin turned the key in shock. The engine roared to life and he jumped, nearly letting the engine die before he slammed his foot back on the accelerator. He jammed the van into reverse and the van powered backwards. The Police Sergeant was thrown to the ground where he immediately began to rise again.

Martin stared at the man on the ground and then he lurched back and then surged forward as they hit the wall behind.

"Shit," he cursed and tore his attention away from the officer. He put the van into first and surged away back onto Main Street.

"What are we going to do now?" Hillary asked, her gaze locked on the rear-view mirror.

"I think it's time we got out of town."

By the time Alan Peters arrived down to reception he knew something was wrong. He had spent enough time in Hotels to know that 6.40 in the morning was mid morning as far as the staff were concerned. When he got to the foyer he could see that the reception desk was empty, the dining room closed and no evidence of cleaning anywhere on his trip down.

He saw an old couple standing uncertainly by the desk ringing a small bell for attention.

Well, at least I'm not totally alone, he thought as he approached the couple, they looked relieved that they had found someone. They were both in the sixties, Peters judged. *Yet another tourist looking for their Irish roots,* he thought unkindly.

"Hello," Peters called as he crossed the tiled floor, wincing as his footsteps reverberated like gunshots in the empty room.

"Hello," the man replied and the woman smiled. "The place seems deserted." The man's southern drawl placed their origins just as accurately as the ridiculous-looking 'Dallas Cowboys' baseball cap on his head. "I'm John Tanner and this is my wife Adelle."

"Alan Peters," he clasped the man's hand tightly and smiled at the woman. "No one around?"

"Doesn't seem to be," the man lifted his cap and scratched his grey hair, "maybe we're too early for 'em. Me an Adelle always rise early, 'specially on holiday." The couple smiled again and Peters was already bored with their company.

Just then a wiry man in an ill-fitting suit appeared through a door behind the desk. He looked tired and harried but forced a smile as soon as he saw the guests.

"I'm so sorry," he said as he straightened his tie. "Bit of a staff shortage this morning, I'm sure they'll be in soon. Is there something

I can help with?"

Peters took the opportunity to escape. "I'm sure our friend will be able to help, if you'll excuse me I have to find a shop to buy some new clothes," he indicated his ruffled appearance. "Unexpected stop over."

They both nodded and smiled again as he headed for the doors and out into the street.

Theresa Winfield replaced the phone on its receiver and sighed. Her office only had one small window and the light barely illuminated the large office. She had grown accustomed to the dark while she made her phone calls but it still seemed to press in on her. The fact that she knew something was happening only served to increase her unease.

She had called everyone she had a number in her files for. That wasn't as many as she would have liked as her uncle had not kept great records; medical histories and notes of visits were all accounted for but personal information was sadly lacking. *He probably knew all their numbers off by heart,* she thought.

She had managed to phone forty patients but had talked to less than half that number. She had no idea whether the other half were fast asleep or dead and the ones that she had reached had probably thought her mad.

She had tried to call Matthews as soon as she got to her office but the phone wasn't making a connection to any number outside of the local exchange. She had even tried one of her patients who lived ten miles out of town and received the same ominous disconnected tone.

There was nothing more she could do so she packed up her medical bag, taking anything that might be of use, and headed out to her car.

Alan Peters stood on the steps of the Hotel and looked around. The Hotel was situated at the end of Main Street overlooking the harbour. Small boats bobbed gently at their moorings, although he could see one or two that had slipped their lines during the storm. A gaudy yellow two-berth was tapping gently against the harbour wall as the waves lapped against it and another larger boat made its way out to sea.

The area immediately in front of the Hotel was covered in leaves and branches and the droplets of water that hadn't yet been seared away by the rising sun reflected millions of tiny rainbows. Peters looked towards the main shopping street but there was no sign that any of the shops were open.

He could see the construction cranes and the metal girders of his building site looming over the street from where he stood. *Bleeding environmentalists* he cursed. He had not had time to visit the site and see how work had progressed since his last trip down over two months ago It was obviously too early to get what he needed in the shops so he decided to walk over and have a look while it was still quiet.

"**Which** way?" Pender asked as they sat at the crossroad.

Whiteshead lies nestled beneath the splendour of the Knockmealdown Mountains which loom protectively around the small town on all sides. The mountains extend, in an east-west direction, for approximately 35 miles and the border between the counties of Waterford and Tipperary runs along the peaks of the range.

There are three routes out of the valley with the main routes running east and west, to Waterford and Cork respectively. The third route takes a northerly direction and spirals up over the range, reaching some 790 metres before coming down into Tipperary on the other side.

They had reached the T junction at the end of the estuary in silence, each of them busy with their own thoughts.

"Theresa said to go to Waterford" she replied and shrugged.

"Fair enough," Pender sighed and checked for traffic. The road stretched for miles to the right but on the left a sharp bend created a well-known accident spot. Normally at this time there would be a huge amount of traffic, commuters getting into the cities of Cork and Waterford before the main traffic rush. This morning, however, the road was clear.

He pulled out and almost immediately the shrill blare of a horn made them all jump. Pender slammed on the brakes and looked down the road at the back of a fast-disappearing Toyota.

"At least we're not the only ones left in the town," he joked as Julie fumbled for a cigarette.

"I was beginning to wonder there for a while myself," she replied as she drew smoke into her lungs and exhaled slowly. Pender checked both directions again and pulled out onto the main road. He checked his rear view mirror and nodded as he saw Johnson follow him.

They started seeing a few more cars as they drove up out of the valley, although they were all going in the one direction - out towards Waterford.

"I've never seen that before," Pender looked over at his wife.

"What?"

"There's usually a steady stream of traffic going towards Cork by this hour in the morning. I've never seen it this quiet."

"It's got to be related to Theresa's phone call. I wonder what's up." Julie stubbed the butt of her cigarette out and laid her hand on her husband's thigh.

The unexpected traffic jam as they rounded the corner made both of them jump and Pender slammed on the brakes, stopping mere inches from the car in front. He quickly checked the mirror to see if Johnson had seen them and sighed in relief as he saw the BMW stop smoothly behind them.

"What now?" he shouted at the car in front as his heart thumped in his chest. "There are no traffic lights on this road."

"It must be an accident then," Julie shrugged.

"Maybe," he replied. He looked past the car in front but whatever was blocking the road wasn't visible from where they were. Johnson appeared at his window.

"What's up?"

"No idea," he replied and opened the door and got out. "Want to take a look?

"Lead on my friend."

He leaned back into the car for a second, "I'll be back in a minute."

Chapter 13

Friday 7.00AM – 8.00AM

"… **and** I understand that, sir, but my orders are to stop any and all traffic on this road. I am sorry but you can't come through here."

Pender and Johnson arrived at the roadblock just as the harried soldier was finishing. The Irish Military were rarely seen on public roads. Except for escorting their own payroll on a weekly basis and the occasional off-campus activity, it was rare indeed to see the dull green trucks at all. Pender never remembered seeing them involved in actual traffic control before.

A number of police officers stood along the barricade but their status was obviously only as a support roll. Three Army trucks were parked on the road and at least twenty fully-armed soldiers stood along a small wooden barrier that had been pulled across both lanes. There was a second barrier on the far side of the trucks, effectively creating a controlled zone in between them.

There were at least fifteen people gathered around the barrier with a large fat man as the focal point. He stood as close as he could to the barrier and leaned over so that his belly rested on the cross beam and his forehead nearly touched that of the Lieutenant who had spoken. His face was red with anger and he raised his finger and jabbed it at the soldier, however he stopped short of actually touching him.

"I don't give a damn about your orders," the man shouted and his voice carried easily to where Pender and Johnson stood, "I have to get my wife to the hospital . . ."

"And I've got an important meeting," another man to his left added to which a number of others muttered their pressing needs to be allowed through.

"Sir," the Lieutenant had to shout before the clamour died down enough for him to be heard. "We are happy to provide medical help," the Lieutenant replied calmly, although his voice had taken on a harder edge than before. "What's wrong with your wife?"

"She was bitten," the man replied and pointed at the car just behind him.

The soldier seemed to stop for a second but then recovered.

"What happened," the soldier asked.

"A bloody dog came up to her when we were out for an early walk and just bit her for no reason," the man's voice was calmer now and his face had recovered most of its normal colour.

The soldier seemed visibly relieved and quickly called for the medic to come forward. Johnson looked over at Pender and raised an eyebrow. The general clamour grew again as others took up the lead and demanded that they be allowed through. The medic arrived and called the woman and man through the barricade and directed them towards a small tent that had been set up on the grass verge. A soldier followed them and took up station at the tent opening.

"You can't do this," another man shouted.

"I'm afraid we can," the Lieutenant held up his hands in a conciliatory pose but the voices continued to rise and drowned out any further response.

"Can they just block the road this way?" Pender asked Johnson. "I've never seen the Army do this before.

"They can't," Johnson confirmed, "but the police can and that's why you see the token Police presence. If you check on the legalities you'll probably see that the roadblock is officially down as a police action, but they're only here for show. This is an army operation all the way."

Pender looked at Johnson for a second and then shrugged. "What would bring them out for this kind of thing, escaped convict?"

"It would have to be more serious than that for these guys to be involved," Johnson confirmed.

"What do you mean?"

"The Cavalry Corps are usually the ones that would help the police with conventional operations. You see that flash insignia on the Lieutenant's arm?"

"The one with the swords?"

"Yep, that's the Fianóglach, which shows they're part of the Rangers. These guys wouldn't be called in for just anything."

"How do you know all this?"

"Let's just say I've been through the same training these guys have had."

Pender considered for a moment but before he could respond there was another commotion at the barrier. The situation was deteriorating rapidly. Three men had grabbed one end of the barrier and were attempting to move it to the encouragement of the others. The shouts built up to a crescendo. Two soldiers levelled their guns at the men and the Lieutenant was shouting for calm.

"Oooh," teased a barrel-chested man, "what are you going to do —shoot us?"

The other men began to jeer and two others joined the group at the barrier and began to lever out of its ties.

Suddenly there was a gunshot and everyone stopped. The silence was immediate and total, as if someone had hit the mute button. A tall man exited the tent with his pistol in his hand. He wore a beret at a jaunty angle and his cropped hair barely appeared below the material. He wore camouflage fatigues like the other men but his battle dress was impeccably tailored, the pips on his shoulders identified him as a Captain.

Everyone stopped what they were doing and waited for the man to reach the barrier.

"Gentlemen and Ladies," he smiled but there was no warmth in his face. "We are sorry for the inconvenience, truly we are. But our orders have been issued by the Taosiseach's office itself and they are very clear. We will continue to carry out these orders until relieved or told otherwise."

"I suggest you all go back home and wait for further word. There is no point in asking my men what is going on as they do not know, none of us do. But let's be very clear about this. We have been ordered to hold this position as a matter of the highest priority. No-one is to pass and we are authorised to use any and all means to ensure that these orders are carried out." He paused as he scanned the crowd and slowly replaced the sidearm he had used to gain their attention.

"Now please move away from the barrier or we will be compelled to remove you forcibly." The other soldiers had quietly taken up positions on either side of the group and all of them now had their weapons levelled at them.

Nobody moved for almost a full minute and then, slowly, the first of them turned away and returned to their vehicles. The more militant among the group remained where they were for a while longer, staring hard at the Captain, but as the group reduced in size even they turned away eventually. They walked slowly back to their cars deep in hushed conversation and Pender shrugged and started back as well.

Johnson laid his hand on his arm, stalling him, and pointed at the small die-hard group. They talked animatedly for a few minutes and then rushed over to their respective cars. They turned around and sped back towards town, one of them, a land rover with four men inside, nearly crashed into some of the other people in their haste.

"What do you think they are up to?" Pender asked.

"Nothing good I'm sure." Johnson replied. "Where do we go no?"

The two men continued to talk as they walked back to their cars. "There's a country road up over the mountains," Pender answered, "maybe they haven"t covered that route."

"Lead on, I'll follow you."

Alan Peters shivered as he walked out of the sunlight and entered a tunnel of plastic sheeting that marked the entrance to the site. He blinked furiously as his eyes grew accustomed to the darker interior and it took a number of tries before he succeeded in sliding the key into the heavy lock that held the chain link in place. The chain was wrapped tightly around the door handle and a metal bar that was inset into the frame. The security wasn't exactly high but then again there wasn't too much anybody could really steal that would fit through the door. The larger entrance, where the trucks and cars entered, was secured by heavy fencing and was alarmed. As soon as he opened the lock he threaded the chain through the handle and the door swung open only to be blinded again as he walked back into the sunlight and into the main site.

The outer shell of the centre was almost complete but there were still a few bare metal girders thrusting naked into the sky. Peters was proud of the design, having spent a small fortune rejecting plan after plan. Finally, he had found someone who had been able to convert his vision and his enthusiasm into an architectural reality.

He looked over the structure and smiled. The early morning sun was slowly drying the soaked deck and a slight haze rose lazily into the air bringing with it a heady smell of sea air and fresh wood. Even as bare as the structure was he could already see that the finished product would be all that he had hoped it would be. The shopping centre was built along one side of the new harbour; in fact the whole west wing jutted out over the water and was supported by cylinder-shaped stone pillars.

Peters had initially tried to reject the idea but his architect had seemed so excited by the design that he had relented. He stood on the small walkway and looked down the line of shop fronts and smiled. The water lapped gently against the pillars below him and he knew that the architect had been spot on. He'd make a fortune in rent for the water fronted properties, they were the perfect location. A restaurant or a bar would pay heavily for this attractive setting.

He moved on. The front doors were locked and the windows had all been installed but there were still a few gaps where it was possible to squeeze through. He walked along the walkway, taking care on the surface that was still wet and slippery from yesterday's storm. He eventually found a gap on the east wing where they had still not sealed the outer lining.

The centre stretched all the way through from the harbour to the main street of the town and was the single biggest structure and investment the town had ever seen.

It's too bloody late to stop it now, he insisted to himself as he looked around. There were three floors in the centre stretching in huge ovals around a large open middle area with plants and water features that complimented the water theme from outside. The entire roof was glass and rose to a spectacular pinnacle in the centre. You could see the building from miles away and at certain times of the day the sun reflected off the roof at just the right angle and sent beams in a blaze of colour over the whole area.

I won't let them stop it now.

He looked at his watch; eight o'clock. He took one more look around; burning the image in his mind. He would have a fight on his hands later today and he wanted to remember just what he was fighting for. The sun had risen higher when he squeezed back outside and he was disoriented as he pulled himself through the narrow opening. He didn't see the figure approaching him until the last minute.

"Is there a problem?" Julie asked as her husband got back into the car. She knew that her voice had more of an edge to it than she had meant but the children had been driving her mad since John had gone to see what had caused the traffic jam. They usually played well together but the unexpected early start and the cramped back seat had been a recipe for disaster and good-natured banter had quickly descended into outright arguments as the minutes had ticked slowly by.

"I'm not entirely sure," John replied as he put his seatbelt on and started the car. Julie felt like shouting at him to tell her more but forced herself to wait. She knew her husband too well, he'd tell her everything but he was still putting the facts in order in his head and there was nothing she could do to hurry him up.

"There's an army roadblock up there," he continued as he put the car in reverse and turned around.

"The army," Julie interrupted, "but they don't do traffic duty."

"I know but they're armed and adamant that no-one gets in or out. Theresa was right it seems. There's certainly something very peculiar going on."

"Are you sure that it wasn't the local part-timers?" Julie asked referring to the territorial regiment that worked full time jobs and played at being soldiers at the weekends.

"No," John replied as he drove back the way they had come. "Dave says they're not just army but Rangers, the elite of the Irish army."

"Rangers! How does he know?"

"That's another strange thing," he looked over at her and she could see that he was worried. "He said something about training with a bunch of them."

"My God, who do you think he is? What is he?" Julie asked as she looked back towards the car behind them.

"I don't know. There's just too much we don't know right now." He sighed and placed his hand on her leg.

"I don't know if we should get too friendly with him,"

"Love," he sighed, "right now I think we should stick as close to him as we can."

Julie looked over at him and cocked a quizzical eyebrow.

"Look, we have no idea what's going on but if it's serious enough to get Theresa to call us at the crack of dawn then I think we can assume it's serious enough. I for one feel we're better off with Dave than on our own."

Julie's head was swimming. The day's events were growing stranger by the minute. *The army,* she thought, *it just didn't make any sense.* The Irish army was just too small to involve itself in local affairs; it would have to be something huge to call them in.

"What do we do now?" she asked.

"I thought we"d try the Tipperary road. If these guys are Dublin-based they might not know of it."

"I'm sure they have maps, dear," Julie replied as she placed her hand over her husband's and squeezed.

"If you have a better idea then I'm all ears," Pender shrugged and kept driving.

"Is that a helicopter?" Hillary asked as she strained her head against the windshield. They had just reached the outskirts of the town. They hadn't seen any more of those things but they had seen a young woman jogging about five minutes ago. They had slammed on the breaks and started shouting at her trying to warn her but she only increased her pace and disappeared down a lane they couldn't drive through.

"You're right," Martin slowed the van as he looked up. "It's army."

"How would you know?" Hillary sneered.

"It says army on the side," he replied and smiled at her, "don't tell me you're not wearing your lenses."

"I can't afford to wear them every day," she pouted, "they're expensive you know. Where do you think they're going? Do you think they know about the things?"

"I'm not sure," Martin replied. "Looks like they're going to land over by the estuary."

"Let's go over and see."

"Are you mad?" he asked incredulously. "With those things around?"

"Look, we don't know what's going on here but it could be happening everywhere. Maybe these guys know something we don't. Maybe they're even here to rescue us."

"Could be, I suppose." Martin bit his lip as indecision gnawed at him. "Okay," he said finally, "we'll head over to the estuary first and see what happens, but if they don't fly us out then I'm driving out of here with or without you."

"Agreed. Let's go."

Constable Denis O'Malley hated Fridays, especially when he had pulled the late shift. He loved his job; there was no question of that. He'd wanted to be a police officer ever since he had seen TJ Hooker on the TV, but nothing TJ ever did had prepared him for Friday nights.

He had served his first apprenticeship out of Store Street in Dublin and thought that he had seen everything. The endless stream of drunks, from the ages of fourteen up, was something you just got used to. Normally they would just patrol in force and their very presence would curtail most of the high-spirited acts. Those that went too far got to spend a night in the cells. The sheepish look of embarrassment on their faces the next morning almost made up for having to clean up the cells after them—almost but not quite.

There had been plenty of nights, though, where there had been near riots and he had often received a bloodied nose or loose teeth during a brawl that had gotten out of hand. He had jumped at the chance to move to Whiteshead when it had come up. He had always preferred the one-to-one elements of the job and the lure of a quiet community where he could be part of the local framework greatly outweighed the lack of prospects that such a position afforded him.

The dream of a perfect community where he knew everybody and they respected him was shattered on his first Friday night on duty. Here the only thing that was different was that the forty and fifty year olds were just as much trouble as the youths. Driving drunk was a major problem in a small town where the lack of major traffic and the closeness of their homes resulted in chaos late at night. The cells were too small to make any impact and so all he could do was walk through the town and hope that his presence would make a difference. Up till now it hadn't.

He sighed; it would be at least another six months before he could realistically put in for another transfer so he'd just have to make the most of it till then. During the day it wasn't so bad, but there really wasn't much to do. There were never any serious crimes; in fact yesterday's accident had been the highlight of the month so far—although he certainly didn't wish for any one to die. Some excitement, however, would be very welcome.

His shift started at four in the afternoon but he enjoyed getting up early and going for a run. The beach was perfect here and the morning was fresh and clear. He quickly dressed in a track suit and headed out, taking a shortcut through the fields behind his rented house and was on the beach within five minutes.

Chapter 14

"Look, it's coming down over there," Hillary pointed over to the right and Martin nodded. He had been tracking the helicopter with one eye as he weaved through the series of turns along the estuary road.

"I see it," he said. The helicopter was the biggest one he had ever seen, admittedly he hadn't actually seen any others close up but he had seen them in films and on the news and this certainly looked bigger than them.

The main body of the craft was green with patches of a darker green and some dull brown splashed across the body in the camouflage colours he had seen in all the movies. There was a rotor at each end of the craft and the noise was deafening as it passed close to them and continued on out to the middle of the estuary.

I didn't know we had anything that big, Martin mused as he returned his eyes to the road and slammed on the brakes.

There were a number of cars already parked along the edge of the road, in fact most were merely abandoned as their owners jumped from their vehicles and ran towards the descending craft. Still more people ran from their homes along the front and poured over the wall as they ran for the helicopter.

"Leave it here and we'll run over," Hillary shouted as she unclipped her seatbelt.

"Hold on a minute," Martin shot his hand out and stopped her just as she was about to jump out.

"What? Come on or there won't be any room left."

"There's something wrong about this," Martin tried to explain himself but he wasn't quite sure what it was that was worrying him.

"Come on," Hillary insisted and pulled her arm away and jumped out of the car. Reluctantly he followed.

There were about thirty people on the sand, some of them running and others merely walking towards the craft. Martin classified these into two categories, those that had seen the things that had invaded the town and those that were merely curious as to what was going on. Judging by the number of runners there were at least half who knew what was going on.

Hillary raced ahead of him but Martin just couldn't summon enough enthusiasm to run. There was something nagging him, something . . .

The helicopter hovered for a minute over a mound of sand and Martin squinted to see what had caused the knoll as the rest of the estuary bed was completely flat. There seemed to be a rounded metal object sticking from the sand but he couldn't be sure. As soon as the helicopter touched down a stream of soldiers jumped on to the sand and created a cordon around the mound and the craft.

The soldiers stood with their weapons raised and Martin slowed his approach. *This isn't right,* he thought, *what's going on?*

"Hillary, slow down," he shouted but Hillary merely looked back and swung her arm indicating that he should follow. The first of the runners were only a hundred yards away from the line of soldiers. Beyond the soldiers four figures jumped down to the sand and Martin stopped. The figures were all dressed in full environment suits, their bright yellow colour and Plexiglas helmets so out of place that even the runners began to slow their headlong advance.

The figures ignored the people and moved over to the mound and disappeared behind the sandy knoll. Just then Martin realised what he had been unhappy about. The size of the helicopter, the markings ... No wonder he had been confused, this was a British helicopter.

What the hell are the English doing . . . ?

Just then the first shots rang out.

Pender slowed as he approached the sharp turning and then accelerated up the narrow road. He had to drop a gear to cope with the initial gradient but the powerful two litre engine easily handled the climb despite the previous day's accident.

"Why don't you try Theresa again," he looked over at Julie and shrugged, "maybe she has some more information on what's going on."

"I tried already," she sighed. "I just get her voice mail."

Pender nodded and turned his attention back to the road. The road was dark; an archway of leaves grew into a canopy above them allowing only patches of sunlight to filter through. The road itself was narrow, its width was just wide enough to take two cars if one of them moved slightly onto the grass verge and there were enough potholes to make the drive interesting.

The signs indicating that the road was winding did not do it justice and Pender found himself constantly moving the wheel as he followed the twisting route. Up ahead he saw the blinking brake lights as a car disappeared around a corner only to reappear briefly before another corner blocked his vision.

"That's one of the cars that were at the barrier," Pender noted as he checked in his mirror for Johnson. "They must have had the same idea."

It reappeared in front of him, brake lights flaring brightly in the gloom. This time they stayed on and Pender applied his own brakes as the car in front came to a halt.

"Shit!" Pender cursed as he saw the familiar green-clad soldiers at another barrier in front of them. There were three cars in front of him; one of them was the Land Rover he had seen earlier.

The soldier approached the lead vehicle and Pender sat back and sighed.

"Looks like we're out of luck we'll j ..." As he spoke the Land Rover's engine roared and it shot off to the right with a screech of its tyres. The heavy canopy of trees opened up just before the roadblock, the soldiers had obviously positioned it in the sunlight to make sure they would be seen.

The Land Rover shot forward and crashed through a line of bramble. The heavy vehicle plunged down into a ditch and with a screech of an over-revved engine powered back up the other side and through the bushes. Its right bumper was ripped off as the car caught a stone on its way out of the trench and then it was up and over. The tyres churned the sodden ground and the car swerved dangerously as it fought for traction.

The soldier ran back to his men shouting orders and they swarmed over the ditch after the car. The tyres sprayed muck over the soldiers as they struggled over the sharp brambles and then, just as the first of them cleared the obstruction, the tyres caught and the Land Rover powered away across the fields.

A second car turned its wheels to follow but a grim faced soldier appeared in front of him and pointed his gun directly at the driver. Other soldiers raced to their own off-road jeep and started to follow through the gap in the hedging.

Pender watched in fascination as the Land Rover powered across the field and felt like cheering when the car turned back towards the road a good two hundred yards further past the road block.

"Bloody Hell, they're going to make it," he said and the children started to cheer in the back.

There was a sudden burst of fire, the sound muffled by the distance. The car swerved erratically in the field and then lost control completely and careered into the ditch. Pender saw the soldiers run towards the vehicle but he couldn't see if anybody in the car was moving or not.

"Can they do that?" Julie asked, her face pale and bloodless from the shock.

"I don't know, love," Pender whispered. "Whatever is going on it must be big."

Theresa Winfield's office was, like most businesses in Whiteshead, just off Main Street. The main street in question was actually more of a square that continued to the east down to the harbour and west to the main Cork Road but everyone called it Main Street. There were a number of people walking on the other side of the square towards the construction site and she sighed.

Maybe she was over-reacting. The sun was already hot even at this early hour and the clear sky promised a beautiful day. A cool breeze caressed her gently and she found it hard to credit the disaster she had been certain was already taking place. The appearance of people walking through the town made her question her initial panic.

She squinted in the bright sunlight, trying to bring the distant figures into focus. There were two men and a woman and all three walked in a line along the road. Theresa had parked her car over past the construction site so her intended route would cross theirs but she was reluctant to hurry. She considered calling to them but Matthew's words kept running around in her head—'the army are going to quarantine the town'—and her encounter with Maguire was too fresh in her mind.

She had done all she could, hadn't she? She knew she had a duty to protect people, to warn them, but there were just too many things that she just didn't know. She had phoned everyone she could and warned them, it was probably too late for her to get out herself at this stage anyway. Until she knew exactly what was going on and whether it was contagious or not she had no intention of inviting trouble.

She altered her direction to ensure that she wouldn't pass too close to the people and crossed behind some parked cars in the centre of the square. She felt stupid crouching behind the vehicles but not stupid enough to warrant standing up.

"They don't have good hearing but they can see you well enough." The voice was low but high-pitched and trembling with a breathlessness that betrayed the fear of the speaker. She snapped her head around and saw a small boy, around ten years old she judged, hiding behind a van to her left. His feet were bare and he wore faded blue pyjamas with "WWE Rocks" emblazoned on the front.

The initial shock of hearing a voice so close to her was beginning to wear off but her heart still thumped loudly in her chest. "Hey there," she tried to appear calm, "what are you doing hiding out here?"

"Same as you I guess," the boy replied with a shrug. Theresa looked at him. He may be scared but he certainly wasn't a fool. "I'm staying away from them," he indicated the figures passing by on the other side of the square.

Theresa nodded and shifted her position to sit next to him behind the van. "Where are your parents?"

She saw a momentary flicker of a lost little boy in his eyes and noticed that his lip trembled slightly. Then, taking a deep breath, the boy seemed to regain control and merely nodded over towards the construction site.

Oh my God, Theresa's face went pale. She looked over at the three figures. Now that they were a little closer she could see that their appearance was dishevelled, dark patches stained their clothes and they walked with a slight stiffness that she hadn't noticed before. Her mouth went dry. Up till now she had been trying to convince herself that Maguire's attack was an isolated incident, whatever was wrong wasn't contagious and that Matthews was being over cautious.

But now, as she watched the figures pass by she knew that she couldn't fool herself any longer. She was in the middle of a serious outbreak. She wasn't entirely sure what was happening to these people, or indeed how it was transferred, but each figure was splattered with blood so it most probably wasn't airborne.

She nodded to the boy and lifted her arm, inviting him to move closer. He looked at her and she could see the indecision in his face. His eyes moved from the place where his parents were and back to her in quick, darting movements. For a moment she thought that he would just stay there but then he threw himself into her arms and she felt his small body shuddering as the tears that had been kept in check were finally released.

The shape appeared from nowhere and Peters lurched back in fright. His mind was already preparing a savage tirade to launch against the figure even as he steadied himself against the wall. He whirled. And then stopped abruptly.

The figure before him couldn't possible be alive, let alone walking towards him. The man was clad only in the remnants of pyjamas, at one stage they had been a light blue but were so thoroughly splattered, and in some places drenched, in a darker, almost brown, colouring.

Is that blood? Peters mind tried to come up with a rational explanation but the terrible wounds on the man's body just wouldn't fit any explanation he could think of. The man's face was torn along the cheek where the flesh had been ripped away; even now a small flap of skin lay pale and shrivelled against his chin. His arm and shoulder had been badly mauled also, as if a large animal had attacked him.

That's it, his mind grasped the thought like a drowning man reaching for a rope. *He's been attacked by an animal.* The man was only five feet from him and had raised his left arm towards him; his right arm lay uselessly by his side, the tendons torn and useless from whatever had attacked him. Peters backed away.

Whatever had attacked him may still be around. Peters scanned the boardwalk but it seemed to be clear. He returned his attention to the man and took another few steps back, keeping just ahead of him.

"Can I help you," he asked gruffly. He had no intention of helping the man but the silence was beginning to get to him and any noise, even his own voice, was better than nothing.

"This is private property you know," he tried again. The man looked straight at him but there was something wrong, other than the fact that the man shouldn't even be able to stand up, let alone walk. He didn't make any noise, didn't ask for help or moan with the pain he must be feeling' He just kept walking, or maybe shuffling was a better way to describe it, towards him.

This is ridiculous. "Move aside," he tried to inject a hard edge to his voice and to push past the man but something stopped him and he backed away instead. Visions of yesterdays attack flashed through his mind. *Could this man have been a victim of a similar attack? Surely not.* He answered his own question. *Surely no man could inflict such terrible wounds.*

He stumbled. He had been backing away slowly but had been unable or unwilling to take his eyes away from the advancing man and he hadn't seen the cable. The first he had noticed it was when it had wrapped around his leg and tripped him. He landed heavily on his thigh and grunted as his side tore along an exposed nail in the wall.

I'll fire someone for this, he promised himself as he scrambled to his feet. His side blazed with pain and his hand came away wet with blood when he groped at his shirt for a better look. The man was closer, too close, so he ignored the pain and scrambled to his feet. Unfortunately, the cable had become entangled in his leg and he fell a second time, knocking his shoulder against hard surface. He looked up—the man was almost on him. He bent forward to untangle the cable but his fall had already stretched it taught. He would have to move forwards to create a little slack in order to loosen it, but that meant moving closer to the blood-soaked man.

He steeled himself and slid forward on his bottom and wrenched at the cable as soon as he felt the slightest loosening. He unlooped the cable around his leg and pulled it free but the man was already too close and he felt his leg being gripped by the man's bloodied hand.

Martin flinched as the shots punched the air. He jumped to the ground in reflex. *They're only warning shots,* his mind screamed at him but he stayed where he was. He looked towards the helicopter and saw that a number of the people hadn't stopped at the warning shots, they hadn't even slowed down.

A second volley of shots rang out and he closed his eyes instinctively. By the time he opened them again all hell had broken loose. The second volley hadn't been a warning. There were bodies lying in the sand in front of the helicopter and most of them were not moving. Some crawled along the sand away from the helicopter with bloodied limbs. Others simply lay where they were and moaned, the screams audible even over the slow sweep of the rotors.

Still others, those lucky enough not to have been injured by the volley, turned and ran back to the road. A brave few paused long enough to assist a fallen friend or neighbour, their eyes never leaving the stony-faced soldiers. Some of the wounded were lifted and removed while others stayed where they were and shouted for help.

Martin could see a few, apparently uninjured; merely kneeling beside the unmoving bodies of those they had known or loved.

Jesus, Martin thought, *what the fuck is going on? When exactly were we invaded?*

"Hillary!" he suddenly shouted as he scanned the beach for any sign of her. He jumped to his feet but there were too many people running past him and he was forced back further.

"HILLARY" he shouted, his voice going hoarse from the volume. He pushed against the sea of people and then suddenly he was alone and he stumbled forward with the momentum. He saw a figure on the sand. His heart thundered in his chest, the hair was the same colour as Hillary's. He rushed forward but kept his eyes on the soldiers. He could see that they were tracking him and he laid his hands out to each side as he continued to run towards the still figure.

He reached her and fell to his knees beside her. She was lying on her side away from him and he gently rocked her back and looked down her body for any wounds. Her body seemed intact but there was a nasty welt on the side of her head and blood seeped from it at an alarming rate. At least she was alive. He looked up briefly at the soldiers and for the first time in his life he actually hated another human being.

"You bastards!" he shouted, heedless of what they might do. His eyes swept the faces before him but he saw no pity or sorrow there. He looked up at the helicopter and stared at the numbers on the tail, burning the legend in his mind before returning his attention to Hillary.

He pulled his shirt out of his trousers and ripped the end all the way around. He found Hillary's bag lying beside her and he poked around and found a pack of tissues. He tore these from their wrapping and applied them to her wound and tied it in place with the remnant of his shirt.

He leaned back and looked at the bandage, it would have to do. He lifted her gently and with one more look of pure hatred at the soldiers he turned away and started walking back. There would be a reckoning, he promised himself. Someway, somehow, there will be a reckoning.

Peters yelped in fear and wrenched his leg back. The man holding his leg lost his grip but was tugged forward by the momentum and fell towards him. Peters scrambled to his left and the man fell heavily in the spot he had occupied mere seconds before.

The man still hadn't uttered a sound and the silence was really getting to him. His side stung like hell from his wound and his chest was beginning to pain him from the exertions so he stood to the side just far enough away from his floundering attacker to allow him to recover. The man flopped about on the walkway like a fish out of water, his injured arm torn and useless by his side, and Peters found himself studying him as he attempted to rise.

The man stared straight at him but his face showed no emotion whatsoever. There was no hate, no sign of pain from his terrible wounds and no look of frustration as his every attempt to rise failed. The man continued his struggle to rise. Peters couldn't be certain but he was convinced that the man's bare chest wasn't moving and the lack of moaning or grunting from the figure was entirely unsettling.

There's no way a normal man could walk around with those wounds, Peters thought as he looked more closely at the ravaged flesh. As well as the wounds on his face and his arm the man also had a nasty injury on his upper thigh. He hadn't seen it before but the man's pyjamas bottoms had ripped as he flailed from side to side and Peters could see that a large chunk of flesh was missing from his thigh.

What the hell did that? The wound had stopped bleeding but Peters couldn't see any clotted blood around it. There was plenty of blood alright, it looked like gallons of the stuff had soaked into the pyjamas and this had dried and caked to the material, but the wound itself was raw. Peters didn't remember too much of his first aid from the scouts when he was young but he did remember that blood clotted quickly. He also remembered that blood loss on the scale he was seeing just wasn't possible.

He snapped out of his reverie as the man finally made it to his feet and lurched towards him. Peters pushed himself away from the wall but the man was faster than he expected and he felt a hand grab his hair and yank him backwards. He slipped on the drying deck and fell heavily once again to the ground. The man followed him down to the deck and they rolled towards the edge and crashed against the wooden railing.

Pain shot up Peters' arm where it struck the wood and he felt a numbing tingling in his hand. The other man struck the railing with much more force but it seemed to have no effect. Peters gripped the man's hands to protect himself but his attacker ignored this and began to lean in towards him, his mouth open.

Peters" eyes opened in shock as he realised what the man was trying to do and the surge of revulsion gave him a rush of energy. He lifted the man away from him and threw him to the side in a rush of adrenaline-induced panic. The man fell against the railing again and Peters heard the crack of splintering wood. He launched himself to his feet and kicked out at the man. His feet pummelled him again and again as anger and revulsion took hold of him.

He stopped only when his feet were too leaden to lift and his chest pains returned. He bent over and sucked great breaths as he rested his hands on his knees and slowly the anger ebbed away. He felt lightheaded as blood pounded painfully in his head. He looked over at the man and his heart missed a beat. The figure was slowly getting back to its feet.

His face was badly mauled where Peters had kicked him but none of the wounds bled. The flesh that had hung against his cheek had been torn away by Peters' shoe but the tear was completely bloodless. Peters watched in shock as the man rose fully and then started towards him again.

Peters shot his leg out and caught the man full in the chest. His attacker stumbled backwards, hit the railing and tumbled over the edge. Peters rushed forward and looked down as the man hit the water. Spray shot upwards and drenched Peters as he looked down but he didn't care. The man hit the water and disappeared beneath the surface. There was no flailing arms, no shout for help—he just disappeared. The water roiled violently for a few minutes, ripples shooting outward and slapping noisily against the concrete struts beneath him, but it wasn't long before the surface calmed and soon returned to its tranquil indifference once again.

The beach was alive with activity. Seagulls screeched their greetings as they floated on the brisk wind currents and the surf thundered around him as it crashed against the rocks that surrounded the small inlet. The smell of sea water filled his senses as he breathed deep and he could detect a hint of the flowers and plants that lay strewn over the beach after the storm.

O'Malley hit the sand running and immediately noticed the strain in his calf muscles as the sand gripped his feet. He struggled on, his breathing already more laboured, and then, suddenly, the going was much easier as he reached the harder, wet sand at the water's edge. He powered down the beach enjoying the cooling spray as his legs splashed through the rolling tide.

This was what made being in this town worth it. There wasn't a soul on the beach, in fact, if it hadn't been for the glass supports of the new centre jutting up over the hill in front of him, he could imagine that the whole county was uninhabited.

His route would take him down past the rocks and then up a small path that brought him over the hill and down towards the new centre. From there he would loop through Main Street and then back to his house, the whole trip clocked in at four miles and normally took him around twenty minutes.

He pumped his legs harder as he reached the incline and powered up the hill. He was out of breath as he reached the summit and he rested for a few minutes as he took a drink of water. The first time he had raced up here he had puked his guts up and had to walk home. The town was spectacular in the early morning. The sun bathed the buildings below in gentle radiance, banishing shadows at a touch, and created fantastic speckles of light as it danced on the gently rolling waves before they broke into tumultuous white foam.

From here he could see the glass top of the new centre as it jutted proudly into the clear sky. At this distance it seemed to loom over the buildings like a tyrant and the cranes that surrounded it were like one-armed, steel sentinels protecting their charge.

He could see the odd figure moving about in the town, although at this distance they merely looked like specs of dirt on a lens. He took another gulp of water and then headed down.

"I'm Theresa," she smiled at the boy with as much reassurance as she could manage.

"Aidan Dooley," he said formally to her in that curious way children had of always announcing their full names.

"Wanna talk about it?" Theresa asked gently as the boy's sobs subsided.

The boy sniffed and ran his sleeve against his dripping nose. He looked at her for a minute without talking; his eyes seemed to penetrate her and examine her inner core. Then, abruptly, he nodded and began.

"I woke up when I heard Danny scream, that's my brother," he paused for a second and Theresa could see the fear and despair in his little face. ". . . was my brother," he corrected. "Mom and Dad were standing over his bed and were taking turns . . ." his eyes filled with tears. "They were eat . . . " he tried again and Theresa hugged him to her.

"It's alright, shush now," she soothed as the boy's body shivered. Her trained mind tried to tell her that what was happening was medically impossible but as she held the boy in her arms she knew that, impossible or not, it most certainly was happening. She had to get the boy to safety, but for now those things were right between her and her car so they'd have to sit tight until they moved away or someone else came to help.

She looked down at the boy and could see him shivering in his light pyjamas; the shock and the cold were draining the boy's energy too quickly - she would have to get him something to wear. There were shops opposite her and one of them even had brightly dressed mannequins in the window but the only one's she could see sported ladies and girl's wear.

Beggars can't be choosers, she thought and shrugged. They might have other clothes inside, either way she had to get him something to wear quickly. If those things didn't have great hearing then she should be able to break in and grab some clothes. She just had to make sure they didn't see her. She looked down at the boy.

"Aidan, I'm going to get you out of here but first we're going to get you something to wear, okay?" He looked at her and nodded. She took his hand in hers and both of them raced across the square.

They reached the shop door and flattened themselves against the small porch that typified the shops along the street. Theresa grabbed the door handle and wrenched her hand downward. *Of course it's locked,* she chided herself as the glass-panelled door stood firm. She lifted her medical bag and rammed it against the glass. There was a loud crash as the glass shattered and she stood immobile as her heart hammered in her chest. She expected a group of those things to descend on her at any second but the street remained empty.

Her lungs hurt and she realised that she had been holding her breath. She looked down at Aidan and could see the tears running down his face. She looked quizzically at him before noticing that her hand gripped his so tightly that her knuckles were white. *Oh my God,* she thought as she released his hand and dropped to her knees to see how he was.

"I'm so sorry," she said as the boy massaged his hand. "Some rescuer I am, eh?"

He looked at her soberly and took her hand again in his and squeezed gently. She wiped the tears from his cheeks and stood up. She reached her hand through the jagged opening and unlocked the door. They walked into the shop together.

Chapter 15

By the time Martin arrived back to the road there were people everywhere. Some were caring for those that had been wounded, some stood around in shock and others shouted their anger and frustration as they watched the soldiers from the safety of the road.

Martin laid Hillary down gently next to the other wounded and then looked about for someone to take a look at her. A small child lay next to them with blood pumping from her left arm. A woman with a bowl of water knelt beside the child and dabbed gently at the wound as she examined it.

Martin knelt down beside the girl. "Don't worry your Mom will fix you up," he smiled at her encouragingly and looked up at the woman. She began to smear a cream on the wound and then wrapped a bandage around it.

"Oh, I'm not her mother," her face remained strained as she spoke, "I just happen to live up there," she nodded towards the houses overlooking the estuary.

Martin nodded and then turned back to the girl. She was about eleven and had white jeans and a pink t-shirt, both of which were splattered with blood. Her face was pretty, though at the moment it was scrunched up with pain, and a splash of freckles ran across her cheeks and nose like a mask. Her hair was clotted with sand and fell in clumps around her shoulders. "Is your Mom or Dad around?" he asked the girl, trying to distract her from the pain.

The girl's eyes filled with tears and she bit her lip but made no reply.

"She was found out there," the woman indicated the estuary behind her, "under the body of a woman. It could have been her mother but we haven"t been able to get a word out of her yet. Now," she said to the girl, "that's the best I can do until we get you to a hospital. Okay, let's have a look at your girlfriend."

"Oh, she's not my . . . " Martin began but the woman was already examining the wound and didn't hear him. Martin looked down at the girl. She was around the same age as his sister. He didn't see half enough of her since his parents had split up and his mother had moved to Dublin. He had stayed in the area, hell he had been here all his life; he had a job and friends here, but he did miss Gillian.

They had always been close but his Dad's drinking and the constant shouting in his house had meant that the bond between them had grown stronger. Gillian would come into his room when the arguments had woken her up, she came to him for advice and support and in turn she gave him a purpose in life. He had been at a loss ever since she moved to Dublin with their mother, finding himself merely living from day to day. But he couldn't just abandon his father, could he?

The girl moaned softly and he shook himself from his reverie. She held her arm to her chest and looked straight up at the sky. Tears welled up in her eyes but she was determined not to cry, he had often seen Gillian do that. The girl's small body shivered, whether from shock or cold Martin wasn't sure.

How the hell could anyone shoot indiscriminately into a crowd of women and children? The thought burned within him as he took off his jacket and laid it over the child. She moved her head and looked up at him briefly and he just smiled and patted her shoulder.

Don't worry," he said, "You're not alone."

"I tell you I can't get a signal," the man insisted as he shoved his mobile phone under the other man's nose.

"Fuckers are probably blocking the signal," another man joined in.

"Don't be daft."

A group of men had gathered at the stone wall and looked balefully at the helicopter as the suited men and the soldiers got back into the vehicle.

"Those bastards are going to pay," another man shouted over the noise of the engine.

"Can anyone else get a signal?" the first man shouted and Martin watched as everyone checked their mobiles and cursed.

"How about the houses?"

"Naw, tried that," another replied, "the lines are down."

"What the fuck is going on?"

"We've been invaded."

"Don't be daft."

"You explain it then."

Martin tuned out the voices and turned back towards Hillary. The woman, he found out later, was called Patricia Kelly and she was a trainee nurse in the local hospital. Patricia had cleaned and bandaged Hillary's wound and pronounced her as fit as she could make her. She warned that there was still a chance of concussion so she should take it easy for a while.

Hillary had woken up a few minutes ago and Martin had filled her in on what had happened. He leaned forward and patted her hand. "I'll be back in a minute," he said and began to rise to his feet. The young girl looked over suddenly and grabbed at his leg, her eyes growing wide in fear.

"I'll only be a minute," he bent back down and took her hand in his. "I have to warn these people before they head into town. I won't leave you." The girl relaxed a little but still looked dubiously at him. "Hillary will still be here, see," he nodded at Hillary and the girl looked over and released his leg. "I won't be long; you'll be able to see me the whole time. Okay?" She nodded and levered herself onto her elbows and watched closely as Martin made his way to the group.

". . . think we should go to the hospital," one man argued.

"No point, there's no power. We should go to the police and report what's happened."

"We need medicine . . . "

"Excuse me," Martin walked up to the man he considered to be in charge. The man was only about five foot seven and extremely overweight but he seemed to exude authority and the other men naturally gathered around him. Martin had noticed that the man had left the others free to talk while he had listened quietly, taking note of all the suggestions.

"Can I help you, friend?" he asked in a surprisingly deep voice. Martin immediately noted the intensity of the man's eyes.

"Yes," Martin answered. "I'm Martin Taylor. You can't go into town."

"And why is that?" the man asked quietly.

"We've just come from there, there's ..." Martin trailed off as he realised how stupid he was going to sound. His mind frantically tried to think of a way to explain what he had seen that wouldn't immediately discredit him.

"Yes?" the man's eyes seemed to bore through him, as if they could read his every thought.

"Look," Martin began again, "this is going to sound strange but there are people in town that have gone mad ..."

"Most of this town went mad years ago," a man interrupted and others joined in but the fat man silenced them with a look.

"You were saying," the man prompted.

"Yes, these people had already killed others in town when we saw them."

"Are you sure they actually killed these people, it wasn't just a fight that you saw?" the man asked and watched Martin closely.

"No, they were standing over the corpses. Trust me, there is no way these people were still alive. We were on our way out of town when we saw the helicopter."

"Do you think there are more of these mad people?"

"I don't know but I only saw five people in town this morning in total, one of them is over there, two were dead and the other two had killed them, I wasn't waiting around to find out. Oh, one of the dead was a police officer and he had been killed by another Officer."

"Interesting, any theories?" the man prompted.

"No, not really," Martin replied, "but I noticed that there were guys in environment suits in that helicopter before they opened fire."

"A virus of some sort then?" the man prompted.

"Could be, something certainly turned those guys mad."

"Okay, thanks for the information. What are you planning on doing now?"

"Thought I'd head out of town as soon as Hillary is feeling better."

The man nodded and held out his hand. "Jack Thornton," he smiled and Martin shook hands. Thornton then turned to the others. "Gentlemen and ladies, you"ve all heard our young friend. I suggest we follow suit and head out of town and see if we can report this situation to the relevant authorities. We also have wounded that need to get to a hospital. Make sure everyone is assigned to a car."

"What"ll we do about the bodies?" a thin man to Thornton's left asked and everyone suddenly looked over to the still forms.

"We'll report what happened as soon as we can and get someone to take care of them properly," Thornton sighed, "but for now we have to take care of those that need our help most." The others nodded, as if relieved, and then Thornton continued.

"Brid," he called over to a woman, 'see if you can find any of the owners of those houses and get some food and drink for these people. We'll settle with them later, keep a list of what we take and I'll take care of it."

Martin was astonished at how quickly the man organised everyone. He caught the man's eye and raised his eyebrows.

"Was there something else?" the man asked amiably.

"Yes, there's a little girl over there by my friend."

"Yes, that's Kim Stanley, what's the problem?"

"Is her father around?"

"No, he left them years ago, she lives with her mother, Caroline I think her name is."

"Oh, you see she's in shock and won't talk but she was found under the body of a woman. The chances are it was her mother."

"Bastards," Thornton spat. "I'll get one of the women to come over and take her with them as soon as I can."

"Fair enough," Martin replied and headed back towards Hillary and Kim. He was surprised at how disappointed he was that someone else would look after her.

Dave Johnson followed the car as it weaved its way back down the mountain road but his thoughts were still pre-occupied with what had happened in the last hour. The soldiers had quickly covered the gap that led to the field in case any others had decided to follow the Land Rover, although there was little chance of that after it had been shot to pieces.

The Captain of the guard had come out briefly and ordered everyone to return to town. A few men in a second off-road vehicle had argued that they wanted to stay and look after their friends but the line of soldiers left no room for discussion as the Captain ordered them to raise their weapons. Johnson's last view of the crashed Land Rover was of bodies being removed, but whether they were alive or dead he had no idea.

Johnson had had many dealings with the military, albeit in England, and this sort of behaviour just didn't add up. There was just no way that sentry or traffic detail would be handled by the Rangers and there was no way they would fire on civilians, even in a mob situation. The repercussions would be fatal to any Government that issued such orders.

There were only two possible explanations that could even begin to make sense. Either the Army had begun a coup, unlikely that they would start such an important event in a small town in Southern Ireland—or there was something going on that was limited to this area but that was so dangerous that they could not risk it spreading, at any cost.

The fact that the radio stations had not mentioned anything since this whole mess had begun pretty much discredited the coup idea. The fact that this had all started the same day they had found the submarine was too much of a coincidence as well. If those canisters had leaked then were John and he infected already? How bad was this poison that the Government had called in the Rangers and were willing to shoot innocent people to keep it contained? Was it so dangerous that they were prepared to infect the whole town in order to quarantine it?

The questions raged through his mind and none of the answers he considered gave any of them much hope. The papers they had found in the submarine might be important to whoever was investigating the sub but he had been unable to get near anyone in authority at either of the roadblocks. He had tried after the Land Rover had crashed but nobody was willing to listen.

His mobile phone was still dead. *They''ve probably taken down the local transmitter,* he thought and shivered. He had been involved in scenarios similar to this during his training and he knew that there were written procedures that covered every eventuality for these situations. There was little they could do for now but go back to …

As he rounded a corner he got a beautiful panoramic view of the town and a thought leapt into his mind.

The sea.

Pender watched as the other off-road vehicle turned into a small lay-by ahead.

"Where are they going?" Julie asked.

"I don't know," Pender replied, "but I'd take a guess that they're planning on hiking it out of here."

"Maybe we should join them."

"Love, if I can guess what they're doing I imagine that our country's finest have too."

"But they might make it," Julie persisted.

"They might, but after that last demonstration I don't want to risk it. They might find it easier to shoot us rather than chase us."

"Surely they won't fire on children."

"They had no way of knowing who was in that car they shot at and it didn't seem to stop them."

They lapsed into silence and Pender took the opportunity to look in his mirror at the children, they had been very quiet since the soldiers had opened fire. He caught Craig's eye for a second and smiled reassuringly at him. The boy nodded soberly but didn't look very reassured. Even Jack hadn't opened his mouth.

Pender really had no idea what the best thing to do was but he was beginning to feel as if they were being corralled like sheep and his investigative instinct was shouting warnings to him. He made a decision and pulled over into the lay-by and parked next to the other Land Rover.

Julie looked over at him quizzically, "I thought we weren't going to chance it."

"I've been thinking," he said as he pulled the handbrake and turned towards her. "This has got to have something to do with the sub, right."

She nodded and he continued. "Okay, if that's the case then going back into town might be more dangerous than going this route."

"In what way?"

"Anything that has the army shooting unarmed civilians rather than letting them past a quarantine has to mean that a)," he held up one finger, "whatever it is they think we have is more serious than any repercussions they might have to endure later or b) they're pretty confident there won't be anyone left to make a complaint."

"Oh my God," Julie whispered and then looked over at the children and then back to Pender. She nodded and opened the door. "What are we waiting for? Let's go."

The shop was dark and gloomy. Faint slivers of light found small gaps in the curtain over the window behind the display and cut through the darkness like tiny lasers. The faint light splashed against a number of mannequins and made both of them jump as a breeze rustled the curtain and the shifting light gave the impression of movement. A long counter stretched along the far wall and piles of neatly folded clothes sat along its length. Theresa and Aidan moved into the shop cautiously, their hearts still thumping from seeing the models.

"See if you can find something you like," Theresa suggested as she crossed to the curtain and pulled the material apart a little more, though not so much that they could be seen from outside. She blinked furiously as the bright sunlight seared into her eyes and destroyed her night vision. She turned away and stumbled over a mannequin, screaming as the face suddenly loomed towards her.

"Are you alright?" Aidan called in a loud whisper and she nodded as she laid the dummy on the ground.

"Did you find anything?" Theresa asked as she crossed over to him.

"It's all girls" stuff," he replied and wrinkled his nose as if the clothes smelled.

"Well you can't stay in those," Theresa insisted as she rifled through the clothes. "There has to be something you'll wear—how about these?" she held up a T-shirt and white trousers.

"Boys don't wear white," he insisted as he lifted the leg of the trousers and let it fall.

"They also don't wear pyjamas outside when they're being chased by dead people. It's either this or you can pick out a nice dress." Theresa hadn't meant it to sound harsh but her nervousness had put an edge on her tone that surprised her. She looked down at the boy and tried to smile reassuringly but the smile only reached as far as her mouth. Her eyes remained fearful.

"Are they dead?" Aidan asked as he took the clothes and began to pull them on. "Those people out there," he nodded towards the window. "Are they really dead?"

"I'm not entirely sure," Theresa looked blankly out the window as the boy's question forced her to consider the situation more closely. Up till now she had been reacting, never really having time, or even allowing herself the time, to fully consider what was happening.

Dead people don't come back to life. She was a doctor and she knew that this was a fact but some of the people she had seen had horrific injuries. Injuries that would have, at the very least, left them immobile if not dead. How do you explain the people walking about oblivious to their wounds and suffering from horrendous blood loss?

But could they really be dead? She forced herself to consider the question. The sample she had taken from Perkins—God was that only yesterday?—showed that the PH levels were below that at which the body could survive. But yet the man had been breathing when she left him. Maguire had been walking around when he had attacked her but his movements had been stiff.

Healthy cells in the body are alkaline. In disease the cell pH is below 7.0. The more acidic the cells become, the sicker we feel. The cells themselves won't die until their pH gets to about 3.5 but blood PH is much more specific. If it drops to 7.2 or below then oxygen can not be carried through the blood and we die.

But why do they turn violent? That man who had been knocked down on Main Street had bitten his victim—Why? His victim had been taken to hospital and according to Matthews had turned feral and attacked everyone around him. Maguire and his son had attacked her. Why attack people, if it was hunger then why not eat . . . ?

A though hit her. "Oh my God," she whispered and Aidan looked quizzically at her. "Come on, we have to go." She grabbed the boy as he was closing the button on his trousers.

"What . . . ?"

"There's no time, Aidan, I have to get to a friend of mine. I think I know what's going on."

Chapter 16

Friday 9.30 AM – 10.00 AM

Dave Johnson pulled in just past the Pender's car and jumped out, his mind already forming a plan of escape. He raced over to John Pender and opened the door for him before he had the chance himself.

"John," he began interrupting Pender before he even had the opportunity to speak. "We can get away by boat."

John Pender stepped out of the car and looked out over the sparkling sea before turning to face his friend.

"Can you sail, Dave?"

Johnson's smile slipped a little, he had no experience on boats at all.

"I'd say the thought hit me about the same time it hit you but we could run into more trouble out in the ocean if we don't have someone with experience with us. For that matter, would we even get a boat? There will be too many people panicking down there once the first of the people get back with the news that we're all trapped. I can't risk the kids."

"Do you have a better idea?" Johnson asked as he sighed his disappointment.

"I figured we could take the trail up over the mountain and see if we can get around the roadblock."

"Don't you think the soldiers will have thought of that? They'll catch you, maybe even shoot first and ask questions later."

"I know but it's a hell of a big mountain and there can only be so many of them. If we stay off the main routes then we might just be able to make it."

Johnson ran the plan through his head and then shrugged. "I guess it beats drowning. We'll give it a shot."

Julie Pender closed the car door and looked around. They had pulled into the lay-by just past the Land Rover but the men from that vehicle had already gone. She breathed in the clean air and lifted her face to catch the faint breeze as it drifted past. The sun warmed her face and shoulders and she could feel faint trickles of sweat running down her legs. She would have preferred shorts in weather like this but there was no way she could have guessed it would be so hot when they had left the house this morning and she was stuck with her choice now.

She looked up at the blue sky and saw a few small puffs of white clouds, like marshmallows, floating past. The mountains surrounded them on three sides and she looked at the patchwork landscape and sighed. *How can anything bad be happening in such a beautiful place?*

The children tumbled from the car, stiff from their prolonged journey. They were quiet and subdued; they might not know what was going on but soldiers shooting at cars and rushed early morning journeys were definitely not normal. John was talking to Dave Johnson and pointing up at the mountain to the north. She squinted and saw movement where he was pointing. *That must be the others,* she thought. *God, that's a long way up.* Was Dave right? Should they try to sail out of danger rather than risk the soldiers shooting them?

She crossed to the children and pulled them close to her, benefiting from their hugs just as much as they did from hers. She didn't mind admitting she was terrified but she didn't know which terrified her more, the soldiers or the chance that there was a deadly virus loose in the town. Were they already infected? John and Dave had both entered the submarine, should she keep the children away from them or was it already too late?

She looked over at her husband and sighed. It wouldn't matter either way she realised, she couldn't leave him even if he was infected. She had nearly made one mistake in her life already that could have torn them apart and she'd be damned if she was going to let anything else threaten them. *Besides,* she thought, *there's been more than enough time for the virus to have spread since last night.*

She wondered idly if they should just do what the soldiers had said. Did they have the right to risk spreading a virus to others outside of the quarantine. She felt the warmth from the children's hugs as they pressed against her and she felt her resolve strengthen. If there was even the smallest chance that they were not infected at this stage then there was no way she could lead them back into danger.

She looked over at John again and smiled when he winked at her. She saw him nod his head towards the mountain trail. The mountain walk was a popular tourist attraction and provided a winding dirt track trail that followed an easy route up over the mountain. The track was mainly cut through heavy forest and was completely overshadowed with large, majestic trees of every type imaginable. The trail was famous for the rare shrubs that were found in the area and further up the trail were spectacular views of the bay, the harbour and the surrounding valley. She took the children's hands and followed the two men into the gloom.

Denis O'Malley leaned up against the wooden barrier that stretched around the building site and waited for his heartbeat to slow. He absently brought his towel to his face and wiped away the perspiration. The sweat on his body cooled rapidly and he shuddered as some trickled slowly down his back. He raised the water bottle to his lips and took a long drink, savouring the cool liquid and congratulated himself yet again for his foresight in purchasing a water bottle that kept its contents cold.

He saw a few people in the distance, wandering aimlessly and shook his head. He still couldn't get used to the lack of drive in the town. Everyone took their time, nobody hurried. He supposed it was him that was the strange one but he just couldn't waste his day doing nothing. He couldn't wait for his time here to be finished and he could transfer back to the city where time meant something and people bustled about their business.

He looked at his watch, 9.40. It was still too early to get a cooked breakfast in the café, it didn't open until 10.00. He shrugged, typical small-town eccentricities. He'd get home, have a shower and then drop down for a fry up. He pushed himself off the wall and continued into town.

Martin watched the bedlam as the people got into their cars and tried to turn around on the narrow country road. Horns blared, tyres crunched on loose gravel as drivers stomped on their brakes as they tried to get through the chaotic circus. Outside on the Estuary the last of the burial party returned with their faces grim and pale.

One of the men, Martin remembered that Thornton had called him Pat, approached him and knelt down beside Kim. He didn't say anything but the look in his eyes was more than enough. Kim's mother was dead. She reached out her hand and gripped Martin's hand in hers and then the tears fell.

Her body convulsed as the feelings she had tried to suppress finally won out and the raw emotion took hold of her. Martin scooped her up in his arms and held her tight as Pat nodded and moved away. The clamour of the cars still filled the air around them but, just for a minute, it seemed that they were alone.

Brid, the woman that was handling the distribution of food and transportation approached them with a second woman in tow. She interrupted them with a gentle cough and Kim turned to her in confusion.

"Jack asked me to arrange transportation for Kim," she began and indicated the woman beside her. "This is . . ."

"No," Kim shook her head emphatically. Her voice was strained and barely audible over the engines around them but the tone was unmistakable, the set of her jaw and the grip of her arms around Martin's neck only emphasised her response.

"But Kim, dear," Brid tried to gently coax the girl away from Martin. "Audrey has plenty of room ..."

"No," she insisted again and pulled herself closer to Martin.

"Looks like we'll have to make room in the van," Hillary said and nodded at the women. "We'll take care of her." Brid nodded and the women withdrew into the maelstrom of engines, horns and shouted curses. Above them the helicopter banked and headed out over the sea.

Theresa ran from the shop back towards their previous hiding place on the edge of the square with Aidan following close behind. Her knees still throbbed from her previous assault and her shoes cut into her toes. She cursed her vanity with each painful step but she forced herself forward regardless. There were more figures ambling around the town than the last time and they narrowly avoided running into one as they left the shop, a second later and they would have been seen.

Just how many people have been infected? Theresa wondered as they knelt behind the car and sneaked a quick glance around. There were six figures visible from where she was; they were well spaced out and didn't seem to be in any hurry and they all walked with a curious stiffness that only served to re-enforce her theory. The silence in the street was eerie, almost as if someone had pulled a shroud over the town.

"My car is on the other side of the square," she spoke in a low whisper just in case their hearing was better than Aidan credited them with. "We're going to have to make a run for it," she looked into the boy's face and saw fear there but he nodded regardless and she nodded back. She didn't think she would have been as brave at his age.

"Okay then, they're spread out at the moment. Stay close."

Theresa launched herself from behind the car and ran towards the car park. Her route took her across the square at an angle and if all went well she should be able to reach the far corner before they were seen. It was the last hundred yards where she anticipated problems.

In the distance, over by the town's only bookstore, a figure noticed her and changed its direction, its previous slow amble now transformed into an almost comical, rushed gait. It was still over a hundred and fifty yards away and no immediate threat but its hurried pace had attracted the attention of other figures that were a lot closer.

"Bastards aren"t stupid," she cursed as she saw other figures turn their heads looking for whatever it was that had attracted their colleague. There was no communication between them but, by the time Theresa was only half way across the square, she had been seen by at least three others that she could see.

She looked over her shoulder to make sure that Aidan was behind her when her heel suddenly caught in a crack in the road and broke. Her ankle twisted violently on her unstable shoe and pain shot through her as she fell to the ground. The searing pain in her ankle was eclipsed briefly as her hands scraped along the ground and the skin was ripped from her palms. Then both her hands and her ankle competed equally for attention as she sprawled to the ground.

Aidan dropped to her side and grabbed her arm, attempting to drag her to her feet. She was about to pull her arm away and snap at the boy for ignoring her pain but as the boy dropped down she could see one of the townspeople only a few feet behind him and the fright steeled her resolve. *He must have been right behind us when we started running,* she thought. *How the hell did I miss him?* She grabbed Aidan's shoulder and leaned on him as she simultaneously pushed her other hand against the ground and forced herself to rise.

Her ankle wobbled and hurt like hell but it held her weight. Her knees and hands throbbed painfully but she used the pain to drive her on. In the time that they had lost with her fall two of the figures had already blocked their path to the car park and she frantically scanned the square for an alternative route. She briefly considered running past the two figures but all she could manage was a fast hobble and if she or Aidan fell the bastards would be on them before they could rise.

They were not particularly fast but their reactions were not exactly sluggish either.

She grabbed Aidan by the hand and ignored the shooting pain as her ankle protested her loping run. They moved away from the man behind them with only feet to spare but already her heart was beating too fast and her limbs felt leaden. She wasn't used to exercise at all, her job had kept her too busy, and so this unexpected flight was already taking a heavy toll. She wouldn't be able to keep running for much longer, she needed to find somewhere safe, fast—but where?

Another three men and two women appeared from the car park area *Where the hell had they been hiding?* She stopped briefly near the centre of the square and looked frantically around. To her right the wooden hoarding surrounding the building site reared to a height of seven feet, to her left lay the car park and ahead led to a dead end.

There was nowhere to go.

Denis O'Malley noticed the first odd occurrence when he ran through the car park. The small area held a total of only fifty cars, if they were parked correctly and not just abandoned like some were prone to do. The car park usually catered for the night time crowd visiting the restaurants and bars along the water's edge. Many people drove into town and then, depending on how the night was going, either drove home or left the car and walked or took a taxi home. This morning there were fewer cars than normal but most of the bars had closed early due to the weather so it made sense that there were fewer cars left in town than normal.

An old man wandered among the few cars as if looking for his vehicle. While there was nothing unusual in itself in this O'Malley did think it odd that the man was having such trouble finding his vehicle when the choice was limited to only six cars. His training immediately made him slow his run; the man might still be drunk. He sighed and decided that a friendly warning might be better than waiting for the man to actually start his car when he would be forced to arrest him.

"Excuse me," he called and approached the small wall that marked the boundary of the park. The man had his back to O'Malley but there were no other sounds in the town so he should easily have heard his call. O'Malley crossed quickly to the man, eager to pass on his warning and finish his run. He grew a little more irritated with every step as the man continued to ignore his hails. Maybe he should just let him start the car and then he could arrest him. He called out a final time as he drew level and then grabbed the man by the arm with a little more force than was needed.

The man spun rapidly on contact and O'Malley stumbled back in shock. The man's abrupt turn was shocking enough but the sight of his face and front covered in blood sent O'Malley reeling. His first thought was that the man had been injured and he instantly regretted his earlier irritation.

He recovered quickly and immediately reached out to try and help the man; his trained eyes scanning for any obvious injuries. The amount of blood was shocking and he was already fumbling for his mobile to call the ambulance when the man grabbed at him.

The man's hand closed on his wrist and O'Malley felt himself being drawn towards the man. The smell was awful, a cloying, sickly-sweet stench wafted towards him and he automatically pulled his hand back. The man lost his grip but his nails tore a furrow along his arms and blood burst from the wound.

O'Malley continued to retreat as he looked down at his arm. "Bastard," he grunted as he pulled his towel from around his neck and pressed it against the wound, the white material was radidly soaked by the blood and small pink tendrils spiralled outward.

What the hell is this guy on? The man kept coming closer. Denis O'Malley was well used to drunks and hard cases, he had trained hard and, while he was no Jackie Chan, he was well able to take care of himself. This time, however, it felt different. The man hadn't uttered a sound since O'Malley had got his attention and the silence was eerie.

The man looked like O'Malley's father had looked before the cancer had finally claimed him. Emaciated flesh stretched taut over bone made prominent by sunken cheeks and bloodshot eyes bulging like cracked saucers.

How the hell is this guy still standing? O'Malley kept backing away until his foot caught on the small wall surrounding the car park and he fell backwards. His arm sent fresh waves of pain through him as he landed heavily. The light material of his tracksuit ripped on the gravel and he cursed. That was the final straw. Sick or not the man had gone too far.

O'Malley jumped to his feet just in time to block the man's outstretched hands. He ducked under the man's reach and grabbed his attacker's left wrist. Pivoting under a vicious swipe of his right arm

O'Malley moved quickly behind his attacker and brought the man's arm deftly up behind him, pinning the arm behind his back.

The man continued to struggle and O'Malley applied more pressure, bending the man's arm further up behind him. The man showed no sign of pain and didn't utter a sound. O'Malley frowned, he had bent the man's arm as far as he dared, any further and he risked breaking the arm and he'd never be able to justify that to his superiors. His prisoner should be doubled up on the ground screaming in pain at this stage, even if he was high on booze or drugs.

O'Malley felt his grip loosening as his hands began to sweat and his arm throbbed where it had been raked by his assailant.

The man suddenly jerked free and O'Malley pushed the man in the back, sending him sprawling to the ground as he considered his options. Fifteen years he had studied martial arts, ever since the day he had run from trouble and left his friend alone to face some bullies. Ever since that day he had sworn he would never again abandon anyone and never again would he run from a fight.

Now fifteen years later he had exhausted all his options, he just didn't know how to handle a situation like this. He took one more look at the strange man as he rose stiffly to his feet and then he turned and ran.

Chapter 17

Friday 10.00AM – 10.30AM

It grew dark as soon as Julie stepped under the canopy of trees, like someone had drawn a veil over them. Immediately she was aware of a cacophony of sound and movement as if someone had just turned up the volume on nature's PA system. Far above trees creaked as they swayed in the currents of air, leaves danced as the wind romanced them and their rustling filled the enclosed tunnel. Birds chirped and branches snapped as wildlife launched themselves through the canopy.

Thin slivers of light darted through the gaps above and lit their way only to be extinguished mercilessly as the leaves shifted, only to suddenly reappear again further along the route. Julie found herself rushing after the beams as if she were on a mad quest to trap the light. She was reminded of stories in her childhood of adventurers searching for the end of the rainbow, almost reaching their goal only to see their quarry disappear and reappear with frustrating regularity.

Craig and Emma held her hand as they walked with their heads tilted straight up. A heady musk of wood and pine wafted around them and, just for a moment, she was able to forget the terrible sequence of events that had brought them here. Ahead she could see her husband walking lopsided while he listened to something Jack was telling him. Dave Johnson walked beside them watching the undergrowth carefully.

She considered the back of their new friend as the susurration of the leaves above heralded the sudden darkness that descended over them. She felt the children's hands grip hers a little more tightly and then relax again as spears of light filtered down further along the path. Jack's incessant chattering continued regardless.

Dave Johnson was an enigma. They had speculated for so long as to who he was before they had met him that she felt that he had been a part of their lives for ages. They barely knew him in reality. He could very well be any of the things that they had speculated on, even a mad axe murderer, but somehow she doubted it.

There was a confidence about him that was very attractive. He carried himself with assurance, his movements were smooth and measured and she noted that his head never ceased in its movements from side to side as he probed for danger. John had mentioned that he had

had training with elite military forces and, as she watched from behind, she could see that he left virtually no trail through the carpet of needles and leaves.

Strangely this did not worry her. Instead she took a measure of comfort from his abilities. If he had meant them any harm he had already had plenty of opportunity before now. Indeed it was not danger that she sensed most about him at all, it was emptiness. There was something in his past that he had yet to come to terms with and, until he did, it would never truly heal.

The path disappeared around a corner and she saw Dave indicate that they should stay where they were while he scouted ahead. She drew level with John and winked at him. Jack continued his liturgical chattering as he questioned his father on every conceivable fact and secret of nature.

Dave Johnson moved forward towards the edge of the tree-lined path. Ahead, the line of trees ended abruptly and light streamed down in a solid sheet like a waterfall. The path continued on up the hill but there would be no cover, no protection from roaming patrols or searching snipers.

He was convinced that there were patrols. The Rangers may be drastically under-funded but they were highly-trained and wouldn't leave such an obvious route open. He paused at the edge of the trees to let his eyes grow accustomed to the brighter glare and then moved out into the scrub on his belly, pulling himself along on his elbows.

He could see a group of seven men forging up the mountain side about two hundred yards in front of him. He cringed as he heard their loud banter as they strode confidently upwards, already convinced that they were clear.

They past an area of long grass and the gentle swaying erupted into violent turmoil as figures suddenly and silently appeared around the group of men with weapons levelled. The men stopped dead for a second and, as one, they bolted in different directions. The soldiers didn't shout any warning but shots rang out and echoed around the mountain, shattering the solitude and sending birds skyward in a flurry of motion and cacophony of sound. The men fell forward as if on cue and disappeared into the long grass, none of them reappeared. The soldiers checked each of the bodies and silently merged back into the grass.

Within minutes the scene returned to the calm of before and Dave Johnson shivered despite the burning of the sun on his shoulders. He returned to the blissful cool of the covered path, remaining on his belly until he was far inside its protective embrace.

"They killed them all?" John Pender asked incredulously. "But that's murder."

"Only if there is someone left to complain after it's all over," Johnson muttered in reply.

"Jesus," Pender sighed and looked over at his family. Johnson had taken him aside to tell him his news and, although he was puzzled when he had done so, Pender was glad now that he had.

"There's no way we can continue on now, we'll have to try the marina after all."

"I've been thinking about that," Johnson replied. "They could very well have a boat out there, you know."

"Maybe," Pender rubbed his jaw as he looked through the trees as if he could see through them and even now scanned the horizon for such a vessel. "But I doubt it."

Johnson looked quizzically at him. "Securing the sea would be part of a normal quarantine and they've followed the book on this one up till now."

"Maybe where you come from," Pender smiled grimly, "but you're basing your assumptions on English capabilities."

Johnson nodded.

"We don't have much of a navy in Ireland. At last count there were only seven ships."

"It only takes one to blow us out of the water."

"True, but these ships are generally involved in patrolling our fishing zones and they have an area of 132,000 square miles to cope with. At a top speed of 20 to 25 knots there's no way they could be out there already. We should still have time."

"You seem to be well informed."

"I'm a reporter, remember. I had to do a piece on drug-running a while ago and I did a bit of research."

"I hope you're right."

"Either I am or I'm not, either way it's our only option."

Martin turned the van by driving up into someone's driveway. The house was empty and the scattered tricycle and skateboard in the yard, normally an indication of fun and activity, somehow portrayed instead an ominous, desolate scene that sent a shiver up his spine. He, Hillary and Kim were in the last vehicle in a line that stretched along the full route around the estuary and he pressed his foot hard on the accelerator as the cars ahead drew further away.

The van boasted one seat in the front stretching the full width of the van, rather than the usual two separate seats. Martin had always liked that feature as it allowed for much more comfort when he brought a girl out and they went up to the mountains to park. It again proved its worth now as Kim had refused to sit in the back and only calmed when she was allowed sit with Martin. Hillary hadn't fancied sitting in the back either, although that had more to do with the fact that there wasn't any seat in the back rather than a desperate attachment to him.

"I was beginning to think there was no-one else left in the town," Hillary said as she watched the cars snake around the estuary.

"Me too," Martin looked over at her in between corners. Hillary was a knockout, despite the tired haunted look in her eyes and the clotted blood in her hair from her injury. He had always thought she was pretty and looked forward to their morning chats if their schedules allowed it. Martin had frequently waited for up to an hour in the town just so as he could give her a lift as she headed home. He had invariably been roasted by his boss on his return for his delay but he had always blamed traffic, to which his boss, Mister Wayne, would always answer, 'three cars do not constitute traffic, dear boy.' Wayne had always been nice to him and could never scold him for long. Martin often felt guilty that he was taking advantage, although not guilty enough to make him miss his rendezvous with Hillary.

He frowned as he thought of Mister Wayne and wondered if he was in the depot waiting for him or was he already dead or rabid? He knew Hillary was a prostitute, of course, although it had taken him a while to realise it at first. He had thought that she worked a night shift initially, but there wasn't any club in town open that late. He had been surprised to realise that it didn't matter what she was when he had found out, maybe it was because he had gotten to know who she was well before he knew what she did, and that let him see past her profession. Either way he was glad she was here with him.

He stabbed the brakes as the car in front screeched to a halt at the crossroads. Ahead, and stationary in the middle of the road, was another car and another in front of that. He engaged the handbrake and jumped out to see what had caused the backlog, idly wondering if Mister Wayne would consider this a traffic jam.

Denis O'Malley ran into the square and stopped dead. He saw a woman and a small boy over at the far corner of the square and at least fifteen figures approaching them. The figures reminded him of the man he had left behind as they walked with a funny stiffness, not straight-legged exactly but they didn't have the fluidity of movement that one expected.

The way to the station and his apartment was clear and for just a second he was tempted to merely continue on home. *Run away, little boy.* The thought sprang into his mind. *You know you want to. You don't owe them anything. Run away.* He suppressed the thoughts ruthlessly and looked over at the woman and the boy.

They were terrified and he saw the woman desperately searching for a way out and, finding none, pushing the boy behind her as she prepared to meet her assailants. He squinted as he tried to make out their features and then sucked in a breath as he recognised the woman as Doctor Winfield. O'Malley witnessed her courage and shame filled him for even thinking of running. He gritted his teeth, took a deep breath and launched himself at the nearest figure with a scream borne more from fear than aggression.

Theresa pushed Aidan behind her and braced herself as the first figure drew nearer. The whole scene was surreal; there was no sound except for her own laboured breathing. The men and women that approached her did so in total silence—there was no grunting, no excited chattering, no breathing. Just an infuriating shuffle of shoes and bare feet on the road.

She shouted, hurling abuse insanely at them just to break the stillness and convince herself that she hadn't fallen into a silent nightmare

—although the pain pulsing through her ankle and knees were sufficient proof that she was wide awake.

Her heart caught in her throat as she began to discern the features of the men and women that shambled closer. Some of the faces were familiar, she had seen some around town and others she had treated and even called friends.

Tears welled in her eyes as she saw a ten year old girl. Amy, her numbed brain supplied the child's name. She had treated her only four days ago when she had fallen on a nail in her garden. Theresa could see the plaster still attached to her leg but it no longer mattered as the girl now shambled slowly towards them, her pretty white nightgown splattered with dried blood and flesh missing from her left cheek and upper shoulder.

The people were still quite spread out but the closest figure was already looming towards her. She ducked easily under his right arm as he swiped at her. The smell of blood filled her nostrils and she cringed as she laid her hands on the blood-soaked clothes and pushed with all her remaining strength.

The man, a wiry bespectacled man she had never seen before, tottered backwards and fell against the next closest figure. Both of them stumbled and fell to the ground but already the next in line was reaching for her. She ducked low again but this time her shoe slipped and she lost her footing. She fell heavily to the ground and tried to rise but the groping hands of the figure above prevented her from getting up. A second figure, her subconscious identified it as Georgina, her pretty secretary that she had sent home early, loomed towards her.

She didn't have time for remorse as the hands gripped her. The cold of their flesh seemed to suck the warmth from her arms and she looked up to see their faces loom impassively towards her and the sun seemed to fizzle and disappear.

Suddenly she felt a blow to her head and a searing light bored into her eyes as the sun reappeared with renewed intensity. Her head seemed to ring with the blow but the things that had surrounded her only seconds before were now sprawled on the ground. She looked at them in confusion and felt hands grab her from behind.

She sat dumbly on the ground, her head just couldn't work out what had happened and the ringing scattered her thoughts and left her bewildered. She kept telling her limbs to move but they ignored her. Dimly she was aware of Aidan trying to lift her but she just couldn't get her body to help him. Around her the townspeople silently regained their feet and began to approach her again.

One figure among them grunted and cursed as he struggled to his feet and she cocked her head quizzically towards him, trying to understand why this particular one could talk and the others could not. The figure was blood-stained like the others but he cursed and kicked at them as he approached her. He crossed the distance quickly and grabbed her by the arm and wrenched her to her feet. She swayed on her feet as her head continued to rebel against her instructions and she braced herself for the pain of his teeth ripping at her flesh.

"We've got to move." His voice seemed to drift around her but the ringing in her head drowned it out and she merely looked at him. She was dimly aware of Aidan pulling at her and then the man grabbed her and shook her shoulders as he shouted directly into her face.

"We have to move and I'm buggered if I can carry you." The violence of his tone finally penetrated the fog in her head and she nodded as she felt the ringing reduce to an annoying buzzing. The man, she was sure she knew his face but his name just wouldn't come, brushed past her, grabbing her hand and pulling her behind him.

The shouting and sounds of a scuffle drew Alan Peters towards the entrance to the site. After his assailant disappeared into the water he had sat watching the surface for quite some time just in case he returned. In that time he had gone over the attack again and again in his head and had come to the only conclusion that seemed appropriate, he didn't consider his conclusion either logical or sane, but it was appropriate to what he had seen.

The man that had attacked him was dead. It may be impossible and completely insane but nothing else he could think of would account for it. The man hadn't been breathing before he slipped beneath the water and there were no bubbles once he disappeared. In fact he hadn't struggled at all and Peters kept expecting the man's ruined features to appear above the lapping swell at any second. Also there was just no way that anyone could still walk around with those wounds, so, he reasoned, the man was already dead.

The main questions now were how did it happen and was he the only one? He had unlocked the door he had entered by and slipped quietly down the enclosed passageway back towards the street. He remained behind the plastic sheeting as he scanned the area. A woman passed by, walking as if she had a sprained ankle but not as stiffly as his assailant. The image of the woman was badly distorted by the sheeting so he pushed it gently aside to get a clearer view. The woman wore jeans and a red top and looked entirely normal from behind.

He was about to call out to her when another figure appeared further along the square. This figure was over a hundred yards away but even at this distance he could see the dark splotches of dried blood on his clothes. That answered question two, there were more of them.

He briefly considered calling out to the woman, to warn her or offer sanctuary, but rejected the thought almost immediately. He didn't want to risk it in case there were other walking corpses outside of his field of vision. He had retreated back through the passageway and locked the door behind him. He had spent the last half-hour or so searching for weapons that he could use if needed. He had amassed an impressive arsenal of pipes, wood cuttings and even a hammer or two that some negligent labourer had left behind.

The sounds of a scuffle outside drew him to investigate, not from any desire to help but it would be pointless to remain where he was if the panic was over and the cavalry had already arrived. He unlocked the door as before and crept along the passageway, a hammer held tightly in his right hand.

He saw the woman and child immediately and watched as the dead slowly surrounded them. The woman looked around her frantically but couldn't see a way out. He could have called out and offered her an escape route but those things hadn't figured out where he was as yet and he didn't want to reveal his position. Anyway, the wooden hoarding didn't look like it could survive a determined assault so they'd probably all die if he called out.

The woman slipped and the creatures descended on her. He was about to turn away from the scene, he wasn't a ghoul after all, when he noticed a man running across the square directly for the group. The man launched himself at the group and his body crashed into them and sent everyone sprawling.

The woman seemed to be stunned and then the man grabbed her and they ran towards his hiding place. Peters had lifted the sheeting to get a better view and as the survivors approached him he let it fall. Too quickly he realised immediately and his heart pounded as he worried that they might have seen him. Two seconds went by and then another and there was no shout for help, maybe he had gotten away with it.

He risked another quick look and saw the man running towards him.

They had seen him. He abandoned his position, even dropping the hamer in his haste, and ran back to the door. He raced inside, turned and slammed the door closed, relaxing only when he heard the click of the lock connecting. He sighed heavily and leaned his back against the door. That had been too close.

Denis O'Malley saw movement behind a sheet of hard plastic. He hadn't noticed it before as it fell flush with the hoarding and the dust and dirt had stained it a similar colour to the hoarding itself.

There's someone there, he thought. Someone hiding and that must mean someone still alive and healthy. Why hadn't they signalled? There was plenty of time to get them safely through before those creatures caught up with them.

The person disappeared suddenly and Denis changed his direction towards the sheeting. He caught the briefest glimpse of a shadow behind the plastic and then it disappeared again. Denis tried to pull Theresa faster behind him but her ankle couldn't support their pace and he had to slow down or she would fall behind. The boy was struggling to support her by allowing her to lean on his shoulder but he wasn't tall or strong enough.

O'Malley sighed. Their assailants were closer now; their strange loping gait was becoming faster as they drew nearer and the doctor was getting slower. They'd catch them in no time. He stepped to Theresa's other side and took her weight on to his shoulder and together they hobbled as fast as they could towards the hidden entrance.

They were only twenty feet away and had increased the gap to the townspeople by a small margin but any delay at the entrance could still be fatal.

The entrance wasn't wide enough for the three of them to fit through so Denis pushed forward first, ripping the sheeting aside while the others hobbled in. They were immediately plunged into a cool, dimly lit passageway that was wide enough only for one of them at a time. It stretched down about fifteen feet and terminated in a sturdy looking wooden door. The door was closed.

As the boy passed the sheeting O'Malley let it fall and the passageway immediately grey darker with only a dim glow penetrating the thick dust. He could no longer see the door but they had nowhere else to go now so he ran down the passage, his arms outstretched, probing for the entrance.

His hands felt the wood moments later and he groped blindly for the handle on both sides. He let out the breath he had been holding as his hands gripped the cool metal of the lever handle and he plunged it downward and pushed.

The door remained closed so he plunged the handle again and this time pulled. His heart sank as the fear he had been harbouring became reality. It was locked. He had known as soon as he had seen the figure dart away from them that it would be locked but he had hoped. *What kind of bastard would lock us out?*

Anger flared within him and he pounded on the door. "Hey in there," he shouted. "Let us in. We're not infected." He didn't really know what to say and he didn't want to drive the person on the other side of the door away. "I'm a police officer and I have a doctor and a young boy with me. Those things are still far enough away. Open the door please."

He tried hard to keep his tone even and reasonable but he knew that they only had another few seconds before those things reached them and this time they had nowhere else to run. They were trapped.

The seconds ticked by and there was no answer from behind the door, no click as the lock was opened. Theresa pushed level with him and laid her face up against the door.

"Hello," she began and O'Malley could hear the terror in her voice. "I'm Doctor Theresa Winfield. I have a small boy with me, please let us in. There's not much time. Please."

The door remained closed.

Alan Peters heard the pleas as he leaned against the door. He shut his eyes tightly and brought his hands to his ears, trying to block out their voices and the screams that he knew would start soon.

He wasn't a complete bastard, he did feel for them. But he just couldn't take a chance that those things would get in. Besides, for all he knew those people were already infected and would turn into those things and turn on him later. He couldn't take the chance. He pressed his hands more tightly against his ears but the cries still filtered through.

O'Malley knew that the person behind the door wasn't going to listen to reason so he gently touched Theresa on the shoulder and eased her behind him. "Doctor, see where they are if you would. I'll take care of this." The woman looked quizzically at him but she shrugged and headed back behind him. O'Malley took a deep breath.

"Okay," he shouted at the door. "I've tried to be reasonable but we've run out of time. In three seconds I'm going to start kicking this door and I'm not going to stop until either you open the door or it falls down, and then those things will get in and we both lose. This is your final chance."

"One." He raised his voice even louder as he spat the word.

"Two." He braced his arms against the sides of the narrow passage and lifted his right leg.

"Three." The final word was punctuated by his foot slamming against the area just below the lock. The door held but the whole passageway shook with the impact. He drew his leg back again.

Theresa hobbled along the passageway towards the shimmering sheeting. Her ankle hurt like hell and she gripped the walls on either side for support. The dirty light filtered through the thick plastic and bathed her in a hot, dull glow. The air in the passageway was humid and sticky and her shirt stuck to her like a second skin.

She approached the sheeting with mounting trepidation, expecting one of her assailants to appear at any second and devour her. Her mind was clearing fast as the adrenaline pumped through her system but she still couldn't quite remember the sequence of events that had brought her here. All she knew was that her rescue would be short-lived if Denis O'Malley couldn't get the door open.

She paused briefly at the edge of the entrance and shifted her feet to put most of her weight onto her good leg. Her foot brushed against something hard and she looked down. The light here was better than back at the far end and she saw the outline of a hammer on the ground. She bent quickly and scooped it up and then leaned further against the sheeting to see beyond its dirt-encrusted surface.

The face that appeared directly in front of her made her jump and her hand snapped back against the side wall grazing her knuckles and forcing her to drop her newly acquired weapon.

Peters was thrown forward by the first blow to the door and scrambled for his footing. *What was the man doing? Didn't he realise that they'd all die if he broke the door down?* Alan Peters was terrified and his numbed brain just couldn't fathom that anyone would rather see them all die instead of accepting their fate and keeping him out of it.

"Go away and leave me alone," he mumbled over and over like a mantra but the words lacked volume and merely came out like a desperate keening. He leaned back against the door just as the second blow struck and his back was jolted painfully.

"Go away, go away . . . "

The blows continued.

Theresa dropped to her knees, her hands scanning the ground blindly for the hammer as her gaze remained locked on the plastic above. She could see an outline and then the sheeting bulged inwards.

"Denis, they're coming," she croaked, her voice breaking with fear. Her hand suddenly felt a shape and she grabbed it. The hammer felt reassuringly heavy in her hand and she slowly rose to her feet. She glanced back towards the others but her eyes were too used to the light and all she could see was darkness.

The first figure lurched into the passage. *At least they have to come one at a time.* She raised the hammer and swung with all her strength at the thing's head. The hammer hit him on the forehead and Theresa heard a sickening, wet crunch as the weapon penetrated the skull. The figure fell at her feet and remained still but the next one was already shambling forward.

She was appalled at how easy it was to cause the damage that she had spent a lifetime training to repair. One side of her tried to reason and argue that these poor souls could be cured and that she had just committed murder, the other side of her urged her to kill everything that moved and sort it out later. The adrenaline and fear fuelled the later side and she swung again at her next target.

O'Malley felt the door give a little. His foot pounded with each kick, the thin runners on his feet were never meant for kicking doors down and offered little support against the impacts. He could hear Theresa behind him grunting as she swung at the next figure. She wouldn't be able to hold them much longer.

"One last chance," he panted, as he took a moment to change his position to use his other foot. "The next kick will do it and then they'll flood in and kill us all. Come on, open up and we'll barricade the door together."

The door remained closed. He sighed and raised his foot again. Just as he was about to kick again he heard a dull click and the door opened a crack. A pale face appeared. "I'll let you in on one cond . . ."

O'Malley didn't wait for the man to finish the sentence. He kicked hard against the door, sending the man sprawling and the door crashing open to reveal the site beyond. The sudden explosion of light blinded him but he turned back towards the darkened passageway. "Theresa, we're in. Stop playing with your friends and get your ass in here."

He powered inside to prevent the door from closing again as it swung back on its hinges and turned to help the boy through. His eyes were slowly growing accustomed to the brightness and he could barely see Theresa. She was still struggling, hobbling on her bad ankle and behind her the passageway was dark with shifting bodies.

"Come on," he urged, reluctant to leave the door in case it closed behind him. The man who had opened the door jumped to his feet. "You have to close the do . . ."

"Fuck off." O'Malley gave the man a baleful stare and Peters recoiled as if struck. Then Theresa was there and he lifted her bodily in through the door and swung the door closed. The door was secured by a slide bolt just under the lock but the padlock that held it closed was on the ground. Their assailants had already reached the door so he couldn't bend down to get it and hold back the hoard at the same time.

He put his foot against the base of the door and leaned his body against it but the sheer weight on the other side of the door was too much. The door began to inch inwards, slowly but surely.

"Somebody get the lock," he shouted desperately and he tried to push against the door. Already a gap had formed and he could see fingers probing through. Suddenly the lock was being pressed into his hand and he looked down to see the grim face of the boy looking up at him.

"Great," he cried in relief. "Here, help me. One big push on my mark. Okay, mark." They pushed together and the door closed a little but not fully.

"Theresa, we need you here." He strained to slip the lock through the hole but they were an inch out and the bolt just wouldn't fit through. The door began to creep inward again. His muscles were screaming at him. His body was weak after his earlier exertions and their flight here had taken the last of his reserves. He felt a heaviness in his limbs and his chest hurt as he continued to brace his body against the door.

His foot slipped as his trainer lost its grip and the door swung further inwards and then, suddenly, Theresa was there, her hands braced against the door. Her body pressed tightly against his back and he felt the inward swing halt and then reverse as the door slowly closed.

He looked down at the lock and saw the bolt would now clear the frame. He threaded the lock through and clicked it closed.

The door strained against the lock but it held. He looked down and saw the damage his kicks had caused. One of the screws had come out and a second was loose. It wouldn't last long but, at least for now, they were safe.

"They killed them all?" Julie's face paled as Dave Johnson related what he had seen.

"They gave them one chance to surrender and when they made a break for it they didn't give them a second chance," Johnson confirmed grimly.

"We have to go back," Julie grabbed her husband's arm, her eyes wide with shock.

Johnson looked over at John Pender and saw his eyes dart towards the path and then back towards him. "There's no way around them?" He asked simply as he stroked his chin.

"You can't seriously be thinking of taking a chance wi…" Julie snapped at him and wrenched her arm away from him as if he had suddenly grown boiling hot.

"Love," Pender interrupted gently and tried and failed to catch her arm. "I'm only asking a question. We have to look at every angle before we decide which way to go."

"You can look all you want but I'm not going out there and neither are the children. Do you want to get them killed?"

"Julie," Johnson could hear the exasperation in Pender's tone. "We have to be sure. We've come this far and there's no telling what we'll find back in town."

"John, they're shooting people," Julie responded with an incredulous grin that quickly became a sneer. "What could we possibly find in town that's worse than that?"

"You're probably right," Pender sighed. "What do you think Dave?"

Johnson weighed up the options. "I don't see any way around them," he began and noted the satisfied grin on Julie's face. "There's just no cover out there to slip past."

"So it's back to town then?" Pender asked.

"I'm afraid so. It was worth a shot though," he added with a shrug.

They turned and headed back through the gloom, the void between husband and wife all too noticeable.

Julie Pender fumed as they walked back towards the car. *How dare he?* Her mind spat the question and the look she shot over at her husband was vitriol. To even consider trying to play soldiers with their children's lives was inexcusable. She was aware that the children trekked silently behind her, no doubt scared and confused at this latest development. Of course they'd see her as the one flying off the handle and their father as the calm, reasonable one as usual but God, these soldiers were killing people. You just can't even consider trying to reason with them.

As she cleared the path and came out into the sunlight the feeling of oppressiveness from the looming trees began to recede and her anger began to wane. She had always been prone to a quick temper but was equally quick to cool off. Her steps became less forceful and she slowed somewhat and let the others catch up. Of course she realised that John would never knowingly let any harm come to the children and she regretted her insinuation that he would.

As she played back the conversation in her mind she cringed as she realised that he hadn't actually suggested that they should try to sneak past, only that he had asked if there was another way. She must be more tired than she thought. She looked at her watch, 10.30—*God, is that all it is? It feels like it should be evening already.*

She looked over her shoulder and caught John's eye, he looked away petulantly. *Hurt pride,* she thought and grimaced as she prepared to apologise. She dropped back and let Dave and the kids walk past her until she was level with her husband.

"Hey you," she said and looked over at him.

"Hey," he answered with a stiff tone.

"Oh come on, I'm sorry okay? It's been a shite morning."

"Yeah, I guess we're all on edge," he shrugged and a small grin appeared on his face. "I wouldn't let anything happen to them you know."

Julie stopped and grabbed his hand pulling him to a stop. She looked into his eyes and kissed him gently. "If there's one thing I know I can count on in this whole world, it's that you love us."

He nodded and they continued walking, their hands clasped tightly together.

Martin joined the throng of people milling about their vehicles. Car doors slammed as the townspeople sought answers. Martin shivered as he walked past the main group and headed for the front of the line. There was no point in staying back here; no-one seemed to know what was going on anyway. If he wanted any information then he'd have to head up towards whatever was causing the delay. As he passed the others he sensed the fear, it was almost palpable. The atmosphere here was dangerous. Curses and raised voices predominated as people began to imagine all kinds of new terrors. It wouldn't take much for a panic to start and he didn't want to be anywhere nearby when that happened.

The line of cars disappeared around a sweeping bend and it took him another ten minutes before he cleared the corner and could see the obstruction. There hadn't been an accident, thank God. The lead vehicle had stopped in the road and Martin could see another line of cars on the other side of the road heading into town. These were stationary also and there was a small group from both parties talking animatedly in the middle of the road.

He could see Jack Thornton and the woman, Brid. He didn't know the others but he recognised a few of them from before so he continued on towards the front and joined the group as a tall, mean-looking man was finishing talking.

" . . . and the bastards shot them. Bloody murder it is. They won't get away with it I tell you."

Martin caught Thornton's eye and raised an eyebrow. "So, they just told you to go back to your homes and wait for them to give the all clear?" Thornton pursed his lips as he ruminated on what he had heard.

"Looks like we're caught between a rock and a hard place. Ah, Martin." Everyone turned towards him as Thornton addressed him and Martin felt embarrassed about his earlier bravado and wondered if boldly joining the group had been the best decision after all. "It seems the army has decided to quarantine our little town and want us all to go back home like good little citizens. Evidently they had as little compunction about using deadly force as our flyboy friends back at the estuary."

"Irish or English?" Martin asked.

"What do you mean?" Thornton cocked his head to the side and a frown scrunched up his face adding many more lines to his podgy face.

"The soldiers in the estuary," Martin replied uncertainly. "Surely you saw the markings on the helicopter? They were English."

"Fuck. No, I never noticed that."

"The bastards on the roadblock were definitely Irish," the mean-looking man interrupted. "They had the police with them too. Those bastards just stood by as the soldiers shot up the van. Someone will hear about this"

"These crazy people you saw in the town," Thornton began, "do you think they can handle vehicles or weapons?"

"They seemed to have limited intelligence as far as I could see. The police officer I mentioned got stuck in the front office and just battered the partition down."

"What crazy people?" the mean-looking man asked.

"It seems there might be a nasty virus loose in the town," Thornton replied. "Martin here saw a number of people kill some innocent bystanders, seemingly without any provocation. It would explain why they've set up roadblocks."

"But isn't killing anyone that tries to get through over-reacting, not to mention in violation of every international law?"

"That, my friend, depends on the virus."

"What do you mean?" Martin asked but he knew the answer already and he could feel icy fingers caress his heart.

"They obviously don't expect to have to answer to anyone when it's all over."

There was silence in the group as everyone tried to come to terms with the news in their own way.

"Well, I suggest we all stay together," Thornton began. "There's safety in numbers. The only question is where will we all fit?"

"How about the Marina?" Martin asked.

"No, it not really defendable . . . Oh I see," Thornton suddenly realised what Martin had meant. "Oh yes, that's brilliant."

"What's brilliant," Brid asked.

"We're going sailing, my dear." Thornton rubbed his hands together. "Lead the way, my friend."

Chapter 18

Martin found himself leading the long line of cars towards the town by virtue of the fact that he was the furthest back of the group. He glanced in the mirror every now and then, trying to judge how many cars were travelling behind him, but the road had too many twists in it. There were certainly over forty cars though.

The main road narrowed ahead and terminated in a T-junction, the Cork road continued to the right and Main Street beckoned from the left. Martin stopped briefly at the junction and considered turning right.

He looked over at Hillary but she was busy scanning the streets. Kim smiled reassuringly at him and he wondered if he was doing the right thing bringing her into such danger. He really didn't want to go anywhere near those things in the town again but he knew that the main road would be blocked and guarded further ahead. The sea remained their only viable option.

He sighed and pulled the wheel to the left and headed towards the Marina. He kept his speed low, not in any respect for the thirty-mile-an-hour limit but because he wanted the other cars to be close by in case anything happened.

They crossed over Baker's Bridge, so called because it used to have an old mill on the bank of the river before modern industry came and dried it out when they redirected it to the Pharmaceutical companies that poured their money into the town. The ruins of the mill seemed particularly desolate this morning as they surveyed the overgrown and neglected riverbed.

They passed Hackett's supermarket where this had all started for him. The doors were open but the interior was dark, forbidding, as if something lurked just inside the door for the unwary shopper. Martin shivered and continued on. The noise of his van's diesel engine seemed to be overloud in the deserted town; its deep rumble bouncing off the buildings in the narrow street and announcing their position as surely as if they blared their horns. *So much for the element of surprise.*

He looked in the rear-view mirror and saw a long line of cars stretching back and disappearing round the corner. Everything was deserted and they still hadn't seen any evidence that anything was wrong, let alone that there were rabid, blood-thirsty creatures roaming the streets. For just a moment Martin found himself wishing that they'd see at least one, just to prove to the others that he wasn't mad and that he had actually seen these things. But then he remembered the terror he had felt and he realised being thought of as mad was a small price to pay if he never had to see those things again.

The main square came into view ahead and he could see a few cars parked along the centre from the night before. As they came out of the narrow street and into the open the sun suddenly swept the car, blinding him momentarily and raising the heat of the interior of the car uncomfortably in a matter of seconds.

Martin fumbled in the dashboard for his sunglasses and rolled down the window at the same time. Cool air wafted in immediately, its clean scent highlighting the oppressive, sour smell of the undelivered milk cartons in the van. His groping fingers finally found his sunglasses and he slipped them on, blinking furiously as he tried to clear the water from his eyes.

"Oh my God!" He snapped his head towards Hillary at her exclamation. Her face was white as a sheet. Her hair, normally full and rich in colour, hung limp and wet against her face. She was looking straight ahead and the look of sheer terror on her face was one that Martin would never forget. He turned his head in the direction of her gaze and knew immediately that he wouldn't have to worry about finding proof anymore.

Martin slammed the van into first gear. The engine screamed as it downshifted and he stabbed his foot on the accelerator. The van responded and shot forward into the square. Ahead of them he could see at least fifty of the things he had seen before. Some walked aimlessly around the square, their clothes ragged and bloodstained, but the majority of them pressed against the wooden hoarding surrounding the building site.

They had to pass close by the throng to get to the Marina, there was a quicker way through the arches, the local name for the ruins of an eighteenth century fort, but that would mean walking and he had no intention of getting out of the van until he reached the water's edge.

He pressed the accelerator harder and brought the van up to fifty miles an hour as he reached the group. Some of them turned from their incessant hammering and shambled towards the fast approaching vehicle, their slack faces and bloodied continences enough to convince Martin that these were no longer normal townspeople.

He was only twenty feet away when three of the figures walked directly in front of him. He shot out an arm to protect Kim and then braced himself as he kept the van directed straight ahead. The whole van shuddered as he hit the people. The bodies of two of them flew through the air but the third, a small boy of around seven, disappeared under the van and caught under the wheels. Martin swerved left and right, trying to clear the obstruction, with no luck. The wheels suddenly lost traction and the van flew out of control careering to the left and crashing against the bank on the opposite corner.

The bank had recently been renovated and boasted a new window-fronted lobby that looked out over the square. The momentum of the van carried it through the glass and most of the way through the office space beyond. Martin felt glass pepper his face and arm through his open window, the pain like hundreds of needles pricking him simultaneously. The noise was deafening; tyres screeched, glass shattered and desks, chairs and computers flew in every direction as the van continued to spin. He lost all sense of direction as they were thrown from side to side and then something slammed into his head and darkness descended upon him in a rush.

Jack Thornton tapped the wheel impatiently. There were twenty or so cars ahead of him and at least the same behind and those in front moved frustratingly slowly. The narrow, one-way streets did not allow overtaking. He sighed heavily and wiped the sweat from his face. His head still thumped painfully, reminding him of the previous night's excesses.

He shifted his considerable bulk in the car and felt his shirt peel uncomfortably from the leather seat. *I really should loose weight,* he thought as his stomach twisted painfully with a mixture of hunger and nausea from the mix of cocktails he had sampled the night before.

The morning had begun strangely and had spiralled quickly out of control since then. He had woken early to a loud ringing in his head. It had taken him far too long to wake from his stupor and the phone had eventually stopped ringing. He was vaguely aware of a beeping noise as a message had been left, but he had drifted back to sleep again.

He had woken a few minutes later as the message reminder beeped again and he angrily stabbed the play button, cursing the caller before he had even identified them. The message had been short, but the hurried communication Theresa Winfield had left had snapped him out of his torpor like a bucket of cold water.

He had met the doctor only recently when he had begun to feel pains in his chest. She had been efficient and likable from the start, and extremely tactful when she explained that the pains had more to do with indigestion that heart trouble. She had also warned him that if he continued abusing his body like he had been doing that he ran the risk of having a massive heart attack. She hadn't minced her words and had made no allowance for his position as the town's Mayor.

Thornton wasn't used to people being so direct, and certainly not used to people telling him what to do. But her attitude was refreshing and he had found himself taking her advice to heart, he smiled as he recognised the pun. He had been good since then as well, except for last night which had been an exception and one he was currently paying dearly for.

When he heard the doctor's voice on his voice mail he had thought for a moment that she had somehow found out about last night and was ringing to scold him but as her words filtered through his befuddled brain he had felt icy tendrils caress his heart.

He had jumped from his bed, ignoring the searing pain as his head thumped from the sudden movement. He grabbed for the phone and dialled the doctor's number, playing her message back in his mind. The phone was engaged. He sat at the edge of the bed, feeling his stomach bubble and his head swim. He cursed himself for drinking too much and for being so unprepared when the town needed him most.

He jumped from the bed, ignoring the dizziness, and stumbled to the shower. He turned the water on to cold and walked into the freezing torrent. He screamed as the water seemed to pierce his skin but he forced himself to stay there for ten minutes. By the time he had walked back into the bedroom he was sober and feeling much better.

He had dressed quickly and tried Theresa's number again but the phone rang out. His mind had gone over the details of the message again and again while he was in the shower and he had decided that Theresa was not the type to over-react. He would take her advice. First he would wake his neighbours and then … It was at that stage that his thoughts had been interrupted by the deep growl of a helicopter landing out on the estuary and the day had gone to hell from there.

His thoughts were interrupted as car horns blared ahead of him.

A Land Rover pulled onto the path and roared past the slower vehicle ahead of it. Another pulled out and then a third and suddenly there were two lines of cars clogging the street. Horns blared as the occupants in the original lane closed ranks and drove up to the bumper of the cars in front, ensuring the new line of cars could not force their way in. The second line of cars came to a stop just before the entrance to the square as a street sign blocked their way and they had try to edge back into the line of cars.

People shouted abuse at each other and the noise was loud enough to wake the dead. The lead car on the path, a large black Land Rover, suddenly saw a small gap, revved its engine and shot forward. The gap was quickly closed by the next car in line and the Land Rover had nowhere to go. It slammed into the other vehicle and continued on into the square regardless, tearing the whole side off the car behind.

The occupant jumped from his ruined vehicle and ran after the Land Rover. The man was fast and the Land Rover was slowed initially by the car in front of it. The man reached the driver's door of the Land Rover and jerked it open. Thornton lost sight of the vehicle and jumped from his car to see what was happening. He heard a loud crash ahead and ran to the front of the traffic jam.

Men were gathered around the lead vehicle trying to pull the torn front wing away from the tyre but the metal was bent too far inwards.

"Lift the goddamn thing out of the way," he shouted at them as he gulped air. "We have to get these cars moving." He ran out into the square and saw two men rolling on the ground beside the Land Rover. The vehicle was buried into a shop front and people were crossing the square towards the scene. Ahead he could see a line of cars stopped at the other side of the square. There were people all around the cars, hammering on the vehicles and blocking their way.

He could see some people get out of their cars but they were quickly swamped by their attackers and they quickly disappeared in a sea of bodies. "Shit!" he muttered. Taylor had been right. He turned quickly and yelled at the men lifting the damaged vehicle out of the way to stop what they were doing.

The situation was deteriorating rapidly. The men moving the car couldn't hear him over the noises of shouting and horns blaring so he started towards them as fast as he could. They were only twenty feet away but they had already cleared the vehicle to the side by the time he reached them and cars shot through the gap as soon as it became wide enough, almost knocking down the people who had just cleared the obstruction in their haste.

Thornton waved his hands trying to stop the cars but panic had begun to take hold. People had sat in their cars too long and frustration and fear overtook common sense. Cars raced out into the square and quickly found that there was nowhere to go. Some stopped and got out of their cars to see what was holding the line up, others raced around the square, driving up on the path, hoping to cut in further up the queue but only succeeded in snarling the traffic further. Still others saw people they knew and approached them only to be attacked by the silent figures that wandered through the chaos attacking and killing as they went.

It was a nightmare and Thornton watched helplessly as cars reversed in a vain attempt to escape only to crash into the cars behind. People ran aimlessly, looking for a safe route but their attackers quickly cornered them with their greater numbers and swamped the poor unfortunates. Thornton couldn't see exactly what these mysterious figures were doing to their victims but they left bloodied bundles in their wake.

He screamed at the people in their cars to pass the word back and get the cars at the back of the line to reverse but word of the chaos in the square was spreading more quickly and people panicked. Cars reversed into the cars behind them and other cars tried to turn around only to get caught mid turn. The screech of metal filled the air and competed with the screams of terror that came from the square. People abandoned their cars and ran in every direction; some even ran into the square, their wild eyes unseeing as they raced blindly past.

Thornton stared disbelievingly around him as people brushed past him. These people were counting on him so he had to regain control and salvage what he could. They could still make it to the Marina if they used the shortcut through the 'Arches' but they needed to stay calm and together. He grabbed the nearest person to him and ordered them to gather up anyone they could. The man looked blankly at him and tried to pull away. Thornton shook the man until his eyes focused on him and then repeated his instructions until the man nodded his understanding.

He grabbed more people and repeated the procedure until, finally, he had a growing number of people around him. He quickly filled them in on his plan.

Denis O'Malley had never in his life felt such hatred before. He stared at the man in front of him and felt such raw emotion that he actually felt himself shake. He wanted to lash out at the man; he wanted to rip his head from his shoulders, but slowly he forced himself to calm down.

The man was whining about the door and the fact that they would all die now that they knew where he was and then something in him snapped. He grabbed the man by the neck and pulled him to within an inch of his face. "If I were you I would shut the hell up," he spat the words with such venom that it was a wonder that the acidic tone didn't burn a hole in the man's face. "We nearly died out there and right now I am considering slowing down our friends outside by throwing you over the Goddamn wall." The man stared hard into his eyes as if trying to determine if the threat had any merit, he obviously decided that it had as he stopped blubbering and sat meekly against the centre wall.

"Are you two okay?" he asked Theresa and the boy and they both nodded. "Any idea what we're dealing with, Doctor?"

"Not really," she answered. "It seems that there was a submarine discovered and some gas . . . " she never got any further in her answer as O'Malley lifted his hand motioning her to silence as he cocked his head and listened. He had heard something. *There,* he snapped his head towards the door, trying to filter out the booming of the fists against the wood and concentrate on the sound in the distance.

He heard the growl of an engine. "Quick," he shouted towards the man, "is there a way into the centre?" The man looked blankly at him. "Come on man," O'Malley snapped, "I need to see into the square. Can we get up there?"

The man nodded dumbly and pointed down towards the decking. "There's a gap half-way along there. Once inside you can use the escalators."

O'Malley nodded. "Okay, let's go. Something's happening out there and we need to find out what it is." Theresa and the boy followed him immediately but the man remained sitting against the hoarding.

"What about him?" Theresa asked as they approached the gap in the wall.

"I couldn't give a toss what he does," O'Malley stated simply.

Theresa followed O'Malley through the gap and into the shopping centre. Despite their predicament she found herself looking around in awe as the light filtered through the prism at the top and shot a myriad of colours around the building.

She felt Aidan's hand dragging at her and she tore her eyes away from the roof and redoubled her speed up the stationary escalator. O'Malley was already running towards the glass front of the first floor and she struggled to keep up on her swollen ankle.

O'Malley pressed himself against the glass with his arms flat against the surface, as if he were somehow impaled there, and Theresa felt her heart beat faster as she approached the glass. She didn't know what she had expected to see but the scene before her surpassed any nightmare she could have dreamt.

The square was in chaos. The small town centre was approximately 100 square yards with shop fronts on all four sides. Four roads led into the square; the northern end led to the Police Station and a dead end, the second, King Street, was the main entrance to the town and fed into the Cork and Waterford main roads, the third was named Bourke Street and led down to the Marina. The fourth was currently blocked with the construction of the new centre.

Theresa looked out over the square and saw a line of cars stretching from the main entrance across the square to the Marina entrance on Bourke Street. There seemed to be hundreds of cars stopped on King Street and the line disappeared back into the distance. There had been an accident on the corner of Bourke Street and the debris had blocked the cars trying to get down to the Marina and the traffic backlog filled the square.

To make matters worse there were hundreds of those slow moving figures attacking the vehicles. Theresa watched in horror as people got out of their cars, whether to shout at them to move or simply because they recognised their neighbours she didn't know, but once out of their vehicles the figures descended on them and tore them to pieces. She watched the scene play out in front of her like some bizarre silent movie.

She could see people screaming, cars screeching as others saw the danger and tried to return the way they had come only to find the way blocked. Cars crashed into shops and other cars in their panic and all of it happened in total silence. The glass in front of them afforded them clear visibility but insulated them totally against the cacophony of terror that filled the square.

"Oh my God," she whispered, her voice sounding loud in the hushed centre. "We've got to help them."

O'Malley was already moving along the glass and she wasn't sure if he had heard her or not. She glanced over at him as he raced along the wall of glass trying to get a better view and checking out different angles and then, as if he had seen what he was looking for, he nodded and waved her over.

Theresa looked around for Aidan and found him pressed against the glass looking out as if in a trance. She laid a hand gently on his shoulder but firmly pulled him away. O'Malley was already talking before they were half-way to him.

"You see that main door down there?" He motioned towards a large gate that led into the street a further hundred yards from the site entrance they had used earlier. The gates were wide enough to allow crane and truck access and stretched a good forty feet across. The gates themselves were wooden panelling with corrugated steel nailed to the front. They were secured by a large chain and lock that threaded through two metal rings on either door.

"Yes," Theresa answered dubiously. "They don't look that secure."

"Oh, we can rig something up to secure it better," O'Malley answered confidently. "The main thing is that we could get a lot of people through those gates to safety."

"We could also let a lot of those things in as well," Theresa replied. She looked over at O'Malley. His manner was a little bit manic she thought as she studied him. Their narrow escape had been highly stressful and he had had to carry her most of the way as she had been out of it but there was something about him that nagged at her. She noticed the drops of sweat on his brow but the heat was quite strong through the glass so maybe she was over-reacting. She was probably just stressed herself. They had to try something to help those poor souls but there was no point in sacrificing themselves for nothing either.

"We'll sort something out," he answered quickly and immediately darted back towards the escalators. Theresa looked back out at the scene below and shivered at the thought of venturing out there again.

Chapter 19

Dave Johnson eased the car over to the side of the road and parked just behind the Pender's vehicle. Ahead he could see a line of cars gridlocked along King Street.

"Looks like we're not the only ones to think of the Marina," he heard Pender comment as the man approached him. Johnson got of his car and stood on the path to get a better view. The cars were hopelessly stuck in the narrow street with at least seven collisions that he could see where cars had reversed into walls or other cars in their attempt to extricate themselves from their situation. The street was eerily quiet and he couldn't see anybody in any of the vehicles.

"It's a mess," he sighed. "So what do we do now?"

"There's a short cut through the ruins in the 'Arches'," Pender replied, "so we can get through all right but if this amount of people have come through already then I doubt if there's anything left that will even float. It looks like we're too late."

"What do you make of that?" Johnson asked and nodded towards the mess of cars. "It looks like they panicked but what could have been chasing them and where are they now?"

Pender looked out over sea of abandoned cars as if the answer was hidden among the vehicles but finally, he gave up and let out a deep breath. "I don't know but we certainly won't find out by staying here. We might as well head over to the Marina anyway, there's bound to be someone there that can explain this mess and we might even get lucky and hitch a ride on a boat."

Denis O'Malley rushed through the centre and out onto the wooden deck. Blood pounded in his head, drowning out the slap of his sneakers on the wooden surface. Sweat broke out on his face as sunlight drenched him once he ran out from under the shadow of the new building. His chest hurt as he ran and his arm throbbed painfully where he had been scraped. He'd have to get Theresa to look at that as soon as things calmed down a bit. He couldn't hear whether she had followed him or not but he ran to the gates regardless, there wasn't much time left if he was going to save those people outside.

He had no idea what was going on. Theresa had been about to tell him something before the cars had arrived outside, something about a submarine and a gas. His head was fuzzy as he tried to sort through the events; first he had been attacked by a maniac, then he had rescued Doctor Winfield and the boy from a group of similar attackers and now there were a whole square full of them attacking the townspeople.

There were no prisons or asylums anywhere near the town so it wasn't an escape. He couldn't be absolutely sure but he thought he had recognised one or two of the attackers from his vantage on the first floor but he was too far away to be certain. If it was a gas of some type then he would have to be careful when dealing with the attackers; he had to protect the victims for sure but that didn't mean that he could lash blindly out at the attackers. They could be just as victimised as the people they were attacking.

He shook his head as he reached the huge gates. *Time to focus*, he thought. He looked around and saw the man that had locked them out sitting off to the side of the wooden hoarding. He seemed to curl into himself further with every blow as the door was pounded relentlessly from the other side. The hammering wasn't as heavy at the moment as most of their attackers had been distracted by the chaos in the square but there were still enough left and their rhythmic beat was ominous, almost primal, and O'Malley couldn't help but shiver as the tolling continued inexorably.

O'Malley briefly considered grabbing the man to his feet and forcing him to help but just then Theresa arrived beside him. She was panting and out of breath but smiled at him regardless. "Where do you want us?"

"Alright," O'Malley said as he snapped back into focus. He tried to smile at her and the boy at her side but he wasn't too sure if he succeeded or not. "I need you to put your weight behind this door," he indicated the right-hand gate. "I'm going to open the lock and slip out and I want you to close the door over. Once I gather up enough people I'll shout and you open the door and let us in."

"As simple as that?" Theresa asked dubiously.

"These people are moving very slowly," he shrugged as if confused at her reticence, "we should have plenty of time to gather up the survivors and get back before they notice us."

"It didn't take them long to surround us out in the square," Theresa laid a hand on O'Malley's arm. "Don't underestimate them,

Denis. They might be slow but they're not stupid."

O'Malley nodded quickly and turned away from her and lifted the heavy chain lock.

"Denis," Theresa turned him around again to look at her. "You're burning up."

"It's nothing," he replied but his voice was much higher than he had intended. "I've been jogging all morning; I just haven't had a chance to cool down yet."

Theresa cocked her head to the side and looked at him. "Hey," she said suddenly as she noticed his arm. "You're hurt. Let me have a look at that."

"After I get those people to safety, okay?" O'Malley snapped as he pulled his arm away and hid it behind his back. "Look," he continued as he forced himself to calm down, "it'll be too late if I don't go now. People could get killed out there if we don't act now."

Theresa looked at him closely for almost a full minute and in that time he felt his body begin to shake. Parts of his body were hot and other parts were cold. He had no idea what was causing it but he knew that if he didn't go now he might not be able to go later.

"Okay, then," Theresa relented, "but you come straight to me when you get back. I've got some medicine in my bag that might help."

O'Malley was already threading the lock through the steel supports before she finished talking.

Jack Thornton shuffled from one foot to the other as he watched his charges stream past. *Too slow,* he thought nervously as he kept glancing back towards the square. He expected to see a hoard of people appear at any second but he had to remain outwardly calm if he was to avoid a panic.

Many of the people he had gathered did not know what was going on in the square, they had been too far back to see but the rumours were rife and there was an almost palpable fear among them that wouldn't take much to turn into blind panic.

He motioned for the rest of the group to hurry without showing too much concern and then finally the last of them passed him. He checked the square briefly. The attackers were still occupied so they should still have enough time to get to the Marina without being seen, providing there weren't more of them ahead.

Thornton walked quickly past the line of refugees. He forced himself to walk calmly but quickly, nodding a warm and reassuring smile at everyone who met his eyes. His head still thumped painfully and the day's heat was already uncomfortable. He wished he could take off his jacket but he could feel the sweat soaking his shirt and he couldn't afford for the others to see how nervous he was.

What the hell are those things? He had been asking himself the same question since he had seen the chaos in the square. If they had been monsters or strange beings from another world he could have accepted that but these things were his neighbours, people he had grown up with, played with when he was young and drank with at the weekends. He had seen them attack people in the square indiscriminately, he saw one woman torn limb from limb and a small boy no more than ten years old bitten until all that remained was a bloodied lump on the ground. The attackers showed no remorse. They seemed to move from victim to victim relentlessly; indefatigable in their single-minded drive to kill and maim.

Thornton continued on towards the top of the line and looked back along the sea of faces, calculating quickly the number of people. *Only forty,* his face went pale. *My God we started off with well over a hundred.*

The shortcut through the 'Arches' took them around the main square and through the older streets of the original village from which the current town had grown. The 'Arches' themselves comprised of the gates from an old fort that had guarded the harbour since the 1600s. Its once impressive stone edifice and towering keep were now crumbled and ivy-ridden but its lost grandeur was still apparent in the surviving main gate and the arched passageway that led to the barbican. Thornton shivered as he passed under the arches and walked through the narrow passage. He looked up at the sheer walls surrounding him and imagined the murder that had taken place here as the defenders reined fire down on helpless attackers.

The group continued on through the ruins and came out to the west of the harbour. Their vantage on the elevated land commanded an impressive view of the Marina and the shopping centre beyond it.

Pat Murphy led the convoy and Thornton smiled grimly as he approached him. Thornton had known Murphy since junior school. They hadn't always been the best of friends but both men were well aware of the other's capabilities and, while they didn't always agree, both men respected each other. Murphy was the local hardware shop owner and he had argued against the proposed shopping centre as it would take business from the local community, his own business in particular. Thornton had argued that major investment in the town would benefit them all. They had continued to argue for months, some of it heated, but Thornton couldn't think of a better man to be beside him in their current situation.

"How does it look?" Thornton asked, wheezing heavily from the exertion.

"Not good," Murphy replied and blinked furiously as the sun danced over the undulating waves and alternatively shot out blinding lances of light as the swells of the water rippled gently in the harbour. "From what I can see most of the craft must have slipped their moorings during the storm. There were at least twenty boats here yesterday, now all I can see are four and two of them are listing dangerously—must have picked up some damage or something. I suppose it could be that someone got here before us but I doubt it."

Thornton shielded his eyes from the glare as best he could and looked out over the water. The harbour looked completely desolate compared to what he was used to seeing. On any given day you would see at least fifteen boats scattered about the harbour, anything from fishing boats up to small yachts. One of the reasons for the new marina complex was to attract the larger mid-range yachts that were too big for the current facilities and that would provide good mooring revenue and attract tourists with plenty of money to spend.

The new harbour would include orderly lines of wooden jetties that would provide easy access to all the boats, currently many of the crew that moored their boats in the marina had to wait for the Harbour Master to bring them out to their craft in a small motorised dinghy.

Now, however, the marina was empty save for two obviously holed small sailing craft and two fishing trawlers. One of the trawlers sat in the middle of the harbour, bobbing gently to the rhythm of the tide and the other, thankfully, lay caught against the harbour wall where it had snagged its mooring line between some rocks.

"We should be able to board that one," Murphy continued as he pointed to the trawler close to the shore, "and use her to bring the other one in."

"Will we have enough room for everyone?"

"We'll fit 'em in. Might be a tight squeeze but we'll not leave anyone behind."

167

Thornton nodded and looked towards the shopping centre. The construction of the centre and the new Marina had necessitated the building of a wired fence between the current harbour and the site, mainly to prevent boats from slipping their moorings and causing damage to the construction. The distance was only about three hundred yards across the water with the wire protruding about six feet from the level of the water. He sighed as he looked at the wooden rows of the new moorings and wondered briefly if attracting such investment had been the best thing to have done after all.

The wooden doors opened inwards as soon as they were freed from the chain and O'Malley was pushed backwards two steps by their sheer weight. He recovered quickly, pushing the doors nearly level again and indicated to Theresa to hold the door on the left while he pushed the right hand door slightly further. The doctor was quick to comply and O'Malley nodded at her and then slipped his head through the gap to look outside.

The area immediately surrounding the doors was clear; however total chaos reigned just a short distance away. There were still a small number of their attackers massed around the door they had entered through but the vast majority of the things were centred in and around the cars that clogged the square.

O'Malley nodded once again to Theresa and then slipped through the doors and out into the street. He stood there for a second wondering if he was doing the right thing. Was he endangering Theresa and the boy or could he actually do some good out here? His head swam dizzily. He knew that his arm was infected, but if he delayed any longer he might never get another chance. The door shut behind him with a hollow finality and the threading of the chain through the metal supports gave him the impetus he needed.

He moved quickly away from the door, if anything happened to him he didn't want to lead them back to the others, and raced towards the square. He crouched down behind the lead car and craned his neck around the vehicle to get his bearings.

The main body of the attackers had moved away from where he was, down to the line of cars that had become hopelessly stuck in the mayhem of the initial charge through the square. The cars were stationary now but the square was filled with people running and screaming. Most had no real plan of escape, some tried to fight their way through the attackers to their original destination and others just ran around the square, blindly running from end to end like some insane game of tip-the-can.

O'Malley could see others still in their cars, white faced and terrified as they were surrounded by their attackers. The air was filled with the thump of fists against metal; the terrified screams of those being pursued competed against the shrill, piercing cries of those that had been caught and through it all O'Malley watched the silent but deadly attackers make their way unhurriedly through the throng killing and rending as they went.

He saw a group near the centre of the square that looked more organised. There were about twenty of them formed into a circle and they held a variety of weapons that they had cobbled together. Their hurried search of the cars around them had produced a strange ensemble, some of the men held cricket bats, *another week or so and the season would have been over,* O'Malley thought wryly. Others held large torches in one hand and slapped their other hands nervously along their length and if to reassure themselves that the weight would make up for the lack of length. He saw one woman holding a metal crowbar and still others gripping a pitiful collection of inadequate sticks that had obviously come from the same cricket collection as the bats. The wooden stumps did not provide the same weight or reach as the bats themselves but they were better than nothing.

The group shuffled raggedly together holding their shape largely by virtue of the shouts and urgings from a large man who held position in the front of the group. He cajoled and encouraged, and in some cases blatantly shouted at the others to keep their formation and, for now, it was working. They made their way slowly away from the cars and lashed out at any attackers that came too close. They didn't seem to have any particular direction in mind as the moved first one way then another but then O'Malley noticed that each time they changed direction the group swelled in size. *He's picking up stragglers as they move about,* O'Malley thought as he recognised the tactic.

There were three attackers just ahead of O'Malley and the group were shuffling in his direction over towards a woman and her two children that were being hemmed in by two other attackers. O'Malley saw two men lurch forward as they were tempted out of the safety of the group but the big man roared at them and they sheepishly returned. O'Malley could see the wisdom in the man insisting they stay together. Individually they were too vulnerable, but at their slow pace they wouldn't make it the woman in time. Making a quick decision O'Malley sprinted from his cover and raced towards the woman and the children.

The three figures ahead of him began to turn towards him but were far too slow and O'Malley powered through them from behind, sending two spinning to the ground and the other stumbling backwards. He caught the eye of the big man in the group and received a quick nod in return. The man could see what he was doing and continued to urge his group onwards.

O'Malley hadn't taken a weapon with him, he had been too eager to get out and save the survivors. He cursed his earlier enthusiasm as he approached the two other attackers as they turned towards him fully and prepared for his attack. O'Malley felt a curious calm descend upon him. His body raged between hot and cold and his arm throbbed constantly but the infection also heightened his senses and he felt the adrenaline flood through his system like a narcotic, deadening the pain and sending euphoria through his fevered head.

This sudden rapture overcame his caution and O'Malley launched himself at the first figure without a second thought. He dodged under the first man's clumsy swipe and kicked at his knees. His foot connected perfectly against the man's knee and he went down silently, however the sharp snap of bone was clearly audible. O'Malley immediately went on to the second figure, his confidence growing. He ignored the fallen man; they may not feel pain but there was no way he was standing on that leg again anytime soon. The second figure was slightly faster and O'Malley reeled backwards as he snapped his head away from the man's attack.

He nearly cleared the man's reach but just at the last moment the man's fingers raked along O'Malley's cheek and pain lanced through his euphoria. O'Malley stopped, the shock reminding him of the danger these things posed. He ducked below the man's next attack and continued on behind him, grabbing his neck in a vice and wrenching violently sideways.

He took no satisfaction in the loud snap of the man's neck and muttered a quiet prayer as the man slipped to the ground. He looked down at the man briefly and saw that his eyes were still open but then the group arrived and quickly enveloped him and the woman and her children into its protective embrace.

O'Malley tried to keep the attacker in view. *What the hell are they? I broke his neck and he's still conscious.* Then the man disappeared behind the press of bodies as he felt hands clap him on his back and heard distant shouts of congratulations. He was dimly aware that someone had pressed a cricket stump into his hands and that the woman and her children were surrounded by a number of women who comprised a protective inner circle. The group began to move back towards the square on its quest for more survivors and he felt someone apply a cream to his cheek. He pushed them away gently but firmly and began to force his way to the front.

The big man continued his constant drone, directing the group with an incessant bellow of "Left, left" in time with every step. O'Malley pressed against the people in front of him, interrupting their rhythm and leaving a wake of people out of step behind him. His cheek stung badly and warm blood caked his face. He felt himself sway as the adrenaline drained from his system leaving him exhausted and pain-ridden in the wake of his mad attack but the press of bodies around him served to keep him on his feet.

He shouted weakly at the big man but the sheer noise of shuffling feet and shouted instructions easily drowned him out. He had to get closer. The pain served to clear his head and he began to use the group's momentum to work his way around to the man rather than force his way against the tide. The group were back into the centre of the square by the time he was close enough to attract the leader's attention.

"That was brave," the man nodded towards him and interrupted his monotonous chant briefly. "Stupid, but brave nonetheless."

O'Malley ignored the comment and shouted with the last of his strength. He explained about the centre, the safety it offered and saw the man nod once. He bellowed a new instruction and the group stopped and then began to move in the opposite direction. O'Malley just had enough time to smile before darkness swept him up and he felt himself falling.

Martin woke to pain. His chest was the worst, although his legs, neck and arms weren't much better. It took a few seconds for his memory to flood back and with it came the realisation of his predicament. *How long have I been out?* He wondered even as he began to move gently, testing his limbs to see if anything was broken. He lifted his head slowly, wincing at the pain but forcing himself to rise regardless.

He looked over at Hillary and Kim and sighed with relief when he saw their chests rise and fall. *They're alive at least.*

He raised his head and looked in the rear-view mirror. It was askew but it gave him sufficient view behind him to confirm their situation. Four creatures approached them from outside the shop. They appeared at first to be almost on top of them until he remembered that these mirrors were designed to make objects appear closer, however they were close enough and getting closer. They were slowed initially by the trail of destruction and their limited mobility but they were making headway nonetheless.

Martin undid his seat belt and cried out as he fell forward onto the steering wheel. He slapped at the door handle and almost fell out as the door swung open, almost flying back to hit him with the momentum. He lifted one leg first and swung it out onto the floor of the office. The van had come to a stop on hitting the back wall but had collected a number of desks and chairs along the way and he had to sweep his foot from side to side to clear a level area. He pulled himself out of the van and stopped for a moment to let the world stop spinning.

He glanced over at their pursuers and saw that two of them had fallen over some debris but were already getting back to their feet. The other two were closing in quickly; it would only take them only another few seconds to reach Hillary's side. He reached down and lifted the mangled spine of an office chair. It was coated in hard plastic but the inner core was metal and its weight was reassuring.

Martin worked his way along the back of the van, keeping his hands on the metal of the vehicle to give him support. His head was still too dizzy to risk walking unaided. He reached Hillary's door a few seconds before the first of them approached. It was a woman, blood drenching her face and down the front of her blouse. Her hair, once blonde and curly, was now matted and limp, the ends still dripping small drops of red as she moved. Martin was again struck by their silence and lack of expression and almost missed her attack on him as he stared at her.

He had a brief view of her arm coming towards him, the once manicured nails were still long but the red covering them had little to do with polish. Her fingers were rigid and bent inwards, more like a claw than a hand and it seemed to loom in front of him before his left leg collapsed and he fell. His fall saved him and the woman's hand raked the air above his head.

Martin stayed on his knees and brought the chair spine up with all his strength. He harboured no illusions about trying to disable the woman without seriously hurting her; it was far too late for that. If they found a cure later he would deal with his conscience then but for now he put everything he had into his swing and nodded in satisfaction as the weapon hit the woman on the chin, snapping her head back violently and sending her reeling over a desk where she disappeared.

The second attacker was still a little behind and he used the time to open Hillary's door and duck inside. He ran his hands quickly over her body, feeling for swollen flesh that might suggest a break. He felt a bruise or two but nothing serious and then gently shook her to bring her round.

She moaned briefly but settled quickly back into sleep and Martin shook her more urgently as he checked on his next assailant. He ducked back out of the car and swung the spine at the man's head. The man stumbled towards him heedless of Martin's attack and then dropped like a stone when the spine caved in the left side of his skull. Martin checked the body briefly and saw that its eyes were closed. The body remained still. *Maybe they can be stopped after all,* he thought and then ducked back into the car to help Hillary.

Hillary lurched from troubled sleep into a nightmare of pain and terrifying reality. Her dreams had been of hideous creatures and shrieking metal but the reality she woke to was no better. The soothing tones urging her to wake were at odds with the violent shaking and she cursed whoever it was with language she didn't realise she knew.

She tried to ignore it at first and fall back into sleep but the shaking continued regardless and finally she was forced to open her eyes. Martin looked down at her and then suddenly disappeared. She blinked, confused and then turned her head to see what had happened. Martin suddenly loomed into view again in front of her and her heart lurched with fright with his sudden appearance

She saw his lips moving but she couldn't make sense out of his words. It felt almost like she was under water but the tone of his voice conveyed enough urgency to penetrate the clouds in her head and she started to pull herself together.

Martin disappeared again and she rolled her head after him to see where he had gone. She saw him swing at another man and saw the man fall to the ground. She was still confused; her mind would snatch at memories only to have them slip away from her before she could fully grasp their meaning. Then, as if a switch was suddenly flicked, her head cleared and she remembered. The creatures, the crash, they had all happened.

She forced herself up, ignoring the pain, and then felt a hand help her. She grunted at Martin, hoping that he took this as encouragement rather than a rebuke, and soon found herself grabbing at the side of the van as her legs collapsed under her. Martin held her tightly and supported her while the strength slowly ebbed back into her limbs. The air was thick with dust from the accident and her throat and eyes felt raw from the grit that still floated in the air. She heard Martin talking but had to face him and concentrate to understand him. " . . . all right on your own? I need to check on Kim." She felt herself nodding and then he disappeared back into the car.

Left on her own she looked around nervously. There were three figures close enough to make her nervous but they were still far enough away to prevent her from fleeing in panic. She inched away from the man at her feet, he certainly looked dead but she wasn't prepared to take any chances. Many of the things she had seen so far had no business still moving about either so she wasn't entirely confident that he would remain dead.

Martin backed out from the passenger door and held Kim in his arms. Hillary was surprised at how relieved she was to see him and wondered if she would still be alive if she hadn't met him this morning. She noticed a line of blood seeping from a cut that was hidden by his hairline and she moved closer to him, parting his hair to get a better look.

"It's fine," she heard him say. "We've got to get out of here before more of those things find us." She nodded, recognising the wisdom but disappointed at the same time that she hadn't had the chance to help him. Up till now it had all been one way with him rescuing her and then carrying her back from the estuary and again here, helping her out of the car and fighting off those things. She owed him more than she could ever repay and the sight of his smiling face as he held the little girl was so infectious that it banished much of the tension she felt and she began to smile in return. He really was quite good looking when he smiled, even if he was covered in dust.

Chapter 20

Theresa waited nervously at the door, praying for O'Malley's safe return. She looked at her watch, he'd been gone for ten minutes now, and then tried yet again to see through the small gap between the doors. It was useless; she could only see directly in front of the gate no matter how she shifted her position or angled the doors. She looked along the line of tools and wooden cut-offs that comprised their arsenal and tried to slow her hammering heart.

She had sent Aidan back into the shopping centre to see if he could see anything from there but he hadn't returned yet. She looked over at the man but he still lay on the ground curled into a ball where he had been since she had kicked him in the balls over five minutes ago.

As soon as Denis had left he had immediately come across to her and helped her close the doors and lock them. At first she had thought that he had decided to help them and she nodded gratefully to him. He smiled at her and motioned for her to hold the chain in place while he slipped the lock through them and turned the key.

She had known something was wrong as soon as he pocketed the key and they had spent five minutes arguing until Theresa had lost patience and kicked him. She had retrieved the key while he rolled on the ground and he had stayed there, eyeing her with hate-filled eyes, ever since. She wasn't worried that he'd attack her again; her father had made sure that she and her sisters had all learned self-defence, but it was a shame as she could have used his help.

She leaned back against the door and sighed, looking up at the sky and watching a lone cloud float across the otherwise empty canvass. "He's joined up with a group out in the square." The voice startled her and she jumped as Aidan relayed his news. She looked down at the boy, God she had to remind herself he was only ten as he was handling the situation amazingly well. *Pity the adults can't be as resilient,* she thought as she looked over at the pathetic figure on the ground.

"Huh?" she looked at him quizzically.

"O'Malley," the boy repeated with a look of exasperation that only the young can master. "He's joined up with a group outside."

"Is he all right?"

"I suppose," he shrugged, "He was fighting with a few of those things but then I lost sight of him in the group. He was on his feet when they reached him though."

"Are they coming over here?" Theresa dug her hands in her trousers for the key.

"Yep, but you better be quick. They've got half the square coming after them."

Theresa nodded and turned to unlock the chain and thread it through the supports. She handed the chain to Aidan and motioned for him to stand ready for when they closed the doors. She pulled the left-hand door open just enough to slip her head through and looked down towards the square. From this angle all she could see was the debris from the bank that lay strewn across the narrow road and the cars beyond it that were hopelessly stuck. There were no creatures in view. She slipped back in to update Aidan and then picked up a large wrench that had a particularly wicked-looking curl at the top. She hefted the weight, nodded and then popped her head back out to await the survivors.

The muffled screams of the people in the square carried on the breeze and left the group gathered on the water's edge in no doubt that their position at the back of the procession had been fortuitous indeed. Jack Thornton stood at the head of the group and watched as the two men and one woman clambered slowly over the rocks towards the snagged trawler. Their curses carried easily across the short distance as the men slipped on the lichen-covered surface and served to lighten the funereal mood that had descended on their audience.

There was even a good-natured cheer when the first of the men touched the trawler but Thornton quickly turned and glared at them, motioning them to silence. The three figures scrambled aboard and two of them immediately disappeared below decks while the woman searched the main deck. Thornton didn't realise that he'd been holding his breath until the two men reappeared and he sighed heavily.

He could see Pat Murphy at the stern of the boat waving and he shaded his eyes from the glare of the sun to read the man's hand signals.

"Okay," he said as he turned to the group, "they want four more volunteers to go get the other boat. Only four," he shouted quickly as a rush of people surged towards the boat. "You'll all get on, don't worry," he continued in a more conciliatory tone and smiled to reassure the group.

He couldn't really blame them; they were really very exposed and vulnerable where they were. His calm and reassurance seemed to have sufficed for now and the group settled back to watch the others anxiously.

Martin set Kim on her feet and supported her until she nodded that she was okay. Her face was pale and she had a raw-looking graze on the side of her head. Her finger was swollen to twice its normal size and he assumed that it had been broken in the crash.

"Are you sure you can manage," he dropped to his knees and looked her straight in the eyes. "We may need to run once we get out there."

She nodded more firmly and he felt happier as he rose to his full height and cocked his eyebrows at Hillary. "How about you? You ready to run through those things?"

He watched Hillary look out into the square and then look at him levelly. There was a definite hardness around her jaw that gave weight to her nod of agreement. He raised the chair spine and nodded himself before leading the way towards the bank's entrance.

The two figures that had stumbled over the debris earlier had just reached the van when they headed out the opposite way. Martin had considered going back and taking care of them but he didn't want to risk any attacks that could possibly be avoided. However, he was still nervous about leaving the two behind them because they effectively cut off any possibility of retreat. History was full of stories showing the folly of a two front plan but he just didn't know enough about these things. Was the contagion in the air around them or did they have to cut or bite you to infect? He could be risking Hillary and Kim by just being near them but without knowing for sure he felt they were better off with him than not. He suppressed his misgivings and continued on out into the square.

The chaos of the square was a shock. They had known that there were a number of the infected in the square but nothing could possibly have prepared them for the mayhem that greeted them as they walked out onto the street. Cars packed the enclosed area, some damaged and buried into other cars or lamp posts along the street and others were merely abandoned. The routes into and out of the square were hopelessly blocked and everywhere he looked he saw people running and screaming.

Bodies lay strewn around the square and through it all he could see the infected townspeople shuffle inexorably and methodically after their prey. Their silence and lack of emotion was in complete contrast to the deafening panic of their quarry. For a minute the three survivors stood in complete shock. Martin had no idea where to begin to formulate a plan. His eyes darted from one corner to another, hoping to see an escape route but all he saw were group after group disappear under the relentless tide of death. His mind was numbed by the sheer violence of the scenes.

"Over there, look" he jumped as Kim shouted out excitedly. He looked down at her and followed the direction of her outstretched arm. There was a large group of people just off the centre of the square that seemed to be holding their own. They were packed tightly together and the outer ring were armed with various weapons and, for the moment, seemed to be keeping their attackers at bay.

There were still quite a number of the infected still closing down other individuals throughout the square but as they completed their grisly tasks more would turn their attention towards this group. He had no idea how long they could last as the number of attackers grew but it was certainly their best option for now.

"Let's go," he urged as he pushed Kim and Hillary ahead of him. "Safety in numbers."

At least for now, he thought despondently.

They had run from the ruins of the bank holding hands to ensure they stayed together. The group were moving slowly away from them but their speed was slow and methodical so they caught up easily enough. When they were only a few feet away it became more apparent that the group wasn't quite as large as they'd thought. There was a large core cluster but these were surrounded by a growing number of the infected who kept pace with them easily.

Now and again one of the attackers would be sent stumbling backwards but few of them were hurt badly enough to keep them down and they rose again and returned to the fray. Martin slowed his pace as he searched for a safe entry point. There was none. He stopped and looked around but there was nowhere else to go. He felt very exposed out in the square and a few of the infected townspeople that had been surrounding the group suddenly peeled off and approached them.

Martin squeezed Hillary's hand and then stepped in front of them and raised the chair spine to meet their attack. Just then the group of survivors seemed to bulge outwards in what looked like a well-practised manoeuvre. The circular shape morphed like an amoeba and a corridor bulged outwards, pushing through the thin line of infected and enveloped Martin and his charges before they quite knew what was happening.

Suddenly Martin saw smiling, welcoming faces in front of him and then he felt himself being pulled back towards the main group. The infected townspeople were pushed aside or sent sprawling to the ground and then the group were reformed back into their largely circular shape. Martin looked around frantically and then sighed in relief as he saw Hillary and Kim beside him.

The group continued on its methodical way as if nothing had happened. They had been pulled into the centre and Martin had no idea where they were going and no way of finding out. He tried to talk to the people around him but everyone was too busy concentrating and he nearly fell a few times as he looked around. He finally gave up and concentrated on his own footing. Wherever they were going, it had to be better than where they'd come from.

Theresa saw the first of the group arrive at the corner. The group came to a stop and some people dashed forward down the hundred yards or so to the gates where she stood. The rest of the group began to surge in different directions and for a minute it looked like it would simply break apart like a flower suddenly exploding into bloom. Theresa could see the infected attackers closing in behind the group and the ragged line would not hold them for long.

Men and women pushed past her, flinging the doors wide open in their haste and hurling Aidan to the ground. She screamed at them to slow down but they ignored her. For a minute everything seemed to come apart and then a voice boomed out and everyone stopped.

"Stop!" The sheer power of that one word was enough to cut through the panic. "Anyone that breaks out of the circle will answer to me." Despite the need to hurry the man who had spoken deliberately remained silent while his words sunk in. "We will all get to safety if we work together. The way is too blocked to allow us all to run, we have to file through or we'll end up killing more of ourselves that those things will."

Theresa was impressed. She had been the resident doctor at many sporting events where the crowd had lost it and panic had caused them to stampede. She knew how easy it was for people to react for their own self preservation. She had never before seen anyone capable of pulling a panicked crowd back from the brink, but this man was doing it.

"All men with weapons will move to the back of the group now," he continued and immediately the group seemed to fall in on itself as the front rank disappeared back into the crowd. "Now! Children first and then the injured. Single file past the rubble and then take up station at the door and be ready to close it over as soon as we are all in. Front file, protect against those bastards until the group is safely inside and we'll withdraw backwards. Slowly," he urged as the front rank began to back up too quickly and parts of the line were left vulnerable.

"I need some of those already through the door to come back out and guard the way further along the road in case we're attacked from that direction." Theresa stared in amazement as a few men reappeared sheepishly from the safety of the site entrance and took up positions further along the road.

My God, she thought. *With that kind of charisma we might just get out of this.*

O'Malley stood beside a barrel-chested man and sucked in a deep breath. He had forced his way to the front of the group, determined to pull his weight. Someone had pressed a baseball bat into his hand and they had begun to shuffle towards Bourke Street and the site entrance beyond like a well-drilled Roman legion.

There was a shaky moment when the whole thing threatened to fall apart but the man beside him had held the panic back and his instructions began to filter through to the people around him. O'Malley had felt the urge to run himself, it had seemed to be almost a tangible thing, almost hypnotic, that touched everyone but reason had prevailed. *Thank God,* he thought. It would have been carnage if everyone had tried to stampede over the cars and rubble that blocked the street, let alone the number of deaths that the infected would have caused among the vulnerable.

Now he found himself standing in a defensive line that retreated slowly and allowed the others to make their way safely to the site entrance. Their attackers gained on them with every step, they may be slow but there were a lot of people to get through the narrow gap and the process was slow. They reached the first of the cars and rubble that blocked the road and the line wobbled as one end moved more quickly than the other.

O'Malley looked along the row and saw that they were dangerously exposed as parts of the line stumbled on the rubble while others continued resolutely backwards, unaware that some of their number had been delayed.

"Steady," the big man beside him roared and the line seemed to snap back like a rubber band. But then the first of the men fell, tripping over rubble that looked secure but didn't hold their weight. The first man fell and then he in turn overbalanced the next and suddenly it seemed that the entire row began to disappear like a procession of dominoes.

The infected were on them in a second and even the big man's shouts of support and encouragement weren't enough. The line broke and panic ruled. Men scrambled over cars and rubble, clawing their way over their own number as the infected attacked from behind. The previously ordered queue, moving down the road and in through the site entrance, took on an urgency that at first had people merely moving more quickly but, as people realised what had happened, they began to run.

O'Malley saw a few fall and disappear under the thunder of running feet. He felt himself slip but the press of bodies around him kept him on his feet. He lost sight of the big man and the screams around him disoriented him, leaving him helpless as he was carried along with the crowd as powerless as a leaf on a flowing river.

They reached the corner of Bourke Street and halted. Once stopped a wave of conversation swept through the group as if someone had just flipped a switch. Hillary only heard snatches of the fevered shouts but she got the gist of it. They were going to head for the new building site entrance. Suddenly the ordered and disciplined group began to waver. Excitement surged through them as people realised that there was an escape route. People began to force their way in all directions, many didn't know which way they should go but the need to move was too much to suppress

Those tall enough to see over the heads of the group suddenly saw the narrow entrance to the site and their shouts acted like a starting gun in a race. People pushed, scrambled and fought their way towards the narrow street, pushing those slower or weaker aside. She felt Martin grip her hand tightly and she clung to him desperately. She couldn't quite explain it but she sensed that her future lay in his hands and there was no way she was losing him now. People screamed and ran towards the site entrance, oblivious to those around them. She saw two women go down in the panicked crowd and their screams were lost in the bedlam.

Kim held tightly to Martin's neck and she could see her white knuckles pressed tightly together. Her face was scrunched up in pain as bodies jostled against them but she didn't cry out, although Hillary doubted that she would even hear her even if she had.

Fear swept through the group and reason was abandoned. No-one knew what was happening. One minute they had been walking in an orderly line and then suddenly everyone had panicked. The doors were only a hundred yards away but their very closeness only seemed to add to the urgency and the pace of the group grew faster.

The press of bodies grew tighter as they approached the site entrance. Both doors were wide open but it was still much narrower than the street and the people funnelled in a mass. Once inside O'Malley felt like he was spat out and he was sent sprawling to the ground. The noise was deafening and the atmosphere intense. People ran to the doors and tried to close them against the tide of people, making the entrance narrower than ever. Others merely stood just inside the entrance, relieved to be safely inside but oblivious to the fact that they were obstructing the incoming hoard.

O'Malley rushed against these people forcing them back, shouting at them until he was hoarse but his voice was merely another in the mad cacophony of chaos that rose from the scene. He wouldn't have thought it possible but just at that moment the noise level rose to another level. The people he had been trying to push back suddenly moved more easily and then began to flee, clearing an area in their wake.

O'Malley was confused by their sudden disappearance and turned back to help the new arrivals when he saw the reason for their terror. The doors were nearly closed now but a number of people were still trying to push their way into the safety of the site. One door was already shut and a growing number of people added their weight to it to keep it that way. The right-hand door was closed far enough so that only a line of two abreast could get through.

As O'Malley watched the people force their way in he saw the reason for the others' panic. Some of the infected had got mixed up with the survivors and a number of them were already attacking the people at the door.

Theresa watched in horror as the flood of people approached her. She could see there would be no way to pull them back so she turned and helped the injured around her to hurry through the doors. Once inside she ensured that Aidan was okay and instructed him to move across to the centre itself and to stay there until she came and got him.

She then turned and began to shepherd the people that were streaming through into safe areas away from the hoard. It worked at first but soon there were too many to control and the area quickly filled with people. She saw some race for the doors and try to close them, their initial efforts being ineffectual but, as more people arrived, she could see the doors begin to inch closed.

She tried to get across to them and stop them but there were just too many people surging through that she couldn't get near them. The group hadn't seemed that big when she had seen it at first, but there seemed to be thousands of people crowding the entrance now. It was at that stage that she saw the first infected person among the throng inside the gate and her heart dropped in her chest.

Once inside Martin immediately forced his way through the crowds to the back of the group. "Stay here," he instructed Hillary and Kim. "I'll be back in a minute."

"Where are you going?" Hillary asked as she grabbed for his hand.

"Those gates are going to have to be closed or those things will get in."

"Let someone else do it, you've done enough. We need you here." Hillary pleaded with him and held his hand in both of hers.

"I won't be long," he insisted as he took his hand from hers. He touched her on the cheek and bent over to kiss her. Then he lifted Kim back into his arms and kissed her too. "Now you stay here okay?" He waited until he saw her nod and then let her down.

He turned and disappeared into the crowd. Hillary was surrounded by people but suddenly felt very alone.

O'Malley gripped his baseball bat and ran to help the men on the door. He grabbed at anyone he saw and shouted at them to help. Some looked at him blankly and he wasted no time on then as he grabbed the next along. Some realised what he was saying and followed him through the crowd but their progress was slow and all the time more of the infected were coming through.

They were hampered further by the stream of panicked men and women that ran against them as they fled blindly away from their attackers. More than once the stream of bodies forced him back and he had to push again and again against the tide. Finally, the last of the panicked mass pushed passed him and an area of about twenty feet in diameter opened out in front of him. Two men stood with him, a further ten strained against the doors and inside the open circle stood nine of the infected.

The men on the door were losing ground rapidly. They had succeeded initially in closing one door and the other had been almost closed but once the infected had breached the opening they had set upon the men. Some had immediately run; others had died as they were attacked from behind and the remaining survivors had been forced back as the press of bodies from outside far outweighed the number of men inside.

O'Malley immediately ordered the two men with him over to the right door to hold the attackers away from the men while they closed the door. They nodded and set off, never once questioning his authority and O'Malley rushed to help the men on the left door.

They're not stupid, he thought as he approached the attackers and noted that only two of them turned towards him while the others continued their attack on the men holding the door. They would have to work quickly, he realised, as he saw another man fall while all the time more and more of the infected poured through the gap.

Theresa screamed at the people in the circle surrounding the gates. There were easily enough people to take care of the relatively small number of infected inside the site and close the doors if they all helped but nothing she said seemed to have any effect. They were petrified and refused to budge. She had started by reasoning with them, trying to explain that they had the advantage but could lose it soon if they didn't act.

They had ignored her so she had tried pleading with them instead but they merely looked away when she tried to embarrass them by looking into their eyes. Finally she had screamed at them. She walked out in front of them and brandished her wrench. "If you won't help then I'll go on my own," she had begun calmly but soon her growing frustration took over and her tone scathed them. "You're not even worth saving, but those men are." She turned and ran towards the gate herself, hoping that her example would motivate them.

Unfortunately it didn't.

Aidan watched as Theresa moved between the people trying to get them to help. She had told him to wait for her in the centre but even he could see that there would be nowhere safe if they couldn't get the gates closed again. He wondered briefly why the others couldn't see what was happening and then shrugged; it must be an adult thing.

He liked Theresa, not only had she saved him but she talked to him rather than at him. He had loved his parents but even they had treated him like a child. He felt a deep sadness inside as he thought of them but forced it away, he'd deal with that later. If he didn't do something quickly he'd loose Theresa as well and he couldn't allow that to happen.

He pushed through the crowd and soon found himself out in front. His heart was hammering in his chest and all he could hear was the thumping in his ears. He looked towards the gates and saw the carnage, saw men valiantly push the gates while others tried to protect them as the infected continued to surge through the gates. He couldn't hear the screams or the crack of bats against bone, all he could hear was the thumping of his heart.

His hands shook and his knees wobbled but he forced himself to turn. He bent to retrieve a hammer from the ground and paled when his knees nearly didn't obey his command to rise. He forced himself up and then faced the crowd.

"Last chance," he said simply, his voice cracked with emotion but carried easily to the crowd. "Just where do you think you'll be able to hide if we don't close the door?"

He didn't wait for a response. He turned and ran after Theresa.

Martin ran towards the gate. Another man ran beside him and a third ran towards the other gate. There were only three of them but it had to be enough. If those things continued to pour through then it wouldn't be long before they'd be overrun and they'd all die.

There were four men straining against the gate and they were losing ground rapidly as they had to divide their attention between the door and their attackers. Martin threw himself against the first of the attackers, taking him low in a rugby tackle. They tumbled away from the gate and Martin surged to his feet. He looked at the man he had attacked and saw that he was already beginning to rise but at a far slower pace.

They were slow but there were just so damn many of them that they had the advantage.

He swung the chair spine at the man, catching him at the base of the skull. He heard a sickening crunch even over the noises around him and the man slumped forward and remained still. Martin didn't feel good about killing them; they might still be able to cure them. But, for now, it was a matter of survival and it was either him or them.

He turned quickly and picked another target, unfortunately there still were plenty to choose from.

O'Malley ran straight through the two infected attackers that approached him. He didn't wait to see if they had fallen or not but ran straight for the ones that were attacking the men at the door. The door was slipping open again as the number of men was reducing so he launched himself at their attackers without thinking. He jumped and spread his arms out wide taking three of them with him as he hit the ground hard.

He lay winded for a moment but the respite had helped and the men at the door and they began to force the door closed once more. O'Malley forced himself up and kicked at the first of the infected. It had only begun to get to its feet and he was able to get a good kick at its temple. He heard a crunch and the figure dropped to the ground again. Again, he didn't wait to see the result. He brought the bat up as he turned and swung at his second attacker just as he made it to his feet.

The momentum carried him too far but he still got good contact against the infected man's shoulder and sent him sprawling to the ground. He knew the damage caused wouldn't be enough to stop it but at least it would give him time to take care of the third attacker. They weren't very fast and they seemed to find it difficult to get back to their feet with any speed. However, they also seemed to be almost indestructible, especially without better weapons. As more and more arrived through the door the odds were very much in their favour.

He turned to the third attacker but he was already on his feet and O'Malley was sent sprawling to the ground. His head cracked against the side of the door and he lay stunned as the other men tried to close the door and not stand on him. His attacker loomed above him and he tried to role out of the way but his muscles refused to move. The sun was suddenly eclipsed as his attacker drew towards him and swiped at his face with his clawed hand.

O'Malley saw the attack coming but could do nothing.

Theresa ran screaming into the melee, more to boost her own courage than to frighten her attackers. She saw that the two men on the right had their area covered for the moment but O'Malley was on his own and she saw him go down.

She was only fifteen feet away but there was a stream of infected coming through the doors between them. There was no way she could reach him in time. The doors had closed over so that only a single body could enter at a time but the real danger lay in letting any more through. She knew what she had to do but that didn't make her feel any better. She launched herself at the doorway.

Aidan watched as Theresa began to swing at the things coming through the door. He longed to help, to throw himself into the fight beside her and keep her safe but he was under no illusion that he could be of any help in such a chaotic battle, he was far too small. Further along the door he saw the man that had saved them earlier in the square. He remembered that Theresa had called him O'Malley but he had never seen him before. He saw the man struck down from behind and then fall against the door where he lay still. *Get up*, he urged silently as he saw the man's attacker shuffle closer.

The man remained still. He was still alive, he knew because he could see him turn his head towards his attacker but the rest of him remained motionless. Aidan could see that there were four of those things between him and the injured man. He weighed up the options in his head, his earlier fear had gone once he had rushed out into the melee and he was able to think clearly.

The infected were dangerous but slow and he was small enough to be able to dodge through them. He raised the hammer and ran as fast as he could. He dodged easily past the first three but the fourth one clipped his shoulder and sent him spinning to the ground. He landed hard and the air was forced from his body, leaving him gasping but otherwise was unhurt.

He could see that O'Malley's attacker was on his knees over the injured man. Aidan remembered a movie he had stayed up late one night to see. His parents were out and the babysitter didn't know that whatever she watched downstairs could also be seen upstairs. It was a weird movie but in it there were people eating other people. A gross idea for a movie but absolutely freaking terrifying in real life. He had no idea if these things were the same but this one certainly looked like it was going to bite O'Malley's face off. He jumped back to his feet and swung at the infected man. The hammer hit him on the side of his head and continued on into his skull.

The hammer got lodged in the skull and he couldn't pull it out but it seemed to have done the trick. The infected man fell forwards and lay unmoving on the ground. Aidan quickly checked behind him and saw the other attackers shuffle towards them. He turned to O'Malley.

"Come on," he urged and pulled at him. "I didn't go through all that so we could be eaten by the others you know." O'Malley seemed to shake his head and, finally, he began to move.

Theresa swung the wrench in an arc around her. She aimed at the head but as long as they went down she was happy. The doors were closing further and the infected had to squeeze through now as the gap grew smaller. There were still a number of them in the site but the survivors seemed to be holding their own. Just then the right hand door slipped.

She looked across and saw that O'Malley was still on the ground and the other men at the gate were unprotected. Another one went down and the door slipped further. She felt the wrench snag on one of her attackers and it was ripped from her hand as the man went down. She backed up. Without a weapon it was suicide to remain but she couldn't let the things swamp them either.

Suddenly another man appeared beside her and then another. One of them passed her a bat and soon there were five and then six. "Glad you could make it," she managed. They nodded to her solemnly and then launched themselves at the infected.

O'Malley felt strong hands grab him and help him to his feet. All around him other men and women were arriving with boards, tools and anything else they could use. More men lent their weight to those still at the door and soon the heavy doors crashed shut.

The infected still in the site were soon taken care of. At first they spent a few minutes hitting them again and again just to keep them down. Then they tried breaking their legs so they couldn't get to their feet but the boy who had helped him had shouted to them to hit them in the head and this seemed to work.

Now that the doors were finally closed and the infected inside were dealt with, a calm descended on the group. Outside, however, the screams continued as those caught on the wrong side of the door were swiftly dealt with by the rabid hoard. He knew that he could do nothing to save them, but the knowledge didn't help much.

Silence again descended as the last of those outside fell. A few minutes later a monotonous banging began against the gates. The sound was methodical and mournful, uncomfortably similar to the peal of a death knell.

Pat Murphy helped the other men onto the boat and he signalled to Crystal O'Mahoney to start the engine. Crystal was by far the most capable person they had to handle the close-quarter work they'd need to fetch the other boat, despite the fact that she didn't own a boat herself.

Her father had been the harbour master and every visiting captain was well used to his daughter tagging along during every school break. She had experience with all sizes and classes of vessels and had a gentle touch that quickly earned her the respect of the most hard-to-please captain. Her mother, and her dedication to American soaps in the eighties, could be thanked for her name.

The deep rumble of the engine spluttered and coughed and then roared as the engines came on line. The noise split the quiet of the day like an explosion and then settled into a constant drone. Pat cringed as he imagined every infected person in a mile radius suddenly stop what they were doing and head towards the noise.

It wasn't far from the reality.

Chapter 21

Jack Thornton shuddered as the engine belched into life. Behind him the rest of the group shuffled uncomfortably and he could hear the buzz of muffled conversation sweep through them.

"All right," he turned and faced the crowd and swept his arms wide to attract their attention. The crowd hushed and he smiled despite their predicament. *I still have it.* "Be patient, we'll all get on the boats, don't worry. We'll be long gone before those things get all the way around to us." He paused as he scanned the crowd, looking for anyone likely to argue with him.

"Don't push at the back," he continued. "Remember we have children in the group."

"That's all right for you," a voice towards the back shouted, "you're first in the queue."

Thornton didn't react, merely scanned the crowd and smiled when he saw the saw his heckler. *James Pierce,* he thought. It would be him. First to complain in every town meeting regardless of whether the topic being discussed directly affected him or not. Many a council meeting had continued on late into the night due to his incessant arguing.

"James," Thornton replied, "If you can convince those in front of you to let you through then I certainly have no objection to you coming up here. It is important that our very brightest are saved first." Thornton waited for the laughter to subside and looked directly at the now red-faced Pierce. "For my part, James, and not that it's any of your business, I will be the last off the dock." The cheers seemed to dissipate the fear that had previously gripped the group and Thornton was surprised to find himself indebted, albeit unintentionally, to his nemesis.

He turned back to the harbour and saw that the now manned boat was making its way over towards the second craft. The way was littered with debris from damaged or submerged craft and Crystal had to move slowly in case they hole their own vessel. Two of the other crew were stationed on either side of the bow of the boat with large poles pushing against the debris and clearing a path while the others ensured that the sides were kept unmolested.

Thornton was impressed by Crystal's skill as she weaved in and out of the small area. He had heard many people compliment her but he had never before seen her at work. There had been many requests that she be made Harbour Master, as her father had been, but these days the council required such a position to be filled by someone with a college degree. *As if learning from books would mean spit in an emergency like this one,* he thought. Crystal would never be able to afford college fees, let alone the time to go off to college. There were seven children in her family and she, as the oldest, had to do her best to bring in as much money as she could.

As Thornton watched he vowed to ignore the current guidelines and promote her to the position immediately, he'd deal with the fall-out later. He smiled as he anticipated the arguments Pierce was likely to bring up.

Thornton was shaken from his reverie as he heard shouts over at the boat and he looked over to see two of the crew jump the short distance between the craft and immediately tie them together. A great cheer rose from the people behind him and one of the men rose and waved enthusiastically at them.

Two more men jumped across, leaving Crystal, Pat and one other on the first boat. A few minutes later the second engine coughed to life and the men untied the lines as the first boat pulled easily away. The second boat reversed slowly, the men with the poles now stationed at the stern, and the boat approached the eager group on the shore.

"Steady!" Thornton ordered as he felt the press of bodies from behind. "Don't push at the back." The roar of the engine was deafening and he had to shout and wave his arms in a calming gesture for those who couldn't hear. The press of bodies eased slightly but not entirely as people craned to see where the boat was.

The boat slid alongside the jetty and the front line surged forward even before any of the crew had secured the lines. Thornton tried to regain control of the group but the boat was just too close and bodies poured onto the deck. Children were thrown up on to the level and then adults scaled the sides to join them.

It wasn't so much a panic but there was certainly no way that the crowd were going to listen to reason. Thornton tried his best to hold people back and to ensure that children weren't crushed but the situation was deteriorating rapidly. The boat filled quickly, already he could see that the upper deck was crammed with bodies and more were forcing their way on to the deck. He forced his way to the front and began to push those still on the jetty back. They resisted at first but his weight was prodigious and finally he forced them away from the crowded vessel.

He had just succeeded in creating a small gap when the screaming began. It started behind him and he turned quickly towards the source. It seemed to come from the lower deck of the boat and was somewhat muted but its high pitch was still audible over the chugging of the engine. Another scream joined the first and then, suddenly, people who had forced their way onto the boat only seconds before began to jump back to the jetty. The small gap quickly filled and soon there was a frantic press of bodies in the opposite direction.

Thornton was carried helplessly along with the crowd. He had no idea what had caused the panic but now everyone was screaming. He saw a number of children fall near him and they quickly disappeared in the throng. He powered his way towards where he had seen them, cutting a swath through the crowd as he forced people from his path.

He reached the spot he had last seen the children and dived down, like a pearl hunter in an ocean, and saw the bodies on the ground. He surged upwards with such force that a gap formed around him and he picked up the two bodies. They were still alive but one of them couldn't lift his arm and the small girl had ugly grazes along her face where someone's foot had trampled her.

What the hell is going on?

Dave Johnson passed through the 'Arches' and heard the roar of an engine as it coughed to life.

"Looks like we're on time after all." He quickened his pace and pulled ahead of the Penders. He reached the edge of the old fort and scanned the area below. There was a crowd of about forty or so people standing on the jetty looking out over the small Marina. Out on the water a mid-sized fishing boat made its way slowly towards a second boat which was adrift further out.

"There's a boat alright," he explained as John and his family joined him. "It looks like they're trying to grab that second one as well. We should all squeeze on if boats are seaworthy." He smiled at the three children. "Have you ever been sailing before?" he asked. The children had been very quiet all morning and he worried how they were handling the situation they found themselves in. Emma and Craig merely shrugged but Jack looked out over the water.

"You can't sail on that thing," he insisted as he cocked his head, "that's a fishing trawler. It has an engine."

Johnson looked at the little seven-year old and smiled despite himself. "You are right," he nodded and tried not to laugh when Jack nodded seriously. "Ever been on a fishing trawler then?"

"Nope, I hope it's not smelly."

"I don't care if it stinks to high heaven," John Pender interrupted as he ruffled his son's hair. "Just as long as there's room."

"Let's go and introduce ourselves."

John Pender held out his hand as Jack began to run towards the crowd. "Hold on there, tiger, we don't want you crushed in the rush. Let's just hang back and let the first boat fill up, we'll get the next one."

Jack nodded and the small group stood about a hundred yards back from the mass of people. The second boat had come up to the jetty and immediately they could see a mad rush onto its deck. None of the crew had the time to tie the boat up and the rush forced the boat away from the jetty causing people to fall into the water.

Shouts of anger, pain and pleas for help rose above the general murmur of the crowd as the deck quickly filled with bodies. Pender looked over at Dave Johnson and raised an eyebrow. "It looks like there are more than half of them crowded on that one, there should be plenty of room on the next one."

Johnson nodded, "I'll head over and see if there's anyone in charge. It doesn't look like it but we'd better check. You guys stay here."

Johnson turned to go just as the first scream rang out.

"Hold on a second, Dave," Pender warned as he looked past his friend. "There's something going on." A small gap had formed around the hatch that presumably led down to the crew's quarters. It was hard to see clearly with so many people moving about but it looked like there were two people on the ground. A third figure stood over them and the circle around this figure grew larger as he staggered forward.

For a second nothing happened. There were about thirty people on the deck but they were all crushed against the sides of the boat while there was a large gap around the two fallen people and the one man in the centre. The figure moved slowly, as if he was uncertain of his footing. Suddenly the figure reached the edge of the circle and panic swept through the group.

People jumped in the water on both sides, screaming as they fell. Some dropped between the jetty and the boat and were crushed as the boat pressed against the wooden supports. Others flapped in the water, their arms wind-milling madly but ineffectually as they dropped below the surface only to reappear and drop again.

Why would people who can't swim jump into the water? Pender looked over at Johnson but his shrug and pursed lip announced his own lack of understanding clearly.

"What's going on?" Julie Pender asked. "What are they running from? My God." she brought her hand to her mouth as she saw a small boy drop below the surface of the water again but this time he stayed under. "Those people are dying, we should help."

"I wish we could," Pender replied, "but we'd better stay out of it until we know more. There's something going on here that we don't know about. There's just no reason for them to panic like this."

"Oh shit," he heard Johnson curse and snapped his head towards him. The remaining group on the jetty were surging back towards them in a panicked stampede. Anyone that fell quickly disappeared under foot.

"Let's get out of their way," Pender grabbed at his family and urged them back towards the keep but stopped short as he saw a ragged line of figures appear through the 'Arches' and shuffle towards them. It took Pender a few seconds to take in the details. His training in journalism had taught him to notice details that others would normally miss, or take for granted, so he immediately noticed the ragged clothes, the bloodstains and the strange expressions. He scrunched up his face in confusion but his body was already acting this new development.

"Quickly," he shouted, "move over to the side or we'll get caught in the middle." He grabbed Jack into his arms and gripped Craig's hand and started forward. He saw Johnson grab Emma and Julie followed behind. There was a small wall to their right. It had once been over twelve feet high and served as the keep's inner protective ring but years of neglect had seen the bricks come loose and, in places, whole sections had fallen inwards, spilling rocks on the grass as if it had been disembowelled.

Pender launched himself over a section of the wall that reached to only five feet and cleared the debris easily despite the weight of his son. The others quickly followed and they turned to watch developments behind them.

The stampeding group were too panicked to check their momentum so they continued on up the incline. The people in the front saw the figures ahead of them and tried to stop or change direction but the press from behind was too great and they were carried forward relentlessly. Pender saw the look of terror on their faces and wondered just what could instil such fear in people.

The second group continued on slowly and soon the two groups merged. Pender watched in horror as a number of the slow figures began to attack the front line of the onrushing group. Screams filled the air and people disappeared from the front line like wheat at harvest time.

The people pushing from behind suddenly realised what was happening up front and then people began to turn hurriedly and push against those behind. The result was chaotic. People screamed as they were crushed or attacked. Others fought their way over the bodies of those ahead of them and the resulting melee was frenzied.

Some people escaped the throng and ran back towards the water, oblivious to the dangers there. They ran out into the water and waded towards the vessel, climbing up its sides and over-balancing the boat dangerously. Pender could see a number of bodies on the deck of the boat and then he heard a loud crash. The driver of the boat had tried to pull away from the shore, trying to protect his vessel against the oncoming stampede. Pender could see the man at the wheel as he pulled the steering wheel frantically away from the shore.

Another figure came up behind him and Pender saw the two fall to the deck. The weight of those trying to get back on the boat along with the suddenly freed wheel sent the boat swerving to the left and then it stopped dead. A loud snap reverberated over the marina and the boat began to list forward.

"Oh shit!" he cursed, "it's been holed." The remaining people crammed on the deck were thrown about like flotsam and Pender could hear some of them scream as they were crushed by the sheer mass of bodies. The boat listed further as water poured into the lower decks and the stern of the boat rose sharply to an angle of 45 degrees as the bow disappeared below the water. The boat plummeted to the bottom of the marina more quickly than Pender thought possible and soon only the tip of the stern was still visible. The screams of those caught unawares by the fast-rising water were cut off abruptly leaving the marina unnaturally silent.

Pender's mind tried desperately to take in all that was happening. It was bad enough that the army had quarantined the town but now it seemed that some of the townspeople had become rabid. While he watched the scenes of slaughter his mind tried to make sense of their situation. It seemed likely that the cylinders they had found in the submarine had somehow infected some of the townspeople. This infection was obviously dangerous enough for the Government to kill its own citizens to prevent the infection from spreading. And now it seemed the infection was able to spread, although whether it was airborne or passed through contact he had no idea.

Either way they had to get away from here. Their current position behind the wall kept them safe while there was such a large group for the infected to choose from but left them terribly exposed if they were seen and the metal fence behind left them no escape route. They had to find a way out.

Dave Johnson looked around him. Their escape was cut off from behind by a high iron fence that encircled the area. The way they had come in was also cut off as more and more of those strange figures appeared through the 'Arches' and joined the melee in front of them. There was only one possible route but that would mean going straight through the chaos in front of them.

"Can the children swim?" he shouted above the screams.

Pender looked at him quizzically but then shrugged. "Emma and Craig can but Jack's only learning. You're not seriously ....?"

"There's no other way. Look," he pointed out over the marina, "There's a way through to the new centre over there. If we can get through then we can get around them and hole up there until we find a better plan.

"But there's a wire fence around the site," Pender protested as he pointed out the supports out in the water.

"If we can get enough people to help we should be able to break through."

"'If' and 'should' aren''t words that fill me with confidence, Dave," Pender looked at him dubiously and Johnson couldn't really blame him. It was a huge risk but they couldn't stay where they were and they were running out of time.

"There's no other choice, John," Johnson replied. "They already outnumber us and more are coming every second."

"What if they can swim as well?"

"Let's hope they can't."

Thornton used his weight to force his way through the crowd despite their panic. Behind him he dragged three children and two women. Panic gripped those around them as first they ran towards the boat and then surged back to the shore. Thornton couldn't see what was happening on the boat but the sheer panic of those coming towards him led him to believe that there must be some of the infected on the vessel.

The jetty was too narrow for so many and most had no real idea what was going on. All they could see was a mass of panicked people surging towards them and all they could hear were the screams of those gripped by terror or being crushed underfoot. The people at the back of the group ran back towards the 'Arches' and, for a moment, the press of bodies eased. Thornton planted his feet firmly on the ground and let the stampede pass around him like a stone in a fast-moving river. The children clutched desperately to him and the two women wrapped themselves protectively around the children.

He was buffeted from side to side but he leaned against the flow and forced the tide around him. The flood of people seemed to go on for eternity but, abruptly, it stopped and he stumbled as his weight carried him forward as the last of the crowd passed. Ahead he could see the boat sinking rapidly but he had no time to wonder at what had happened. He looked out to the second boat but there was no way it could get in to them with the wreck of the other vessel.

The second vessel hovered out at the mouth of the marina but it was too far to swim, especially for the children. He could see Pat Murphy waving his arms frantically as he pointed at the water and out to sea. Thornton frowned and then felt a surge of anger flood through him as the boat turned and began to chug out to sea.

The bastards are leaving us, he thought as he stared at the departing vessel. He looked frantically around. There were a lot of bodies in the water, most of them floated face down but a few bobbed in the gentle waves shouting for friends or family members. Behind them the survivors that had flooded past him suddenly stopped their headlong flight and began to surge back towards him. On the incline Thornton could see a sea of shambling figures and his heart sank.

The noise of the boats have brought half the town after us. Where do we go now? He looked out at the fading vessel shook his head. There was no hope.

He felt a hand on his shoulder and he whirled quickly, belying his weight, and prepared to strike his attacker. The man held up his hands in a calming gesture and began to shout. Thornton looked at him in confusion. He could hear the words but his brain was just too numb from the day's events.

" . . . the tide is going out. We need to find somewhere safe for a few hours."

The tide is going out, hope flared in his heart as the words finally began to make sense. They hadn't been abandoned, that's what Murphy had been trying to say with his hand signals. The tide was too low to allow the boat to come close enough to get them out. He looked at the man in front of him.

"Where can we go?"

"Over there," the man replied and Thornton's heart sank again as the man pointed out into the water towards the building site. "There's no way through."

"Yes there is, if we can get enough people to force a way through."

Thornton looked at the fence and then at the mob. There were only about twenty people still on their feet and most of them were so terrified they merely ran blindly towards the water and then back towards the incline, *My God, there's so few remaining.*

"We've got to give them a focus," the man was still talking to him. "I'll get their attention but I need you to hold it. Can you do it?"

Without thinking Thornton nodded dumbly. He wasn't sure if he could hold a panicked crowd's attention anymore but he had to try. He had always prided himself on his leadership skills to get him ahead in business and political life despite his size and unattractive features. Now all of their lives suddenly depended on those skills.

"Are you sure?" the man looked him in the eyes, as if searching for something. Thornton felt a calm spread through him and he nodded more positively. "Yes, I'm ready." The man nodded as if satisfied and then suddenly turned to the crowd.

The shot rang out, splitting the air with its loud retort and commanding everyone's attention. Even the infected seemed to stop their relentless advance while the looked around for the source of the explosion.

Dave Johnson lowered the gun and nodded at the fat man he had been talking to. He had taken a chance on the man but he had been the only one that had showed any sign of calm in the confusion as he desperately fought to save the children around him. Johnson had been trained in human behaviour, how to recognise traits in people that he might be able to use when he was under cover.

Johnson knew that he could get everyone's attention but holding it and getting everyone to listen to him, a stranger, was unlikley. He needed someone with presence, someone that was known and trusted in the community. He could see some of those traits he needed in this man; he just hoped it was enough.

Thornton jumped when the gun went off. *Who is this guy?* The thought flashed through his mind but he didn't have time to dwell on it. The man with the gun had promised to get their attention and he had lived up to his promise, now it was up to him. He looked over the small group and felt an uncharacteristic fear wash over him. He could see the infected townspeople on the incline about thirty feet from the back of the group and some of the survivors were already dividing their attention between him and the slowly approaching hoard—there wasn't much time.

"The boat has not abandoned us," he began with what he hoped was a positive. "The tide is going out so they have to pull back out past the harbour line. Those of you familiar with the tides know how quickly they change; if they had stayed they would be grounded by now."

"They will be back for us as soon as they can but we need to find a safe place first." There was a muttering in the crowd as some agreed and others shuffled uneasily as the infected drew closer. "We have an idea but it will take all of us working together. We can't have a panic or some of you going off doing their own thing; if that happens we'll all die." He scanned the faces making sure he was getting through to them and then nodded when he saw what he was looking for.

"We're going to head out into the water together," he held us his hand as protests rang out. "We don't have time to argue. We will head out into the marina. The undertow is very strong when the tide changes so make sure you plant your feet, don't run. Children will have to be carried by adults. Once we're at the fence we will focus on one part and force our way through. We can use the site beyond to hole up until the tide changes again. There's no time for questions, let's move."

John Pender nodded at Dave Johnson as the large man finished his instructions. The group of townspeople behind them were only a few feet away now so he grabbed Craig's hand and lifted Jack into his arms and started forward. Johnson came up beside him and took Craig and lifted him under one arm. Pender nodded his thanks and waded out into the water. He looked behind as the other survivors began to file in behind them, their pace rushed but not manic.

The water was freezing and he could feel his lower limbs begin to go numb as he continued out into the marina. His left foot was suddenly whipped from under him as the undertow sucked at him and Johnson reached out and grabbed him, steadying him just before he dipped below the surface.

"Thanks," he gasped as the cold water reached up to his chin. Johnson nodded and looked back at the group of townspeople on the shore. "What the hell are they?" he asked as he saw the direction of Johnson's gaze.

"I have no idea but there are a lot of them. I bet it has something to do with the gas on the sub. I hope they can't swim."

He saw a number of people slip below the surface as the strength of the current surprised them too. Pender could see the fat man, already laden down with three children, dip his massive hands into the water and pluck bedraggled, spluttering survivors out of the water and steady them again.

Pender marvelled at the man's courage and then he paled as the first of their attackers reached the water's edge. They didn't pause at all, merely plunged straight out into the water after the small group of survivors. He heard a scream as a woman in the back row realised how close they were and then a second scream rang out. Pender could feel the atmosphere change among the group. It was almost palpable and for a second he feared that panic would take hold and condemn them all.

"Steady," the big man's voice rang out clear from the rear of the group. "Stay together and we'll make it." The moment passed and the group held their positions as they continued out into the water and then the first of their attackers slipped silently below the level of the water.

A second disappeared and then a third. Pender stopped in the water and stared as the entire front flank suddenly fell below the water. Some resurfaced but were unable to gain their footing and the strong tide pulled at them and carried them further out towards the open sea. Others stayed under the water and disappeared completely.

The ones behind didn't pause as their companions disappeared but continued out into the water, lemming-like, as they pursued their prey. A great cheer rose from the small group as more and more of them slipped and disappeared silently into the cold water.

"Keep moving," Pender snapped his head towards the fat man. "Some of them may get through. Keep moving at the front."

"Come on, he's right," he heard Johnson urge him on and he turned reluctantly and continued on.

The fence was only a few feet away and, as they approached, Johnson was already scanning along its length for any signs of weakness. The wire was stretched across the marina for a distance of some two hundred yards and held in place every ten feet or so by metal poles that stretched about ten feet out of the water.

The current pulled at him and the water reached up to his neck as he drew level and began to pull at the wire to test its strength. It was temporary, meant to keep the boats from slipping through to the site and causing damage there, but strong nonetheless. The wire was soldered onto the metal poles so they couldn't just pull them apart.

"Craig, you hold on to your dad for a second while I look below," he passed the boy over to Pender and then dived below the surface. As soon as he lifted his feet the current gripped him and pulled. His snatched out his arm and wrapped his fingers through the wiring and then eased himself down towards the bottom, keeping a firm grip on the wire all the way.

The poles terminated in squares of concrete that held them firmly rooted to the harbour bed. *At least they're not drilled in place,* he thought and tested the weight. He planted his feet on the bottom of the harbour and gripped the wiring just above the concrete shoe and pulled. The pole and its support lifted about a foot off the bottom but then stopped as the weight of the poles further along prevented it from moving further.

He eased the weight back down and then climbed the fence to the surface. "It's held in place by a concrete weight," he began as he surfaced and was startled by the number of people crowded around. "It'll only lift about a foot because of the poles further down. I reckon we can lift it enough if we have someone here and on the either side. I'll take the far end."

"I'll do the next along," Pender announced and ignored the look of concern on Julie's face.

"I'll take the middle," the fat man nodded and then handed off the children to those able to take them.

"Be careful of the current," Johnson warned, "you'll have to keep hold of the fence at all times or you'll be pulled out to sea. When you get to the far side we'll need three of the men to come back and help us through." He looked at the faces around him and nodded "Okay, let's do it."

Julie Pender slipped beneath the surface of the water with Jack held tightly to her chest. Jack was terrified of water and she had spent a full five minutes trying to convince him that he'd be fine but it hadn't worked. The group by the fence dwindled rapidly as the survivors dived under the fence and came up on the other side safe and sound.

"You're next," the fat man had interrupted her and she was shocked to see that she was the last to go. "Some of them have figured out how to walk through the water," the man nodded towards the far bank and she saw that their attackers were beginning to make their way towards them. Some still lost their footing and slipped quietly away but others had learned and were already half way across.

"Mom, I can't go under the water, I'll drown," Jack pleaded and she could see the terror in his eyes. "Maybe if we try to climb over the fence," she pleaded with the big man beside her.

"There's no time, you have to go now," the man insisted and then reached out one hand for Jack. She resisted at first but she could see no malice in his face and she passed him forward.

"Look, little guy," the man began, Julie could see the strain the man was putting himself under while he held the fence with one hand but he kept a smile on his face so as not to scare Jack further. "Those people behind us want to hurt us and we don't have much time. You don't want your mom to be hurt do you?" She saw Jack shake his head solemnly. "Good. Now I'm going to hold the fence for you and your mom is going to dive under with you." She saw the fear come back into his eyes. "If you don't go then we'll all die because I'm not leaving without you."

Julie could see the truth in the man's eyes, *My God, he doesn't even know us.* She felt a flood of relief as Jack nodded firmly and the man nodded back and handed him back to her. "Are you ready?" she asked him and he nodded and sucked in a big breath. She plunged down, feeling Jack struggle as soon as the water covered his face. She felt the bubbled pour from his mouth but she forced herself down further. She gripped him harder as he opened his mouth and forced herself to ignore his wide eyes as he pulled water into his lungs.

It was quicker to go back but she knew that the three of them would die if she did. She felt his small body buck violently as he struggled for air but she ignored it. Tears welled up in her eyes as she continued down the fencing and then suddenly there was a gap. She plunged through and then pumped her arm, dragging them to the surface as fast as she could. She felt the current take them away from the fence but she ignored it in her struggle to get to the surface. Her heart hammered in her chest as she felt Jack's struggles grow weaker. Her own arms were growing heavier with each stroke as the freezing water sapped her strength. Exhaustion swept over her but Jack was depending on her and she forced herself on. The surface seemed to be tantalisingly close and then suddenly she was through and she gulped air into her lungs and looked down at Jack.

His eyes were closed and she bent towards his mouth and forced air into him. She was vaguely aware that she was being pulled out to sea but her attention was on Jack. She sucked in another breath and pressed her mouth over his and blew hard. She massaged his small chest as best she could with one arm while she threaded water with the other. The current pulled at her like a jealous lover and she slipped beneath the undulating surface countless times. Her lungs burned for air but every mouthful she managed to gulp she immediately exhaled it into her son's still body. She felt her vision cloud as she forced more air into his mouth and then suddenly a mouthful of water shot back into her mouth as Jack coughed.

Relief flooded through her as the boy sucked air and she pressed him to her as the tears flowed down her cheek. In her relief she wrapped both arms around him and immediately slipped below the surface. She panicked and gulped water into her own mouth, the coldness immediately making her cough and suck in more liquid. She tried desperately to pull them back to the surface but her arms just wouldn't work. She slipped further into the water's cold embrace and then suddenly felt a sharp pull on her hair. Her neck snapped back as her momentum was stopped abruptly and she felt a hand grip her shoulder and pull her backwards against the current. She was dimly aware of the pressure on her hair easing and then she broke through the surface again and her body was heaving.

"Are you okay?" she was dimly aware of someone's face above her. She thought for a moment that she recognised him but then the memory slipped away. She felt Jack being taken from her and she tried to resist but her arms had no strength left. She felt his weight lift from her chest and suddenly she could breathe. Air flowed more easily into her starved lungs and the dark patches in her vision began to recede.

"You're going to have to help me," she could see the worry on the man's face and she smiled at him, or thought she did. He pulled her towards the fence and set her on her feet. "Can you manage from here?"

She nodded dumbly and began to wade towards the wooden deck of the new shopping centre. She stumbled a few times but the man was there beside her each time she fell. In truth she realised that she wasn't really much help at all. Her legs were numb and her arms leaden but she tried as best she could to move forwards. She looked to the side and saw Jack wrapped around the man's neck and she smiled.

She was surprised to see so many people on the deck. *Surely there weren't that many of us?* She thought and shrugged. She could see Emma and Craig out front, tears flowing down their cheeks. Already men were coming out through the water to help.

She felt hands grab her and pull her out of the water. She felt something warm being wrapped around her and then two heavy impacts as Emma and Craig wrapped themselves around her. Everything felt blissful for a second and then she felt herself falling and everything went black.

Chapter 22

Friday 12.00PM – 1.00PM

The decking surrounding the shopping centre was packed with people. Some lay on the wooden slats shivering in their soaked clothes while others craned over those in front trying to see the new survivors who had arrived from across the water.

Theresa pushed her way through the crowd and finally emerged at the edge of a circle that ringed the newcomers. For a moment the gap between the two groups was more than the physical soaking of the boards but Theresa crossed to the first of the bedraggled survivors and the act seemed to act as a catalyst. Suddenly a flood of people surged forwards helping some to their feet, taking jackets off and wrapping them around the survivors or directing those that were uninjured away from the small area to allow for the treatment of those that were.

Theresa moved from person to person, checking them quickly and moving on while leaving instructions in her wake for their treatment. Suddenly she saw John Pender over at the edge of the water and for a second their eyes met. She saw the worry and fear in that glance and immediately made her way over towards him.

"Theresa! Thank God," he sighed as he led her over to a figure on the ground. "It's Julie, she's collapsed." Theresa merely nodded and ran her eyes over the still form of her friend. Her fingers felt for a pulse automatically and relief flooded through her as she felt a flutter at her neck. Her skin was too cold though. "What happened?"

"Jack panicked while they were underwater and then the current pulled them." Pender spoke rapidly and the words tumbled out in one long stream. "How's Jack," she asked as she rubbed vigorously at Julies limbs to generate heat. "Get some dry clothes. Beg, borrow or steal them, we have to get her dry." She barked the order even as she pulled at her clothes. Julie's skin was blue and her eyes were dilated. She had to hurry.

John Pender rushed off and Theresa wrapped the naked form of Julie Pender in the jacket that someone had already provided. A man sat beside her with Jack in his arms. He looked exhausted but he had already pulled the wet clothes from the boy and was rubbing at his pale skin in strong vigorous motions. She could see that the boy's skin had already lost the pale blue colour. As he moved she saw that his back was soaked with blood. The water that had drenched him had been so cold that it had slowed the bleeding but now that he was out of the water it had begun again.

"Are you a doctor?" she asked as she continued to rub heat into Julie's body. He looked over at her as if seeing her for the first time.

"What?" he asked as if waking from a dream.

She nodded at Jack. "He'd be dead now if you hadn't got the heat back into him. You're obviously familiar with trauma."

The man shrugged and smiled, despite his ragged appearance he managed to look confident. His eyes were a clear, pale blue and his longish hair lay in wet rings against his head. "No," he replied, his voice was deep and breathless from his exertions. "I have had a little field training though."

"You"ve met out resident hero then," John Pender returned and handed a bundle of clothes to Theresa and Dave Johnson and each of them immediately set to work dressing their charges. "How are they?"

"They'll live," Theresa nodded and then stood. "Now let's get you out of those clothes."

The man handed Jack to John Pender and held his hand to his heart in mock fright. "My, she is forward isn't she, John? We haven"t even been introduced yet."

Theresa felt herself blush and scolded herself. She had heard that joke so many times she usually ignored it but this man's roguish smile had set her heart hammering.

"Look," she tried to instil a touch exasperation in her tone but wasn't too sure if she pulled it off or not. "That back of yours is bleeding and needs attention. How did you do that anyway?"

"He saw Julie and Jack being carried away by the current and dived under the fence to get them, that's how," John Pender interrupted. "That's two I owe you, Dave."

Theresa helped the man to remove his shirt and noticed the pain in his face as he moved, despite his joking. His back was torn ragged by the fencing with deep furrows in three distinct lines from the neck all the way down. It must have been agony to pull himself through the narrow gap and he had practically carried both Julie and Jack to the decking as well.

She dipped into her bag, marvelling that she still had it after the day's events, and set to work.

Friday 6.00PM – 7.00PM

"**How** is he?" Pender asked as Theresa came back into the main foyer. There was little light as the early evening gloom pressed in on them and she appeared more like a shade than a person. They had all worked hard since the dramatic events of the day, securing their defences and caring for the injured. The afternoon had taken a particularly heavy toll on Theresa, however, as she seemed to take her patients pain as her own. Pender motioned for her to join him and she shuffled over to him and slumped gratefully to the floor.

He could see that her normally bright eyes were dulled with pain and exhaustion. They had forty three survivors in total of which fourteen were injured with numerous cuts, broken bones or pulled muscles. His question had referred to Denis O'Malley who had collapsed soon after they had all arrived and was by far the most worrying. Pender didn't know the police officer but knew that many of the people in the group owed their lives to him. He had also been first out into the water to help Julie to safety so Pender had a vested interest in the man's condition.

"Not good," Theresa replied, her voice strained with fatigue and frustration. "He's dying right in front of me and I can't do anything about it. I just don't have the equipment to help him."

"Is he contagious?" Jack Thornton asked from across the foyer.

Pender cringed at the question but understood its importance, if not the callousness of its asking. He had talked to Thornton earlier in the day and knew that it wasn't that he was an uncaring man but that his bluntness was due to his concern for his surviving townspeople.

He felt Theresa stiffen beside him for a second and then sigh. "I don't know," she replied and kicked at her medical bag in frustration. "There's a small scratch on his arm, that's all it took. They didn't even have to bite him. It must be some pathogen or virus for it to transfer that easily. How the hell are we supposed to survive if we can't even survive a scratch?"

"Is it airborne, will any open wound get infected?" Johnson asked, concerned about the wound on Theresa's arm.

"I don't think so," she looked up and saw him looking at her arm. "There's too many of us with similar wounds and none of us show any signs of infection."

"How long does it take?" Pender asked.

"I don't know for sure," Theresa sighed, "but he was scratched about five hours ago so it's quick. The patients that first showed these symptoms seemed to have inhaled the original gas and they got sick almost immediately. It was seven hours before they died."

"So they are dead then?" Pender asked as he got to his feet and paced the floor. "What exactly are they? I mean are we talking zombies?"

"I'm not entirely sure," Theresa turned and looked over the small group gathered around her. "I don't have the test results to be sure one way or the other but they have cravings are animated so they have to be alive, don't they?"

"But can they be cured?" Pender slammed his fist against the glass and looked out over the square. The dull slap of his flesh on the glass made everyone jump. "Are we killing our friends and neighbours here or are they merely mindless creatures?"

I just don't know. If we can find a cure …"

"But we need to be sure if …"

"If you let me finish," Theresa interrupted and stared hard at him. "As I was saying, I don't know if we can find a cure but I can tell you that even if we can stop the cravings these poor creatures have they certainly won't ever be the same again."

"What do you mean?

"Well for one thing they have all lost a huge amount of blood, far too much in some cases to be able to move around like they are doing. Secondly, they must be raging with blood poisoning as the different blood types mix in their systems; that should be enough to kill any normal person. On top of that they have a PH rating that is far too low so there will be no oxygen getting to their brains. Their higher brain functions, the area where cognitive processing is done, will have atrophied."

"Can we have that in English?" Johnson asked as he picked up her medical bag and began to tend the wound on her arm.

"The body is a complex organism," Theresa began slowly as she searched for the right words. "Normally our bodies produce acid as a by-product of normal metabolism. This is the result of our bodies burning or using alkaline to remain alive. Since our bodies do not manufacture alkaline, we must supply the alkaline from an outside source to keep us from becoming too acidic and dying."

"The way we measure this is by measuring the pH of the body, for example, the body functions best with an internal chemistry being slightly alkaline, between pH 7.0 and 8.0. However, the pH of the blood is even more specific. A normal pH would be around 7.35 while a pH of 7.2 would mean death, it's that tight." Theresa looked around her but no-one asked any questions so she continued on.

"We use food to replenish the alkaline in the body. Foods are of two types, acid or alkaline, although this designation refers more accurately to the ash value of a food; the residue that remains after the food is digested and processed. If there is an acid residue the body must neutralize this acid to keep the blood from becoming acidic. The acid is neutralized with alkaline."

"Ideally there is adequate alkaline in our normal diet to do this. However, if there is not, the body must extract alkaline from its own cells to neutralize the acid. This, of course, causes the cells to become acidic, and thus diseased. If the blood is too acidic then it can't carry oxygen around the body. This would go a long way in explaining their slow and awkward movements if their muscles are starved of oxygen. Their brains, more importantly, have been affected badly by the lack of oxygen and only the base functions of their lower brain stem seem to be operational. I can't prove it but I think the reason they are attacking us is to drench their systems with our alkaline-rich blood. They can't think for themselves so they're relying on primal instinct."

"That was English?" Pender shrugged at Johnson who shrugged back.

"They're basically vegetables."

"So they're no longer the people we knew?" Pender pressed her. "They can't be cured?"

"I don't see how," Theresa sighed. "This gas seems to have changed their systems quite drastically. I can't be certain but from my earlier examinations I don't think they're even breathing anymore."

"Does the pathogen you talked about re-animate the body if it's dead?" Pender's voice was a little muffled as he faced the glass.

"I can't see how." Theresa replied and then gasped as he turned away from the window. The man had gone completely pale. "Why?"

"But if they were infected before they died, could it cause them to get up after death?" Pender insisted.

"I suppose it's possible if the pathogen had enough time to change the cells before they died. Why?" she looked quizzically at him and noticed that others were growing as concerned as she was.

"If it can," Pender rubbed at his eyes as if he couldn't believe what he had seen, "then we can expect reinforcements to arrive in the next two hours or so, and they won't be ours."

"Oh my God," Theresa got to her feet slowly and looked out over the square with its broken vehicles and motionless bodies strewn everywhere. "There are hundreds of them," her mind raced to comprehend the implications of Pender's statement. "The gate will never hold them all."

"We've got to get out of here before they rise and join the party." Pender stated. "Now, has anyone got any ideas?"

A sea of blank faces stared back at him.

"**Hey,** nice pants," Aidan Dooley blushed as Kim and Emma remarked on his white jeans. It wasn't so much the jeans themselves as the floral pattern that snaked up each leg that had caught their attention.

"It was either these or a dress," Aidan complained and then giggled himself as he saw he wasn't going to win. They sat in a circle on the other side of the foyer from the adults, close enough to be seen but far enough to have their own space.

"I'm starving," Jack complained, "I haven't had anything to eat since breakfast."

"We're all hungry," Craig assured him, "but there's no food here and we can't get any until those things out there go away."

"Do you think they will?" Kim asked as her face grew serious again.

"I don't think they're about to go anywhere, not as long as we're here anyway," Aidan shrugged.

"But the army will come and rescue us," Emma assured them. As the oldest she thought it her responsibility to keep things positive.

"I wouldn't count on the army helping," Kim replied sourly, "they killed my mother."

"Oh my God," Emma put her hand on Kim's arm and squeezed gently. "When, what happened?"

"Up at the estuary," Kim felt tears begin to well up in her eyes as the memory suddenly burst through her carefully prepared defences. She had tried all day to keep her thoughts on anything but her mother's death, and thus far she had succeeded. But, now that things had quietened a little, she could feel her control slipping. "Those bastards just shot her and left us trapped here with those things," she looked around at the others and shrugged. "So don't go pinning your hopes on the army, that's all."

Emma looked around at the others and felt despair grow heavily over them. "Hey," she began as an idea struck her, "the estuary. That's where we should go. We'd be safe in the Keep." The others looked at her but their faces didn't hold quite the enthusiasm she had hoped to see.

"How do we get there, Einstein?" Craig jeered. "In case you hadn't noticed there are hundreds of zombies out there."

"Don't call them that," Aidan snapped. "My parents are out there. They're not zombies, they're sick, that's all."

Craig looked over at the taller boy and sighed. "I'm sorry, man," he began, "I didn't mean anything. It's just …. Oh I don't know it just seems that they're awfully like that movie, you know the .."

"I know," Aidan snapped, "but it's not the same. They're not dead, right?"

Craig looked at the boy and saw the fear and despair in his eyes. He was pretty sure that they were dead but his father had always thought him to consider other people's feelings so he nodded. "Yea, you're probably right."

"Is there food at the keep?" Jack piped up. "Cause if there is then I'll go and if any of those zom…" he looked over at Aidan for a second and then continued, "..sick people try and stop me then I'll bash them."

"Who are you going to bash, Tiger?" They all looked over at Pender as he appeared from the other end of the room.

"The zom . . . sickos outside if they try and stop us going to the Keep."

"The Keep?" Pender looked at him quizzically.

"Yea, Emma said we should go there and defend it like King Arthur," Jack mimed a big sword in his hand and brought it crashing against imaginary foes.

"The Keep," Pender repeated and seemed to drift away in thought. "You know," he said at last, "that's a brilliant idea. Stay here." He turned suddenly and disappeared back to the other adults at a run.

"And you thought it was a stupid idea," Emma beamed and fixed her brother with a look of triumph. Craig groaned and braced himself for at least an hour of 'I told you so's.'

All of the survivors were gathered together in the foyer, including the children and the injured. Those well enough to move by themselves did so and anyone else was carried into the circle. Pender looked across at Denis O'Malley and was shocked by how sunken his face had become.

"Okay," he began and the wave of conversation abruptly stopped, leaving him the centre of attention. "Many of you don't know me. I'm John Pender and that's my family over there. A few of us have been discussing our options, as I'm sure many of you have been doing, but now it's time to put all the cards on the table and see what shakes out." Pender had spent the last hour deep in conversation with Theresa, Dave Johnson and Jack Thornton. It wasn't that they excluded the others, just that it was impractical to discuss their options until they actually had something to offer.

Pender looked around at the faces before him. They were just ordinary people thrust into an extraordinary situation. Some of them, like O'Malley, would shine through as true heroes, putting others first and pay a high price for their bravery. Others would find in themselves strength or weakness in their characters that would define who they were and how they would act over the next few hours. He looked over at his family and hoped he was up to his own challenges.

"As you have probably heard it's not practical to remain here. If more of those things do get back up and join those at the gate then we won't be able to hold them back. Once they get in here there's no retreat."

"How likely is it that they will get up again?" Pender looked for the speaker and nodded at the man as he pushed through to the front. A woman and a young girl hovered close beside him.

"We just don't know for certain, Mister ..."

"Taylor, Martin Taylor,"

"But from what Doctor Winfield has told us, and considering the wounds that these things have, it seems likely that they will get up. We have to move from here as soon as we can. Besides, we have no food either so we've come up with a plan that just might work. However, we're all in this together so it's time to fill you in and put it to a vote."

"Who put you in charge?" another voice rang out as a second man shouted the question.

"No one did, Pierce," Jack Thornton announced before Pender could answer, "but if you have a better idea we'll vote on that too."

James Pierce harrumphed but could find no argument against this.

"There is a boat out in the bay that will come in for us once the tide has changed and it's safe enough to do so, but that won't be until the morning. There are a lot of those things out there so we're going to need volunteers to lure them away while the others make a run for it."

"Where to?" a woman asked and a rumble of nervous conversation rippled across the group. Pender balked for a second, he hadn't wanted to address the group. He had thought that Thornton was better positioned to get the townspeople's trust but it had been his idea and the others had unanimously voted for him to do it.

He took a deep breath. "The Keep."

There was a moment of total silence and then a torrent of questions and shouts rushed at him.

"Hold it!" he shouted with such volume that he surprised himself and shocked his audience into silence. "Thank you," he continued more calmly. "You will all get a chance to ask questions later on. For now please listen to what we've come up with."

"We're going to let those things in." He waited for the initial explosion of horror to subside and then continued. "They're all gathered in the same place so we'll let them in and use the pedestrian entrance further along the road to slip out. We'll split into four groups. The first group will consist of two people and they will let the infected in and then run through here and join the rest of the group. The second group will cross the square and head towards the cars on King Street. There's a shop near the back of the traffic jam and they will load up any cars they can use with food and head for the estuary. This group will consist of about ten people."

"The third group, and this will be the main bulk of us, will head directly to the Keep using as many cars at the back of the line as we can. If the cars don't have keys just walk, it's not too far and those things can't move very quickly so we should be alright. The Keep is much more defendable than here. Its walls are solid and there are gates re-enforcing the entrance."

"What's to stop those things surrounding us? How will we get to the boat then? And what's the fourth group going to be doing through all of this?" Pierce smiled as he heard murmurs of agreement behind him.

"Ah, that's where the second part of the plan comes in. We're going to blow the dam up at the mouth of the harbour once you all get into the Keep. The water will flood back into the estuary and surround you with a moat that those things won't be able to get past. Once the dawn comes the boat can come up to the estuary and take you all aboard to safety."

"You say that as if you won't be with us," Martin asked and Pender took a moment to look over at his wife. He knew by the look on her face that she had already figured out what he was going to say.

"Someone has to blow the dam," he said quietly. "It's my plan, so my responsibility."

There was silence as everyone realised what this meant. "Daddy, no, you can't," Emma tried to run over to him but her mother kept a tight grip on her arm and drew her back into her arms.

"How will you know we are in the Keep?" Pierce shouted as he felt the audience sway towards the stranger front of them. He expected to hear shouts of agreement and hopefully a call for a new spokesman, a position he would feel honour-bound to accept. Instead, though, people looked with disgust at him. *This wasn't going at all as he had planned. How could he have misread them so badly?*

"My colleague has a gun. There are eight bullets remaining. The signal will be two shots in succession, just in case you need to use it on your way. Just make sure that you keep at least two shots for the signal."

"If we were in America, you know, we'd all have guns and this would be a lot easier," Dave Johnson announced trying to lighten the mood.

"Guns," Martin grinned, "we'd probably have a few armoured cars as well and a machine gun for the children."

There was a brief ripple of laughter but it soon dried up as people realised they had to make a decision.

"Alright, I know it's not perfect but I believe it will work." Pender scanned the faces and what he saw there gave him the courage to continue. "We need to vote now, people. Those of you in favour, raise your hands."

There was no point in asking for any not in favour as a sea of hands reached high in the air.

"Now comes the hard part," he muttered to Dave Johnson as he walked towards his family.

"**Why** do you have to go?" Julie Pender looked at her husband through her tears.

"You know why," Pender sighed, "it was my idea. I can't ask anyone else to do it."

"But you'll be killed. And where are you going to get explosives anyway?"

"Jack says there's a blasting shed on the site that should have enough. And anyway we might be able to swim out to the boat afterwards."

"Don't lie to me just to get yourself off the hook, John Pender. You know as well as I do that the current will suck you under faster that you can spit out in that harbour. I suppose Dave is going too?"

"That's the plan," he answered meekly. "He's just telling Theresa now."

"Shame," she said as she threw her eyes towards heaven.

"What?"

"They made a nice couple for all of five minutes."

"She"ll find someone else," Pender was beginning to loose patience. He had expected her to take his volunteering badly but he hadn't expected her to be so cold.

"It's not that easy, you know."

"You didn't seem to have much trouble." As soon as the words were out he regretted them. She didn't deserve that and the pain and shock in her eyes pierced his heart more surely than a knife.

"I'm sorr . . ." he began.

"You knew," her face was pale with shock. "All this time and you knew. How?"

He shrugged sheepishly, "I'm a reporter. I make my living studying body language. It wasn't hard to see once I took enough time to notice something was wrong."

"You never said," he could see the tears run down her cheeks and he ached to hold her to him. This really wasn't going the way he had planned.

"There was no point," he sighed. "It was as much my fault as yours. That's why I wanted to move. Start again. I wasn't going to give you up without a fight."

She smiled a little as she wiped the tears away. "Nothing happened you know."

"Doesn't matter," he began.

"Yes it bloody does," she interrupted and pulled him towards her.

He wrapped her in his arms and squeezed. She, in turn, gripped him with all her strength and they stayed that way until Dave Johnson tapped him on the shoulder.

It was time.

He pulled back, kissed her nose and she smiled. "You don't even know the first thing about explosives."

"No, I don't," he admitted, "but superman here does."

"Is there anything our mystery friend doesn't know?" she cocked her head towards Johnson and winked at him.

"It seems not," Pender admitted.

"I don't care if you are SAS or Captain bloody Britain. You keep him safe or by God you'll answer to me, Dave Johnson."

"British Intelligence, Ma'am. Retired," he smiled as he bowed to her. "And I'll bring him back to you, don't worry."

"It would be nice to see you come back as well,"

"I'll do my best."

"I don't give a shit what you think, I am the obvious choice," Denis O'Malley collapsed back onto the bed, his outburst having taken more out of him than he cared to admit. "Anyway," he continued more amenably, "you know I'll only slow you down and to what purpose? I'm dead already."

"Don't say that," Theresa snapped at him. "We don't know for sure."

"I do," O'Malley insisted. "The infection is spreading; I can feel it run through my veins like acid and it hurts like hell. I can't even walk for God's sake. And what about the colour of my skin? Or did you think I had gone Goth?"

Theresa just stared at him and wiped a tear from her eye. She knew he was right but it just wasn't right to leave him behind. She looked away at the others in the group but no-one really knew how to respond.

"Look, I'm sorry, Theresa," O'Malley relented as he saw how upset she was. "But, let's be serious."

"But you won't be able to hold the doors and unlock them on your own," she felt she should at least have one more go at convincing him, though she could see the logic of his argument.

"Then get someone to help me. Then they can run back and join you while I take the first wave with me."

"What do you mean, 'take them with you'?"

"You know as well as I do that there just isn't enough time to get everyone out through that narrow passage before the first wave of those things catch up with us. So Dave has given me a few sticks of dynamite and we're going to strap them to my chair and slow 'em down a bit. Once the doors are open I'm going to light the fuse and blow those fuckers up. You didn't think I'd let them eat me alive did you?"

There was silence in the foyer as the gravity of the situation hit home. While the plan was a good one it was still relying on a lot of luck. "So now all we need is a lunatic brave and stupid enough to join me. Any takers?" O'Malley smiled at the group around him.

Theresa looked around. She knew that a few had already volunteered but some like Martin Taylor and Jack Thornton had been refused as their talents were judged to be more useful elsewhere. Martin had come to them as soon as the vote had been cast volunteering for anything and everything despite the pleading of the young girl and woman with him.

O'Malley had immediately refused his help and asked him to lead the group that were to forage for food. Thornton was needed for his leadership skills and had to remain with the main group, he was too large to run the distance required anyway.

The group of people suddenly found their feet to be of enormous interest as they tried to avoid eye contact. She couldn't really blame them. Most of them were family men and women who had children to protect. The seconds ticked by and she heard John Pender sigh beside her. It would have to go to a lottery.

"I'll do it."

Everyone turned to face the man who had spoken and Theresa gasped as she recognised the man who had locked them out of the site earlier in the day and whom she had kicked so brutally. He didn't look the same man. He stood straight and his head was held high, a far cry from the snivelling wreck they had encountered earlier.

"Looks like I owe you an apology," she heard O'Malley say. "I had you down for a coward. Why the sudden change, if you don't mind me asking?"

"I've been a shit most of my life but something like this makes you examine yourself more closely than I was ever prepared to before. I didn't like what I found so I'm going to do something about it. Anyway I can't let you guys have all the glory. I believe heroes get all the nice women."

O'Malley laughed and then ended up coughing instead. "That they do Mr. . . . ?"

"Peters, Alan Peters."

"I hope you can run fast, Alan."

DAY 4
Chapter 23

The night passed slowly. People drifted about the foyer as if lost. Others paired off for some privacy, their urgent couplings over-loud in the empty rooms of the centre. Families found quiet corners and huddled together or talked in quiet tones depending on their needs and outlook. Those that were alone tended to drift into groups of other singles, these groups seemed to offer companionship and comfort but delivered neither as the disparate groups were full of strangers who were too scared to offer anything but their own fears.

Outside the wind picked up and whistled as it blew through the unfinished centre. Wood creaked and metal groaned; sounds that would normally pass unnoticed were suddenly strange and terrifying. And all the time the relentless press of bodies against site gates tolled their threat of death in a monotonous pounding.

Saturday 6.00AM – 7.00AM

The groups organised themselves quietly. There were no shouts of 'Good Luck' and no 'Goodbyes', merely the occasional nod of a head and a few tears. Everyone knew the risks. Martin led his group through the narrow passage that led to the pedestrian entrance. Behind him filed eleven people including Hillary and Kim. He had spent a full twenty minutes trying to convince them to stay with the main group but they had ignored his arguments, his shouted orders and finally his pleas. They now tramped behind him with victorious grins.

As he looked back along the line he could see the grim faces of each of the others. They all held what weapons they had managed to scrounge from the site, amounting to pick axes, wrenches and wood cast-offs. For a moment he was tempted to laugh as he was reminded of the dwarves in 'Snow White' but the moment passed and the reality of the situation took hold of him again.

The group approached the entrance quietly, shuffling carefully along the darkened corridor enclosed by the grimed plastic. There was still the chance that some of the infected were on the other side of the door and if so then they would have to deal with them quickly and quietly.

Martin slipped the key into the padlock and turned it while he held the lock in his other hand. The lock opened easily and dropped into his palm. He laid it aside and then gripped his own weapon, a large wrench of about two feet in length, and pulled the door open rapidly.

The face that appeared in the gloom in front of him seemed at first to be disembodied, its pale visage seemed to shine in the darkness, but then Martin could make out the vague outline of its dark clothes.

The face showed no surprise, no reaction at all, and Martin swung the wrench hard against its head and reached for the body as it fell to help it to the ground. Ahead he could see the entrance to the passage and beyond that the square. He moved quietly along the last few feet, craning his neck to see as much of the area around the entrance as he could without revealing himself.

There were a few infected wandering in the square but the majority of them were still gathered around the main entrance. Their silence was eerie and the monotonous pounding on the door sent a shiver through him. The main entrance was a good hundred yards from the pedestrian one but there were so many of the infected that their numbers stretched almost to the smaller door.

Martin motioned for the others to stay where they were and he looked at his watch.

Five minutes to go.

He lowered himself to his knees to offer the smallest possible target and looked out over the square. He noted with mounting trepidation that there were certainly far fewer corpses on the ground then there had been the night before.

"Looks like their reinforcements are arriving sooner than we'd like," he muttered to himself and began to count off the remaining minutes.

Denis O'Malley reeled in his chair as another wave of pain swept through him. John Pender and Dave Johnson had rigged together a chair they had found on the site. They had strapped O'Malley upright with a length of cord and strapped two wheels, which they had found attached to an old shopping trolley that had somehow found its way onto the site, to the back legs of the chair. It was a bit lob-sided but it did allow Alan Peters to move him into position with the minimum of effort.

O'Malley looked at Peters and nodded once. His heart hammered in his chest as he stared at the bulging doors in front of him. He was scared to death but he knew that he was dying and this way was a lot better than what waited for him. He fingered the Zippo lighter Theresa had given him with one hand and held the fuse for the explosives in the other. His hands shook so badly that he wondered if he'd be able to light it when the time came.

"It's time," Peters announced gently.

"Okay," he sighed. "Unlock it and get away as quick as you can. I'll take it from here."

O'Malley watched as Peters unlocked the gate. Immediately the doors flew inwards and the infected poured inside. Peters stumbled backwards as he was taken by surprise and he fell heavily to the ground behind O'Malley's chair. The first of the infected reached him and O'Malley flipped the Zippo and struck the wheel.

He felt their hands on him, groping urgently at him, and then the smell of paraffin reached his nostrils. He couldn't tell if Peters had got clear or not but he could wait no longer. Agony flared in his arm as teeth tore at the flesh and a wave of dizziness threatened to pull him under. He forced his arm to the fuse and smiled in relief as he saw the sparks fizzle.

The light faded around him as more and more of the infected surrounded him. Pain wracked his body as they tore at him with teeth and nails sending his nerves into a paroxysm but finally a curious calm swept over him at the last moment.

"Fuckers," he croaked just before his throat was ripped apart and then everything went dark.

Alan Peters crashed through the glass of one of the shops as the blast picked him up and threw him like a rag doll across the decking. He landed heavily and felt the glass beneath him cut through his clothes and rake his skin. He looked back briefly at the entrance and saw the two doors hanging wide open. A mass of bodies lay strewn on the ground but already the next wave was stumbling through.

He pushed himself to his feet, wincing as glass cut into his hands, and swayed slightly as he fought against the dizziness that swept over him. The first line of the infected was already clear of their dead and Peters turned and rushed through the foyer.

Ahead of him he could still see a queue at the pedestrian entrance. The escape was taking much longer than planned. They had assumed, when they had planned the escape, that they would be able to clear the people out through the entrance before the infected could see them and so buy plenty of time as their attackers wandered through the large complex. Unfortunately something was delaying them, whether it was negotiating the narrow passage or problems out in the square, Peters didn't know. Either way they were in trouble.

The infected coming up behind him had already seen the route he was taking and couldn't miss the large crowd over at the other doorway. If he continued on he would be condemning everyone still in the complex to death.

Alan Peters had never been a man to do anything unless it benefited him directly and always made sure of the widest publicity possible. His last act on Earth was so totally incongruous to his life that the casual observer would be forgiven for assuming that another person of the same likeness had suddenly appeared in his place.

Peters made a decision and changed direction to the far side of the foyer and continued on deeper into the complex, moving slowly enough to ensure that all the infected followed him.

He knew that there would be no escape from the complex but at least this way he would save the others. He wasn't quite sure what made him make the decision but, curiously, he felt exhilarated as he led the hoard away from the small group of survivors, like some modern day pied-piper. It was the ultimate irony that his greatest achievement was the least publicised, in fact only one person saw what he had done, and this by purely by accident.

But Theresa Winfield vowed to herself that his act would not be forgotten, and in that vow Alan Peters finally achieved the piece of immortality he had always craved.

The dam that had drained the estuary had been built at the mouth of the harbour. Huge amounts of rocks and soil, excavated from the site when digging the foundations of the new centre, had been deposited across the narrow entrance that led to the estuary. Dave Johnson watched as the first group led by Martin rushed across the square before turning his attention back towards the dam. The new land mass formed a narrow bridge between the harbour and the far side of the estuary but there was only one way to get to the dam and, unfortunately, the infected lay between them and their goal.

John Pender and himself sat on the first floor of the centre and waited for their allotted time to pass. Both groups; 'Martin's scavengers' as Kim had dubbed them, and the main group led by Jack Thornton, would escape across the square. Once they had safely left the centre, and once the infected were inside, Pender and he were to head over towards the dam.

It was hoped that by that stage the majority of the infected would be spread out sufficiently to allow Pender and himself to work their way past them and onto the end of King Street. Once there, they had only to continue on down Chapel Lane, through the old Gas works and then onto the pier.

It wasn't so much the getting there that was worrying Johnson, it was more the getting back. He ran the plan through his head yet again, and while he had sounded confident while he explained it to Theresa, he wasn't sure that she had believed him. He looked out again at the main site entrance and paled at the sheer number of the infected all along King Street. He began to wonder if they would even be able to get to the pier let alone blow it up.

There were so many more of them than they had thought. He turned back towards Pender when the force of the explosion at the gates ripped through the glass behind him and sent him flying across the floor with thousands of pieces of jagged glass.

He pulled his arms over his head and landed heavily. Pain shot through him as pinpricks of glass peppered along him arms and his neck. He forced himself to wait a few more seconds and then raised his head and looked around. The room was covered in a layer of broken glass, shards as long as his arm mixed with small, diamond-like nuggets that reflected the day's morning sunlight like a kaleidoscope.

Shit! He thought as he looked around the room in search of his friend. He heard a low moan and looked over to see John Pender roll out from under a sea of sparkling glass. "Are you alright?" Johnson asked as he gingerly pulled himself to his feet trying to avoid the glass.

Pender raised his face towards him and smiled. There were quite a few cuts on his face and the back of his hands and blood flowed freely from a number of the lacerations, though none looked particularly deep.

"I'll live," he replied and accepted Johnson's help to rise. "How much explosives did you use?"

Johnson shrugged, "I'm used to C4 not this industrial stuff, and I wanted to be sure it didn't just maim poor Denis. I didn't want him to feel anything."

At the mention of the constable the men shuffled uncomfortably for a moment and then Pender walked over towards the open window. A fresh morning breeze whipped about him and he shivered as the chill cut through his clothes and caressed the cuts on his face. The blood dried and caked to his face making it seem as though he was wearing a thin mask.

The scene below him was one worthy of Dante's descriptions of Hell. A sea of the infected where swarming through the ruined gates, their mute advance all the more frightening by its single-minded relentlessness. There was a wide circle of bodies, most of them contorted or dismembered directly in front of the where the gates had been but, already, the hoard were swarming over the bodies, heedless of their dead. "Jesus! He took out hundreds of them," Pender whispered and looked over at Johnson.

"But there are still too many left," Johnson sighed. "We'll never get past them." Below in the centre they could hear the shuffling of feet in the foyer as the infected poured in and still many more hundreds continued through the gates. "I never thought there'd be so many," Johnson continued. "We should have gone last night before the bodies revived. We'll never get to the pier now."

"We have to," Pender insisted. "Otherwise the others will be surrounded in the Keep and they'll be swamped in no time. There has to be a way around them."

"Not unless you can fly," Johnson replied and turned away from the window to keep an eye on the stairs. It wouldn't be long before the infected made it up here.

"It's not quite flying," he heard the excitement in Pender's voice and turned back, "but it might just get us past them." Johnson followed Pender's outstretched finger and smiled.

The crane towered over the site like a mighty one-armed sentinel. It sparkled in the early morning as the sunlight reflected off the droplets of dew that clung to its surface despite the growing heat from the rising red orb that had already cleared the horizon far to the east. Its long arm stretched towards the centre far above them and a metal wire, some two inches in diameter, dangled enticingly before them as the wind carried it to and fro.

"You're not serious?" Johnson cocked his head towards Pender and raised his eyebrow.

"It's either that or we wait here for those things to find the stairs and tear us to pieces."

"As you put it that way, it looks more attractive by the minute. We'll never jump that far though."

"I know that," Pender replied a little testily. "We need to get something to increase the swing and bring the wire closer. See if you can find a plank of wood or something."

Johnson shrugged and they split up in the search. The centre was practically finished so there were no spare planks of wood lying around, however Pender was determined and he probed and pulled at any fitment that looked to have anything like the length he required and soon returned to the window with an odd assortment of door jambs, plastic piping and curious metal tubing.

Johnson, for his part, merely managed one piece, a wooden countertop, and he struggled back to the shattered window under its weight. The plastic piping proved too short, as did the metal tubing. The door jamb just about reached the wire but they had no support to push against the wire, despite Pender leaning dangerously out over the window.

The countertop was shorter than the door jamb so there was no way it would reach and for a moment Pender slumped despondently on the floor, oblivious to the glass beneath him, as he stared out at the wire.

Behind them they could hear the shuffling of feet on the stairs. It wouldn't be long before the infected reached them; however Pender's thoughts were not for himself, he was more worried about what would happen to his family if the dam wasn't blown.

He turned to Johnson suddenly and launched himself to his feet. "We can throw the countertop at it and start it swinging." His enthusiasm was infectious and Johnson found himself nodding and lifting the heavy wooden panel immediately.

"We'll only get one chance," Johnson warned as they lined themselves up on either side of the window. Pender nodded soberly and they began to swing the panel towards the window and back, gaining sufficient momentum until, with a nod from Pender, they launched the panel up and out through the window.

For a minute it looked like they had pitched it too high and it would arc to quickly and fall short. The two men watched, their hearts thumping loudly and their attention riveted on the heavy panel as it flew through the air. At the last moment it dipped at the front and missed the hook at the end of the wire by barely and inch. Pender began to shout his frustration when the panel dipped further and the back of the panel swung into the metal hook with such force as to send it back at least five feet.

For a second Pender stood unbelieving and almost missed the reverse swing of the hook. Without thinking he launched himself out of the window and stretched outward for the hook. His fingers brushed past the hook as he misjudged the swing and then suddenly it slammed into his hand. The metal was wet and cold and he grabbed at it desperately as his body-weight pulled him downward. He almost lost his grip as he snapped in the opposite direction to the swing of the wire and then he was swinging with the motion of the wire and he began to pull himself upward.

He paused for a rest as he managed to get his feet on the metal ring that supported the hook and he looked over at Johnson. He could see the heads of the infected behind his friend as the first of them reached the top of the stairs. Their slow, jerky movements of yesterday seemed to have gone and their gait, while still slower than normal, seemed to be a lot more fluid. *They'll be impossible to stop if they manage to run,* Pender flexed his legs and pushed towards the window and then relaxed as the wire swung backwards, flexing again on the downward swing. The first swing to the window wasn't far enough and Pender could see Johnson watch the swing and check how close the infected were alternatively. Pender used all his weight to force the wire closer and wrapped one arm around the wire while he stretched out with the other.

Johnson jumped. Everything seemed to slow for a moment; his friend appeared to float in mid-air and the wire seemed to halt. And then Pender grunted as Johnson crashed into him. He lost his footing and kicked helplessly as he groped for a handhold. Pain seared through his palms as his flesh tore but he gripped harder regardless. Johnson slipped down his body and grabbed at his clothes, stopping his own fall by grabbing at the belt around Pender's jeans.

"Climb up," Pender gasped as he gritted his teeth against the pain in his hands. He closed his hands and mind to the pain as Johnson pulled himself slowly up his body. The pain seemed to go on for an eternity and then, suddenly, it was over and he felt himself being pulled back up. His feet gained their previous foothold and he opened his eyes to see Johnson's smiling face.

"Piece of cake, just like you said."

Although the sky was brightening rapidly, the square held onto its shadows like a lover reluctant to break an early-morning embrace. As soon as Martin heard the explosion he forced himself to wait a further minute to allow the hoard to filter into the centre. He muttered a quiet prayer for Denis O'Malley's soul and then moved to the end of the passage.

The main group of the infected were clambering over each other to get in through the ruined entrance, although their slack-faced blank looks were incongruous to their obvious haste to enter the site.

Martin nodded to those behind him and slipped out into the square. The wind hit him like a slap as he cleared the passage, icy fingers seemed to pour over his body and suck the warmth from him. He glanced nervously behind him to see if the main group had seen them yet but their attention was still focused on the main entrance.

There were still numerous mounds on the ground, and Martin wondered if these bodies were indeed dead or whether they would suddenly lurch back to life, or whatever passed for their animated existence. The bodies seemed to cloak themselves in the few remaining shadows and each pool of darkness seemed to exude malevolence.

Martin tried to lead his group around the bodies but there were so many that they had to pass close to some of them. The wind whipped at one mound and seemed to ripple its clothes and Martin felt his heart stop as he imagined the body moved.

He skirted the body only to come across another and he stumbled as he tripped. Everyone in the group gasped as the body rolled over and exposed a neck torn to the bone by blunt teeth. Martin gasped as he recognised the pale features of Joshua Hackett, the shopkeeper he had seen attacked at the start of this nightmare. His skull was split open and his glazed eyes were empty.

Around him he saw a few bodies move, but whether this was the wind or new, demonic life, he wasn't sure. He motioned the others to hurry and they crossed the square as quickly as they could.

The supermarket entrance seemed as dark and forbidding as it had the last time he had been here. Fruit and vegetables lay strewn about the entrance and a nauseating scent of decay lay heavily in the air, though it did not seem to come from the produce. Martin motioned for the others to follow as he walked into the gloom.

Although it had been cold outside in the wind the interior of the shop seemed to suck at his very soul and he shivered uncontrollably. He looked over at the counter where he had seen Mr. Hackett viciously attacked but all that remained was a red stain that covered the floor and bags of potatoes in the immediate area.

He looked around and saw that the others were already collecting food and bringing it outside. He had sent Hillary, Kim and another man he did not know to find a car or van and sighed with relief as he heard an engine cough into life in the distance.

He shook himself out of his reverie and began to collect food and bring it outside. His stomach growled noisily as he smelt the food but forced himself to concentrate on the task at hand. By the time Hillary appeared around the corner they had a small mountain of food waiting for her. Martin smiled in relief as he saw Kim and Hillary get out of the car, she had chosen a large seven-seater SUV and the group set to work folding down the last two seats and loading the back of the car.

Martin looked down the row of cars and could see the other larger group make their way through the line of vehicles and head over towards the estuary. *Looks like everything is going according to plan,* he thought.

"Why does nothing ever go according to plan?" Pender fumed as he pulled himself up the metal wire. His hands were torn to shreds but it had to be him that climbed to the crane's cab as he was the only one with any clue as to how to operate it. Not that he really knew how to operate it but he had done a story on being a crane driver at Christmas for the paper a few years ago and part of the research had necessitated his going up into the cab and spending an hour with the driver.

He remembered the views perfectly but couldn't say the same for how the crane operated. He did remember that there were a lot of levers though. He lost track of time completely as he concentrated on lifting one hand over the other. He refused to look up or down but instead merely closed his eyes and continued to climb, muttering every curse he knew as a mantra.

Typically, he was rewarded for reaching the top by slamming his head against the cab door and he let loose a stream of new obscenities that he had not used on his climb up. He blinked furiously to get rid of the stars that appeared in front of him and his eyes watered as the light of the sun stabbed at them relentlessly.

He found the handle to the cab and turned it counter-clockwise. He had been told by the crane driver that he had interviewed that they never locked their cabs, relying on people's fear of such heights and the site security to ensure that nobody operated the equipment illegally. However he did reveal that they kept the key hidden just in case someone defied the odds and broke in. The driver had sworn Pender to secrecy and Pender had honoured the trust the man had shown him by keeping that fact out of the story. Pender prayed that the hiding place used by the crane operators in the city was the same as that used by their country cousins.

He pulled himself into the cab and immediately reached out the window, feeling along the sill as his hands groped under metal for the small, magnetised box he desperately hoped he would find.

His hands were frozen from the dew and the lacerations on his skin made his fingers numb but he sighed with relief as he brushed past a small box and he gripped it tightly and pulled it into the cab. He opened the box and tipped the key into his palm, watching it reflect the light as he thanked God for their good fortune.

He stabbed the key into the lock and smiled as the low hum of electric power flooded through the cab. The lights in front of him blinked on and he sat looking at the levers as he tried to remember their correct sequence.

His first attempt dropped Johnson ten feet before he realised what was happening and his second swung his friend helplessly against the building where he crashed through another pane of glass before Pender managed to find the control to pull him back.

He leaned out and looked down at his friend and shrugged an apology. The third attempt, however, worked perfectly and swung Johnson out over the hoard of the infected and out over the site gates.

He lowered the hook to the roof of a building on the street and watched as his friend clambered to safety.

Now all he had to do was slide down the wire himself. He looked down at his ruined hands and shrugged. "Beats being eaten."

Theresa Winfield watched the last of her group clamber into a car and drive off towards the estuary. She saw Julie Pender's face in the window just before the car disappeared around the corner and then she turned to Jack Thornton.

"Just us left then," she commented and nodded towards the two other men that had stayed with them. Pierce McGrath was over towards the junction with the square, checking that the infected were not following, and Pat Maguire was opening cars and checking whether the keys had been left behind or not.

They had been lucky so far and had found quite a few cars at the back of the traffic jam that still had keys in the ignition and they had run through the survivors quickly, packing them into the vehicles. Julie Pender had insisted that she stay with Theresa but she had finally convinced her to leave on the last vehicle.

Jack Thornton nodded, "Yep, we've been l . . ." he was interrupted by McGrath shouting as he ran towards them waving his arms. They couldn't quite hear him but his agitation was clear.

"There's a gro . . . " McGrath panted as he drew level with the others, "group of them coming this way." He paused as he sucked in another breath, "I'm not sure if they know we're here or not but they're moving faster than yesterday."

"Pat," Thornton shouted to the other man searching through the stationary cars, "any luck? We're a bit under pressure here."

Maguire looked over and nodded and then disappeared back into a nearby car.

Theresa felt surreal standing on the side of the road with the other two men, it almost felt as though they had merely met in the street and were passing the time of day. "Should we be helping?" she asked and shrugged.

The other two men shrugged back and were about to move when Pat shouted over to them.

"The keys are either buggered or so badly jammed in that we'd never get them out. We'll have to walk."

"But it's a fifteen minute drive," Theresa went pale. "The dam will be blown by the time we get there."

"The road goes around the estuary but we can cut across country by the industrial estate and get there in ten minutes no problem," Maguire explained. "It'll be tight though."

"We'd better hurry, then," Thornton agreed and pointed back towards the square. "We don't want those buggers seeing which way we're going."

The others looked back and saw a mass of bodies already filling the end of the street.

Jesus! They are faster than before. Theresa turned away and hurried to keep up with her companions.

The estuary spread out before them as the car pulled off the main road and began its winding journey along the coast road. *Back where we started,* Julie Pender sighed as she thought about the events of the last twenty four hours. The children slept in the cramped confines of the car despite their awkward positions and she smiled despite her worry.

There had been no conversation in the car for the fifteen minute journey, as each person considered their own worries and fears. Julie knew the odds were very slim indeed that she would ever see John again, it would practically be a miracle if they even got to the stage of blowing up the dam, let alone make it safely back to them.

She thought back to all the wasted time, days and even years they had squandered as they lived their separate lives and she wished to have even a fraction of them back. She had always thought that they would be together forever, they had even joked about all the time they would have when the children had grown up and left home. Now, it seemed, they would be lucky to see tomorrow's dawn.

She caught a glimpse of the centre across the bay as they pulled up near her house and wiped away a tear as the children began to wake. Their young faces were so innocent in sleep and she wondered what they had done to deserve such a bleak future.

The other occupants scrambled from the car and she was left alone for a minute with the children. He mind wandered for a moment and she wondered if she would have the courage to take responsibility for them if they were over-run by the infected. She smiled reassuringly at the children as they stretched and yawned and she vowed to herself that no God-forsaken bastard would lay a finger on them, not alive anyway.

They exited the car together and followed the train of people out ono the hard sand. In the distance they could see the Keep rising out of the sand like a lonely sentinel. The clear early-morning sky had already given way to a dull cover of sickly grey cloud. An occasional ray of sunlight cut through the thickening cover to bath the eastern side of the structure in golden sunlight. However, the rest of the edifice was cloaked in shadow and looked more forbidding than welcoming.

The sky grew dark and menacing as a storm rolled in from the sea. The earlier sunshine that had seemed to promise hope and new beginnings suddenly seemed to change its mind and instead rumbled angrily at the small group as they made their way across country towards the base of the estuary.

The wind whipped at them, snatching at their exposed flesh and sucking the heat from their bodies with each frigid caress. None of them had coats or warm clothing of any kind, the unusually warm weather of the last few days having taken their minds from such matters.

Theresa leaned into the wind and followed the figure in front of her. She looked at her watch and saw that five minutes had passed. She had no idea where she was, so she could not tell whether they were on schedule or not. She walked directly behind Thornton, using his ample frame to shield her from the elements but she could still feel the occasional drop of rain as the wind lashed against her face. *Great!* She thought miserably, *now it's going to fucking rain. What else can go wrong?*

Her eyes were scrunched shut and it wasn't until she slammed into Jack Thornton's back that she realised that he had stopped. She mumbled an apology but saw that he wasn't even aware of her. His gaze was locked on something in front of him, something that his broad back blocked from her view. She moved out from behind him and gasped.

The sudden slam of freezing air was a shock to her already chilled body but the sight before her sent a shiver far deeper than any cold could reach. They had finally reached the estuary and were currently standing on what used to be the bank before the water had been blocked. They were on the town side of the large area and she could see the road winding its way around the coast on the far side.

The road seemed to be alive in the poor light, its surface undulating and writhing like a snake pit. She tried to focus her eyes harder by scrunching them tightly against the wind but it was too far away. The clouds above her roiled across the sky malevolently like some dark Jeanie suddenly released from its bottle. The dark clouds shut out the pale morning light as effectively as a blanket drawn across a lamp. In the distance she heard a deep rumble.

"What is it?" she asked, having to shout as the wind increased.

"The road is full of them," she heard Maguire say and she looked quizzically at him. "They must have seen the cars head this way and followed them."

"Who?" Theresa asked as she looked again into the gloom but couldn't make out any details.

"They must be coming from the factories," Thornton's face was grey as he spoke. He looked over at Theresa and saw her confused frown. "They must have been working the late shift last night. There must be hundreds of them, thousands even."

Theresa looked back to the road and began to see individual shapes now that she knew what to look for. The road was clogged with them. There had been hundreds at the centre but there were far more here. They seemed to move as one single organism along the road and already those in the lead disappeared into the distance.

"We have to warn them," she shouted over the wind. "They won't be expecting so many."

"There's no way the Keep will protect them from that many, either way they're all dead," Maguire sighed and went to turn away.

"We have to try," Theresa grabbed him and turned him back to face her. "Jack," she looked over at Thornton for support, "tell him we have to try."

Thornton looked alternatively between Maguire, Theresa and the road as he considered their options. The silence seemed to go on forever and Theresa shook uncontrollably from the cold. "We have to try," he said at last and Theresa exhaled with relief. "You three run on ahead and I'll see if I can slow them down a bit."

"What?" Theresa grabbed Thornton, "you can't, you'll be killed."

"Theresa," he took her hands gently in his, "there's no way I can run that distance. I'll only slow you all up and then we all die. Now you're wasting time, get going. Pat!" Theresa struggled at first as Pat led her away but his urgings finally got through to her and she followed them out onto the sand and into the dark mouth of the estuary.

She only looked back once and saw Thornton wave briefly before the darkness swallowed him up.

How many more of us must die?

The rain began to fall as they ran. It began slowly, more an irritation than anything, but it soon grew heavier until sheets of water lashed at them in the wind. Within minutes, she was drenched and her legs ached as the once firm sand began to grow soggy in the relentless downpour. The dark outline of the Keep had already disappeared behind the sheeting rain and her two companions were merely wraiths beside her.

She fell, slipping on seaweed suddenly slick and slippery in the rain. She landed heavily and felt the wind driven from her body. She tried to cry out for help but her mouth filled with sand and water and she retched instead. Her companions were nowhere to be seen, already far ahead and oblivious to her falling.

She forced herself to her feet and stumbled on. She wasn't entirely certain she was still running in the right direction now but she had to try. In this visibility the survivors in the Keep wouldn't even see their attackers until it was far too late.

Pender stood at the end of the pier and looked back at Dave Johnson as he removed the bag from his back. "Will the rain affect the explosives?"

"I'm not entirely sure," Johnson replied, "I'm not really that familiar with this type."

The rain had begun just as they reached the pier and they had greeted its arrival with mixed feelings. On the plus side it would cloak them from the infected as they moved out into the open but it would also make negotiating the slippery surface of the temporary dam very dangerous.

"We'll have to make sure that they're well covered just to be sure then." Johnson nodded his agreement. The dam stretched at least a mile from the harbour to the far side of the estuary and Pender had hoped that they would be able to plant the charges close to the harbour end and run for it.

Unfortunately, as Johnson had explained, they did not have enough explosives to destroy the dam so they would have to plant the charges where the most pressure was being put on the structure and hope that the force of the sea would do the rest. This, of course, meant that they would have to plant the explosives as near to the middle of the dam as possible. It would also mean that that they would have little hope of getting off the dam before the explosives blew.

The surface of the weir was an uneven collection of rocks and dirt layered and packed tightly together by machines and sealed by the power of the sea. It was only six feet wide and rose to a height of ten feet above the level of high tide.

There had been some shelter from the weather on the pier but, once they set foot on the dam, the wind caught them with its full force. Spray from the sea lashed against them as the waves crashed against the barrier below them and sent torrents of water upward. The wind snatched at them, driving rain into their faces and threatening to snatch them from their precarious footing as they attempted to make their way out to the centre.

Pender's eyes stung as the salted water swept over him and his feet fought to retain their footing on jutting rocks made slick with water. He tried to call to Johnson but his words were snatched by the wind and whipped away out to sea. He tried to turn his body sideways to the wind but out on the dam the wind seemed to be able to change direction at will and he felt his body pushed and then pulled as if the wind were playing with him.

He heard a deep rumble above and looked up briefly at the black, angry clouds above. There was a sudden illumination, powerful enough to light even the ebony darkness of the storm, and he shivered. The storm was almost overhead and growing worse by the minute. He thought of Julie and the kids and how they would die if he failed and forced himself on out into the darkness.

He looked back but already the mouth of the harbour had disappeared in the gloom. Just how they were supposed to know when they were half-way he had no idea. Even if they did get there he had no idea how they were meant to hear the signal?

There were two entrances to the Keep but only one of them was practical from their position. The main entrance was designed to be approached during high tide when a small boat could be safely steered around the moat of jagged rocks that surrounded the structure. There was, however, a smaller door, or iron grating to be more accurate, set below the water line that led to a series of stone steps that spiralled up into the Keep.

Martin examined the gate, noting the rust and sea-encrusted life that covered its surface. The lock was useless; even if they had a key, the mechanism was too badly rusted. He wondered briefly what the door had been used for as the sea would have rusted it beyond all practical use within a year after it was set in place. He pulled at the gate but it did not move at all. He looked at the supports on each side and saw that each hinge was rusted badly.

"I don't suppose we brought along a chainsaw," he quipped as he looked back along the line of cold survivors. He had left with the first car loaded with food and had arrived just after the larger group had reached the estuary. Nobody had seemed to be in control as he arrived and the weather had been threatening at the time. He had quickly ordered everyone to take some of the food and make their way on foot out towards the Keep.

The food they had brought would see them through 2 days, more than enough for their needs. They would either be safely aboard the boat at that stage or dead. It had taken far longer to get to the Keep than he had expected but eventually they had arrived and made their way to the lower gateway.

"It had to be put here for a reason," Kim pushed past him and examined the gate. "They had to be aware that it would be below the water most of the time." She continued to scan the gate and the area surrounding it carefully as she spoke.

Martin smiled at her; she had certainly come out of herself since he had first met her at the estuary the previous day. She was still reluctant to be apart from either himself or Hillary, but she was a lot brighter than before. He still worried, though. He had not had the time to talk to her about what had happened and her eyes still retained a distant, haunted look that he would have to address. For now though, she seemed to be coping and that was as much as any of them could do at the moment.

She reached through the gate and padded the steps and surrounding walls. "There has to be a .. aha," she yelped excitedly as her fingers found a part of the wall to the left of the gate that protruded further than the rest of the wall. She pressed against it and there was a deep rumble below the gate. For a moment nothing else happened, but then the stone base split and parted from the step. The gate seemed to hang for a second before it slid easily down into the crevice along ridges that suddenly appeared along the length of each wall. The mechanism was so slick, even after all these years that Martin stood staring at it long after the gate had disappeared.

"How the hell did you know?" he asked incredulously.

"There are lots of secret entrances in old castles and Keeps like this one. Sometimes the most obvious of escape routes proved the most successful." Kim grinned as she moved into the Keep. "Aren't you coming?"

"But how did you know?" Martin insisted as he beckoned for the others to follow.

"You don't live here all your life without knowing the legends surrounding this Keep. Hey, maybe we'll find treasure too."

"I'll settle for sanctuary," Martin replied and continued up the stairs into the building.

Chapter 24

Jack Thornton fought for breath as he ran towards the road. He had no real plan as to what he would do when he got to the pedestrian access down into the estuary but at the moment all he could think of was getting there.

There was no way he could have run to the Keep. As it was, he wasn't sure the others would make it in time anyway. Anything he could do to distract or slow the infected townspeople down would give his friends precious minutes to prepare for the deluge that approached them.

His chest hurt with every step and his lungs burned from lack of oxygen as he laboured to draw breath, but he forced himself on regardless. He ran close to the road to ensure he didn't miss the entrance but the rain fell in sheets around him and he could have already passed it without knowing. The storm raged above with lightening illuminating the dark sky in staccato flashes. It was as dark as night although it was still early morning and Thornton couldn't recall a worse storm in all his years. *It was so damn dark.*

It was almost as if the storm knew what was happening in the town and had come to wash away everything and start again. The sand grew soggy beneath him and sucked at his feet as he ran. Suddenly he saw figures in front of him.

The pedestrian entrance to the estuary lay to his left but already a stream of the silent figures poured out onto the sand. He shouted at them but the wind roared around him and the rain thundered against the sand and drowned him out.

He stood bent over with his hands on his knees as he sucked in air. Tears of frustration burned down his cheeks. He was too late. Now nothing could stop the tide of death that streamed towards the Keep.

He forced himself straight and shouted again but then a pain gripped his chest and his shout of rage turned into a strangled gasp. His head felt light and bright specks flickered in front of him. His right arm felt leaden and dropped to his side as his chest burned with agony. He fell to his knees as his legs lost their strength and then found himself pitching forward towards the sand.

His face struck the sand and he was dimly aware of the course texture on his cheek before he felt something burst inside and darkness slowly enveloped him.

Theresa staggered through the darkness. Her ears were full of thunder and her eyes were lashed by rain but she ran on oblivious to it all. There was a vague shape ahead of her and she sighed with relief as she forced herself on, desperate to catch her colleagues. She seemed to be gaining on the figure faster than she expected and she slowed a little as she drew level, worried that they had been injured.

"Pat," she called out, "is that you?" She didn't know if he had heard or not so she reached out to touch him on the shoulder. The figure turned and lashed out. She was so shocked that she fell backwards as she tried to dodge away from the blow.

She caught a brief impression of her attacker as lightening flared above revealing a pale image with dead eyes and blood stained cheeks. *My God! They've gotten in front of us.* She jumped to her feet and continued backing away as the figure followed her. It moved more fluidly than the figures that had attacked her before and it gained on her with frightening speed.

Her thoughts were jumbled, panicked and she ran blindly into the rain, desperate to get away from the thing that chased her. Suddenly there was another vague outline ahead through the rain, and then another beside that. Lightening flared again and the scene before her was burned into her vision long after the light had faded. There were figures all around her. Somehow she had wandered into their midst in the dark. Ahead of her lay the Keep. It was only about a hundred feet away; though it may as well have been a hundred miles for all the good it would do her.

The figures around her had seen her in the light of the last flash and she could see their dark outlines turn towards her. *Not like this,* she prayed. *God, don't let me die like this.*

Dave Johnson slipped as the wave crashed over him and he fell against the rocks on the narrow ledge. He snapped out a hand and gripped a rock as a second wave suddenly engulfed him and pulled greedily at him as it withdrew back into the roiling sea. He felt his hand slip and then, suddenly, the rock was gone and he was falling.

He felt a sharp pain in his head as it was snapped upward. Water washed over him, filling his mouth and stinging his eyes. He coughed and then sucked in more water as he gasped for breath. He could see John Pender as a vague outline as his eyes stung from the salt. He groped upwards trying to catch his out-thrust hand but his vision blurred and he wasn't sure if he was stretching in the right direction. The pain in his head continued and he realised dimly that Pender had snatched a handful of his hair as he had fallen.

The waves were icy cold and for a moment he was tempted to slip into its embrace. No more worries, no more pain over Kate's death. All he had to do was let the wave take him and he'd be able to see Kate again. The pain, as Pender wrenched at his hair again, snapped him back to himself and the moment passed. He reached out again, flailing blindly towards where he had last seen his friend. He could feel his strength wane as the cold and the lack of oxygen took its toll. He felt his hand drop but then suddenly he felt a strong hand grip him just above the wrist. His lungs burned, crying out for air, and he felt his vision blur again and was dimly aware that he was moving upwards back on to the ledge.

He had swallowed too much water and he lay retching on the rocks as his body shivered uncontrollably. His chest felt like it had been put through a vice and he had to breathe slowly, despite his desperate need for air, or he would pass out from the pain. He felt the reassuring presence of John Pender beside him and he forced himself to take the time to recover.

"If I go bald," he spluttered in between coughing and had to shout to be heard over the thunder of the waves, "I'll know who to blame."

Pender grinned half-heartedly but Johnson could see that the near fatal accident had shaken his confidence. He wiped the salt water from his eyes and tried to see how far they had come but the dam disappeared into the darkness behind them. He had tried to keep track of his steps initially but he had lost his count quite some time ago. Now, he had no idea how far they had come.

The bag on his back was soaked through and he hoped that the plastic sheeting they had wrapped around the explosives was keeping out the water; otherwise it would all have been for nothing.

He nodded to Pender. "Keep a look out for somewhere to plant the explosives; I reckon we've come far enough." Pender nodded in reply and then they continued on in single file, keeping their eyes down as they searched for a crevice.

It was about five minutes later, although it felt more like an hour as they trudged through the storm, that Pender held up his hand. Johnson moved up level with his friend and looked to where he pointed. There was a small crack in the dam where dirt had been washed away by the storm. The rocks were lodged apart by small piece of wood. Johnson nodded enthusiastically, shrugged the bag off his shoulder and knelt beside the crevice.

He reached in and pulled at the wood and grunted with satisfaction when it stayed firmly in place. He opened his bag and withdrew the wrapped explosives. His hands were numb with the cold. He nearly dropped the package as he grazed his hand against the rock, only preventing it from falling into the sea by falling forward and using his body to trap the package before it disappeared over the edge.

He eased himself back to a kneeling position and carefully brought the explosives towards the crevice. He knew that he would not be able to take the explosives out of the protective covering so he tore a small hole in the bag and applied the electrical cable to one of the sticks within. He played out the rest of the cable and handed the other end to Pender who towered above him using his body to shield him from the worst of the water.

Johnson lay flat on the ground and lowered the package as far into the crevice as it would go. He stuffed the bag he had carried the explosives in on top of the package to try to keep it as dry as possible and then sat up.

He motioned for Pender to hand him his own bag and Pender shrugged off the shoulder harness and passed it to him. He opened the bag carefully. Inside he could see the detonator. Luckily it was manual, using the physical twist of the handle to generate the spark that would feed down the cable to the charge. If it had been a battery or an electronically powered one, he feared the storm would have rendered it useless.

Pender handed him the cable and he used both hands to take it. His fingers were almost useless, the cold having frozen them into gnarled claws, and he spent what seemed like an age trying to place the bare ends of the cable into the holes required and then twist the screws shut to hold them in place.

Finally, he sighed in relief, the cable was attached and he lifted his hand towards Pender. Pender nodded and helped him to his feet. "Okay," Johnson shouted over the storm, "that looks like it. There's not much cable I'm afraid but we might as well use what we have."

Pender nodded and they moved past the crevice towards the estuary side of the dam. All too quickly they came to the end of the cable and they turned and looked back.

Martin stood on the western battlements and strained his eyes as he tried to penetrate the gloom that lay heavily around him. Rain lashed against his face and the wind howled its fury as it pushed and pulled at him forcing him to grip the slick, cold stone to prevent him falling to the sand below. He had organised the survivors as best he could. The majority were under shelter, preparing food and keeping the children warm with the few blankets they had found in the shop, but he had ordered some of the men out onto each side of the Keep to maintain a vigil.

He knew that it was next to useless in the current weather but Thornton and Theresa were still not back yet and the rest of the group were happy to defer to someone. Martin wasn't entirely sure that they needed to keep watch but he felt it was something they should do and, in the absence of someone better, he would do as he thought best. He had also stationed one of the women at the gate, just in case Pender and Johnson came back, although he realised now that this was doubtful.

He looked at his watch, they were already fifteen minutes late. He had no idea what could have happened to them but was realistic enough to realise that fifteen minutes was far more time than they could afford. He raised the gun into the air. He doubted that it would be heard over the thunder or the howling of the wind but it was part of the plan and he would complete the task just in case.

He whispered a silent apology to Theresa and her group, knowing that the signal would seal their fate if they were still out on the estuary, and pulled the trigger. The recoil slammed the gun back into his numbed hand and he almost dropped the weapon over the wall. As he glanced down into the darkness he thought he saw movement below on the sand.

Johnson had been trying for some now to think what he would say to Pender at this stage. He had wanted to say so much; to thank the man and his family for giving him something to live for again, for reminding him that life continued on, even after the most tragic circumstances. All these things and more swam through his mind but in the end he wasn't sure how to say any of it so he merely nodded and gripped Pender by the shoulder.

Pender, however, knocked his arm away and wrapped both arms around him in a tight hug. Water streamed down Johnson's face as tears joined with the rain and when they broke to look at each other, both men were smiling. Johnson lifted the detonator between them and they both placed their hands on it. Pender gripped the base and nodded. Johnson nodded in reply and then twisted the handle.

Martin leaned over the edge, forgetting the second shot, as he searched the gloom below. *There!* He saw something else move and then another. Suddenly the darkness seemed to be alive with movement. He still couldn't see clearly but there were far too many figures for it to be his lost friends. Suddenly the sky was lit up and the scene before him was burned into his vision. The estuary was full of dark shambling figures. *There must be thousands of them*, he thought as he raised the gun and fired into the crowd below.

Theresa heard the shot and whirled around to its source. She had been heading in the wrong direction and immediately doubled back. A figure loomed out of the darkness and swiped at her, catching her hair and pulling her down to the ground. She landed heavily and kicked out at her attacker's leg, feeling satisfaction as she heard a sharp crack and saw the figure fall to the sand.

She rolled to her feet and ducked below another figure as she ran. A second shot rang out and she corrected her course slightly and ran. There were people all around her, most of them were oblivious to her but, as she passed by, they turned and followed after her.

She ran blindly ahead, dodging figures as they suddenly loomed before her. She fell twice more and each time she rolled back to her feet and stumbled on. She could see a larger shape before her rising out of the darkness and she sighed in relief as she saw the pointed walls of the Keep.

She twisted violently to the left as one of the jagged rocks suddenly loomed before her and she crashed directly into a dark shape. She knocked her head against the figure's shoulder and sent both of them sprawling to the ground. She tumbled and felt a searing pain in her side. She rolled away from it and slammed against another rock. Her side burned with pain and she lay on the ground for a moment as she tried to catch her breath.

She placed her hand to her side and gingerly examined the wound. Her fingers were too cold to be certain but she was sure she could feel a ragged tear that began just below her right breast and continued down to her hip. She desperately tried to remember whether her attacker had scraped her or whether she had rolled over a rock but she just wasn't sure. Her heart pounded as she thought briefly about what would happen to her if she was infected but then she forced the thought from her mind as she saw her attackers draw closer.

Theresa forced herself to her feet, ignoring the pain shooting through her side, and continued on towards the Keep and safety.

There was a dull thud and then the upper part of the dam blew outward sending rocks tearing past them at ferocious speeds. They felt the ground beneath them shudder violently and they were pitched to the side but then, just as suddenly, it stopped and all was quiet. Except for the roar of the storm and the waves.

"Is that it?" Pender shouted, "I was hoping for more."

"We'd need far more explosives than we had to blow it completely," Johnson shouted to his friend, although in truth he had expected a far greater explosion himself. "The sea will do the rest," he tried hard to instil confidence in his tone but Pender's dubious look spoke volumes to him.

"We should use the time to continue on," Johnson shouted and Pender nodded, taking one more second to look at the crevice. Johnson could see his worried frown and shared the man's fears. If the dam didn't fall then the others wouldn't stand a chance.

Martin's excited shouts had everyone on their feet long before he burst into the main room. Hillary watched the soaked figure appear and noted immediately the change in him. Outwardly he looked bedraggled, his skin was almost blue from the cold and his hands shook but he looked confident and in control as he commanded their attention. He stood tall as he strode through the door, his eyes blazed with an inner fire that was a long way from the shy figure she had known. He barked orders with an authority she doubted even he had known he possessed.

Hillary looked at the people around her and saw the fear in their faces but also their resolve. They had gathered in the room almost twenty minutes ago and had already made it habitable. Jobs had been assigned efficiently and without complaint. Food had been the first priority and she had organised a few of the women to that task as soon as Martin had left with the first shift of guards. She wasn't sure if they obeyed her because of her relationship with Martin or because she had been prepared to take control, but either way she had the people assigned to jobs in no time.

Those that had been injured had been assigned nurses; luckily the only injuries that had been sustained were clean cuts or sprains. Others had been assigned to look after the children, although Kim had resolutely refused to be considered a child and had demanded a proper job. Hillary smiled to herself as she thought of how defiant she was feeling now that she had stationed her to guard the entrance they had come in through. She would leave her there for another fifteen minutes or so and then send one of the others to relieve her.

She looked around the room as she checked on how things were proceeding. The room they were in had once served as the dining area, or so Kim had informed her. The room was almost a perfect square, with a slight bulge at the eastern end of the room to accommodate a huge stone fireplace that stretched at least twenty feet in length and ten in height.

The room was freezing and the bare stone walls seemed to suck any heat from the survivors' bodies. Kim had informed them that the walls were seventeen feet thick around the Keep and the fireplace would have been the only source of heat when it had been occupied.

There were stairs leading up to a few small bedrooms and arrow loops dotted the walls along the stairs, their simple vertical slots may have allowed their predecessors to protect the Keep with a rain of arrows but now only served to allow the bitter wind entry to the already cold room.

"We're being attacked," Martin's words snapped her from her reverie and she looked over at him as he continued.

Martin saw the fear on the faces in front of him but he would need everyone to play their part if they were to survive. "Take what weapons you have and take up positions along the battlements. There are only two ways in that we know of so we'll concentrate our forces there. I will need someone at each of the other walls just in case. Hillary, can you take two others and cover those areas?" He continued to deliver specific instructions to each of the group, dividing up his small force as economically as possible.

He knew Hillary would be furious that he had sent her to the other walls but he just couldn't bear to put her and Kim in direct danger. He'd handle her anger later; if there was a later. For now though, he didn't give them time to debate his orders and hurried them all out into the storm.

The Keep consisted of a central building that stretched some twenty feet in length and nearly that again in width. Surrounding this was an outer wall that rose some thirty feet from the sand below and encircled the Keep itself, except for the large gate that served as the entrance. These walls served as battlements for the defence of the structure and included a fighting platform that ran along the inside of the wall.

The walls were staggered in the classic battlement style with crenellations that allowed the defenders to lean between the merlons and defend the Keep from attack. Martin directed his forces to every third embrasure along the wall and these splayed openings allowed them to see down to the sand without exposing themselves unduly to the ferocious wind that whistled as it tore through the gaps in the structure.

At each corner of the structure there were flanking towers that provided access to the battlements and taller look-out areas. These structures were D-shaped and rose a further ten feet over the battlements. Martin had quickly discounted the towers as useful as they were too high to see anything in the poor light and were too far from the main gate to be of any use if the entrance was breached.

Martin took his position on the battlement at the main gate and checked around to ensure that the others were in position. He could barely even see the battlements on the far side of the Keep from where he was but he knew that Hillary would not leave her post no matter how angry she was. He wondered briefly which would be worse; the oncoming attack or the scathing she would give him if they survived.

Kim sat on the stone step and cursed. Her bum was frozen but the area at the gate was too low for her to stand and she had grown tired of bending over as she guarded her position. She hadn't really expected Hillary to actually assign her a job, let alone guard duty, but she was stuck with it now. She had considered leaving her post in a sulk but knew that the situation was far too grave for petulance.

She looked around the tiny area and sighed. For years she had stood on the bank of the estuary and wished that she could enter the mysterious Keep. She had dreamed of searching through its deserted halls and exploring its buried secrets. Now that she was here, however, she would give anything to be home again.

It was so damn cold. *How the hell could anyone have lived here*, she thought as she wrapped her arms around herself. Just then she heard a shot and snapped her head to the side. *Must be Martin,* she thought idly and settled back to her boredom.

Just then she heard a noise from outside and shifted her position closer to the gate. *Was someone out there?* She knew that Theresa was late with her group but knew also that no-one really expected them to arrive at this stage.

She strained her ears but the small corridor only amplified the rumble of thunder and the sheeting rain from outside. She soon grew bored and returned to sitting on the step.

After a while she heard a second shot but paid little attention to it. She began to hum quietly but stopped suddenly when she heard a cry out beyond the walls. She rushed back to the gate but the wind whipped the sound away before she could get a proper fix on its position.

"Theresa," she shouted and waited. Nothing! "Theresa, Mr. Thornton, are you out there?" She listened again and then she heard a scream. Her heart hammered in her chest, pounding so loud it even drowned out the thunder above. *Theresa is out there.* She rushed to the gate and shouted as loud as she could and then forced herself to keep quiet long enough to listen for a response, but none came.

The gate wasn't easy to find, it had been designed as a secret entrance after all, and Kim knew that Theresa could be ten feet away and not see it in the poor light. She bit her lip and then shouted again but only the wind moaned in response.

She reached behind her for her bat. She had to let Theresa know where she was. She knew Hillary would kill her if she found out but there were four people in Theresa's group that would die if she just sat and did nothing. She had argued to be treated as an adult and now was the time to show that she could act like one. *Anyway*, she told herself, *I'll only be a second. What harm could it do?*

She pressed the brick and watched the gate slide down its grooves. She took the bat and lodged it into the groove on the left, just in case the gate decided to close behind her, and slipped out into the rain.

Julie Pender held Jack close as she looked out over the walls of the Keep. She wondered briefly how John was, if he had gotten far enough to plant the explosives or if he lay dead in the gutter somewhere with all their hopes dying with him. Jack peeped through the embrasure and Julie automatically gripped him by the neck of his jumper and pulled him back.

Craig and Emma were off on the other side of the Keep working as runners for Martin. She had been reluctant initially to let them go but the groups' needs outweighed her own selfish feelings and they really did need everyone to play their part.

She had felt listless since leaving John. She knew she had to be strong for her children's sake but she just couldn't help herself. As long as there was even a small chance of his surviving she just couldn't stop herself worrying about him. She looked out into the dark, over to where the estuary joined the sea and, although she couldn't see anything, imagined John out on the dam planting the explosives that would end his life but possibly save everyone else's.

She looked down at Jack and pulled him to her. The children were too young to go through such ordeals but fate had dealt them this hand. They had no choice but to play it out, whatever the result.

Lightening flashed above and illuminated the area surrounding the Keep. The figures surrounding them had once been her friends and neighbours but now craved the blood that flowed through their veins. Their fate now lay in the hands of her husband and a man that, until two days ago, they knew nothing about. Despite her own feelings she prayed that their mission would succeed and their deaths would ensure that her children would have a future.

The first of the infected reached the main gate just as the sky lit up and thunder roared overhead. Martin could see a faint lightening on the horizon, more of a dark grey than the ebony darkness of before. The gate at the main entrance spread fifteen feet across and rose to the full height of the walls. From his position in front of the gate it towered over him and seemed to disappear into the darkness above. It must have been very impressive in its day but now it was dulled and rusted by the weather. It still looked strong and sturdy from up on the battlements though. However, Martin was more worried about the lower section that had been under water.

The metal on the last fifteen feet of the gate was badly corroded, whole pieces of it had flaked off to his touch when he had examined it earlier and he doubted whether it would stand up to much punishment.

The first of the infected arrived at the entrance and pressed their hands through the ornate designs that spiralled through the body of the gate. Their arms brushed against a loop of metal and many of them bent or cracked and fell through to fall with a dull thud at Martin's feet. The things pushed harder, running their arm through deeper and trying to grab at him. The gate seemed to be holding. But for how long? More figures materialised out of the gloom and soon the gate was filled with their slack-faced, silent visages.

It was eerie standing there watching pieces of the gate fall through to the ground. Each thud of ruined metal on the ground seemed to be a portent, like a bell tolling their impending doom. After the initial damage the gate seemed to hold but the sheer volume of bodies were already straining the gate supports badly enough that the metal shrieked like tortured screams.

The older children acted as runners, carrying messages of numbers and positions from each of the guards to him and his replies back to them. The rain seemed to intensify as the figures surrounded them as if it too was aware that a climax was coming.

"Theresa!" Kim leaned out further but kept her hand on the cold stone, as if reluctant to abandon its cold comfort. She could see the high, dark shapes of the rocks immediately in front of her but everything else was lost in the darkness.

She moved out further, finally letting go of the wall. Her heart thumped in her chest and the pounding distracted her as she strained her senses. She heard a scuffle to her left and she jumped and snapped her head towards the sound.

"Theresa," she whispered to the darkness and then felt foolish. There was no way any of the infected could have followed them this quickly from the town. "Theresa, over here," she called out with more volume but refrained from shouting despite her own reassurances.

The sand sucked at her feet as she walked further out from the Keep and then suddenly a shape loomed at her through the darkness. There was no way she could avoid the figure and she had a brief glimpse of Theresa's terrified face before they collided and fell to the ground.

Theresa fell on top of her and for a moment she couldn't breathe. Then, just as quickly she was gone and Kim lay on the damp sand sucking in air and coughing as the deluge of rain poured into her open mouth.

"Come on," she heard Theresa beside her, her tone urgent and demanding. "They're just behind me."

Kim thought about asking who exactly was behind her but Theresa was pulling at her arms and her terror was obvious. Kim rolled to her feet and pushed past her as she led the way back towards the entrance.

"We thought you were dead," Kim shouted behind her as she searched for the small gateway. The dark seemed to close in around her and for a brief moment she thought that the gate had been swallowed up somehow. But then she saw the opening and gratefully passed through into the corridor.

Theresa entered literally on her heels and Kim leaned back to remove the wooden support. Theresa, not expecting her to lean back, stumbled against the wall and smashed against the brace. She heard a loud snap and saw the bat collapse in on itself as it broke in two.

"Shit!" Kim cursed as she examined the damage. There wasn't much light to see by but what there was showed her that the upper half of the wood had been driven into the groove in the wall too far to be able to get a good grip and the rain made the small portion of wood protruding too slippery to pull. She depressed the hidden stone but the gate remained lodged open.

"What's wrong?" Theresa asked as she nervously scanned the darkness outside.

"The gate won't close."

"Shit, here they are," Theresa looked at Kim, "we'll have to leave it, they'll be here any second."

"But we can't," Kim replied desperately. "They'll get in."

"Move over and I'll have a go," Theresa squeezed past the girl and bent towards the gate.

Kim moved back further into the corridor but leaned out over Theresa's hunched form as she kept watch. She saw the darkness move and then coalesce into the figure of a man.

"They're here," her voice came out more as a squeak and she pulled back from the opening as the figures drew closer.

"Hold on," Theresa grunted as she pulled at the wooden obstruction, "I think . . . aaagh," she screamed as her hand slipped and slammed against the stone. "It's no good," she said between gritted teeth, "it won't budge."

"They're here, come on," Kim scrambled up the narrow stairs and navigated through a warren of corridors before exiting into the courtyard. From there it was a short walk to the large doors of the main hall. She burst through the doors shouting her warning and suddenly stopped and stared around her.

The room was empty.

Kim. Hillary felt her pulse quicken as she suddenly remembered that she had left her longer than she had intended. She wasn't used to being responsible for others and in all the excitement of the unexpected attack she had forgotten about her charge. She looked along the battlement and saw Julie Pender as a vague outline in the distance to her left. The Keep was surrounded but the majority of the infected were at the gate on the other side.

No-one will miss me, she thought. She must be terrified with all those things roaming about. It would only take a minute anyway. Hillary walked down towards the tower and crossed to the Keep itself. She could see a number of the survivors standing in front of the gate and beyond them a sea of bodies that disappeared back into the darkness.

She caught a quick glimpse of Martin's tall frame before she reached the door and stepped into the room.

"Hillary, Thank God!" She jumped as a bedraggled figure ponced on her and flung their arms around her. "They're coming. I'm sorry, they're coming," Kim clung to her as she sobbed into her chest.

"What's wrong?" she tried to ease the girl away from her so she could hear her properly but the child clung tighter.

"It's my fault," Hillary jumped for a second time as another figure suddenly appeared beside her.

"Theresa, is that you?" Hillary looked at the woman and noted her dishevelled appearance. Her hair hung heavily on her shoulders in dirty clumps and her clothes were covered in sand. "We thought you were dead. Are the others with you?"

"We got separated," Theresa said quickly. "Listen, the gate is broken and those things are already in the building we've …"

Hillary lost the rest of what she said as thunder cracked above them but she had heard enough. "We've got to warn the others." She said and turned immediately and walked back out into the storm.

John Pender cursed as he bent into the wind. They had failed. The explosives hadn't been enough and the dam remained in place. He had run out of ideas and all he could think of was getting back to his family so he could be with them at the end.

The sky was a little brighter on the horizon but the storm overhead hadn't abated at all. Wind pulled at him and then changed direction and pushed as if playing with him like a cat with a mouse. Rain lashed his face but the cold had numbed his skin long ago and its viciousness only served to blind him. His hands had frozen into claws and his soaked feet had lost all feeling long ago.

He could see the far side of the estuary as a looming shadow in the dull light but it was impossible to determine how far away it was. He had long ago given up looking back to see if Dave Johnson was still behind him as he feared that if he stopped to look back he wouldn't be able to get moving again.

He would gladly give his life to save his family but there was no way he'd throw his life away for nothing. He was determined to make it to the Keep and nothing this damn storm could throw at him would prevent that.

He wasn't sure how long had passed since the explosion had failed to blow the dam. It seemed like a lifetime. He felt a deep rumble beneath his feet and the narrow surface wobbled beneath his feet. At first he thought the vibration was from the thunder that cracked around him with such regularity that he barely noticed its violence. But this time it was different. This vibration came from below and he could feel its power even through his numbed feet.

He continued on but was forced to stop as he felt something grip his shoulder.

Johnson smiled at him as he turned to face him and Pender frowned at his high spirits. "It's starting," he heard the man shout over the noise of the crashing surf. "Make a run for it."

Pender stared at Johnson uncomprehendingly and watched his friend move ahead of him as he broke into a limping run. Pender had no idea what Johnson had meant and for a second he stayed where he was, lost in the ferocity of the storm. Then the dam shifted again beneath his feet and he heard a loud cracking as rock fractured and broke with the force of the quake.

The rock beneath him opened between his legs forming a gaping maw that disappeared into blackness below. *It's breaking up,* he thought. *My God! It's working.* He broke into a run as the dam beneath him began to tear itself apart.

The wave screamed its defiance as the lower left hinge was forced from its housing. The weight of bodies against the ancient barrier was proving too much. It still held for now but the remaining brackets were already showing signs of failing. Martin sent Craig Pender to the battlements to call his watchers down, there was no point in them being cut off if the gate fell and there was little they could tell him now that he didn't already know. They were surrounded and down to the last defensible position.

He turned just as Hillary approached. He smiled at her despite their predicament. She still wore the same clothes as before but someone had donated a shirt to cover her skimpy top. Her hair was matted and the drenched shirt clung to her but to him she was still gorgeous. Her face was tight with fear and he felt his smile slip as he saw Kim and Theresa wear the same terrified expressions.

"They've got through the gate," she said simply, but in those few words his world collapsed. He didn't bother to ask how, it didn't really matter. He nodded his understanding and called the remaining runners to him and passed his instructions to them. He marvelled at the children's ability to function in such circumstances and he watched them race to their tasks proudly.

"Okay," he turned back to Hillary and touched her cheek with his hand. *She was so cold.* "Get the others on the far battlements and bring them back to the main hall, we'll make a stand there." Hillary leaned forward and kissed him before turning and disappearing into the darkness.

Martin took one more look at the hoard outside. The gate had lost another bracket and bulged precariously inwards.

Overhead the storm intensified.

Julie Pender saw Emma rush towards her and immediately feared the worst. "Is Craig alright?" she shouted before her daughter had the chance to speak.

"He's fine, mother," Emma always used 'mother' when she was exasperated. "We've got to go back to the hall."

"What's happened? Has the gate fallen?" Julie was desperate for news. Martin may have thought he was doing her a favour putting her out here but the isolation had been worse than any of the dangers the other side of the Keep threatened.

"They don't tell us anything," her daughter replied as she pulled at her mother. "They just use us to carry messages."

Julie let herself be pulled towards the stairs as her mind raced. Retreating so soon back to the hall was a bad sign. It meant that they were in the final stages of the siege and with the dam still in place she knew that they were in serious trouble.

"I'll be back in a minute," Emma said as she began to move away from them. "I'll just make sure that guy knows we're moving to the hall."

Before Julie could react, her daughter had run off towards a figure ahead of them. At this distance she couldn't tell who it was but something about the figure's stance troubled her.

"Come on, Jack," she whispered to her youngest, "I don't like this."

Ahead she could see Emma's white shirt approach the darker

shape of the figure. Her heart was beating more quickly as the two figures drew closer. She wanted to shout out a warning but if she was wrong then Emma would resent her for her interference. It was her job to carry the message to the others after all. There was nothing to suggest anything out of the ordinary but she couldn't shake the feeling that something was wrong.

She bit her tongue and decided not to call out but she increased her pace regardless of what her daughter had said to her. When she heard the scream she broke into a run.

Emma ran towards the figure. *Her mother was so clingy,* she thought as she left them further behind. She could easily have waited for Jack and her mother to catch up before delivering her message but she'd only try to take over. *Besides,* she thought, *it's my job, not hers.*

She couldn't tell who the figure was as she drew nearer but by their build she surmised that they were male. She called out to attract his attention but the figure didn't hear as he remained oblivious to her.

"Excuse me," she called out more loudly, "we have to get into the hall. Mar . . . " the figure turned towards her and she stopped dead. The dull light revealed a face heavy with shadows. The man's face was so gaunt that that it seemed to be more a collection of sharp angles that the smooth features she was used to. It was the dead eyes, however, that brought her to a stop.

The figure reached for her and she screamed as his bloodied hand swiped at her. She stumbled and fell backwards. The breath shot out of her and she felt her hair gripped tightly and her head wrenched upwards.

She screamed again and used her feet to try to push herself away from the figure but his grip was too strong and she felt herself being drawn inexorably towards him. Suddenly the grip on her hair eased and she flew backwards with her momentum. She recovered quickly and began to rise to her feet but froze as she saw her mother follow through on her first attack.

She swung the bat in her hand and caught the figure across the head. The man flew backwards, actually rising off the ground with the strength of the blow. Her mother didn't allow the man any time to recover and stepped quickly to the fallen figure and brought the bat down again on the man's head.

Emma was dazed, the attack had happened so fast, and already her mother was turning towards her with a worried frown on her face. "Are you okay?" she heard her ask and she felt her own head nod. Jack rushed up to her squealing with excitement. "Did you see that? Kapow!" he mimed his mothers actions with an imaginary bat. "Mom's a superhero."

She nodded dully at her brother and regarded her mother in a new light. She had spent the last year or so trying to prove her own independence, forcing a gap between them that neither really wanted but that pressure from friends had required. She took her mother's hand and let her pull her to her feet. She saw the love and concern in her mother's face and suddenly missed the closeness they had always shared. She threw her arms around her and hugged her as she used to do when she was little. They had somehow grown out of the habit as she grew older. It was never too late to start again.

Dave Johnson ran as the ground beneath him convulsed and bucked as the force of the sea tore through the weakened area behind them and ripped the dam apart. He had hoped that the explosion would weaken the structure but the violence of the quake suggested that the dam was breaking down far more quickly that he expected.

The ground lurched again and he fell, pain lancing through him as a jagged rock tore into his side. The ground continued to move beneath him and he forced himself up and continued running. The storm increased in volume around him, or was that the rumble of the dam shaking itself apart—he wasn't sure?

Suddenly the ground beneath him disappeared. It didn't move or shift like before, it actually disappeared and, for a moment, he was left suspended in the air like some demented cartoon character before gravity took him and pulled him down into the raging sea.

His body went into shock as soon as he hit the freezing water and immediately the waves crashed over him, filling his mouth with iced water. The current pulled him down relentlessly and his soaked clothes inhibited his ability to pull himself back to the surface.

His muscles tired quickly as the cold sapped what little strength he had left. His lungs burned for oxygen until the pain was the only thing keeping him conscious. Finally, even the pain was taken away by the cold and darkness swept over him.

Martin heard the roar in the distance and looked up at the sky. There was something wrong, the usual cracks of thunder continued to rumble and then faded before the next onslaught. But this time the noise seemed to continue for far too long and then began to grow louder, like an approaching train. The ground shook beneath his feet and the roar became deafening, making it hard to think as it filled him with dread.

The Dam! The thought suddenly popped into his head. *Jesus, they've blown the dam.* He shouted at those around him to hurry but his voice was lost in the growing cacophony. He rushed to the last of his group and urged them on to the hall. He could see figures walking in the distance but their unhurried gait marked them as infected rather than members of his charge and he ignored them.

Behind him the gate suddenly collapsed and a deluge of infected swarmed into the Keep. He ran and pushed those slower than him ahead. A figure suddenly appeared in front of them and grabbed at him. His jacket tore as the man's fingers raked the material but Martin powered past the figure and left it with only a torn fragment of material gripped in its gnarled hand.

The door was only ten feet away when the wall of water struck the outer structure. The water hit with a roar that sounded like someone had fired a cannon right beside him. The force of the sound made him stumble with its violence and the ground heaved beneath him. The air was filled with a deep rumbling that seemed to go on forever and was so loud that he couldn't order his thoughts. He remained rooted to the spot, staring as the water broke violently against the outer battlement. Water crashed high in the air over the southern wall and lashed against the inner structures, sending bricks and torrents of water cascading over the inner Keep. The wall survived the initial assault from the water but many of the crenellations had been ripped away and the remaining battlements looked like broken teeth as the water surged past. Through the gate Martin could see the deluge of water smash into the hundreds of infected still on the outside. One minute the gate was teeming with their silent shapes and the next they were simply gone. Water poured in through the gate and Martin shook himself as the level quickly rose to his knees.

He turned and fled the remaining distance to the hall. As soon as he was through two people at the door slammed it shut and immediately threw everything they had that would soak water along the threshold.

"Quickly," he shouted, "move everyone to the upper floor. Get a few people at each of those arrow holes and see what's going on."

As he started up the stairs the first dull thud of a fist against the wooden door rang out. They weren't out of the woods yet, too many of the infected had gotten into the Keep before the water had arrived.

Julie Pender offered up a prayer for her husband as she heard the water crash against the Keep. She felt sick. Why did it have to be him? Why did she have to loose her husband and her children lose their father? The questions burned inside her and she suppressed the urge to scream her rage and frustration at a God that had seemingly forsaken them. But she forced herself to remain calm. John had done what was needed and given his life for them so she owed it to him to make his sacrifice count. She would mourn him later, for now she had to be strong for their children.

She instructed the children to go into a nearby bedroom as she took up station at one of the arrow holes but they followed her regardless and remained quietly beside her. She briefly considered forcing them to go but then relented. *It's better that we stay together anyway, whatever happens from now on.*

Outside she could see the water continue to crash against the outer battlements. Water surged high into the air as it struck the stone fortification. White spray splashed through to soak her as the water vented its fury at being balked by the ancient stone.

Below, in the courtyard, she could see figures stagger against the onslaught of water. Some fell under waves of water that seemed to leap over the outer walls and plunge down into the Keep but they soon rose again and continued on. There were so many of them that she couldn't count them. There were far fewer than before but still far too many for them to hold back. Luckily, the door into the hall only allowed four abreast so the door was holding for now. Eventually, though, their sheer weight would prevail.

Their idea of holding up in the Keep had assumed that the infected would not breach the outer defences. Now that they had, the small party of survivors had nowhere else to go. This was their last stand.

She looked down into the hall below and saw that the water level had risen quite markedly and already covered the entire floor area. She wondered briefly which would get them first; the infected or the rising water. Outside the storm began to abate and the sky brightened a little but the thunder of the water continued relentlessly.

Suddenly she heard a thunderous crack and snapped her gaze back to the courtyard. The southern wall of the battlement had cracked down the centre and already some of the merlons along the top has snapped off. She saw one of the heavy stone slabs fly across the courtyard with the power of the water and crash against three figures. The slab struck the infected and then carried them with it as it slammed against the far battlement wall.

The crash of the stone was lost in the cacophony of noise that filled her senses. More slabs of rock flew from the wall and crashed into the outer wall of the hall sending violent vibrations through the whole building. She could see Jack and Emma screaming but their voices were drowned out in the maelstrom.

Below, the door was struck by another piece of the wall and it burst inwards taking the ruined bodies of the infected with it. For a moment the doorway remained clear but then the soaked, bedraggled figures of the remaining infected began to appear. Outside, the wall finally bowed to the power of the sea and it collapsed inwards as a huge wall of water filled her view as it came directly for them.

Martin saw the wall of water just before it hit the hall. Water gushed through the arrow holes all along the walls and their power sent the people stationed at them reeling backwards. The whole building shuddered and part of the roof was torn off like paper. Debris and water rained down and many of the survivors were struck by wooden beams and concrete supports.

Martin tried to shout orders but his voice was lost to the violence all around them. He looked down into the hall and saw that the water was already half way up to the upper level. The infected below were having trouble making their way over to the stairs and many of them sank beneath the surface. He could see their dark shapes moving about under the water, unhindered by the lack of air but at the mercy of the water's current as they were carried helplessly with its flow.

The surge of water against the hall seemed to be endless. Water began to seep through the stones but they held fast against the onslaught and Martin found himself marvelling at its builder's skill. There was nothing he could do except guard the stairs and hope that the rest of the roof didn't give way and crush them all. He held tightly to the gun. The last three bullets were unlikely to turn the tide but its weight was reassuring nonetheless.

He watched the infected that had reached the stairs begin their slow shamble up its steep incline. There were around twenty visible either on the stairs or making their way there through the rising water. This did not include those under the water but Martin dismissed those as an immediate threat. Some of them slipped on the slick stone and fell into the water below but there were still enough of them in the room to take their place. Outside the others had been swept away with the water so it came down to those he could see.

He looked around at the survivors. Nobody was free of some injury or other and they looked pathetic with their torn, wet clothes and various injuries tied or bandaged with rags and remnants. There were fifteen of them left, of which three were too badly injured to be of any help. *Fifteen out of a population of fifteen thousand,* he thought with horror.

He was about to say something, anything to inspire them and ask that they give one more effort when he saw them rise to their feet and join him by the stairs. Each one, even the children, wore expressions of resolve and pride. They had endured the horror and heartache of seeing their friends and loved ones die and rise again. They had struggled through pain and injury, storms and raging seas and still they were ready to step up to the challenge one more time.

He looked over their faces, some of which he had known for years and others he had just come to know in the last few days and he felt the tears roll down his face. A few days ago tears would have marked him as weak but now it showed his pride and respect. He could see by their reaction that they too understood and he saw them stand straighter and raise their weapons in readiness.

Hillary and Kim took their positions beside him as he turned to face their attackers. They were ready.

The stairs were wide enough to allow five people to walk abreast so the group took their staggered their positions with the strongest at the front. Julie Pender stood in the second row behind a man she still did-n't know. It was strange that each of them had shared so much in the last day but had had no time for the simple introduction of a name. The children were at the back of the line but they too held their weapons ready. There would be no shirking of responsibilities and no concessions for age if they were overrun.

She offered up a short prayer to the God she had ranted against earlier. She hoped that he would be forgiving of her earlier frustration and that he would deliver them from this final trial. She asked, not so much for herself, but for all the children that remained in the group. She looked up at the sky through the torn roof as if expecting to see or hear an acknowledgement but the sky remained slate grey and the rain continued to fall in sheets. *At least,* she shrugged, *it's finally getting brighter.*

She couldn't see what was going on in front but she saw the man in front of her tighten his shoulders as he prepared to lash out and she stood ready to replace him if he fell. She heard the sounds of a scuf-fle, men grunted as they swung their weapons followed by the dull slap of wood against flesh or the dull crack of bone splintering. Her heart thumped in her chest as she watched the man in front of her as he swayed forward and then back with each attack.

She heard whispers of fear, grunts of pain and exclamations of joy but felt somewhat removed from it all. There was a sudden shaft of light to her side as the man to her right fell but it disappeared as the woman beside her shuffled into position.

There were three loud explosions as Martin used the last of the bullets and she jumped with each one as if she had been his target. The fighting continued for what seemed like an age but then, sudden-ly, the man in front fell to the ground and one of the infected lurched towards her.

She didn't have time to think. She brought up her bat to block the thing's blood-stained hand and drove the bottom of the bat into his stomach. The thing bent over and she brought the bat crashing down on its head with all the force she could muster. The infected man dropped like a stone and she stepped forward over both corpses as she filled the breach.

The man beside Martin fell with a startled grunt and pitched forward down the stairs. Even in death the man helped his colleagues as his body fell against one of their attackers and sent both of them over the edge into the water. They had stopped seven of their attackers but had lost three of their number in the process and another man had a nasty scratch across his face.

At this rate of attrition the infected would win by sheer volume.

Suddenly pain shot through his arm as one of the infected grabbed it and bit into the flesh. He pulled his arm back but his attacker had locked its jaws on his arm and the flesh tore in a lump of bloodied flesh. Blood jetted high into the air from the wound and he swore and slapped his other hand over the injury. He kicked out at his attacker and sent him reeling into those behind, giving him a moment to catch his breath.

He examined his arm briefly. The bite had torn deeply into his arm and blood pumped freely. He didn't need a doctor to tell him there was no hope. If he didn't die of blood loss the infection would turn him against his friends. Already he could feel his head begin to swirl. There wasn't much time but maybe he could do still do something to turn the tide.

He rushed forward with his arms outstretched and forced their attackers back with his momentum. At first the attackers resisted and he thought for a moment that he would fail but then his momentum won out and they began to slide backwards until, finally, he fell himself stumble forward. He ignored the cuts and bites as his body was raked by nails and teeth and continued to force them back relentlessly.

He collapsed at the end of the stairs as the pain and blood loss finally took their toll and they landed in a heap at the foot of the stairs. The cold water revived him briefly as he summoned the strength to rise one more time and kick at his attackers as they floundered in the water.

He heard the others rush down the stairs, attacking any that had fallen through his mad advance. He saw his friends arrive at the end of the stairs and saw the infected fall to their furious attacks as they used their superior height on the stairs to attack their water-bound foes.

He smiled briefly. *They had done it. They had won.* He felt himself fall forward and was aware that someone had caught him. He blinked furiously against the enveloping darkness and, for a moment, he saw Hillary's face in perfect clarity. Beside her Kim knelt beside him and wiped at the blood on his face. He smiled at them and their faces faded to black. For a while longer he was aware of their hands caressing his cheeks, he could hear them call to him but they sounded distant and then he felt himself rise as if weightless and then the darkness came and carried him away.

Epilogue

Julie Pender watched the clouds break. The rain had stopped earlier and now the sun shone weakly through the small cracks in the cloud cover like laser beams. The sea lapped angrily against the walls of the fortress, its violence reduced but not totally spent, and rocked the boat brutally from side to side. She had never been a good sailor but surprisingly the pitching motion didn't make her sick today.

She looked back at the Keep as they pulled farther away. The outer walls had been shattered by the sea and rocks lay strewn about the courtyard like discarded toys. There was a gaping hole in the main battlement wall and jagged rocks on either side of the breech seemed to stretch forward as if trying to close the mortal wound it had sustained. They had won. Although she wondered if it could really be considered a victory at all. They had merely survived she amended and the cost had been deplorable.

The boat had arrived an hour or so after the sea had assumed some sort of calm and her crew had been shocked to see the pitiful number of survivors. They had buried their dead in the Keep, using the large stone slabs as cairns for their dead colleagues. They still had no idea if they could escape out to sea but for now it was enough to know that they had somewhere to go. She wondered what would happen next. Were the infected dead, crushed by the power of the water, or were they merely washed further down the inlet where even now they gathered to launch their next attack?

Would the soldiers at the barricades be able to stop them if they turned their attention outside the town? All the questions raged through her mind and she was surprised to realise that she didn't really care. She had no doubt that she would once again have cause to concern herself with these matters, but for now she accepted that they were out of her control. She was too tired to think anymore.

"Mommy look," Jack jumped up on the deck and pointed out into the sea. At first all she could see was the undulating grey waves topped with white as the sea still roiled with the memory of its previous fury.

"What is it?" Emma asked as she came to stand beside them and shielded her eyes to the glare of the light on the waves.

"Somebody's out there," Jack replied and almost fell overboard in his excitement.

Julie could see nothing but then the boat rode a swell and she could see a shape. She forced herself to remain calm but inside her heart almost burst. She ran to Crystal at the wheel and pointed towards the shape.

It was too much to hope for but it wouldn't hurt to look. By the time they neared the shape the whole boat were gathered along the starboard side. They could see that the shape was the ruined hull of one of the boats from the harbour but they had come this far so all had decided to check it out fully.

It would be too cruel if it proved empty but Julie was well aware that that was the most likely outcome. They drew level with the shell of the boat. The keel was angled towards them and they spent a few more agonising minutes trying to turn their boat around to see inside.

"It's about time you got here," Julie collapsed against Emma as she heard John's voice. She could see that he lay along the boards, his left leg at an unnatural angle beneath him. He was pale but alive. There was a second shape stretched out beside her husband and she saw Theresa lean forward over the side to see.

John saw her worried expression and broke into a smile. "He's alive. I think he swallowed half the ocean but I fished him out and gave him mouth-to-mouth. He's a horrible kisser by the way," he winked at Theresa.

Julie waited patiently on the boat as the others helped the injured men aboard. She held the children tightly to her lest they run forward too early and send everyone into the water. Finally, John was lowered to the deck and the children rushed forward as one, swamping him. Julie considered briefly whether she should retain at least some dignity for her family and then decided 'to hell with it'. She launched herself forward and wrapped her arms around them all.

Maybe it could be considered a victory after all.

The End

Derek Gunn lives in Dublin, Ireland with his wife and three children and is the author of the post-apocalyptic thriller series, *Vampire Apocalypse*, widely praised on both sides of the Atlantic. The first two books in the series are; *A World Torn Asunder* (2006) and *Descent into Chaos* (2008). The third Vampire Apocalypse book, *Fallout*, is due out in 2009. An adaptation of Derek's first book is under option and is currently in active development as a major movie. Derek is a member of the International Thriller Writers Association and the Horror Writers Association. Visit his website at www.derekgunn.com

Permuted Press

delivers the absolute best in **apocalyptic** fiction,
from **zombies** to **vampires** to **werewolves**
to **asteroids** to **nuclear bombs** to
the very **elements** themselves.

Why are so many readers turning to Permuted Press?

Because we strive to make every book
we publish feel like an **event**, not
just pages thrown between a cover.

(And most importantly, we provide some
of the most fantastic, well written, horrifying
scenarios this side of an actual apocalypse.)

Check out our full catalog online at:
www.permutedpress.com

And log on to our message board
to chat with our authors:
www.permutedpress.com/forum

We'd love to hear from you!

The formula has been changed...
Shifted... Altered... *Twisted.*™

THE RAGE PLAGUE

A NOVEL BY ANTHONY GIANGREGORIO

An unknown virus spreads across the globe, turning ordinary people into ravenous killers. Only a small population proves to be immune, but most quickly fall prey to the infected.

Isolated on the rooftop of a school near the outskirts of Chicago, Bill Thompson and a small band of survivors come to the frightening realization that, without food or water, they will perish quickly under the hot sun. Some wish to migrate to a safer, more plentiful refuge, but the school is surrounded by rampaging murderers. Without a plan, Bill and his group don't stand a chance.

Their only hope lies in their one advantage over the infected: their ability to think.

ISBN: 978-1934861196

MONSTROUS

20 TALES OF GIANT CREATURE TERROR

Move over King Kong, there are new monsters in town! Giant beetles, towering crustaceans, gargantuan felines and massive underwater beasts, to name just a few. Think you've got what it takes to survive their attacks? Then open this baby up, and join today's hottest authors as they show us the true power of Mother Nature's creatures. With enough fangs, pincers and blood to keep you up all night, we promise you won't look at creepy crawlies the same way again.

ISBN: 978-1934861127

Permuted Press

The formula has been changed...
Shifted... Altered... *Twisted.*™

www.permutedpress.com

AFTER TWILIGHT
WALKING WITH THE DEAD
by Travis Adkins

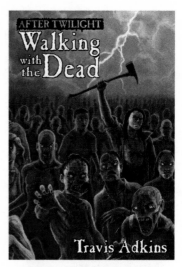

At the start of the apocalypse, a small resort town on the coast of Rhode Island fortified itself to withstand the millions of flesh-eating zombies conquering the world. With its high walls and self-contained power plant, Eastpointe was a safe haven for the lucky few who managed to arrive.

Trained specifically to outmaneuver the undead, Black Berets performed scavenging missions in outlying towns in order to stock Eastpointe with materials vital for long-term survival. But the town leaders took the Black Berets for granted, on a whim sending them out into the cannibalistic wilderness. Most did not survive.

Now the most cunning, most brutal, most efficient Black Beret will return to Eastpointe after narrowly surviving the doomed mission and unleash his anger upon the town in one bloody night of retribution.

After twilight,
> when the morning comes and the sun rises,
> will anyone be left alive?

ISBN: 978-1934861035

Drop Dead Gorgeous
by Wayne Simmons

As tattoo artist Star begins to ink her first client on a spring Sunday morning, something goes horribly wrong with the world... Belfast's hungover lapse into a deeper sleep than normal, their sudden deaths causing an unholy mess of crashing cars, smoldering televisions and falling aircraft.

In the chaotic aftermath a group of post-apocalyptic survivors search for purpose in a devastated city. Ageing DJ Sean Magee and shifty-eyed Barry Rogan find drunken solace in a hotel bar. Ex-IRA operative Mairead Burns and RIR soldier Roy Beggs form an uneasy alliance to rebuild community life. Elsewhere, a mysterious Preacher Man lures shivering survivors out of the shadows with a promise of redemption.

Choked by the smell of death, Ireland's remaining few begin the journey toward a new life, fear and desperation giving rise to new tensions and dark old habits. But a new threat--as gorgeous as it is deadly--creeps slowly out of life's wreckage. Fueled by feral hunger and a thirst for chaos, the corpses of the beautiful are rising...

ISBN: 978-1934861059

DYING TO LIVE
LIFE SENTENCE
by Kim Paffenroth

At the end of the world a handful of survivors banded together in a museum-turned-compound surrounded by the living dead. The community established rituals and rites of passage, customs to keep themselves sane, to help them integrate into their new existence. In a battle against a kingdom of savage prisoners, the survivors lost loved ones, they lost innocence, but still they coped and grew. They even found a strange peace with the undead.

Twelve years later the community has reclaimed more of the city and has settled into a fairly secure life in their compound. Zoey is a girl coming of age in this undead world, learning new roles—new sacrifices. But even bigger surprises lie in wait, for some of the walking dead are beginning to remember who they are, whom they've lost, and, even worse, what they've done.

As the dead struggle to reclaim their lives, as the survivors combat an intruding force, the two groups accelerate toward a collision that could drastically alter both of their worlds.

ISBN: 978-1934861110

EDEN
A ZOMBIE NOVEL BY TONY MONCHINSKI

Seemingly overnight the world transforms into a barren wasteland ravaged by plague and overrun by hordes of flesh-eating zombies. A small band of desperate men and women stand their ground in a fortified compound in what had been Queens, New York. They've named their sanctuary Eden.

Harris—the unusual honest man in this dead world—races against time to solve a murder while maintaining his own humanity. Because the danger posed by the dead and diseased mass clawing at Eden's walls pales in comparison to the deceit and treachery Harris faces within.

ISBN: 978-1934861172

Permuted Press
The formula has been changed...
Shifted... Altered... *Twisted.*™
www.permutedpress.com

THE UNDEAD
ZOMBIE ANTHOLOGY

ISBN: 978-0-9765559-4-0

"Dark, disturbing and hilarious."
—Dave Dreher, *Creature-Corner.com*

THE UNDEAD
VOLUME 2
SKIN AND BONES

ISBN: 978-0-9789707-4-1

"Permuted did us all a favor with the first volume of *The Undead*. Now they're back with *The Undead: Skin and Bones,* and gore hounds everywhere can belly up to the corpse canoe for a second helping. Great stories, great illustrations... *Skin and Bones* is fantastic!"
— Joe McKinney, author of *Dead City*

The Undead / volume three
FLESH FEAST

ISBN: 978-0-9789707-5-8

"Fantastic stories! The zombies are fresh... well, er, they're actually moldy, festering wrecks... but these stories are great takes on the zombie genre. You're gonna like *The Undead: Flesh Feast...* just make sure you have a toothpick handy."
— Joe McKinney, author of *Dead City*

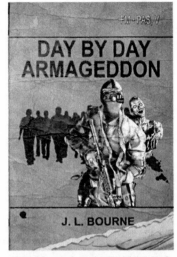
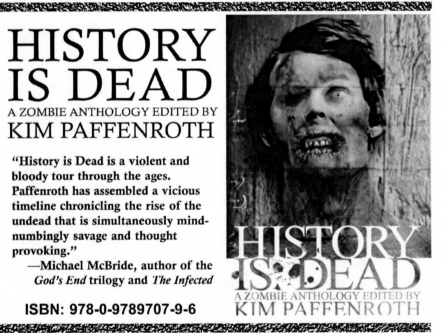

THE PLACE TO GO FOR ZOMBIE AND APOCALYPTIC FICTION

  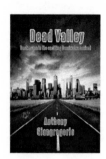

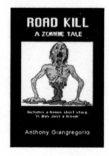  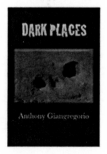

LIVING DEAD PRESS
WHERE THE DEAD WALK
www.livingdeadpress.com

Breinigsville, PA USA
02 February 2010
231741BV00002B/2/P